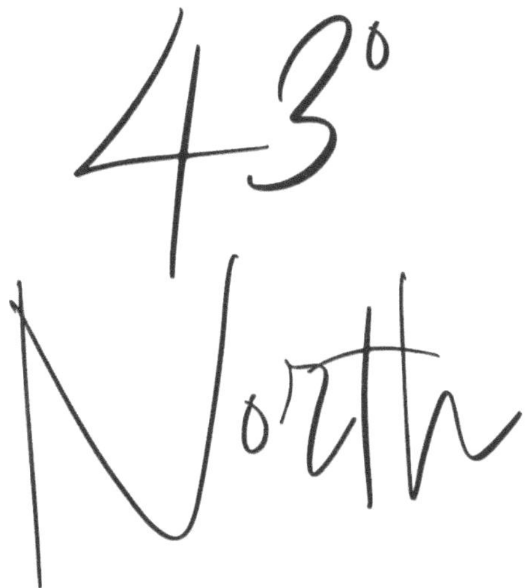


# THE NEWFOUND LAKE SERIES

# ALANNA GRACE

First e-book edition April 2024

First paperback edition April 2024

*Book cover and interior design by SGA Books*

*Cover photograph © RedTea via iStock*

*Editing by Plumfield Editing*

ISBN-13 (paperback): 979-8-9883296-3-3

ISBN-13 (e-book): 979-8-9883296-2-6

www.alannagraceauthor.com

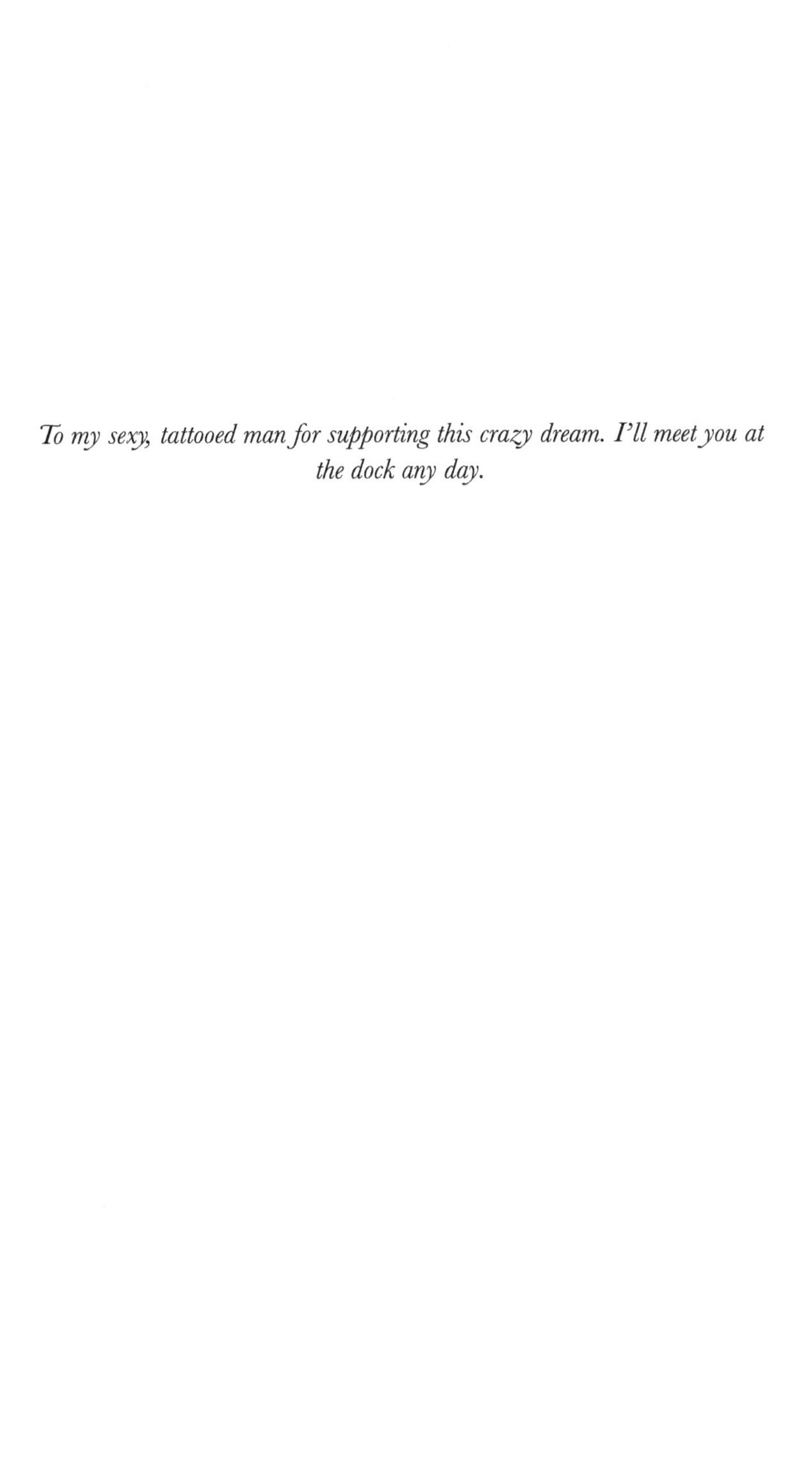

*To my sexy, tattooed man for supporting this crazy dream. I'll meet you at the dock any day.*

# also by alanna grace

Solia Anderson will do anything to save her family's remote log cabin from sale. Tired of her Rhode Island life where, at any moment, she might bump into a reminder of her bad taste in men, she bravely trades creature comforts for untamed adventure. Suitcase (and stubborn determination) packed, she retreats to the quiet shores of Newfound Lake, New Hampshire, where she lazed away her childhood summers.

However, her plans for an uncomplicated, solitary life fall short when she crosses paths with Jackson Christianson, town heartthrob, while she loads the bed of her truck in the lot of the local hardware store.

As sparks fly and romance takes root, Jackson's well-guarded secret threatens their burgeoning passion. When his longing for Solia becomes unbearable, he must choose between mending his heart or shattering their newfound love.

In this compelling narrative of burning desire, heartrending loss, and joyous self-discovery, Solia and Jackson's journey is a testament to the power of true love.

**_Available in e-book and paperback from your favorite retailers or direct from AlannaGraceAuthor.com._**

# prologue

Before I Signed: August

*Shannon*

"I thought you said Richard left town?" Madison whispers in my ear.

I cradle the phone in the crook of my neck and tug my crocheted blanket tight under my chin. "He did. He told me point-blank he's renting an apartment by Lake Winnipesaukee. Not far enough, but at least it's not Meriden."

"He was with another biker at Caitlyn's a while back asking about you, plus I've seen him tooling around downtown several times. What the hell is he still doing here? What doesn't he understand? Your marriage is over. He needs to move on."

"Apparently, easier said than done. He's not banned from town. Was he drinking again?" I roll over onto my back, the metal mattress coils groaning in resistance, and stare up at the white paint chipping off my bedroom ceiling.

"Shannon, are you serious? I don't think I've ever seen Richard without a drink in his hand, and his breath was wretched. He's a mess."

"I wish talking about divorce was enough to knock sense into him. I'm sure he thinks I'll let him come back."

"What do you mean, let him come back? Why would he

think that? Shannon, don't tell me you haven't signed the papers yet."

I place my hand over my eyes at the sting of tears. I'm not about to lie to my best friend. She's seen it all—the tears, the agony. Madison has witnessed me sweeping the shards of broken glass under the carpet every time Richard has shattered a dream of mine. On more than a few occasions, I've held a trembling pen over the dotted line, never allowing the ink to touch the page. Almost twelve years of marriage washed away with one stroke is a heartbreaking reality. "I will. You don't have to say anything. I know how pathetic it is."

"Shannon, you gathering the strength to walk away from Richard is the bravest decision you've ever made. I know you love him, but he isn't going to change. We've been through this."

"I know. Thanks for letting me know he's asking around."

"If you need me, I'm here. And Nate is always a phone call away, whether he's on duty or not. Just ask. Love you."

Drying my tears, I force down the pressure forming in my throat. "Love you too." I slide the phone under my pillow and close my eyes, pushing back against emotions trying to bubble to the surface. Madison has been through the mud with me, always the bridesmaid and never the bride. She's been by my side since we met all those years ago, and if there is anyone who deserves a happily ever after, it's her.

Not only has Madison been on me for years about Richard, but my mother is worried sick twenty-four seven. The weight of her anxiety is slowly suffocating me.

Hours later, I wake to the sound of the revving Harley I'd know anywhere. I rub my eyes, push the frizz away from my face, and grab my bathrobe from the end of the bed. I run my hand along the wall through the darkness and drag my feet to the front porch. As August winds down in the Lakes Region, whispers of cool air begin to push the mugginess aside.

The rusty screen door thwacks shut, and I press my body against the leaning post and adjust myself on the sagging deck boards. Squinting to see in the darkness, I can make out the silhouette of my soon-to-be ex-husband hunched over his handlebars.

"What are you doing here, Richard?"

He rests his forehead on his hands and then looks up. "You can't give up, Shan. Every time I leave the bar, my bike automatically drives up Lake Street. Nowhere else will ever feel like home. Come on, baby, you must miss me. I know you haven't signed the papers because if you had, I would have them."

I hug my arms tighter around my body and absorb the truth of his words. "Listen to what you're saying. You just left a bar … again. You've got a problem, Richard, one I can't fix. I've tried. Everyone's offered to help, but if you aren't reading the writing on the wall, no one can read it for you. This isn't what I want, but our marriage is long gone. You need help. You shouldn't be here." I look up at the cloudless sky and wonder what happened to all the wishes I've sent up to the stars. "What time is it, anyway?"

Richard slides his hand off the handlebar and reaches across to his jeans pocket. Seeing his sleeve of tattoos reminds me of the hours we spent curled up on the sofa sketching designs together late into the night. As though time is standing still, it seems like yesterday we had our whole lives ahead of us, a beautifully written love story, vivid dreams for our life together. He was my happily ever after, until the drinking became more important than me, than us, than everything.

God knows I tried. For years, I begged, we held family interventions, but everything failed. Richard needs help from someone other than me.

We were high school sweethearts, destined to be together, and we made a promise of *for better or worse* over a decade ago.

But I can't do it anymore. I can't stand by and be the wife of the town drunk any longer. It's unbearable. With every drink he's swallowed, I've watched my dreams of love, family, and happiness disappear. The countless nights of worry, wondering where he was, if he was dead in a ditch somewhere, how long it would be until he lost his job. The burden of worry became too heavy. I never thought I'd be thirty-two years old, sitting on this front porch alone.

"It's a little after midnight. Come on, baby, let me stay. You don't want me driving, do you?" He kicks the stand to the ground, leans his bike, and swings his leg over. His boots crunch through the dirt driveway, and I take a step back toward the door. Things with Richard never became physical, but I'd be lying if I said the fear didn't simmer in the back of my mind. When you've loved someone for this long, it's hard to imagine them hurting you. But then again, no one ever imagines the heartache that lies ahead. I never considered my marriage ending a possibility.

"Richard, you're right. You're drunk. Let me call Judah. He'll come get you." Richard stops dead in his tracks at the bottom of the porch steps, the ones he renovated eight years ago when we purchased this dated Victorian beauty.

"I don't need a goddamn ride, Shannon. What I need is for you to realize it's you who quit. You're throwing our life away, and for what? Some rich corporate asshole? It's bullshit!"

Fire burns behind my eyes and every muscle in my body tightens. "Are you serious? I quit? Richard, you left this marriage a long time ago. We only get one life here, and I'm tired of watching it slip through my fingers. I need more. I want to be happy. I want a family, Richard. The life we dreamed of all those years ago is gone. We both know this marriage is over."

Richard drops to his knees. Like an episode rewound and played again, he jams his fists into his eyes and begins to bawl.

"Baby … you know I love you. I can get a new job, I'll get cleaned up, just don't sign the papers."

Knowing exactly what's coming next, I straighten my back and reach for the screen doorknob. "No, Richard, we've reached the end of the road. I'm not leaving you for someone else. I'm leaving because I deserve better."

He looks up from his hands, eyes filled with an anger I am all too familiar with. Trying to balance himself, he stumbles to a standing position.

"You think this guy is gonna give you the world? You think you're going to rub some guy down and he'll grant you your every wish? I'm not the only one broken. Go ahead, Shan, whore yourself out to some loaded asshole and live happily ever after. I should've seen through your bullshit. It's all about money. Fuck you, Shannon. His rich dick is going to realize you're nothing but a small-town piece of ass. You'll be begging me to come back."

And just like that, we once again have crossed the line from desperate to delusional. His words no longer sting. Tears no longer fall. "Richard, I'm getting my phone and calling Judah." I lock the door behind me from the inside, run into my bedroom, and flip on the light. Scrolling through my contacts, I press Judah's number and simultaneously hear Richard's bike roaring to life.

Phone in hand, I run to the front window and watch Richard peel out of the driveway, middle finger in the air, leaving nothing but dust, dirt, and disaster in his wake.

"Hello? Shannon?"

Judah's voice transmits through the phone, and I press the speaker button. "Sorry, Judah. Richard was here, drunk as usual. I was hoping you'd come get him, but it's too late. He took off."

"Shannon, you've done everything you can. I don't want to see him dead on the side of the road, but he's his own worst enemy. We've tried. I'll take it from here. Go back to bed."

"Thanks, Judah." I end the call, double-check I deadbolted the front door, and pull the blinds over the front windows. Judah is one of only a few of Richard's friends who I can say still has a handful of functioning brain cells.

Grabbing a mason jar from the cabinet, I pour water from the faucet and slump into a wooden chair by the kitchen table. Hearing Richard refer to Nick shook me. Meriden is as small town as you can get. I shouldn't be surprised. But money is the last thing I'm out for, and Richard damn well knows this when he's sober. Sadly, those days are far and few between.

Less than a foot away sits the divorce paperwork. My box of memories rests on top. I grab hold of the corner of the stack of papers and pull them and the box toward me.

Months ago, I dug what's basically a time capsule out from the back of my closet. Inside, mementoes sit dusty and reminiscent of early years. I dump the contents on the table, and my sobs begin before I have a chance to contain them.

I want these memories to be enough. I want the dreams we shared to mean more than his disease. Running my fingers along the metal band of the claddagh ring he gave me sophomore year transports me to that night under the glow of the campfire after our friends had left. He was waiting for his dad to pick him up. He handed me a little wrapped box, and I was giddy. This ring was the first real gift I'd ever received from a boy. I was certain it was love.

There are our old prom photos taken along the Newfound Lake shore, our eyes full of life, possibility, and excitement. A champagne cork rolls along the edge of the wooden table, holding the memory of our graduation party when we snuck to the Meriden Town Beach and shot the cork into the air, sending it sailing where it plunked into the water. I'll never forget all of us racing into the lake to be the first to save this nostalgic cork from drifting away. Richard found it and passed it to me for safekeeping.

We swam under the glow of the moonlight for what seemed like hours, passing around the cheap bottle of bubbly and riding the euphoria of our high school years behind us. None of us realized it would be the last time we'd be together on those shores. Life changed, and we each traveled the paths we were destined for. Some of us stuck around, but many ventured outside the confines of our quaint New England town.

I've looked through this box more times than I'd like to admit, thinking these memories would somehow fix what's broken, give me answers, or fulfill my prayers. But I've grown wiser. Things aren't going to get better. This box is filled with memories, moments that helped form the person I've become, but they are also a reminder of the life I wanted. Instead of happiness, excitement, and love, it's been nothing but worry, tears, and fear year after year.

I'm done. I'm ready. It's time to create a new box, one of my own, and step out of the shadow of toxicity. My parents have been urging me to do so for years. They've respected my need to exhaust every effort, but they knew a long time ago this marriage was headed for a dead end.

I dry my eyes on my bathrobe sleeve, clear my throat, and reach into the junk drawer behind me for a pen. Sweeping up the cork, ring, photos, and everything else, I place the lid on the box, leave the pen on the table, and walk to my bedroom closet. Moving on doesn't mean I need to forget. Standing on my tiptoes, I push the memories as far back onto the top shelf as I can and collapse to the floor. My chest heaves as I try to focus on the ceiling, but my tears have liquefied my vision.

I hear people compare a divorce to grieving a death. I never understood the sentiment until now. Memories remain, but new ones can't be made. "We" are gone, dead, and there is no more life between us. I've never been so alone and weak and yet completely certain I'm doing the right thing. Richard was my whole life, and leaving him is like severing an artery.

Deep breath, I peel my body off the carpet and take one step at a time back to the kitchen. With the twenty-pound pen in my hand, I sign on the dotted line. The pen falls like lead onto the table. I fold the papers, seal the envelope, and say a silent prayer.

Unable to shake the chill from my body, I tug my bathrobe belt tighter and crawl back under the covers. The faint rumble of a string of bikers on Main Street echoes off the surrounding mountain ridges. Inching closer to my bedroom window, I lift the shade to peek into my driveway and search for headlights. Thankful for nothing but the pitch-black of night, I let go and hope sleep will come.

# 1



*Shannon*

"Tell me what's been going on." Mary leans back in her polyester office chair, smooths her gray curls down onto her forehead, creases the wrinkles in her checkerboard, knee-length skirt, and searches my face for some hint of emotion. Starting therapy was the easiest and best decision I've ever made. Mary understands me. Being able to say whatever comes to mind without filtering or worrying about hurting someone's feelings is a breath of fresh air.

I reposition myself on the soft leather couch, tucking a pillow under my neck and turning to look at Mary as she lowers her glasses to the tip of her nose. "Honestly, I'm so much lighter. Signing the divorce papers was like hurdling over a six-foot gate. Once I was on the other side, I started to believe I did the right thing. My parents are thrilled I worked up the courage and finally took the step. I mean, I think about Richard, I worry he'll be drunk and drive home, or he'll go to sleep and never wake up. I'm sure these thoughts won't disappear, but I've been able to compartmentalize them. I took your advice to sort out events into the things I can't control and ones I can. And speaking of things I can control, I kind of met someone."

"Go on."

I release a deep sigh. The image of Nick appears in front of my eyes: tall, chiseled jaw, dark brown hair, seductive eyes, his designer suit tailored perfectly and hugging all the right spots. From the moment I laid eyes on him, I knew he was trouble in all the best ways. One glance at his ass in that suit was enough to ignite embers I thought had stopped smoldering a long time ago.

"Remember the green energy company that came into Meriden and attempted to turn this small town into a wind farm? Well, Nick is the CEO."

Mary, professional stoic always, uncrosses her legs, recrosses the opposite, and leans forward, positioning her fist under her chin. "Interesting."

"I know what you're thinking."

Mary shakes her head. "I'm not thinking anything. This is a safe space."

Our laughter fills the room. Nick's company was enemy number one for the summer. I clear my throat, pull my legs off the cushion, and sit up. "Even though I wanted to knock him out each time he sat on the town hall stage spouting the benefits of green energy and wind farms, I couldn't deny something was going on between us. A chaotic attraction formed, and I couldn't ignore it.

"After the turbine deal collapsed, Nick approached me in the parking lot. Long story short, he asked me out. I said yes without even thinking it through. I haven't been on a first date since Richard in high school. It's pathetic how quickly I answered. Mary, this guy is smoking hot and so out of my league."

"What makes him out of your league?" Mary's eyes cast doubt, sending my thoughts into a spiral.

"He's a city boy. Nothing about him fits into our small town. His shoes probably cost more than my monthly groceries. I don't think he owns anything other than designer suits, he drives a Cadillac SUV, and he's probably never stepped foot in a lake."

"And you were compelled to say yes to going on a date with his man because …"

I touch the emptiness of my left ring finger and immediately stop myself from becoming too emotional. "Because he asked me. Because I haven't been asked out on a date in over ten years. Richard and I married right out of high school. But this new man, who I should be disgusted by, leaves me breathless. My life is a mess, so why not? Besides the fact most people want to escort him out of town for what his company tried to do, including my brother. Jackson has made it abundantly clear that he's not a fan of Nick. That day Jackson rescued Solia from the lake, Nick was standing next to me, and you'd have thought we were making out the way Jackson reacted. I mean, if looks could kill, Nick would be dead."

"Remember, he asked you out, not vice versa, so clearly, he's interested. Lead with confidence, and remember, you said yes for a reason." Mary checks her watch and taps its face. "Time's up. I'm here if you need me. Call if you want another appointment."

I nod in response and use both hands to pry myself off the sagging cushion. "I sure will, and hopefully the next time you see me, I won't be a ball of nerves."

Mary jots down a few notes and then holds the thin wooden door open, allowing me to exit.

"Thanks, Mary." As usual, my footsteps are a little lighter than they were an hour ago, and I'm ready to take on the day. I have exactly four days left in my summer. After Labor Day weekend, reading logs, math worksheets, and tying shoes will be my eight-to-four life. The forecast for the holiday weekend couldn't look better, sunny and seventy-five, which means Newfound Lake will be a comfortable eighty degrees. Most vacationers have gone home, leaving the locals to soak up the last days of the sunshine season before preparing for autumn and winter.

I get behind the wheel of my truck and pull out my phone. Maybe the girls are around for lunch on the boat today.

ME TO SOLIA, MADISON, BROOKE:

Hey, girls, anyone around for some R & R? I was thinking we could sneak in lunch and a boat ride.

SOLIA

I'm in! Do you care if Mia comes with? She's in town.

MADISON

Sounds good to me. What time?

BROOKE

Yes!

Of course Mia can come. Okay, pack a lunch and meet me at the marina for 12? I'll bring drinks.

SOLIA

K.

BROOKE

Can't wait!

MADISON

I have a couple errands to do but I should be able to get there for noon. See you then.

I pass a cruiser parked by the lake. I slow down and see Nate behind the wheel. He spots me and waves.

Pulling into Gray Lodge Marina, I scan the dirt lot for an empty spot. I sneak into a tight space near the boat launch where my pontoon, *Lake Girl*, awaits, and I'm immediately thankful for a few more boat days.

September is the shining star of the calendar year in the Lakes Region of New Hampshire. The water's warm, the crowds thin, the weather is less humid, and an aura circulates that invites relaxation. I haul the cooler I threw together before walking out the door, filled with waters, a few bottles of Lake Daze, a few spiked seltzers, and a grilled chicken salad, and my boat bag with my hat, sunscreen, beach towels (in case the girls forgot), and my wireless speaker.

As I walk down the dock, I note several of the boat slips empty, but many vessels have their covers buttoned up, readied for winter. Four years ago, Richard and I bought *Lake Girl* from a neighbor. Richard thought it was a waste of money, but living on these shores and being able to cruise whenever I want was a no-brainer. Unfortunately, Richard prefers the confines of a dark bar room to the open waters and fresh air.

"Hey, Shannon!" Solia shouts from the marina building. She is a burst of sunshine, a blessing to have in our lives. Jackson was two seconds from leaving Meriden forever to escape dealing with the loss of his former girlfriend when Solia rode into town and captured Jackson's broken heart the minute they met, anchoring him here. Their love story is one for the ages. They can't get enough of each other, and I've gained a friend and an amazing colleague in the process.

"Hi!" With Mia, Solia's best friend who lives out of town, in tow, they climb aboard. "Hey, Mia. Good to see you."

"You too! I can't get enough of this place. Figured I'd spend the last couple days of summer up here. Thanks for letting me join."

I spot Solia rolling her eyes and laugh. "I'd love to think I'm the reason you're up here, but we all know you have other motives."

"Tyler is the cherry on top of my visits. Well, let's just say he's more than a cherry on top. He's more like …"

"Got it. We got it." Solia tosses Mia a beach towel.

"You know you're welcome anytime, and Tyler is a good guy. I've known him since we were kids. If you can keep up with him, you might be a match made in heaven. Put your stuff wherever, and we'll give the other two a few minutes."

"His energy is crazy. I mean, the other night we were out to dinner and before we even got back to his place, we had to pull over and—"

"Mia, seriously?" Solia says.

"What? Oh, I forgot—I can't talk about sex? I'm not dating her brother, you are. So maybe Shannon isn't offended. Shannon?" Mia asks as she snaps her fingers and tosses her hair behind her shoulder.

"I'm not a prude, and I'll be the one needing pointers soon." I immediately have both sets of eyes glued to me. With my teeth clenched because I've said too much, I'm relieved when Brooke and Madison sneak up behind me and jump aboard.

"Hey! Sorry we kept you waiting. I texted Madison that I'd pick her up and then stopped at Basic Ingredients for a sandwich and chatted with Judy for a bit. Time flew by, I looked at my watch, and was like, crap! Gotta go! And then I went and grabbed Madison and here we are." Brooke throws herself down on one of the front cushions in the sun. Laughter erupts from us all. Brooke's sentences string along until she runs out of air. If we want to talk about energy, Brooke has more than all of us combined. And as tiring as she can be, her authenticity and kindness more than compensate.

"You made it." I slide their bags under the bimini top and into the shade.

"Yeah, you're right on time. Shannon was just telling us that she needs some sex pointers." Now instead of two sets of eyes, I have four searing into me.

"Oh, I'm sure she's joking around." Madison bites her bottom lip and tries her best to guide the conversation away from this topic in an effort to shield me.

"It's okay, Mad, I let it slip. I was going to tell them, anyway. I do need pointers. It's been a long time since I've gone on a date."

"Wait, back up the bus." Solia stands and moves a couple seats closer to me. "Who, what, when, where, and how? Go."

I pull my clunky boat keys out of my back pocket and turn the ignition. "How about we get out of the boat slip and onto the lake and then I'll fill you in?"

"Sounds good. In the meantime, anyone want me to continue the story about my roadside romp?" Mia looks around, gauging the interest level.

"Oh, Mia, every time I see you, I'm desperate to live vicariously through you. Spill it. Going out to dinner has me nerved up to the point of exhaustion. Do you know what I mean? It's probably why I haven't had a serious relationship since high school. What do you—"

"Brooke, take a breath. We'll analyze you after. Mia, tell your story."

Brooke zips her lips, pulling more laughs from the group, and awaits Mia's story with bated breath.

"So, the other night, Tyler and I left the Mexican place downtown. We'd had a few margaritas ..."

I keep my eyes on the shallow water ahead as I guide the boat through the narrow channel, careful not to snag the propeller on any tall weeds and watching for rocks. As we round the corner, the lake is calm with only a few scattered watercraft—a light green sailboat in the distance and a few kayakers to the left of us hugging the shore for safety. I steer to the right, close along the shore to Pike's Peak, before heading out to the sandbar.

"We were feeling good, but then again, I had more than he did. I was craving dessert, so we stopped at that cute little shop on the corner and grabbed a box of cupcakes. Well, the plan was to eat them back at his place, but let's just say we didn't make it that far!"

Madison asks, "What do you mean? Like, right there on the street? In the middle of downtown?"

Out of the corner of my eye, Solia's hand cups her cheek as she shakes her head in disbelief. Oblivious to her reaction, Mia continues. "Well, my hand started to wander into his shorts a little while he was driving, and he *obviously* liked it. Once we were off the main road, he pulled over to the side, grabbed one of the purple-frosted cupcakes, yanked my top down, and smeared the frosting everywhere. Before I knew it, he was on my side of the truck, devouring the frosting like he'd never eaten before. God, it was freaking hot. Ladies, I'm telling you, I'll never look at a cupcake the same way again.

"After that, all bets were off. We're just lucky the cops didn't drive by. They would've gotten quite the show. We were a hot, sticky mess. Thank god for vinyl seats."

I pull the throttle back and idle a second to catch my breath and look over at Mia. "Are you serious? You are crazy in the best way possible. I mean, I'm not sure if I'm more shocked about the frosting or the fact it was on the side of the road. But hey, no judgment from me."

"What's the craziest thing you've done, Shannon?" All the girls' eyes focus on me as I search my memory for something, anything. The heat in my core rises and a sweat forms on my brow. "Listen, I'm the old married one in the group. Same guy, same bed, forever. I'm certainly not the one to be talking about the crazy things I've done. I'd have you asleep in two minutes."

"First of all, you aren't married anymore, and things are about to change for you!" Madison stands, walks over to the cooler, pulls out the water bottles, and passes them around.

"You finally signed, huh?" Solia offers me water.

"I did. Sorry, I figured Jackson would've told you. It's been a long time coming. I mailed them, Richard needs to sign, and then we wait the ninety days until it's official."

"Ninety days?" Brooke's eyes bug out.

"That's what the law says. So yeah, crazy sex is not part of my vernacular," I add. "I do, however, have a date tomorrow night."

"I want all the details. Who?" Solia moves to the cushion directly in front of me and pulls her sunglasses down to the end of her nose.

The girls gather around wide-eyed, on the edge of their seats. "Why can't we talk about Madison now?" I ask. No one responds.

"I have nothing to share. Let's think—my choices are either the janitor at school or … yeah, that's it." Madison scoops up a handful of lake water and tosses it at me.

"Fine. Remember the CEO, Nick, from Green Breeze Enterprises?"

"I remember Nick. And I remember the way he looked at you during the town council meetings. Installing wind turbines wasn't the only thing he was interested in drilling," Solia says, surprising me.

"Seriously? I had no idea it was obvious. After that scary day on the lake, when things settled down, Nick asked for my number. I was shocked. It's been over a decade since anyone has shown interest in me. He handed me his phone, I tapped away, and the next thing I knew, I'd agreed to a date for tomorrow night. We're going to dinner."

"Wait, why is this guy still in town? He was here for the wind farm, but the deal fell through, so he should be back in Boston by now. Right? Is this a good idea? I mean, come on, the guy almost destroyed Meriden." Brooke scratches the back of her neck, squints, and crinkles her nose.

"You would think. But it seems like he fell in love with the lake while he was trying to destroy it. Next, he was spotted house-hunting. He's staying at the bed-and-breakfast up the road."

"Does Jackson know?" Solia asks. I'd anticipated this question. "I'm happy for you, if this is what you want. I hope he's a good guy and all. He was a jackass through this whole green energy ordeal."

"I'll handle my brother. It's one date. I'm sure that'll be all it is. I'm still torn about it. The guy almost stole your cabin from under you and would've put an end to my family's orchard in a matter of a few years." I push the throttle forward, stirring a small wake behind us, and head toward the sandbar on the west side of the lake. "Nick is a bit of a mystery. He gives off bad-boy energy, but there's something about him. Maybe I shouldn't go."

Mia pounces to the edge of her seat and sits like she's wearing a back brace. "Bad-boy energy is hot. This is good for you, Shannon. Since he wants to stick around, maybe there's a little Small Town USA deep inside him. I can guarantee he's good in bed. He might rock your world. You want me to get you a few cupcakes for later?"

"Mia! Shannon's going on a date with the guy, and you already have her shacking up. I'm not sure if he's the guy to go out with, but …" Solia to the rescue again.

"She left a man who she's been with for a decade. She said her sex life was boring as fuck. She deserves to be shown what she's been missing," Mia retorts. "No offense, Shannon, maybe your sex life was great, but—"

"Ummm, no. I'd say it's been drought season over here. I'm not sure I'm ready for bad-boy energy, nor am I ready for cupcakes." My stomach constricts and I laugh so hard it actually hurts.

Mia leans forward, close enough for only my ears to hear. "Keep your options open."

"Thanks for the advice. I'll do that." I can understand why people, especially Solia, gravitate toward Mia. Her energy is infectious and her spirit endearing. "Let's head out to the sandbar. The school bell is about to ring for some of us, and we'll be counting down the days till summer again before we know it."

We cross the lake at a snail's pace to avoid casting a wake toward a few paddleboarders. It doesn't take much to lose your balance on one of those. The sandbar is a local hangout where the water is still deep enough to keep the boat from beaching. Everyone's anchor is thrown in and secured. Boat engines are off, music is dialed up, and people hop off to swim in the shallow water, float in tubes, or lie on the sand with a cold drink in hand.

The best part about the sandbar is everyone is there for the same reason—to chill and let loose—and that is exactly what we do for the next few hours. We swim, dance, drink, eat, and laugh more than I have in a long time. I feel lighter, braver, and tanner.

Solia and I are sitting on a beach towel on the back of the boat, feet dangling in the water as Madison, Brooke, and Mia play football with a crew of guys on the sandbar. The day heated up, but the water feels warmer than the air, common for September.

"Will you be at Trinity's memorial on Monday?" Solia turns to look at me as she pulls her feet out of the water and tucks her legs into her chest.

"Of course, I wouldn't miss it." I pause, throat tightening.

"Solia, you've helped Jackson in so many ways. I never thought he'd be able to move past Trinity's death. Meeting you is the best thing that's ever happened to my brother." The tears gathering in my eyes catch me off guard. I've been wanting to thank Solia for a while, but it never seemed quite right until this moment.

Solia tucks her arms around her knees and leans into me. "Thanks for saying that, Shannon. Your brother is the best thing that's happened to me too. The stars aligned and brought me here. I know he'll never forget Trinity or the accident, but he's healing and casting the guilt aside. I'm glad he was open to the idea of a memorial. I think he's realizing you can still remember and honor someone who has passed, but also allow yourself to experience the life you've been given."

"Well said. Do you need me to do anything?"

"No, we're keeping it simple. We've had her name and a simple message engraved on a memorial marker that we'll put in the grassy area by the flagpole. Jackson invited Trinity's parents, who were extremely receptive and thankful. They're going to say a few words. I'll bring flowers, and we can have a moment of silence."

"Beautiful. I can't believe it's been a year. I can't think of a better way to celebrate her life and provide closure for Jackson and this town. How's Jackson holding up?"

"He's been a little off the past few days. I'm giving him space. The farm is taking up so much of his energy, as you'd expect this time of year. I'm hoping your dad lays off on the guilt trip about Jackson staying. I hate being part of the reason there's a rift between them."

"My dad can be tough. He was pissed that Jackson left him hanging, but don't get it twisted. The cider business is booming, and they'll be fine. I think my mother is secretly happy he is staying. Dad will come around."

I drape my arm over Solia's shoulders and squeeze.

"Enough about that. Are you ready for tomorrow?"

"I'll be fine. I won't lie—I'm nervous, but I'll survive." I shake out my ponytail. "Come on, let's get the girls and go in."

After several attempts, we manage to get the gang on board and head back to the marina. "Why does summer have to end?" Solia tightens the beach towel around her body and tucks a corner into the top to hold it in place. She shakes her hair into the breeze, releasing droplets.

"All good things come to an end, but we always have next summer to look forward to, right?" Madison slips her feet underneath her body as she kneels on a cushion at the bow and wraps her towel around her shoulders. "I love summer, but there's something unique and special about all the seasons."

Brooke settles into the seat across from the captain's chair, allowing the small windshield to block the slight breeze. "I took up skiing a few years back. I love winter so much more than I used to."

"I want to get back into skiing. Our parents used to take Jackson and me all the time when we were kids. All the way up until I guess when I got married. I haven't skied since." I grip the steering wheel a little tighter and bite the inside of my lip, instantly tasting metal.

"Well, we'll have to change that. You'll have more time to be adventurous. We can plan a girls' ski weekend. What do you think about that?" Brooke looks at me like she's hoping I'll grab the lifeline she's throwing and stop myself from drowning in sadness. Her infectious smile can make anyone's day brighter.

"Sounds great, Brooke. Right, girls? A ski weekend—you'd be up for that, right?" I nod my chin toward the bow.

"I'm in. We'd have a blast. But I would personally like to add men to the invite. Someone needs to keep me warm on a snowy mountain. Just saying," Mia adds.

"Totally. Although I'll enjoy the fall before we plan for snow." Solia rolls her eyes in my direction and giggles.

My brother and Solia are in the honeymoon phase. I'm hoping she's the one. She already feels like a sister; we get each other, and witnessing how happy she's made Jackson melts my heart. "I'm with Solia. Let the leaves turn first and then we can plan for snow. Madison, can you get the buoys ready?"

"Sure thing."

A few other speedboats pull into the channel toward the marina, so I lower the throttle and cruise safely behind them. Taking the last few deep breaths before heading into my slip, I remind myself how lucky I am to live here, to have this day with my friends, and to know everything will be okay.

"You're good. Toss them over."

Madison throws two buoys over the side to cushion the boat against the dock. I kill the engine and hop off to tie the ropes to the deck handles, remembering that the last time I was here, Solia almost drowned. Most of Meriden were here on these docks, leaving the town meeting to make sure one of their own was okay.

"You good, Shan?"

I lower myself and sit cross-legged on the dock to finish tying the rope. "You know what? I'm making this too easy on Nick. It's pathetic I said yes. He's an asshole. Maybe I'll test him out at the farm, you know, see how he handles himself at the orchard. Make him squirm a little before I let him take me out for dinner."

"I see where this is going." Madison slings the cooler over her shoulder and hops onto the dock.

"Yeah. I'll text him and see if he has a few hours to go apple picking. If he can't handle that, he can get lost."

"Is that Richard?" Madison leans forward with her hands on top of the windshield, straining her eyes toward the sun to somewhere behind me. I hear the rumble of a bike and whip the rope around the hook, pulling as tight as possible. I turn to spot the back of a man peeling out of the marina parking lot and up the road.

"Was that him?" I look from Madison to Brooke and then to Solia.

"It sure looked like him. What the hell would he be doing here?" Madison's eyes are ablaze. If looks could kill, Richard would be dead in the dirt lot. She climbs onto the dock and finishes tying the back knot as I continue to stare at the empty road.

My heart is in my throat and all happiness drains from me, replaced by a flood of panic. Richard has no reason to be here unless he's following me. The last thing I need is him lurking in the shadows.

# 2

Nick

This cell of a room smells like fucking mothballs. I can't believe people electively stay at this so-called bed-and-breakfast. The floral wallpaper ungluing at the seams and the creepy wooden rocking chair in the corner had me skeeved out from the second I walked in.

I'm staying in Meriden for the weekend to finish up looking at a few lakefront properties. What started out as an investment conversation between my executive board quickly became a genuine interest the more I learned about the Newfound area. The guys have been razzing me ever since. Fuck 'em. This place got me thinking that my life didn't always need to be in the fast lane.

Add to it, my mother's breast cancer diagnosis this past year caused me to further examine my life choices. Thankfully, they caught it early, but having a place to relax and enjoy extra family time will be a good thing for all of us. I've been putting the family business in front of my actual family for too long. And Mom will love it up here—city living was never her first choice.

Although the new boutique hotel by the lake was filled to

capacity, I'm glad someone was smart enough to open it, giving people a better option. Maybe there needs to be another, since it was booked solid for the foreseeable future. This ass-backward town doesn't have another hotel anywhere, unless I were to stay two and a half hours north in the White Mountains, thus why I ended up in a decades-old bed-and-breakfast.

Sucking it up in this hellhole of a room is not my idea of a weekend getaway, but it's a means to an end. My father would never have stepped foot in this place—he only settled for the finer things in life. The prospect of living on Newfound Lake, the most beautiful body of water I've ever seen, and the chance to lay eyes, and possibly hands, on Shannon, are what's keeping me within the town limits.

And I need to spend some of this fucking money. Having a place up here will be an investment, or that's what I'm telling myself. If it sucks, I'll get my money back twofold, so it's a no-lose situation. I'm not moving up here for the fine dining or shopping. And being only ninety minutes from the bumper-to-bumper traffic of Boston is a plus. It'll make it easy to drive up and spend the weekends.

Being at the lake will force me to slow down. I've been running nonstop on the treadmill of life since I took over my dad's company eight years ago. We learned upon his passing that one of his heart valves had been ninety-five percent clogged for years. Whether he was aware, we'll never know. My father always assumed I'd run Green Breeze Enterprises one day, given I'm the oldest child in the family, not that my brother or sister were interested.

I tried to drop hints of disinterest, but they were either unnoticed or ignored. No one stood up to my father, and I certainly wasn't going to put my foot down at eighteen. I thought I had more time. I knew I was going to have to get a college degree; that was never up for discussion. But photography is my true passion, and I was working up the courage to follow my dreams. Dad's sudden heart attack pivoted my life onto an irreversible course.

We never discussed what I would study or where I wanted to live. My father had those decisions chiseled in stone. And no one ever lifted the stone to see if I had any other dreams buried underneath. I played along, thinking maybe I could have both my father's approval and photography. Maybe there was a way to balance both. I knew surviving on photography alone was a long shot, whereas my father's plan guaranteed excellent money.

My undergraduate years at Northeastern and graduate years at Boston University's business school prepared me. I had a knack for academics—school came easy. Every year spent in the classroom and every summer interning alongside my father was another layer of dirt thrown on top of my dream of one day owning a photography studio. With the passing of time, I hoped to unearth it one day, but knew it wasn't in the cards just yet.

Despite my extensive education and training, a few more years of having my father's guidance would've been better. Losing him was a gut punch to me, my family, and the company at large. From the moment he died, I never gave any other dream another thought, even when my mother—she never forgot my creative side—tried to tell me I didn't have to follow in my father's footsteps.

There was no way I was ready to hear her words as we lowered my father into the ground. He worked to build this company from the ground up, and he would be irate if I walked away to click pictures of nature. He was a man of few emotional words, but I'm sure he'd ream me out and I'd be climbing the corporate ladder as fast as possible to get him to stop.

Even through the steep learning curve, I've earned the

respect of the most senior members of the board. If I learned anything in the brief time interning with my father, it was to be ferocious. Everything is fair in business and take nothing personally. Making Green Breeze a continued success is my mission, and up until now, I didn't give a rat's ass whose town I needed to plow through to make it happen. Nothing mattered more than making my father proud and continuing his legacy.

When I stepped into my father's Bottega Veneta shoes, I knew there was no looking back. I've got my penthouse apartment in the Seaport area of Boston, which isn't too shabby. The nearby culinary scene is first class, and the women aren't too bad to take out for a night or two. But my life had become predictable, unemotional, and successful. It wasn't until I was forced to come visit our redneck neighbors in New Hampshire, as my father liked to call 'em, that I realized it had been forever since I'd heard silence and thought about life outside of the fast-paced city.

Despite Hogan fucking up the deal after failing to do enough research to discover we were encroaching on conservation land, I managed to remember a part of myself that had gone dormant long ago. The lake and the mountains surrounding it were breathtaking—and I caught sight of one of the sweetest asses north of Boston. I'm not exactly sure what women like Shannon do in these parts, but I didn't think twice about asking her out. I've never had a woman turn me down for a date. Maybe once in eighth grade?

Nevertheless, I thought Shannon may have been the first woman to decline, given I nearly stole her family's multigenerational apple orchard out from under their feet for pocket change. Or perhaps because her brother's anger fired from his eyes with an intensity that could've bored holes into my skull. It's neither here nor there because she said yes.

Last night she texted to ask if I'd go apple-picking with her this morning for an hour or so. I thought she was canceling dinner, but this was in addition to. I don't understand why we are picking apples, but I wasn't about to say no. I can do anything for an hour.

My driver, Harold, took quite some time locating a restaurant for my date tonight. Reservations are set for seven o'clock at the Six Burner Bistro up in Plymouth. After showering in what resembles a coffin, I get dressed.

"Harold, change of plans. I need you to drop me off at Christianson's Orchard at ten. I'll be there for about an hour and then back here. Dinner is still as planned."

"You got it, boss. I'll be out front at nine forty-five."

Harold is the man. He was the doorman of our building when I was growing up. My father's driver left, and he asked Harold to fill in. He's been with us ever since. His wife passed away early in their marriage from cancer, no kids. Despite the number of years he's been around our family, I know very little about his life outside of Green Breeze. He's in his midfifties, single, and the easiest-going man I know.

"What the fuck? Doesn't anyone fill in these goddamn holes?" My head slams into the headrest after our front tire dips into yet another pothole in the dirt road leading to the farm. Harold has no choice but to hit each one since both sides of the street are loaded with parked vehicles. This many people can't seriously be here for apples.

"You sound more and more like your father every day. We aren't in Kansas anymore." Harold holds the wheel steady.

The dirt driveway is loaded with pickups, a broken-down tractor, and four spare tires in a pile. One of the sexiest farm girls anywhere sits on the tailgate of her pickup, which is the last thing I thought I would find sexy. Her tanned, toned legs swing off the gate. She's wearing brown boots caked with mud. A tight blue tee with the "Live Free or Die" logo hugs her chest, the fringe of her jean shorts barely visible.

"Sir, are you getting out?"

I don't realize I'm staring at Shannon while Harold has the passenger side door open, waiting for me to exit. He clears his throat and peeks into the back seat. "Sir, she seems to be waiting for you."

I look back at the truck and see she's hopped off and is walking my way.

"Wow, a driver and all. Hi, I'm Shannon." She introduces herself to Harold.

"It's a pleasure to meet you, miss. I'll be here waiting, if that's all right."

"Harold, huh? Do you go everywhere with Harold?" She raises her hand to her hip.

I follow her eyes and look toward my driver, standing by the door. His eyes meet mine, and he tilts his head and turns his back to us. "Pretty much. He's been with me forever. When I decided to spend a little extra time up here and look around, it wasn't even discussed. His room was booked, and here we are."

Shannon covers her mouth, red nail polish matching her cherry lips as she addresses Harold. "Waiting? As in, waiting to drive Nick home?"

"Yes, ma'am. If that's all right. If not, I'll park elsewhere and return in an hour."

Shannon looks from Harold to me and back. "Do you not drive?"

I straighten out my pants and clear my throat. "Of course I do. But Harold is my driver."

With another laugh, Shannon's forehead crinkles, and she lets out a deep exhale. "Man. Okay. Well, Harold, I'm sure you'd rather explore the town or something? Or you're welcome to join us and then drive city boy back to the castle where he came from when we're done here."

Harold's body stiffens, and he looks to be holding back a response. "Boss?"

Trying to avoid sounding like a dick, I nod and wave him off. "I'll call you when I'm ready."

"Sure thing, boss."

He climbs behind the wheel and reverses the SUV, leaving me standing in a dirt driveway more out of place than I've ever been. The smirk on Shannon's face has me wondering what she's up to.

She stands with both hands on her curvy hips, eyes trailing my body. "Little overdressed, aren't we?"

I tug at the collar of my button-down blue-and-white-print shirt, adjust my leather belt, and follow her gaze to my pressed khaki pants and leather shoes. "I left my cuff links in the room," I tease, suddenly aware I look ridiculous.

"You're about to get filthy." She winks, her long lashes sweeping across her undereye.

I see where this is going. "I wouldn't have expected anything less." I follow close behind, watching her ass jiggle under her minuscule jean shorts as we navigate the holes in the driveway.

Apple picking may not be on my résumé, but getting filthy is.

# 3

"Well, who do we have here?" My grandfather holds out his World's Best Grandpa mug. Both my grandparents are rocking on the front porch as per usual.

"You remember Nick from the meetings this summer?"

"Sure do. Put it right there, son." He eases himself to standing while my grandmother holds the arm of his rocking chair steady. "What brings you to the farm this morning? You can't be stupid enough to be scouting this land for something else, now, would you?"

My grandmother whacks the side of my grandfather's leg with the newspaper crossword section. "Now, Earl, that's no way to welcome a guest. Shannon, honey, are you showing him around?"

"Yes, I figured I would pick a few baskets for Jackson and give Nick the lay of the land he almost destroyed."

Nick's jaw is rigid, his chest heaving with deep inhales. "I regret meeting you under those conditions. For what it's worth, I'm glad the deal wasn't meant to be. This is a beautiful farm. You must be very proud. I can't wait to see the rest."

"Dressed like that? No. Grab him a pair of my boots out of

the barn, will you, Shannon? Those"—he points at Nick's shining dress shoes—"will be mucked up in no time."

"No need. I can get them cleaned." Nick winks at me, sending chills up my spine.

"I insist. Don't be a fool." Grandpa shoos us toward the barn.

"We'll be back."

"No rush, honey. We'll be right here. Earl, don't make the young man uncomfortable. He must be here because he fancies Shannon."

"Grandma, we can hear you." I turn and laugh. At twenty feet away, she's practically yelling her words.

"What?" she hollers back.

Nick follows me into the barn. I watch him look up into the rafters and past all the tools and farm equipment, and decide to have some fun with this.

"Here we go." I sift through the pile of old boots that are rotting away in the corner, complete with cobwebs and dried mud. "What size?"

Nick leans over my shoulder, eyeing the pile. His aftershave or cologne is intoxicating, and despite looking out of place, there's no denying that he's the sexiest guy I've ever laid eyes on. Between his trim, muscular body, deep-set eyes, and well-defined jawline, he's the essence of hotness.

"Eleven and a half." His breath is close to my neck, and tingles erupt between my thighs.

"Here we go. Eleven and a half. Perfect." I pull a dirty pair of old brown, worn boots from the pile and nod to the wooden bench by the barn opening. At least he follows directions.

I can't help but laugh at the sight of this guy looking fine as hell with scrunched-up pants and dirty boots. It's priceless. I enjoy the view a beat too long, and Nick picks up on my stare.

"I'm looking too good, huh?" He spins around, giving me a view of his butt, another scrumptious piece to the puzzle.

"Let's go. Grab two apple pickers from the wall over there. I'll grab two baskets."

We sweep around back, and Jackson is nowhere to be found. That's probably a good thing. It's bound to be awkward. He's likely out in the fields somewhere. We have about four seasonal employees on the weekends in the fall. Some years we get quite a crowd for the apple harvest. It all depends on the foliage and the number of visitors we have scouting the area. This year seems less than usual, but if I had to guess, I'd say there are about forty people picking this morning.

Christianson's Apple Orchard has been in our family for generations, and each year, the apple blossoms return as beautiful as the last season. We have ten varieties with space for more. Most visitors pick the lower-hanging fruit in the first couple rows, especially if they have kids in tow. It's such a magical place.

I'm sure most people pick and buy more apples than they can eat, but it's a special experience to navigate the orchard. My childhood was spent roaming the rows of apples, begging my father for hayrides and helping my grandmother peel and core in preparation for pies. So much work goes into sustaining a farm, and this land is part of the backbone of Meriden.

"I thought we were picking apples with"—he pauses and hikes the apple-picker pole into the air—"with these things?"

I have one foot up on the tractor's running board, and I see Nick's eyes float to my butt. I know I'm blushing and use the steering wheel to shimmy onto the seat. "Throw the pickers in the wagon. I'm taking you across the field where most people don't go."

He tosses the poles in, causing the metal to bang against each other. It startles a few pickers in the row next to us.

"Easy, killer." I'm suddenly aware of how tight the seat in the front of this tractor is. His thigh rubs against mine.

"Says the woman who has me in a riding lawn mower attached to an empty wooden wagon driving me to the back fields where there are no people. You either can't wait to get me alone, or you're planning on using those rusted poles to end my days right here where I tried to install turbines."

"Isn't that an interesting idea?" I shake my head and smile. "It's not a lawn mower, by the way."

Nick leans back into the seat, spreads his legs wide, and ropes his arm around my shoulders. "So, I'm supposed to trust you, huh?"

"Yup." I turn the key and steer the tractor up the hill to the back of the orchard.

The sun is shining, not a drop of humidity in the air. We get a few waves and strange glances from the guests. I park on the hillside, the highest elevation on the property. Anyone who denies the beauty from this vantage point needs to go home.

Nick walks to the peak and crosses his arms over his chest. There simply isn't a better view. Newfound Lake is in the center, solid blue and stunning. Leaves painted with vivid colors fill the mountains surrounding the water. It's breathtaking.

"Pretty, isn't it?" We stand side by side, taking in the fresh mountain air. "Growing up here was magical. These fields were our playground. I could never leave."

"I've got to admit, it is an awesome view. Now, why did you bring me all the way up here?"

Nick is now facing me. My heart races—why did I bring him to the top? Maybe part of me wanted to show him what he almost ruined, what would've been lost, or maybe part of me wanted him away from the crowd. I'm not quite ready to be seen with enemy number one.

I choose to lie instead. "No one ever comes up here to grab these apples. Too long of a walk. I figured we could help by grabbing a few baskets." This is not entirely untrue.

Nick lifts the poles from the wagon. A man with initiative— one point for that. "Where to?" he asks. I catch myself staring a few seconds too long and a smirk appears. "These poles are long."

I burst out laughing because he said *long pole*. What the hell is wrong with me, honestly? It's like I'm back in middle school.

The next few minutes I spend actively trying to focus on the apples instead of Nick while he reaches the pole up into the trees to grab hold of the apples. For a city boy dressed in an expensive shirt and khakis, he does surprisingly well. His basket is half full of Gala apples in a matter of ten minutes.

"What does your family do with all these apples?"

I rest the end of my picker against the ground and lean in. "The majority goes to local restaurants and markets. We use a bunch for apple pies and cider for the country store. My grandmother and Lucas are in charge of that, although lately, Lucas has been pulling most of the weight. The rest is shipped to New York, where my parents run the hard cider company. One big family operation."

Nick continues picking as he listens. Beads of sweat have formed on his brow. He's working hard to fill his bucket. "It's an impressive business."

"The funny thing is, it's never felt like a business. It's just what we do. I was the odd duck in all of it. I wanted to be a teacher. I still have my hand in things, but not as much as Jackson, obviously. I'm sure you feel the same about your business. It's a job but also a passion."

Nick gives the picker a break, wipes the back of his hand across his forehead, and walks over to my basket. "I'm not sure

I'd call it a passion." He looks over his shoulder at the mountains in the distance for a second and then turns back. "Yours is not nearly as full as mine. I thought you'd be a pro at this."

"That sounds like a challenge."

"Maybe it is. I'm all about healthy competition." Without another word, he grabs each basket handle, dumps the apples into the wagon, and returns my basket to the ground in front of me.

"What the heck did you do that for? They're all going to roll around the wagon and bump into each other."

"Is that you trying to talk dirty?"

That damn smirk again.

"The apples, Nick, the apples." I'm blushing for sure, no question. I haven't had this much fun in as long as I can remember. "Why did you dump the baskets?"

"Because we are going to have a healthy competition."

God, he's hot. He's got the muscles. He's got the height. He's got every feature I find delectable in a man. I need to stop staring. However, I don't think I've looked at a man the way I'm looking at Nick since … ever. Richard was the only man.

"As I was saying …"

He snaps me back to reality. "You choose the apples we pick. We'll each have ten minutes to fill the bucket. Whoever picks the most wins."

He's got a picker in one hand and his bucket in the other. Nick is all business, and for once, I'm totally into this plan.

"Okay, but what's the prize?" I ask. Within seconds, ten different inappropriate ideas flash through my mind. All I can think about is how Mia would react in this situation. I choose silence and spare myself the embarrassment.

Nick's fingers tighten around the pole. I'm not sure I understand why I'm suddenly admiring how strong his hands look.

"The winner picks dessert tonight." A small smile curls his lips and his eyebrows tilt enough to make me avoid eye contact. I bend to grab my bucket.

"Let's head to the Empire row. The next row over."

He programs the timer on his watch. I scan the treetops to find the one with the most fruit. I leave my bucket on the ground and ready my picker in the picking position.

"On your mark. Get set. Go."

It's a frenzy, like I'm a kid again. Running around the tree, feverishly poking the pole, knowing full well my aim is off when more apples cascade to the ground, a few bumping my head on their way down. I glance over at Nick. Mr. Calm, Cool, and Collected. He's a man on a mission. Pole, poke, pull, and place, over and over, filling his basket. It's kinda hot, I'm not going to lie.

When his back is turned, I ditch my pole, run to his basket, and tilt it over. The apples start sliding down the aisle between the trees. I swing around and run.

"You did not!"

I'm back at my tree. Nick's eyes dart to my basket. I snag it from the ground and start running.

"You said whoever has the most when the timer goes off wins," I yell behind my shoulder and keep running. He's gaining on me the best he can with his clunky work boots.

"Then I better not catch you!"

I duck and dart between the trees and across a second row.

He's going to get me; it's just a matter of time. I need to last until the timer goes off. He's a few steps behind me, and I'm giggling like a teenager. I cut across another row, lose sight of him, and then hear a scream pierce the mountain air, chilling my body to its core. It's a woman.

My feet dig into the ground, eyes scanning left and right. Again, a high-pitched scream.

I bend down and look to my right. Nick. I see his boots

through the tree stumps. I run to him, and then I spot my brother, Jackson.

"Holy shit." I drop the picker and shield my eyes from my butt-ass naked brother standing next to the large tree on the hill with his hand covering his goods.

"What the fuck, man?"

"Oh my god."

"You failed to mention your brother likes to have sex with his girlfriend behind trees up here. Is this a family thing? I knew we weren't here to pick apples."

# 4



What a difference from the last time I met Jackson. Butt-naked behind a tree was not what I had envisioned. And by the look on his face, he wasn't too pleased we ruined the mood. I've got to hand it to him—fucking behind a tree isn't something I've tried. But hey, whatever you're into.

Today was the first time in recent memory that I can remember laughing so hard. My phone was off, no confines of office walls closing in on me, no expectations, just freedom. Every minute I spend here, the more I am discovering old parts of myself.

I've changed into dark gray dress pants, a crisp white button-down shirt, and black loafers, hoping it's not too much. Harold will meet me out front in five.

"Ready, sir?" Harold asks as he opens the back door to my black Cadillac SUV.

"Sure are. We're headed to Lake Street."

"I'm aware. I did a little digging and a drive-by already. The Wi-Fi in town is unreliable, and I don't want your date waiting."

"Thanks, Harold."

The sun descends behind the mountain range in the distance, casting a golden glow over the landscape. The air is comfortable and cool compared to the heated, exhaust-heavy odor of Boston's downtown core. Main Street is desolate, except for the couples finishing an evening meal at the local Irish tavern. Everyone else is tucked into their modest homes on the side streets or in log cabins along the mountain ridge.

Meriden lacks most of the conveniences of a modern city, but no city can hold a torch to the beauty of this landscape. And although I had no problem going forward with the wind farms, I did understand the pride these people have for their town. The more time I spent scoping out large pieces of property, the more the nostalgic charm of the area seeped into my bones. An offhand comment by an executive board member turned into a real consideration, and I found myself wondering what it would be like to own a piece of Newfound Lake. Why not? Why not me?

As Harold pulls up to the old white Victorian, I round my shoulders and push my back into the seat. I take in the slanted porch, overgrown lawn, and chipping paint and wonder if I've made a mistake. As I look toward the roofline, the wind picks up, and a few apples from the tree in the front yard shake loose and fall to the ground. I'm watching one roll toward the driveway when Harold opens my door, signaling for me to exit and go to Shannon.

After I brush off any missed lint and straighten the creases in my pants, I cross the dirt driveway, attempting to avoid loose pebbles caked with mud to preserve my shoes as much as possible.

When I'm halfway, the screen door swings open, and I stop dead in my tracks. Shannon leans her hip on the doorframe. She's wearing a short, flowing yellow sundress with thin straps over her tanned shoulders and tan flip-flops with a too-small-to-make-out tattoo on her right ankle. Her jet-black hair shines like the silk of a custom gown as it cascades down her neck, onto her shoulders, and down her arm.

She raises a hand and waves. "Hey, city boy! Come on up."

She looks even better than I remember. I knew she was a knockout when I first spotted her at the town meetings this summer. But now, without the stress and town's eyes lasering in on me, I am suddenly aware of just how stunning Shannon is. She could be standing in front of a barn, and it wouldn't take away an ounce of beauty. She possesses the kind of innate sexiness that leaves you gasping for air. Her deep brown eyes are impossible to avoid.

"Hi, Shannon." I put my arm around her waist and kiss her cheek gently, eyes drifting down to her chest at a perfect angle to see nothing between her breasts and the fabric of her dress. "Are you hungry for dinner? I had Harold make a reservation for us."

"Harold again, huh?" She cranes her neck in view of the driver's seat and waves.

Shannon sweeps her long silk strands behind her shoulder and gives me a thorough once-over, starting with the buttons on my shirt, all the way down to my Gucci loafers. "Am I underdressed, or are you overdressed?" She giggles, grips her hem, and tosses the gauzy yellow fabric left to right, revealing her tan, toned thighs. I imagine what lies underneath.

"You look amazing, and you don't need to change a thing. Shall we?" I hold out my hand and am met with a satisfied smile. She turns to close the door behind her, leaving the scent of peach conditioner in the air, and slips her hand into mine. Her soft palm sends shivers through me.

Settled into the back seat, she crosses her legs and leans in my direction, allowing me to inhale the intoxicating fragrance of cinnamon and vanilla lotion she must've lathered on her legs. The perfect combination of sweet and spice. Apparently,

Meriden women can smell delicious, despite the many local fields of cow shit.

"Where are we headed?"

"Harold made reservations at the Six Burner Bistro in Plymouth. They have a little of everything, and the reviews are excellent."

"Great choice."

"You've been?" I ask, wide-eyed.

Shannon's laugh is adorable in the sexiest way. "Small-town girls sometimes leave town, city boy."

I'm suddenly aware of every fingertip gracing my thigh. "Of course you have. Sorry. I didn't mean to imply … I'm glad Harold chose well."

As I look out the window, one farm after another streams by, each one with a different tractor as a lawn ornament, reminding me of our earlier encounter. "So, that was quite a show today."

"That was unexpected, to say the least. I don't think I've ever laughed so hard."

Her shoulder vibrates from the erupting giggles.

"You and me both. That isn't something you farm kids do on the regular?"

Her hand flicks onto my chest.

"I remember being in high school and knowing Jackson and his girlfriend hid up there from time to time. I never asked for specifics. But I can't believe I didn't spot the tractor. Sorry about that."

"No need to apologize. I've got to give him props. It's kind of reckless. I like it." I'm not sure having sex on the ground has ever sounded appealing before. However, the mental picture of bending Shannon over behind the tree out in the wild sounds fucking amazing.

Watching the country roads wind through the mountains, I'm acutely aware of how unsettled I am around Shannon. I usually have women eating out of my hand within the first five minutes. But Shannon's self-confidence and straightforward manner have me reeling, and I wonder about this foreign sensation in my stomach.

I glance at her and find her deep chocolate eyes melting the tightness in my jaw and igniting all five of my senses.

"So, word around town is you're looking for a lake house? True, city boy?"

Something about the way she calls me *city boy* has me wanting to flip up her dress, unzip my pants, and have her ride me until she's begging for more. "Sure is. I have to admit, this place took me by surprise. The views around Newfound are jaw-dropping. It'll be nice to get a reprieve from the city chaos occasionally. Once I got a taste of it, I wanted more."

"You're right about that. The lake and mountains are the reasons most of us have never left. There are some beautiful lakefront homes. They seem to get bigger and more grandiose with every new build. Do you live in Boston full time?"

"I do. Penthouse suite in the Seaport District. Headquarters are located around the corner. Are you a Boston fan?"

"I haven't spent much time in the city. Only on a few occasions. But I'm a New England sports fan through and through—Pats, Bruins, Celtics, and Sox. Love them all."

*Sexy and a sports fan? Hot.*

We pass Plymouth State and Harold pulls against the curb. Dusk is upon us, casting a soft glow through the small-town street as the lampposts illuminate every third yard. Couples stroll hand in hand, in and out of restaurants and shops lining the cobblestone sidewalks. Despite the high ratings of the Six Burner Bistro, I realize with every person who walks by that I am overdressed. In Boston on a Saturday night, you'd never step out dressed in casual summer attire, at least not in the places I dine. The locals look a hell of a lot more comfortable than I feel.

I shrug it off and reach for Shannon's hand as we walk through the propped-open door and into the dimly lit restaurant. The atmosphere is charming and possesses the right amount of romance.

The hostess seats us at a bistro table for two in the corner facing the bar area with our backs to two bay windows that display the lit sidewalks and passing patrons. "This okay?"

"It's perfect." Shannon drapes her jean jacket over her chair, revealing the backless dress and her clearly defined back muscles. The waitress delivers our menus and starts us off with a carafe of ice water.

"Can I get you anything to drink this evening?" the waitress asks, scanning the street in the background.

"Shannon?"

"A glass of Pinot. Thank you." Her forearms rest on the table and her lips curl into a soft smile.

"And for you, sir?"

"I'll do American Honey on the rocks." I answer without my eyes ever leaving Shannon's lips.

"Sure thing. Be right back to tell you about our specials."

"Great, thank you." I place my menu on the table and stare at Shannon while she scans the meal offerings, her soft, sweet smile shining with a coat of lip gloss. I find myself wondering what her lips taste like. "So, tell me why a woman as beautiful as you hasn't been scooped up. I'd be willing to bet every man within a thirty-mile radius of Meriden has asked you out."

Shannon places her menu down and leans forward on her folded arms. When she tilts her chin down, I wish I could yank those words out of the air and stuff them back into my mouth.

"That's kind of you to say, really. And I was wondering how to word this if it came up. I was, I mean, I am—I guess I am technically married."

The oxygen in my lungs disappears, leaving a sense of suffocation. I lean back in my chair and search her face for understanding.

"No, wait. What I should've said is I'm going through a divorce. It's been over for a long time, and if I'm being honest, this is the first date I've been on in over ten years."

I process the information as it replays in my head and try to readjust my preconceived notions about Shannon. She must sense my discomfort because she reaches for my hand and squeezes my palm. "I'm sorry. I probably should've told you this when you asked me out. I wasn't thinking straight. Your invite caught me off guard, and I figured, why not say yes? Looking back, that was selfish of me to not be up front with you."

I undo my cuff links and roll my sleeves to my elbows and look over my shoulder, suddenly wondering if someone turned up the thermostat. I've dated divorced women in the past; that's not the problem. I just hadn't expected this from Shannon. Meriden already fucking hates me, and now I'll have some hick who'll want to kick my ass for asking out his soon-to-be ex-wife? Why would a man willingly fuck up a life with her? Especially someone willing to live in the middle of nowhere.

"Did small-town life get to him?"

Shannon leans back and squints at me as the waitress returns with our drinks.

"Here we go. Would you like to hear today's specials?" Without an answer, she recites the list from memory while I watch Shannon's eyes trace my arms from wrist to elbow with intense focus. She shifts in her seat and recrosses her legs in the opposite direction, never taking her eyes from my forearms. Her stare and slight smirk stir embers of desire from deep inside. The sensation is so foreign, I'm starting to question if I'm hungrier than I realized.

After the waitress gives us another minute to decide,

Shannon looks up. "What is a guy like you doing with two sleeves of tattoos? This is the last thing I expected."

"I guess we've both been surprised tonight." I lean forward, leaving only twelve inches between us, and reach for her hands. "Let's start with your past having nothing to do with your future, and a nicely dressed man doesn't mean he's not a little rough underneath. Being divorced doesn't bother me in the least. Do tattoos bother you?"

She turns her hands over in mine and caresses my skin with her thumbs.

"Nick, maybe I'm supposed to be more careful in what I say on a first date, but you'll have to excuse me since it's been a while. You look great, and I'm sure I don't have to tell you that, but my interest piqued when you rolled up your sleeves. This"—she traces her fingers along the muscles in my forearm—"is sexy as hell.

"And booze ruined my marriage. It was nothing that could be fixed. We'd been together since high school. It's sad, but I'm ready to move on. I want to be happy."

I watch her nail trace my father's name inked into my forearm and realize how she's only been with one man since her teenage years. This turns me on. It also sounds like she's put up with a bigger burden than she should've been expected to carry.

"What about you?"

I'm in the trenches of thoughts running through my head, imagining how many different things a woman like Shannon deserves in and out of the bedroom, when the waitress reappears with bread, oil, and balsamic vinegar, ready to take our orders. I release my hand, maintain eye contact, and tug my pants to the side underneath the table to make room for my bulging desire. I notice Shannon's smirk and wonder if I made my adjustment too obvious.

How does this woman have me on edge twenty minutes into our first date?

We order our entrees and resume conversation while someone in the back lowers the dimmer switch. The waitress lights the small candle placed between us. Every table in the restaurant is occupied by couples, and all six barstools are filled. The bartender mixes and pours as soft jazz streams from the camouflaged speakers in each corner. The atmosphere couldn't be more opposite from the crowded, noisy five-star restaurants on the streets of Boston. My livelihood resides in the city, but this place has lowered my blood pressure and set my body at ease.

"Me? Never married. I date occasionally, but it's tough with work and traveling. I haven't been in a serious relationship in years, mostly just dates to work events, that sort of thing."

"Oh." I sense Shannon's unease as she shifts in her seat, and I'm wondering if I just cornered myself, if I sound like a playboy.

"I'm not like a serial dater or anything. I spent some time on a dating app, but I won't get into that. It's mostly coworkers who set me up." I don't know why I'm explaining myself, or why I'm concerned about upsetting her.

Shannon's sweet smile returns as dinner arrives, and I'm thankful for sustenance. I order another round for the two of us, instantly regretting it, thinking of her ex. "Sorry, I should've asked first."

"No, it's totally fine. I'm not the one with the drinking problem."

Her words prevent the dread from seeping in, and I unclench my teeth and let the buttery scallops melt in my mouth. Not half bad.

The rest of dinner is spent learning about her teaching career, her love of everything outdoors, and Meriden. I don't think I've ever given a shit to listen to a date talk before. I couldn't tell you what any of them do for a living. I'm always too worried about the next board meeting, the next acquisition, to focus on anyone else's life stories.

And yet I find myself completely entranced by the way Shannon recalls her childhood, her heartfelt anecdotes about her grandparents, and her loyalty to these small-town streets. Her world is foreign to me; for every slowed-down family meal and excited home football game, I recall the speed of growing up at uncomfortable business dinners with my parents while being mesmerized by flaming crème brûlée. My mother never wanted a swanky lifestyle, but she would've followed my father to the ends of the world. She loved his high-rolling ass until his last breath and still does to this day.

"So, how does a busy city boy, tattooed from wrist to who knows where, find himself in a small-town restaurant with a small-town girl?"

"Am I sensing you'd like to know where my tattoos end?"

Shannon's cheeks turn a deep red, and she returns her eyes to her plate.

"Because if you are, I'm flattered. And your small town has some charm. I've forgotten that life doesn't have to feel like someone has their finger pressed on the fast-forward button continuously. There is something about you that caught my eye from the minute I spotted you in the audience at the town hall meeting. I regret the circumstances under which I met you, but I'm hoping we can have a fresh start."

"I think we can try. Fortunately, your plan fell through, and we don't have to revisit the reason you initially came to town. I can look past your business model for now, but I can't speak for the rest of the town, especially my brother. And for the record, I wouldn't have said yes to this date unless I wanted to."

She leans forward enough for the fabric of her dress to separate from her skin, revealing her rock-hard nipples. The embers ignite into a full-blown bonfire, and I know I'm going to get into trouble here.

The waitress delivers the check, I pay, and then text Harold to bring the Cadillac around. I search for a reason to extend the night, but my options are limited. There is no way in hell I'm inviting her back to the bed-and-breakfast.

When I place my arm around her waist, the string of her panties under her thin dress presses against my thumb. "I had a great time tonight." I'm hunting for a clue that she doesn't want this evening to end.

She leans against the brick front of the restaurant while Harold pulls to the curb.

"I've got it." I signal that I've got the door. Before Shannon slides into the back seat, she brushes against my chest, and I freeze, stone solid.

She slides her hands up to my elbows, fingers under the fabric, and says, "How many more surprises do you have up your sleeves?"

"We don't have to end this night. And you forgot our bet. You were supposed to choose dessert." I cup her chin, tilt it up, and pull her gently to my lips, savoring every sweet inch of her skin as her body warms against mine. The intensity of the kiss surprises me, more passion in these twenty seconds than I've felt in years. Holding her against me, she feels like a fragile glass vase that needs my protection.

She tilts her head and bends forward to enter the vehicle and I want more than anything to press the pause button, rest her chest on the seat, and fill her from behind. I haven't had sex in a while, and I'm finding Shannon more desirable than any woman I've met in recent years.

"Want to stop by the Binn, city boy?" Her eyes are mischievous as she slides across the leather seat.

*The Binn?* I'd follow this woman into a bucket.

"Sure. I'm not sure what that is exactly, but I'm certainly intrigued."

"It's a local bar just east of the lake, off the main drag, near Basic Ingredients."

"Spoken like a true New Englandah." I shake my head and give her a slight eye roll because no matter if you're a city or small-town New Englander, you *pak the ca* and use buildings to give directions.

She seems slightly surprised by my willingness to go, but she smiles and holds my hand in the back seat. It transports me to a time when holding hands was a huge leap with a girl and would leave me dreaming about her when I was alone in bed.

Harold relies on Shannon's directions. As expected, our navigation system doesn't work in the mountains.

"I don't think I've ever seen a place so dark." Outside the windows, I see nothing but a few taillights in the distance. "Wait. Look over there." I lower my window. Shannon slides closer and leans to peer out the glass. Harold reduces his speed. "I swear I saw fireworks."

Shannon squeezes my hand. "Not a night without fireworks in these parts. If you stick around long enough, you'll hear the blast echo off the mountain ranges, and if you're lucky, you'll spot them through the tree line. It's part of the landscape. I don't even hear it anymore."

"Really? It's so loud."

"You get used to it. Do you notice all the honking and sirens on the Boston streets each night?"

"Good point. I don't. It's interesting how you become part of your surroundings and how certain aspects go unnoticed because it's an everyday occurrence."

Harold pulls into the dirt parking lot, hitting several potholes. Shannon is crushed against my shoulder, laughing hysterically as I grip the "oh shit" bar.

"This lot is a mess," I say. Surveying our options, it's clear there's nowhere to park. "How about you swing down the side road and I'll text you when we're ready?"

"Maybe Harold wants to come in and grab a beer," Shannon says, looking to Harold for confirmation, and he instantly turns to me for approval. Never dawned on me that he may want to come in. I simply nod.

"Don't mind if I do. It'd be nice to grab a beer in one of these—is this what they call a dive bar?"

"That sounds about right. Spot ahead." Shannon cranes her body forward, pointing straight at a four-by-four backing out. "Tyler is leaving."

"You know the guy backing out?"

"Yeah, he's one of my brother's best friends. It would be odd if I didn't know who that was. I'm sure you saw him at some point this summer."

I never considered who I'd be running into—ramming into Shannon is my only agenda item. "Is your brother here?"

Shannon turns and shrugs. "Not sure. I guess we'll find out. If you'd asked me a couple months ago, I would've laughed. But Solia turned his world upside down in the best way possible. He's smitten with her, so he's often here with her and the guys."

Shannon loops her arms through both mine and Harold's as we cross the dirt lot. My shoes dip into some god-awful mud hole, soaking my socks, and all I can do is laugh at myself. I need practical shoes.

Harold pulls open the tavern door and the sounds of an acoustic guitar float toward us. I might as well be walking into a foreign country. Everything is dimly lit, dark wood, and possibly antique. There are old iron beer company signs hanging from nails on wooden posts, Christmas twinkly lights strung from the rafters, and the smallest wooden platform of a stage across the room.

"If you live around here, you have to know the Binn and everyone inside."

I plaster on a smile and hide my uneasiness. It only takes a second before eyes bore into me. I'm in the line of fire. Their glares are darts, and I'm the bull's-eye. If I were the betting sort, I'd wager the man standing at the bar has been doing target practice for months, just waiting for a moment like this.

Jackson. At least this time he has clothes on.

# 5

You'd think I walked in with two circus clowns. The entire bar turns and stares in our direction. When you're not from town, they know you're not from town. I spot Jackson as soon as my foot crosses the threshold. His eyes say it all: disbelief and fury. Every barstool does a forty-five-degree turn in our direction and time suspends. Maybe I didn't think this through enough.

Jackson slams his beer down and walks toward us with Ryan close behind, who shakes his head in warning. "Look what the cat dragged in. If it isn't the guy who tried to destroy this town and my sex life. You decided to swim with the bottom-feeders and have a beer where we'd all be. Great thinking, man."

I untangle my arms from Nick and Harold and step forward, closer to Jackson. "First of all, I invited them. And earlier was your own darn fault. That was more than either of us wanted to see. You're lucky I love Solia." I hold out my arms in their defense. "Nick's looking to buy a summer house here. You'll be seeing him around." I'm trying to make eye contact with Jackson, but he's looking past me and straight at Nick.

I back up so the three men face one another. "How about we have a do-over? Nick, this is my brother, Jackson. Jackson, this is Nick, and his driver Harold."

Jackson turns to Ryan. "His driver, for fuck's sake. Did she really say that?" Jackson is in hysterics, bent over, his hands on his knees.

I see Nick straighten his back and rub his knuckles together. Harold smirks and eyes Cindy behind the bar, seemingly unfazed by the verbal exchange.

"Don't be an ass, Jackson. Shake hands, move on. The deal fell through. There are no wind turbines being installed. Harold, that's Cindy. How about I take you over there and we let these two figure out their shit?"

Both Jackson and Nick look at me as if to say, *"You're leaving us alone—together?"* Nick fidgets with his dress collar and Jackson's facial muscles twitch. I leave them both standing there and walk with Harold over to the bar.

"Hey, Shannon, who's your new friend?"

"Cindy, this is Harold. He works with Nick. We stopped in for a quick drink. This is Cindy, our resident bartender. If the Binn is open, Cindy is working. She'll have your order memorized by the time you leave." I wink at her, and she smooths the bumps in her high ponytail and offers her hand.

"Nice to meet you, Harold. What'll it be? Let me guess, you're a bottled-beer drinker, not tap."

Harold's forehead wrinkles in surprise and soft dimples form in his reddening cheeks. "You don't mess around, ma'am. I'll take a Heineken."

"Knew it. I might be getting older, but I still got it."

"You can't be a day over thirty." Harold lays it on thick.

"Well, aren't you a charmer. Honey, I'm the energy I want to be. My birth certificate is the only thing telling me I'm forty-six." Cindy winks and turns to me. "Shannon, Pinot? And what about the other gentleman?" She points over to Nick, who is now shaking Jackson's hand. Neither man looks thrilled by the peace agreement, but at least it's a step in the right direction.

"American Honey on the rocks, and yes to the Pinot."

"Coming right up. Go grab a high top. I'll be over in a sec. Hey, I meant to ask Jackson—how are your grandparents doing?"

"They're good. Same old, same old. I saw them earlier today rocking away on the porch."

"I miss seeing them in here. I'll be sure to swing by soon."

"They'd love that, Cindy." My grandparents used to frequent happy hour until driving at night became stressful.

"I can stay. You go ahead, Shannon." Harold keeps his feet firmly planted on the plank closest to the bar while he watches Cindy bop behind the counter, pouring, uncorking, gathering ice. If I'm not mistaken, seems Harold might be a little captivated by our Cindy. They're close enough in age, this might be interesting. Come to think of it, I haven't seen Cindy on a date in some time, nor have I asked her for an update. I need to check in with her.

I choose a table and slide onto the round-top stool. Nick's arm brushes against my shoulder, and he takes the stool adjacent to mine. "Well, that was civil," he says. "No blood was drawn."

"Perfect. Now we can carry on with our night." I place my hand on his forearm, sensing the stress pulsing through his veins. Harold joins us, Heineken in hand and Cindy by his side with the rest of our order.

"You must be the famous Nick I've heard so much about. It can't all be true if our sweetheart Shannon is here with you." Cindy offers her warm smile and friendly laugh, cutting the tension.

Nick inhales deeply and drops his shoulders from his ears. "I'm not sure I'll agree to the famous part, but we're on the same page about this girl." He extends his hand to shake Cindy's. "It's nice to meet you."

"Same. Don't worry about the townies. They'll come around. It just might take time. You did try to ruin our town and all."

"You're absolutely right. I did almost ruin it. It's easy for me to say it's just business, nothing personal, but after being around for a little while, I realize how deeply personal it was. Luckily, for Meriden, Green Breeze barked up the wrong tree this time." Nick shrugs and takes a lengthy sip of his whiskey.

"There's nothing more personal than trying to take someone's land from underneath them. I hope you stay away from all the trees in our state. Just saying." Cindy sends me an exaggerated eye roll, tightens her ponytail, and heads back to the bar.

Nick shifts his focus to the tavern walls, observing all the license plates, photos, and antique liquor and beer signs. "This place certainly has an interesting aesthetic." He smiles, his dimples on display as he tries to change the subject.

I wasn't thinking about kissing him again, but I am now.

"An aesthetic? Meaning?"

"Cozy, like home, I'm not sure. I like it. It's—different." His eyes trail my lips as he shifts his stool closer to me. "Yeah, it's cool."

Harold watches Cindy walk away and then turns to join the conversation. "No offense, Shannon, but this is a far cry from the big-city bars."

Nick begins to reply, but Harold is now looking past the two of us, focused on a vacant barstool. "You two mind if I head over and sit at the bar? I think there's a game on."

Harold is halfway across the room before either of us responds. "I don't think I've seen him watch a game ever. What the hell is that about?" Nick squints up at the television screen. "Isn't that a replay of the summer's Masters' tournament?"

Giggling at Nick's cluelessness, I turn my head and point at Cindy behind the bar. "I'm pretty sure he's not watching a game."

Nick looks from Harold to Cindy and back and nods.

Now that we're alone and most people in the Binn have turned their sneers away, the desire eases back to learn more about Nick.

"How does someone end up working in the wind turbine business?" I'm so out of practice with men. I'm sure work is the last thing he wants to talk about, but I'm at a loss and hate awkward silences. Nick leans forward, resting his elbows on the round top, allowing a breeze of his spicy pine scent to waft my way, immediately making me tingle in places I forgot existed. I cross my legs to trap the heat and lean closer, desperate to consume as much of him as I can.

He takes a sharp inhale and looks up at the rafters, making me wonder if I've just opened Pandora's box. "I always knew I'd work for the family business. My father started this company decades ago, at the start of the green energy boom. I'm the oldest of my siblings—my sister is twenty-six and my brother is twenty-two—and my father never hid the fact he wanted me to take over the company one day. I didn't have much say in the matter."

As his words fill the air, my heart feels heavy and my teeth dig into my lower lip.

"I went to Northeastern for my undergraduate and studied business and then went on to Boston University for my MBA. Naturally, the next step was to begin working for my father, learn the company structure, and see what side of the business I was best suited for. I spent all my summers interning in different departments. A few months in, my father died of a heart attack. No warning, no signs, just gone." He snaps his fingers and slumps his weight forward.

"I'm so sorry, Nick. We don't need to talk about this."

His hand returns to the table and reaches for mine. "It's fine. He's been gone eight years. I miss him like hell, but time has given room for some peace. It's unfortunate you've seen the negative side of things first. I've worked tirelessly to learn this business and make him proud."

His words give way to a softness in his eyes. A piece of resentment deep inside me chips off and floats away. He's a man, a man who lost his dad and desperately wants to make him proud. Don't we all want to make our parents proud? He didn't choose this line of work; it chose him.

"I don't doubt for a second he is more than proud of you. You are successful and business is good. Right?"

His eyes cast downward and a slight darkness washes over him. "Yes, it is. I just …" He pauses and tilts his chin in the opposite direction, inhales, pushing the air out of his nose and returning his focus to me. "I haven't stopped. My life has been a whirlwind, meeting after meeting, budget sheets, inspections, the list is endless. Listen, I don't want to sit here and complain because I make a great living. It wasn't until my mother was diagnosed with breast cancer this past year that I began to wish I had a little more time to breathe so I could spend part of my life doing other things I love."

My grandparents' advice holds true: *never judge a book by its cover*. It never ceases to amaze me that, despite how people present on the outside, you never know what someone is going through under the surface. Nick's rock-hard facade and demeanor are armor protecting him from painful loss and imposed expectations.

"Nick, I'm so sorry. Your mother, how is she?"

"We are very lucky. They caught it during a routine screening and at the very early stages. She had a lumpectomy and a few rounds of radiation. She's on some long-term medication, but since all that, she's cancer-free. It was a real wake-up call."

Upon relaying her positive prognosis, Nick's relief is obvious.

"Losing a parent and taking over a family business is a lot to deal with, and add a medical scare to it … yikes. You and Jackson have a little more in common, regarding the family business end of things, than you both realize. No one expected me to take over the family business. But Jackson, he was always the one. Whether it's on the cider end or the farm end, he was the golden child. Thank god because I wasn't cut out for that.

"Luckily for me, Jackson lives and breathes the farm air. Nowhere he'd rather be. My life plan was always teaching and family. It was pretty simple. This divorce has me rattled and in desperate need of uncomplicated."

My words are the brutal truth. The next thing I know, Nick's lips are on mine, and he is standing over my stool, one hand grasping my nape and the other holding my chin. His tongue explores my mouth, and my legs go weak. Wild sensation spreads through me, every inch of my skin on high alert. His body inches forward and his hand leaves the base of my neck and travels down my spine. I've never been so thankful for a backless dress. His strong hand grazing my skin is enough to set me loose.

I forget where I am, who I am, and for a moment, I just live. If this is what I've been missing, sign me the hell up.

The heat of the moment reaches a fever pitch and, as if on cue, his lips softly close and he gently pulls away. His cheek rubs against mine as he moves his lips to my ear. His teeth nibble my earlobe and he breathlessly whispers, "If I don't stop now, I don't trust myself." A blue flame shoots through my body, desperately wanting more. Nick pulls away, leaving a void I want to fill with every inch of him.

My eyes readjust to the light, and I'm reminded of where I am. The fire coursing through me is quickly extinguished when I see several sets of eyes focused on the two of us. I break into laughter and the fire makes its way to my cheeks. It's been a long time since I've kissed anyone like this, if ever, and I can sense the shock waves vibrating throughout the bar.

Nick settles back into his seat without letting go of my hand. "Sorry. I embarrassed you."

I smile, lean over the table, and plant a soft kiss on his lips, hoping to reassure him embarrassment is the last thing I'm concerned about. And for now, I'm going to forget how we met.

"How about we finish these drinks and head back to my place? Maybe I'll claim my win for dessert." As soon as the words fill the air, I want to shove them back. *Who am I? What the hell?*

Nick's mouth curls and he runs his tongue over his top teeth. His playboy smile appears as he presses his hands together between his knees and leans in. He is one of the best-looking men I've ever seen. He's got a jawline chiseled from stone, and don't get me started on his deep-set dark eyes with lashes for miles.

He holds his glass, jiggles the ice, and downs the rest of the whiskey. "I'm ready whenever you are." He winks and pushes his barstool, grabbing it to prevent it from crashing to the floor.

Harold is at the bar, immersed in conversation with Cindy. Nick leans close to Harold's ear and Harold nods in response, but I'm too far away to hear the conversation. Harold hands the keys to Nick, who then stuffs them in his pocket and heads back in my direction with a swagger and confidence I'm not accustomed to. I'm not sure I can handle a man like Nick.

*What am I even doing inviting him back to my house?* Nerves rage through my body, making me a little off-balance. I contemplate rescinding my offer.

"Harold is going to stay. Apparently, he's enjoying himself, and your friend, Cindy, offered him a ride home," Nick says as his fingers comb through his dark locks, his gaze on my lips. As if lifted from my chair by an invisible force, I down my wine and head for the door, hand in hand with a man I've basically just met.

Mentally, I scan through my house: *Did I leave it a mess? Did I make my bed? Are there gross dishes in the sink? I don't even know if I have anything to offer him to drink or eat. What am I doing?*

With Nick behind the wheel instead of Harold, this is more like a real date. "Damn, this man is tiny." Nick adjusts the seat several inches, tilts it back, and spreads his legs to get comfortable. He then looks over at me and grins. I practically melt, my mind reeling, thinking of what he could do to me if he already has me this excited.

Placing one hand on the steering wheel, he reaches for mine with the other. I'm hoping the nerves and excitement pulsing through me aren't channeled through our physical contact. Today's country hits play in the background as the night breeze wafts through the windows, and for the first time in a long time, I'm right where I'm supposed to be. Being on a date with the town's number one enemy was unexpected, but I'm willing to overlook that given Nick's sex appeal and what seems to be genuine interest for this town and slight regret for upsetting so many. Learning he was thrown into the family business upon his father's death has shifted my mindset completely. I think others would see Nick differently if they knew.

The streets are deserted. Meriden is a small lake town whose population quadruples in the summer and empties out like a concert hall in the fall. There is nothing that compares to Newfound Lake in the summer, but each season has its own appeal and beauty. Labor Day weekend is beautiful if you like the peace and serenity of nature.

As we make our way down Main Street, Nick squeezes my hand and breaks the silence. "What are your plans for the rest of the weekend?"

"Tomorrow is kind of heavy. Jackson's girlfriend passed away in a boating accident on the lake last year over Labor Day weekend. We're having a memorial service tomorrow in memory of her. Jackson and Trinity's family had a small stone monument made. I'm pretty sure it was Solia's idea, but she'll never take credit. Regardless, it'll be special for Trinity's family and will provide needed closure for Jackson."

"Sounds like a perfect idea. I'm sorry for his loss."

"Yeah, it was tough going for a long time. Jackson came close to moving to New York and working for my parents. Actually, that was right about the time you rolled into town. In a weird way, the whole wind turbine project brought Meriden together, more specifically Solia and Jackson. And by Jackson meeting Solia, he was able to heal in ways no one thought possible. Divine intervention right there for you."

"Is this thing tomorrow private?"

"No, not at all. Anyone can come. It's at noon."

"I might. In most people's eyes around here, I'm an enemy. We all got off on the wrong foot. Plus, if it's important to you, I'd like to be there."

*Where did this guy come from? I take care of people; people don't take care of me. Is this how other people feel? Supported?*

"Sure, you are more than welcome." I swallow hard, hoping I didn't just set him up to fall into a snake pit. What was I supposed to say? No, you can't come?

With the light of the full moon illuminating the street, we turn onto Lake Street. When my driveway is in view, a shiver takes over my body and I hold my breath. *What the fuck is Richard's bike doing in my driveway?*

"Are you expecting someone?" Nick puts the vehicle in park, scans the bike, and turns to me as I sit paralyzed in the passenger seat.

"No, not at all." I lean forward, squinting to get a better glimpse, but I can't see Richard anywhere.

"Whose bike is this?" Nick points at the Harley leaning on the kickstand at the top of the driveway.

"That would be Richard's, my ex."

"Does he stop by often? Is this going to be a problem?" Nick's energy has shifted. His body is tight, his jaw clenched.

"No, there is no reason for him to be here. This is definitely a problem."

Nick releases my hand and reaches for his door handle. There's no way I'm letting him find Richard before I do. I push open my door and hightail it to my front porch without looking back. I forgot to turn on the porch light. As soon as I'm about two feet away, I see the glow of a cigarette and the soles of biker boots hanging off the steps. I hear the gravel of the walkway under Nick's feet as he closes in behind me, and I sense the wine and part of my dinner making its way up my throat.

Richard is lying back on the porch, legs hanging off the steps, blowing exhaled smoke into the sky. I take in the scene, wishing I could press freeze, haul Richard's ass out of here, pretend like everything's cool, and go rip Nick's clothes off. I'm startled out of my fantasy when Nick places his hand on the small of my back and I'm forced to confront the situation.

I kick Richard's boot, instantly getting his attention. The muscles in Nick's arm go rigid as Richard lifts himself to a seated position, using his free hand to hold himself up. His eyes dart from left to right, taking in the scene in front of him. He puts the cigarette out on a porch plank and tosses the butt into the grass.

"Well, I'll be damned. Looks like you've already moved on, sweetheart, spending the night with pretty boy. That didn't take long."

Nick's arm leaves my back, and he covers his fist in the opposite hand. Sensing shit is about to hit the fan, I step in front of Nick, hoping to stop whatever is going to happen next.

"Richard, what the hell are you doing here? Get off my porch."

"This right here is still my front porch, Shannon. I can show up whenever I'm in the goddamn neighborhood." He uses his fingers to rake through his disheveled beard. The bandana tied around his forehead is caked in dirt. He needs a shower.

"Stop by and what? You're drunk, Richard. Seriously, it's over. You can't show up whenever the hell you want. We agreed the house was mine."

"Man, she's asking you to leave. Let's go."

"Who the fuck is this Ken doll? Screw off, buddy. This is my wife."

"Ex-wife, Richard. Ex-wife."

"Not until I sign those forms."

"You told me you signed them and mailed them in."

"Why the fuck would I do that? And just forget this place like I didn't pound the walls of wood myself and make the place what it fucking is? Bullshit, Shannon. You're a piece of motherfucking work."

My eyes are glued to Richard as fury builds inside my chest, my lungs practically bursting at the seams. His words no longer sting nor do they make any sense—they just piss me off.

Richard's eyes are lopsided and droopy. He coughs a nasty chest full, spraying his cheap beer smell into the air and then rolls onto his side, his beer belly bulging out from underneath his shirt. I close my eyes and take a deep inhale, trying to calm down. There have been so many nights he's come home drunk and then passed out—it's the same scene on replay.

Within seconds, Richard is snoring, leaving Nick and me standing in front of him like audience members.

I turn to Nick, my excitement of the evening replaced with dread and disappointment. "I'm so sorry."

"What are we going to do with this guy?"

"We're going to leave him right where he is and he'll be gone by tomorrow morning."

"You can't be serious. Leave him there? All night?"

"I have two choices—leave him here or take him inside. He's too drunk to leave. When he gets this drunk, he sleeps it off and is up before the roosters. I'm sorry you had to see this. I can't believe he showed up here."

I push my fingers into my eye sockets, wishing I could fix this scene with a magic wand. "I'm sorry about all this, but I'm going to have to take a rain check."

"It's not safe leaving you here."

"I appreciate you watching out for me, but here's the thing. I've done this before. All I have to do is text Officer Russell that he's here and they'll do a couple drive-bys, probably even park at the end of my driveway most of the night. He'll be gone in the morning."

"What about your safety?"

"I've changed the locks, he doesn't have a key, and like I said, he'll probably pee himself before he even wakes up. Nate Russell and I go way back, so he's got me covered. You don't need to worry about anything. What I don't want to happen is for him to wake up and see your Cadillac parked in my driveway. I don't need to aggravate this situation any further."

Nick pulls me against him and gently moves the strands of hair away from my eyes. "You were planning on my vehicle being here in the morning, were you?"

Once again, I realize I've spoken without thinking. "Well, I … it's just—"

"I'm not complaining, Shannon." He leans in, his lips grazing my forehead. "I'll go if you want me to, but I don't love the idea of leaving you here with a drunk on your porch."

"It's all good, I promise. I'll walk you back." Silence fills the night air as we make our way to the end of the driveway. As Nick pulls open the door, he looks to my front porch and shakes his head. "I'm right down the street if you need me, okay? And I'm going to wait here until you are inside with the door locked. Deal?"

"Thank you. Yes, deal. I'll be fine and like I said, Nate will be back and forth all night. They know the drill. Maybe I'll see you tomorrow."

"Yeah, I'd like that. Thanks for tonight." Nick leans down, obvious disappointment in his eyes, and kisses my lips like they're part of a fragile package. "Good night. And if you change your mind, I can come back."

I force myself up the driveway, up the front porch, look back to the bright headlights and then down at a sad sack who no longer resembles the man I once knew. "This is the last time, Richard. You've got to get your shit together. I won't stand for this anymore. Figure this the fuck out." I walk through the front door, turn the keyhole lock and dead bolt, flick on the front porch light, and watch Nick's headlights disappear.

*Damn it. Tonight could've been good.*

# 6

Nick

The morning sun beams through the paper-thin curtains of my bed-and-breakfast shoebox sauna. I have no choice but to rise and shine. Despite the bed feeling like a concrete slab, I slept surprisingly well. I parked at the end of Shannon's road last night until I spotted the cruiser doing a drive-by. I didn't want to stick around and upset her, but I wasn't comfortable leaving until I knew a local officer was notified.

Joints creaking, I walk over and peel back the curtain and take in the view of sunshine and empty sidewalks. I'm not sure I will ever be accustomed to this level of quiet.

The main room smells of corn bread and scrambled eggs. Each wooden table is covered with a floral cloth, mismatched to the floral curtains hanging over the colonial windows. The B&B manager brings me a coffee because apparently, she's also the waitress. Talk about a one-woman operation. She remembers my name and asks about my night. I'd be lying if I didn't admit she makes me feel welcome, like being in someone's home.

After a corn muffin and coffee, I head to Harold's room.

We have a nine thirty appointment with the real estate office to finalize everything, and I want to get to the lake for the memorial service at noon.

The shag-carpeted hallway is reminiscent of the 1980s. I knock on room six, hoping Harold is ready. A few minutes pass. I raise my fist to knock again, but the door inches open, a set of eyes peering through the crack. "Harold, you ready? We have an appointment at nine thirty."

Harold opens the door enough for his body to squeeze through the opening and for me to see there is someone under the blankets behind him in bed. He steps into the hallway, pulling the door shut without a sound. "Sure, sure, let me get dressed. I'll pull around front."

"Hold up. Is someone in your bed?"

Harold moves in front of the door, crosses his arms against his chest, and lifts his chin to the ceiling. "There may be."

"The bartender? I knew she was giving you a ride home, but …" Awes fill me. I've never seen Harold with anyone. He's never even mentioned going on a date that I'm aware of.

"You guessed correct, boss." Harold looks like a teenager caught drinking.

"Give me the keys. I have things I need to do. You take the day off."

Harold uncrosses his arms and wrinkles his forehead. "I got it. Give me five."

"Give me the fucking keys and go back to …" I wave my hand at the closed door.

"I appreciate that, Nick. As long as you're sure."

Before I have a chance to answer, he slips back inside and returns seconds later holding the keys out into the hallway. I grab them and give him a thumbs-up, which he almost slams the door on. I'm happy for the guy. Shocked, even. At least someone's getting laid.

A t my meeting with the real estate agent, the paperwork is in order, the search is behind me, and I'm an official resident of Meriden. After, I drive along the lake road and pull into the first available spot toward the end. The brilliant sun reflects off the lake water. A few kayaks are scattered around the shoreline, a red sailboat is off in the distance, and several families dot the beach with blankets and coolers.

It's amazing how different life is only an hour and a half north of Boston. Meriden seems to flow on a different vibration. I'm itching to dig out my camera and see what the light captures. This view is worth every single penny I paid. I can't remember the last time I was this excited about something. Leaving the hustle and bustle of the city behind, even if only for the weekends going forward, will give way to so many possibilities it's almost unsettling.

I think having a vacation home here is what I've needed. The gas pedal of life has been flat to the floor for years. It'll be nice to slow down. And if it sucks, I'll squeeze every penny back and more if I decide to resell the lakeside property.

The only person who will love this as much as I do is my mother. She's nonchalantly dropped hints here and there about me following my other dreams, reminding me that I don't have to work myself into an early grave. My father was so dedicated to his company, but my mother had more freedom to pursue her passions, since money was never an issue for her. She inherited a large estate from her parents when they passed. My great-grandfather founded and sold one of the largest beer companies in the country, so he took care of my grandparents and they, in turn, left a sizable trust fund for their only grandchild. So Mother didn't need my father's money or success.

If she'd had her way, she would've sold Green Breeze. I

simply couldn't and wouldn't listen; I always knew I was to be CEO as part of the family's business succession plan. Granted, no one thought my father would drop dead a year after the plan was finalized. In hindsight, I should've listened to my mother. I thought I had more time.

I walk toward the beach. Ahead, a crowd of about twenty have gathered in the center around a flagpole, each person facing the lake. I recognize Shannon's grandparents, sitting on the wooden bench holding hands, wrapped in jackets and a blanket. Hoping to be unnoticed, I stand toward the back in view of Shannon, who stands next to Jackson, Solia, and Madison, and I assume the late girlfriend's parents.

Jackson points at two loons in the distance. He turns to Solia and says something I'm too far away to hear, and Solia leans her head against his chest, then reaches up and rubs the tip of her nose against his.

These two are definitely in love.

After a few words, a short prayer, and placement of the dedication monument, the crowd disperses. It's only then Jackson and Solia spot me, eyes wide with curiosity. Shannon traverses through the group toward me. Jackson and Solia help their grandparents off the bench and to their truck.

"Hey, thanks for coming."

She's beautiful in her flowy pale green floral skirt and emerald T-shirt. Her light makeup accents her natural beauty. "Of course. I wanted to be here. I didn't want to upset anyone. I figured I'd be safe in the back."

Shannon's smile tugs at my heartstrings, sending an unfamiliar surge through my body. "You're good. Everything went according to plan. The monument looks beautiful, Trinity's family loved it, and Jackson seems lighter." As if on cue, Jackson and Solia appear behind Shannon, giving me a once-over.

"Hey, man," Jackson says through gritted teeth and extends a hand.

"Hey. Listen, Shannon told me about Trinity. I'm so sorry for your loss."

"Thanks. Yeah, it's been a rough road, but I've managed." Jackson smiles and wraps his arm around Solia's shoulders. She looks at him with a soft smile. "I'd say I'm in a good place. It's only up from here." Solia wraps her arms around his waist, and I'm certain no woman has ever looked at me that way.

Through the calm, we turn our heads to the growl of a motorcycle engine, getting louder by the second. A pit forms in my stomach as the bike materializes, the same bike that was parked in Shannon's driveway. *What the fuck?*

"Looks like we've got company," Jackson says, stepping in front of Shannon.

"You're kidding me. What is he doing here?" She flattens a hand against her forehead.

"Let me take care of this," I say. "Last night was one thing, but again? What is this guy doing? Stalking you?"

"What do you mean, last night?" Jackson looks at me, then his sister.

"He was at her house after we went out for dinner. He reeked of booze and passed out on the front porch."

"Seriously, Shannon? Why didn't you call me?" Jackson doesn't take his glare off the approaching bike.

Shannon's eyes glaze over as tears form. She wraps her arms around her stomach, as if willing her emotions to obey. "Jackson, Nick was there. I called the station and talked to Nate. He was on patrol and kept an eye out. Everything was fine. It was unsafe for him to drive. What if something had happened? I couldn't make him leave drunk."

Jackson's fury seems to be boiling over, his hands fisted. Solia has her fingers on the back of his T-shirt in an effort to pull him closer to her. "I've had enough. This ends here."

I step forward, my feet in line with Jackson's, creating a unified front as Richard steers the bike in a sharp turn on the spot. The guy looks like he hasn't slept in days, hair like a ratted pile of black wire, enough facial hair for a small critter to hide in. Once again, the stench of alcohol permeates the air from a few yards away. His baggy jeans sag off his body, his brown T-shirt splattered with bleach stains. A metal chain hangs from his pocket with a pack of Marlboros sticking out.

"Look what we got here. Are we double-dating already? This is fucking fantastic. Even my brother-in-law approves of this dickhead boning his sister. One minute you're taking him home to fuck him in my house, and the next, you're at a family gathering. Beautiful. Fucking beautiful." Richard stumbles closer, obviously having already downed several beers before ten a.m.

"Dude, you need to go home. Don't make a scene." I take a few steps forward, broadening my shoulders and cracking my knuckles.

"You want me to go back to my front porch? It's only a matter of time before she begs me to her bed, and I slide inside that pussy of mine." Richard tosses his head toward the sky and laughs.

I haven't thrown a punch in over ten years, but this guy is asking for it. Shannon senses my anger and steps in front of me. "Richard, leave." Her voice quivers as she tucks her hair behind her ears.

Richard proceeds to move forward, arms extended toward Shannon. Jackson grabs hold of Shannon's arm and pulls her behind him. "Richard, cut this shit out. You're drunk, yet again, showing up where you weren't invited. If I see you showing up again or talking about my sister that way, I'll fucking pound your face in."

*Bam*! Without any warning, Richard's fist lands square into Jackson's jaw.

"You motherfucker," I say under my breath. Without hesitating, I lunge and deliver my best shot to Richard's gut, dropping him to the ground. Both women yell and people are standing on their front lawns, watching the show. I clearly hesitate a moment too long and miscalculate the situation because before I have time to react, Richard careens into me, sending me rolling off the pavement and onto the sand.

"What do you think, man? She's going to suck your corporate dick?"

I slam my fist right into the bridge of his nose and hear something crack. "You motherfucker."

"Stop!" Shannon yells in the background, but Richard is not going down without a fight. The strength of a drunk guy should not be underestimated. He swivels left and right, aiming for anything, his meaty fist connecting with my jaw. Goddamn it.

What happens next is a blur, punches and kicks flying. One minute Jackson delivers a blow and the next I finally have Richard on his stomach, face down in the sand. I've got to give it to the guy—two to one, and he went down swinging.

I'm kneeling on Richard's back, locking his arms behind him and looking up at the beach road where Shannon stands, cheeks wet with tears. All hope for peace seeps into the concrete. Madison steps in and wraps her arms around Shannon's waist. That should be me. I want to be the one comforting her.

Only then do I realize blood drips from my jaw and stains the sand. I wipe the excess on my shoulder just as sirens flood the air, growing louder with each passing second. Solia tucks her phone into her shorts pocket and heads over to the cruiser. Two additional officers pull in behind the first.

In a matter of minutes, they have Richard off the sand. His shirt is ripped, both eyes swollen and nose bleeding, and he's handcuffed and secured in the back of the cruiser. Jackson and

I both decline medical assistance and talk to the attending officers. We give our statements and are told they'll be in touch. We're left sitting on the sand, hands in our laps, with two sobbing women. Talk about a fucking emotional morning.

"I am so sorry. Come here." Shannon kneels in the sand in front of me. Her deep brown eyes attempt to drain the pain from the corner of my right eye and the burning sensation in my jaw.

"It's all good. I'm fine. Jackson, you good?"

Looking like he escaped the tussle far better than I, he lifts himself off the sand and moves to Solia. "Thanks for your help. We should've had this guy's ass carted away a long time ago. What a pathetic piece of shit. He needs help. I know you just got here, but Shannon's been trying to get him help for years. He's lucky he hasn't killed anyone yet, driving drunk around this town. But now he's showing up at her house unannounced and throwing punches. He needs his ass thrown in the slammer or checked into rehab so he'll leave my sister the hell alone. It's a good thing I got my grandparents out of here when I did. This would've ripped their hearts out."

"Everyone else okay over here?" Nate takes off his police hat and presses it against his chest, standing wide-legged like only an officer of the law would. "Ladies?"

"We're fine. He only got to Jackson and Nick." Shannon stands, wipes her eyes, and walks to Nate. "What happens now?"

"We'll take him down to the station. Don't worry about the rest. I'll talk to these two about pressing charges."

"Nate, don't let him get away with this. You should've heard the stuff he said to Shannon." Madison is getting choked up.

Nate signals Madison to join him with the tilt of his chin.

"I've never seen you so angry," Solia quietly tells Jackson. "It's kind of hot." A dirty smirk replaces her sweet smile. "Let's go. I think we've had enough for one morning." Solia grasps Jackson's arm, pausing only to ask, "Are you two all set, Shannon? You good?"

"Totally, yes. I'm sorry this happened, Jackson." Shannon frees them of any obligation of staying and watches them walk down the street. Shannon's eyes cast downward. Knowing how important today was, it breaks my heart to see her this way.

"Don't you feel the need to apologize to anyone. You are not responsible for him. Come on, I've got something I want to show you."

She lifts her head, curiosity sneaking in, and her lips turn slightly upward. "First, we need to get you cleaned up. I have a first aid kit in my truck."

"You drive around with a first aid kit?"

"When you live in these parts, boating, hiking, and biking, you need to be prepared. Madison, you good?"

After a moment, Madison turns away from Nate and waves. "I'll text you later." She turns back around and leans against Nate's cruiser. I hope Richard is pissing himself in the back seat.

Shannon waves. I walk behind her up to the beach road to her truck. Despite the fact I'm soaked in blood and pain, I still can't stop thinking about my hands tracing her curves. I've never met anyone who drives around with a fucking first aid kit, and unbeknownst to me, I now find her even hotter.

She lowers the tailgate and instructs me to sit. She then unzips her magical medical kit and offers the first of her remedies. "Punch this ice pack and then put it along your jaw. This might hurt a bit, but I'm going to clean that cut with water and swab some ointment on it. It will sting, and then you'll need a bandage to cover it."

As she leans forward with the supplies, I tilt my head so I'm eye level with her chest as she stands in front of me, tending to my wounds. Her fitted emerald-green tee hugging her chest distracts me from any sting.

"You okay?"

Placing my hands on each of her hips, I close my eyes as she applies light pressure. "I'm more than okay."

"It was pretty sexy taking on Richard, I can't lie. I don't think I've ever witnessed a fight, never mind be the cause of one. It's just so freaking sad what booze can do to someone. When he drinks, he's a different person. He never talks that way when he's sober. The problem is, I can't remember the last time he wasn't drunk."

I give her hips a squeeze and my heart sinks. "No one should ever talk to you that way, drunk or not. He's a piece of shit. Sorry, but it's true. At this point, it is who he is." I stand, my hands still on her waist, and tilt my eyes downward in the hopes my words will sink into her soul. "No woman should have to take care of a man like he's a child. He has a problem, and it's his problem to fix. You've done all you can. He needs to hit rock bottom before he'll be ready to change anything. Maybe this is it. And even though I've never been married, I sure as hell know that's no way to treat a woman."

Shannon's eyes well up with tears for the second time today. She leans forward, pressing her body against mine, her head against my chest, arms wrapped around my waist. The way she's holding on to me is so intimate. I barely know this woman and yet, I find myself wondering why sex hasn't been on my mind today. I actually give a shit that she's sad and I want to make it better.

A warm breeze over the lake reaches us, blowing Shannon's silky hair forward. I slide my fingers through the loose strands and scoop all her locks at the base of her neck. I place my lips over hers, gently opening her mouth to taste her. My excitement gets the better of me, and I'm seventeen all over again. Her hands slide down my back, our kiss intensifies, and our bodies cement together.

A horn blares, followed by "Get a room!" Our lips pull apart, and we both look in the direction of the passing vehicle.

"What the hell?"

Shannon is bent over in hysterics, trying to catch her breath. "That's Gerry," she says in between bouts of laughter. "You must remember him from the summer. You'll need to work on smoothing things over with him."

Taking her hand in mine, I realize I'm on a lot of shit lists around here. "I'll work on it. It seems Gerry has a sense of humor. Come on—are you good leaving your truck here? I want to show you something."

"He's the best. Don't you want to get cleaned up?"

"Nah, I'm good. Ready?"

"Sure. Where to?"

"You'll see."

I settle my hand over my pocket against the edge of the keys to my new lakeside home. Making quick decisions is not something I do, but this house is exactly what I envisioned. Everything about this decision is like puzzle pieces locking into place.

Upon looking over at Shannon, I note the despair has left her eyes, but exhaustion seems to have replaced it. Her window is rolled down, her arm dangling in the breeze, her head against the headrest. I reach for her other hand and give it a gentle squeeze, allowing her to take up a little more space in my heart.

"Shut the hell up!" Shannon stares at me as I park and jingle the newly cut keys before me.

"Come on. I'll give you a tour."

Shannon walks around the back of the Cadillac and down to the water's edge. The house was built a few years ago by some business tycoon who has since remarried and moved. It's located on the edge of a cove called Loon's Landing, elevated on a plot of land large enough for a three-story, twenty-one-hundred-square-foot house, two decks overlooking Newfound Lake, and a boathouse complete with an apartment and dock. Large pine trees edge the property lines, allowing for complete privacy and a one-hundred-eighty-degree view of the water.

"This is amazing!" Shannon stands at the base of the dock, absorbing the energy from the sun.

"It's a far cry from the city skyline, that's for sure." The water laps at the sand, absorbed instantly. A pontoon boat skims the water as it gently travels through the channel markers without creating a wake. "You want to see inside?"

"Yes, of course." Shannon's eyes scan the royal blue shaker panels and she follows me to the staircase leading up to the second-story deck and to five sets of floor-to-ceiling sliding glass windows. As I put the key into the lock, reality sets in—this house is mine. I welcome a calm, centering breath I didn't realize my lungs needed until now.

"This is your house. You bought it?"

"Sure did."

"I assumed you were checking out places, not buying one. Holy shit, Nick. This is insane. You must have dropped serious cash on this place," she states while taking in the three cedar fans hanging from the cathedral ceiling, the floor-to-ceiling stone fireplace in the center of the room, and wrap-around couches on all sides, waiting to be sat on to either embrace the warmth of the flames or to sit back and look out over the water. "It's already furnished."

"What good is money if you don't spend it the way you want to? That's the way I'm starting to see it, anyway. It was offered as completely furnished. I figure if I want anything different, I'll hire an interior designer to take care of it. I don't want to waste time shopping. Decorating is not my thing, so I might as well find someone better equipped to handle it."

Shannon runs her hands along the brown leather sectional and heads to the built-in bookshelves in the front of the room. Her dainty, pink-painted fingertips glide along the hardback books on the shelves. I can't remember the last time I read a book willingly. Probably a textbook during grad school.

"There are so many classics here. I could read all day out on that deck."

"Let me show you the rest." I guide her through the chef's kitchen, complete with an eight-burner stove with a handcrafted hood, double ovens, sprawling quartz island with eight stools, and a completely stocked refrigerator.

"Did you shop?" Shannon's mouth is agape upon observing the rows of water, seltzers, juice, and lemonade bottles lined up like soldiers marching. There is enough food in here to feed an army.

With her back to me and her eyes on the food, I wrap my arms around her waist and lay my chin on her shoulder. "Do you want to see the rest, and then we can grab a snack?"

She leans her head to the side, causing her hair to intertwine with mine, and the aroma of her shampoo fills my nostrils. *Do all women smell this good? I've never noticed before.*

I lead her through the shiny wood-planked hallway off the kitchen that leads to two bedrooms facing the lake. Each has floor-to-ceiling windows and a set of sliding glass doors, a king bed, a wall-mounted television, and a plush white throw rug, as well as an en suite bath. The bedroom across the hall is the size of the other two bedrooms combined, complete with two full-size beds. One has a twin bunk over it, plus there are two additional sets of twin bunk beds and a full entertainment system outfitted with all the latest tech gadgets and game systems.

"This is enormous. I'm not even going to ask what you spent on this. Who is going to use this space? Do you have three kids and an ex-wife you forgot to tell me about?" Shannon inspects the bathroom, complete with a whirlpool tub and massaging capability.

"I'm a smart financial planner. I'd never buy anything I can't afford or that isn't a good investment. I did my research. There aren't many properties for sale on the lake. I learned quick when properties pop on the market, they get snatched. This one fell into my lap. It went on the market, the buyer fell through, the inspections were complete and clear, and I loved it."

"It's amazing, but do you always buy such expensive things impulsively?" Shannon walks back into the other bedroom across the way, sliding open the door and stepping onto the deck. "Don't get me wrong, there are some things in life that never get old, never lose their magic. This lake is that for me. To see this view every day from your bedroom is going to take your breath away. You'll never want to leave."

"It's safe to say this place quickly dug its claws into me. I agree, it's breathtaking. Buying a place here would never be a bad investment. By the way, this isn't the master bedroom. You haven't even seen half of the house."

"And who did you say is coming here?"

"My mother, Claire, lives in Rosendale, just outside of Boston. She'll be here off and on, probably more than I'd like. She loves to get out of the city when she can, and even more so now that my father has passed. My sister Ashlyn works as a wedding photographer. She's busy, always going one hundred miles an hour, traveling here, there, and everywhere. With weddings, there are lulls in the year, and hopefully she'll come up from time to time. Brett is the baby of the family and I'm sure he'll be up here with his buddies any chance he can, but he lives out west. He works as a firefighter—wants to become a hotshot."

Shannon turns to face me and leans against the deck. "A hotshot?"

"Yeah, it's what they call firefighters who fight wildfires in the remotest spots. There's intense training and it's crazy dangerous. Don't ever get my mother started on the subject or she'll give you an earful. Let me show you upstairs."

I lead her back to the kitchen and toward the front foyer, where a rustic chandelier hangs from the ceiling. A black steel-framed staircase on the left leads to the second floor. "This is quite an entrance."

"After you." I extend my hand and follow her up, my eyes never leaving her ass. At the top sits a small sitting area with a couple leather recliners and beachy side tables, coasters, and reading material for anyone who might be interested. A modest television is mounted on the wall. "If you go left, you'll see the sitting room. To the right, my master bedroom. You choose."

Shannon's eyes dart from left to right as she seems to contemplate her choices. I decide to spare her. "Go right." She follows close enough for me to inhale her scent. I push open two white oak doors, giving way to a bedroom sliced right from the pages of *Architectural Digest*. The back wall is glass, overlooking the lake. We are high enough to peek above the tree line, leaves far and few between. A living area hosts a small pale blue couch and two mismatched, perfectly placed chairs, an entertainment center, a bar area equipped with a wine fridge, and an elegant light fixture that looks to have been crafted from driftwood.

"This is gorgeous. I'd never leave!"

I'd be perfectly content with her staying.

Shannon walks to the king-size bed that, with the press of a button, can be sectioned off with white curtains that close around the backside of the bed and/or along the wall of windows. She sits at the end of the mattress and looks out over the lake. "This house is amazing, Nick. I've never seen anything like it."

I can't keep my eyes off her. Her ass is on my bed. It requires all my strength to restrain myself from crashing my body over hers.

"I'm glad you love it. I was shocked a house this nice lasted on the market for five minutes." I sit by her side and place my hand on her leg. She turns her head toward me, and I go for it. I wrap my fingers around her face, feel her soft strawberry-tasting lips on mine, and run my fingers through the bottom layer of her hair. I don't know what it is about her hair, but it's intoxicating. Soft as silk, so fragrant, and I want to take a fistful, pull her head back, and kiss every inch of her neck while she gasps for air. I would have a field day driving her wild.

I take the liberty of trailing her jawline with my tongue and guiding my way down her neck. I hold on to the strap of her tank top and guide it off her shoulder. Her chest pulls inward as she takes in a sudden intake of air.

She whispers, "Nick," and I harden on command. My hand finds her breast, cups its fullness, and BAM! A cell phone rings from somewhere, and it isn't my ringtone.

*Goddamn it, seriously?*

Shannon yanks up the strap of her tank, rubs her eyes, and tucks her hair behind her ears. "I'm so sorry, that's mine. I should get that." She fishes through her bag on the floor, locating her phone. I throw myself back on the bed, eyes trained on the ceiling, my excitement deflating like a helium balloon.

She remains almost mute, beside a few words, "Hi … Yes, of course. No, I understand. I'll be right there. That's good news, right? Okay, of course." She stands, ends the call, and looks at me lying on the bed. "I'm so sorry, Nick. I have to head over to the station. I don't know all the details, but

Richard is getting out on bail. That was my mother-in-law, or ex-mother-in-law. She said he wants to get help. This is huge. He's never done this before. I need to go."

I sit up the instant I hear Richard's name. "That's great that he wants help, but why do you need to be there?"

"Something about me being the one who carries the medical insurance, and I'm still technically his wife and emergency contact. I'm so sorry, but I need to go."

Without a moment for me to grasp what she's just said, she's up and out the door.

*I guess we're leaving now. This guy is a motherfucker even from the police station.*

Not much is said on the way back to the lake. Without a goodbye or plan set, Shannon jumps out. "Thanks so much for the ride. I'm so sorry, I had no idea this was going to happen. Call me?"

Before I can answer, she's halfway to her truck. "Yeah, sure, I'll call." Is this what it's like to be someone's second choice?

# 7

Leaving Nick and running to Richard's side was the last thing I wanted to do, but I had to. After more than a decade with someone and a phone call from a relentless, dysfunctional mother-in-law, how can I not cooperate and get him the help he needs? The divorce isn't final and won't be for eighty more days. I was finally able to convince him to sign the divorce papers and hand them over, and I mailed them. Whatever is left to deal with, our lawyers will handle.

And Nick and Jackson agreed not to press charges after the fight the day of the memorial, contingent upon Richard getting the help he needs.

More than anything, I wish Richard would've hit rock bottom a long time ago. Maybe that's partially due to my enabling his behavior. Regardless, he's enrolled in a detox program in Lincoln, New Hampshire, about twenty minutes north. He's been there for ten days.

My soon-to-be ex-mother-in-law is a piece of work. You'd think she'd take over and figure it out. But she sat back and expected me to read the fine print and sign off. I need to remove myself from his emergency contact info and figure out the insurance situation.

In detox, Richard has limited access to the outside world, including no cell phones. We were told this facility has an excellent recovery rate. I'm allowed visitation but haven't gone yet. I'd like to think if the old Richard has resurfaced, he's sick with remorse for the scene he caused at the lake. I'd also like to think his family would step up and visit, but that's not going to happen.

I haven't seen Nick since I left for the police station that day. With the chaos of the new school year starting, I've texted a few times, not hearing from him until this morning. He's back in Boston working. This man might make more money in a year than I make in a decade of teaching, but I don't think I would trade. Don't get me wrong—his house is a dream, and life seems a little easier with that kind of money, but the hustle and stress that goes with it doesn't appeal to me whatsoever. Besides, after learning there is a lot more stress and emotion behind the hustle makes me want more in life for Nick.

Pulling into Basic Ingredients, I'm surprised at the lack of cars for a Friday afternoon. Usually, this place is jammed with tourists stopping by before heading to the water. The wooden edge surrounding the screen door slams against the frame behind me as I inhale the scent of blueberry muffins, cinnamon scones, and countless other baked goods Judy whipped up this morning. Everything she creates has an extra special dose of scrumptiousness.

"Hey, Judy!" I lean over the small wooden ledge to an opening into the kitchen where customers are usually lined up to order. "Where is everyone today?" I spy behind me to see a few customers browsing the Newfound Lake sweatshirts and custom trinkets, while others pour iced coffee at the beverage station in back.

"I'm short-handed. A few of the girls had college

orientation. They helped prep over twenty dozen sticky buns, which flew off the shelves. Gerry came in and bought two dozen for the library crew for their book sale. It's been steady ever since."

This is not surprising. Judy is famous for her sticky buns. Locals and visitors alike go wild for them.

"If you are ever in a bind, let me know. I'm happy to help in a pinch."

"Thank you, Shannon, but you are doing more than enough working full-time and helping plan Run Your Buns Off. I couldn't do that without you. Plus, the tourist season is winding down.

I've volunteered for the Run Your Buns Off committee for the past two years. The New Hampshire Marathon is held in Meriden every Columbus Day weekend. Runners can choose between running the full marathon, half, a five-kilometer, or complete the Family Fun Run, a one-mile run/walk. The race starts downtown, travels the circumference of the lake, and ends back in the center of town. Not only is it one of the most scenic races in New England, it's also a huge fundraiser for the local community center and food pantry. Most of the planning occurs in the summer when I have free time.

"Give me a second and I'll run to the back. I have a few designs I want to show you so we can get the shirts ordered and check that off the list."

"Sure thing. I'll grab a coffee. Take your time."

A few minutes later, Judy pushes through the swinging accordion doors from the kitchen, holding a box she places on the round table in the center of the store. "Okay, we've narrowed it down to this bright yellow Dri-FIT long-sleeved, the neon blue Dri-FIT short-sleeved or long-sleeved, or the hot pink in either style."

She displays each choice, flipping from front to back, showing off the New Hampshire Marathon logo in the middle of the outlined shape of Newfound Lake on the top left front. On the back is the design we agreed upon—three runners with sticky buns for bodies—I mean, who won't think that's hilarious? A local artist, who also works at the Audubon Society, did a great job with our vision. It's the right mix of realism and humor.

"I'm a sucker for blue. They are all great, but I think we should switch it up this year and do blue. It's still bright enough for a runner to wear and be spotted, and the past two years we did a bright purple and orange." I hold up the blue against my chest, waiting for her reaction.

"Perfect, I'm with you. Let's get these ordered." Judy packs the samples into the box without folding or organizing. "Here, you can keep the ones we don't want and order the shirts."

"Sure thing. Long or short sleeves? How many runners do we have signed up?" I ask, sliding the box off the table.

"You choose. And I wrote the numbers on the box, but we always need to account for last-minute registrations. We have a little under four weeks, so let's get at least twenty-five of each size in addition to the current numbers. I spoke to Carol at the print shop. After they get this initial batch, we can update them if we need more. She's flexible, and I prefer to keep business local. We may be paying twenty-five cents more per shirt, but it's worth it."

"I agree." Tilting the box, I see the registration numbers written in red Sharpie. One hundred adult extra-large, two hundred fifty large, five hundred medium, two hundred twenty-five small, and one hundred youth mediums. "This is over a thousand runners. That's more than last year."

"Sure is," Judy says, looking at the elderly couple entering the store. "Ever since we joined forces with the town, this race has taken off like a shot, no pun intended. You have a lot to do with that." She smiles and her eyes light up with pride, melting me in a way only Judy can. "And listen," she says as she steps closer so her words don't reach the customers' ears, "I heard about Richard. I'm sorry it's come to this, but I hope you know it's for the best. Rehab is the best place for him—that took strength. When he gets out, I have a few friends who attend a local AA meeting here in town. I've been to a few of them for special anniversaries, when they earn their pins and whatnot. If Richard needs a group to join, which he should, let him know there's one right here in Meriden. If not here, they're everywhere."

"Thank you, Judy. I had no idea. I've been meaning to visit Richard soon and if it comes up, I'll definitely mention it. Honestly, I reached the end of my rope. He needs to figure out the rest for himself." There's an invigorating strength behind my words.

"It's probably too soon for him to look for a group, but keep it in your back pocket if needed. There is also a group for family members who need support if you haven't tried that already."

"Sure thing, thank you. I'll keep that in mind and get these taken care of. Talk soon."

Judy is already halfway to the kitchen as the couple makes their way to the ordering window.

With the box of shirts stowed in the back seat, I take a few deep breaths and allow the uneasiness of not having visited the rehab center to settle in. Love is strange like that. After every shitty thing Richard has done, every mean insult he's thrown my way, and every night and anniversary that's been ruined, I still want the best for him. Sobriety is what's best. I'm the only one who remembers what's buried underneath the booze.

I scroll through my inbox for the rehab confirmation message; I remember seeing visiting hours. Here it is. Friday hours are two to four. I'll take it as a sign. It leaves me enough time to stop by the print shop, place the order, and head to Lincoln for a quick visit. *It won't do any harm, right? He's in rehab, alone, probably thinking everyone has forgotten about him. That's a shitty feeling.*

~

As I pull up to the Lincoln Rehab Center and Urgent Care, I note the tidy landscaping, the shrubbery trimmed at sharp angles, and blooming perennials, but not a human in sight. This place instantly gives me nursing home vibes. I'm thankful my grandparents are healthy and living on the farm.

A white-haired woman with thick glasses sits at the front desk. She takes my name, asks who I'm here to visit, and radios a guard to walk me down. Everything inside reminds me of a hospital: white, sterile, and filled with the stench of rubbing alcohol.

"Right this way, miss." Another woman appears, her arm muscles larger than the width of my leg. Her hair is slicked into a bun and she's wearing a set of royal blue scrubs. A name tag indicates she goes by Mo. I wouldn't mess with Mo if you paid me. She's all business. She walks like she's encased in a back brace and has a sharpness to her voice that would bring any opponent to their knees.

I simply thank her and follow, looking at every door lining the hallway. Each has a small window in the center and the patient's name and current caretaker appear to be listed under the room number.

"Do you have any alcohol or narcotics on your person?"

Standing outside of room 125, I whip my head back to Mo, who is standing with her hands on her hips, waiting for an answer. "Of course not. I'm here visiting my alcoholic husband. Ex-husband."

"Sure. To be clear, all visitation rights will be denied if

anything were to be brought in and you would be reported to our facility's administration."

"Got it. We're good. I have nothing, so no need for concern."

Mo spins on her heel and walks back to the lobby, calling over her shoulder, "Sign out when you leave."

I'm standing outside the door, contemplating my next move. The only thing separating Richard and me is a single knock. I take a second to convince myself that this visit is the kind, responsible thing to do.

I gather the energy swirling in my belly and knock, more forcefully than intended. As my fist meets the cold metal, I'm alerted to a text message. Yanking my phone from my back pocket before Richard opens the door, I scan the message and see it's from Nick.

NICK

> Hey, beautiful. I have a client cocktail hour and reception event in a couple weeks. I was wondering if you'd accompany me to Boston for the night. It's October 6. Hope you can make it.

Accompany him? I don't think I've ever been asked to accompany anyone somewhere. My mind spins with excitement—cocktails, Boston, a dress—when the door opens and Richard is standing in front of me.

"You came." The sadness in Richard's eyes is enough to melt the anger in any villain's heart. The dark circles appear permanent underneath his eyes, his shoulders slump forward, and the lines etched in his forehead have him looking decades older than the last time I saw him.

"Yes, Richard. I wanted to stop by and see how you were doing. Can I come in?"

"Yes, of course. It's not much." Richard pushes the door

open, revealing a twin bed against the wall with a small wooden nightstand by its side. A brown cloth recliner against the opposite wall looks antique. Several books and magazines decorate a small round coffee table, and a wooden door leads to what I assume is the bathroom. Richard's attention follows me around the space as I inspect his dwelling.

He's almost unrecognizable. He's wearing black scrubs, and his wiry black hair is wet and slicked smooth against his head. There are no chains or bandanas in sight.

"Not too shabby, huh?" Richard lets out a half-hearted laugh and sits on the edge of the twin bed like a little boy waiting for bedtime. I follow his lead and have a seat on the recliner.

"How are you holding up?" I cross my legs.

He pauses and looks up at the ceiling and returns his gaze to me. "This place ain't the greatest, but after the first few days of hell, I'm a new guy, and they say it's only going to get better from here."

"Were you sick?"

"Yeah, I was sick. I was flattened by a steamroller. The only method used around here is cold turkey. I would've preferred to cut back. No need to turn my insides out. A drink or two isn't going to hurt."

This is not what I thought I'd hear. Despite looking like shit, he seems calm and rational. I forgot how he was before the booze stole him. "I think that's the point of being here. To quit."

"Sure. And I love talking about my feelings with strangers, sleeping in a twin bed, and eating lumps of paste on a goddamn lunch tray. But hey, it's better than sitting in a jail cell, right?"

"Has your mother been by?"

"My mother? Are you joking? She won't step foot in this fucking place."

"I see." I push myself back, the recliner's worn fabric scratchy under my thighs. I don't want to be the only person Richard has. Leaving him was a no-brainer, but I'm not heartless. Richard's friends had better step it up.

"Shan, shit is real in here. I'm clean. They keep trying to make me talk about my demons and search for a higher power. F that. I'll do my time and get out."

This is not going the way I had hoped.

"Remember the day we hiked Inspiration Point all those years ago?"

He can't be serious. We're time traveling to the day he proposed? We can't do this right now.

"It was so cloudy that day. Drizzling, remember? You complained up and down about going, but I dragged your ass." Richard kicks his leg forward and belly laughs.

This whole topic doesn't sit right with me. "Listen, I'm all for memories, but let's talk about you and how you're doing, not the past."

"Yeah, yeah, sure. It's just, I was hoping now that I'm here …"

I get up and walk to the door. "I'm not doing this. I came to be a decent human and see how you were holding up. It looks like they've got things under control."

My phone vibrates in my pocket. "Hold on a sec." Jackson's number lights up the screen. I never hear from him during the day. "Hello. What? Oh my god, okay, where? Where's Grandpa? How bad? Yes, I'm on my way."

Tears instantly spring to my eyes and lightning bolts of terror pulse through me. "I have to go, Richard." I grab my bag from the coffee table. "Syl fell and she's being rushed to Plymouth Hospital. I have to go."

Richard follows me to the door. "Shit. Yeah, of course."

I'm out the door and driving down Route 93 with the speedometer way over the posted limit. My grandparents,

Sylvia and Earl, are the pillars of our family, our steadfast, go-to people, the ones who will always give an honest response and are free with their wisdom. Losing one of them will tip our world off its axis. We won't spin properly. One doesn't belong without the other; they are a set.

Tears stain my shorts faster than I can wipe them away, but closing the valve on this stream is impossible.

In under twenty minutes, I've parked in the emergency room lot and am running through the automatic doors. A young woman sits at the front desk, her back pin straight. "Name?"

"Mine? Hers? Whose?"

"Take a deep breath. Either or both." She clicks on the computer screen as I search for my brain.

"My name is Shannon. I'm here to see my grandmother, Sylvia Christianson."

She types away and scans the screen in search of my grandmother. I'm digging a hole so deep into my cheek, I'm certain my tooth will drill all the way to the outside. "Got it. Looks like she's being prepped for surgery. I believe your—"

"Surgery? For what? I need to see her." I don't realize how loud my voice rings through the hospital entrance until I witness multiple people stop in their tracks and stare at the front desk. "Sorry, go ahead. What were you saying?"

"You're upset, it's okay. I believe your family is in the waiting room. The surgeon will update you whenever she can." This woman is perfect for her job. Her delivery is empathetic as she ushers me to the waiting room.

Sitting in the blue plastic chair in the middle of the row is my grandfather, Earl, his head tilted forward, shoulders concave, and arms resting on his thighs. He's wearing his predictable pair of dirt-stained jeans—never too old to be getting work done around the farm—and a ratty Raubuchon Hardware T-shirt. Next to him is my brother, Jackson. He stands immediately, and my grandfather looks at me, revealing tears. This sight is enough to bring me to my knees. Grandpa never cries. He's our backbone, tough as nails. I kneel on the linoleum square by his side while my brother returns to his seat.

"What happened, Grandpa?"

His eyes are long and drawn, needing a week's worth of rest. "I was out back hosing down farm equipment and went inside for a glass of water. Right away, I knew something was wrong. I should've checked on her sooner. You know your grandmother—she's in that kitchen without fail every night, whipping up supper. She wasn't there, and the house was silent.

"I found her face down on the bathroom tile. She must've fallen getting out of the shower. There was blood everywhere. She was alive, that I knew for sure. Through all the pain, she was straining to say my name. I called 911 and waited by her side. They told me not to move her until they arrived." He finally takes a breath and puts his fist to his mouth. "She can't leave me."

Even at ninety-two years old, the tremor in his voice signals the need for reassurance that he did the right thing.

I touch his leg. "You did everything right, Grandpa. Thank god you found her when you did." I won't get into the fact that Jackson and I have been nagging our parents to replace the ancient tub/shower combo with a more accessible bath setup. Sylvia and Earl are both unsteady on their feet and getting older.

Keeping my hand on Grandpa's leg, I turn my attention to Jackson. "Have you called Mom and Dad? And what are the doctors saying?"

"Yes, I called, and the doctors haven't said much. All I know is she was alert and responsive upon arrival. She definitely broke her hip and now they're prepping her for surgery. At least that was the plan when I arrived."

"How long have you been here? How did you know?"

"Take a seat, Shannon. There's nothing you could've done. You're here now. I guess when the ambulance arrived, it was Tara and Sean, and I'm assuming they asked Grandpa where I was. Next thing I know, Gerry marches down the aisle to get me. Oddly enough, I was helping your man choose a drill. I'm pretty sure he's never been in a hardware store."

"You were helping Nick? And he's not my man, by the way."

"Sorry. The guy you're dating looked lost."

I push past Jackson. I don't have time for this. Sylvia needs us right now. Everything else can wait.

Grandpa's eyes are trained on the double doors leading to the patient wing. While holding his hand in mine, I say a silent prayer for Grandma. She has to be okay.

The waiting room is vacant besides a couple sitting in the back corner huddled around the most recent copy of *People* magazine. They exchange a few words and giggle. The man looks up and catches me staring and offers a small smile. I inhale a deep breath, trying to stuff my worry deep inside, and turn my attention to the double doors, but not before I spot a man walk to the front desk, a man who looks an awful lot like Richard.

"What the hell is he doing here?"

Jackson is up and heading to the counter before I have a chance to blink.

*Oh, shit.*

# 8



One minute I'm standing in the tool aisle with Jackson, and the next Gerry's scuffling toward us, keys dangling in hand.

"Answer your phone. Earl called."

Gerry leans over onto his knees and sucks in a deep breath. He lifts his head and panic is etched into every wrinkle.

Jackson rips his phone from his back pocket. "I've got to go. Sylvia fell. I need to get to the hospital." He's out the door without another word.

Gerry and I stand in the aisle. The last time we were face-to-face was at the marina when Jackson saved Solia from the lake after a microburst. The times before were the town council meetings to discuss the wind turbine project. Neither event shone a positive light on me. Gerry and I aren't exactly on good terms.

I'm no fool, however—it's clear that if you're not on Gerry's good side, you're not on anyone's good side. His family has been in town for generations, and everyone respects him. If I'm going to be spending any sort of time here, I need to sand our relationship to a smooth surface.

"Do you have any idea how bad it is?" I place the drill back on the shelf, in line with the other forward-facing boxes, careful not to disturb the order of the neatly placed products. I came here to buy a power drill so I can unfasten and pull my dock from the lake before the weather changes. For now, the dock can wait. Gerry crosses his arms against his chest and clears his throat while following my every move.

"Unfortunately, I don't. Sylvia is in her nineties, and anytime someone that age goes down, it's not going to be easy to rebound. Syl is one of the strongest women I know. She'll pull through. I'm going to drive over and check on things. Is there something you need?" Gerry asks, deadpan.

"No, I'm good." I put my hands in my pockets and walk toward the door. "What hospital is she at?"

"Plymouth." Gerry turns back and shuffles to the cashier line.

"Thanks. Have a good day." My words fall on deaf ears, and I leave without the one thing I came for.

I didn't need to think twice about going to the hospital. Despite being put off the night of our first date, I'm not ready to throw in the towel. Shannon has been with a loser her whole life. Something about her has me wanting to be the one who shows her what a real man is made of. Additionally, she needs to be treated to a night in my bed. I'll erase the memory of Richard right out of her.

Jackson has Solia, and Shannon is probably looking after their grandfather, so this is an opportunity to show her my heart is bigger than my pile of money.

The drive to the hospital is less than half an hour. Every place around here is on a dark, winding road edged with pine trees. The number of Moose Crossing signs spooks me out. *Do they actually cross the road?*

At least moose are a little more obvious than the freaks jaywalking on every turn in Boston. Sure, signs are needed to warn people about gigantic mammals crossing. There aren't any signs warning us about Bostonian morons.

I forgot how much I despise hospitals. The automatic doors glide open, forcing a wave of emotion over me. The last time I stepped foot in a hospital was when my father passed away. A slight pounding in my chest recalls back those final moments of sitting in the waiting room, holding my mother as the doctor delivered the words, "We did everything we could." Despite my strength, I had no choice but to crumble to the floor with her in my arms. He wasn't supposed to leave us. From that day forward, my entire life changed.

I arrive at the front desk behind a man dressed in black scrubs. The woman working the desk points him in the direction of the waiting room and says, "The Christiansons are over there on the right."

My attention snaps across the lobby and sure enough, Solia, Jackson, Shannon, and Earl are sitting in a row of plastic chairs against the stark white wall. I head over on the heels of the man in front of me. As we approach the first row of chairs, the man in the black scrubs turns and a dark cloud emerges over the waiting area.

*What the fuck is he doing here?*

I didn't recognize him without the bandana, stench, and bike.

Shannon's jaw all but drops to the floor. The shock and confusion spread across everyone's face, including my own. She releases Earl's hand and charges straight for Richard. "What are you doing?" There's a fire in her eyes amid the tears.

"What am I doing here? What the fuck is he doing here?" Richard's voice is far too loud for a hospital waiting area.

My biceps flex and testosterone surges. "What the fuck am I doing? You're the one who agreed to rehab, asshole."

Jackson stands next to Shannon, one hand on her shoulder.

"I was at the hardware store talking to Jackson when Gerry came and told him about your grandmother."

They both stare at me with looks of confusion and turn to Richard. "You haven't answered the question." Jackson inserts himself between his sister and her ex.

"Shut the fuck up, Jackson. I'm goddamn family. When I heard Sylvia fell, I signed myself out. I'm clean."

"Richard, that's bullshit. I don't need you, you're not clean, and you need to leave."

*Did I hear her correctly?* "You were just with him?" *I'm so fucking confused right now.*

"Everyone, calm down. I went to visit Richard. I felt bad he was alone."

Richard throws me a wink. That motherfucker.

"While I was there, Jackson called. Richard, why would you check yourself out? What are you thinking?"

Richard angles his thumb in my direction. "I can do whatever I want. You can't be serious about this douchebag."

"Man, she asked you to leave." I take my hands out of my vest pockets and angle my shoulders toward Richard.

"What's all your money gonna do in a situation like this, asshole?" Richard's puffed chest is inches away from mine, his beer gut leading the charge.

"Maybe there's a better hospital somewhere. I can arrange transport with the snap of my fingers. What about you? Did you bring a six-pack to sit and watch the show?"

"That's a low blow, man."

"I don't need either of you. I didn't ask anyone to come. What I need is for the two of you to go and let me concentrate on my family. Enough is enough."

"Shan, baby, come on. I'm family, I want to be here. Sylvia's been in my life forever. I love her too."

"If you loved her so much, you would've treated her granddaughter with a little more respect. Huh, buddy?"

Jackson steps in between us and puts a hand on my chest. "This isn't the time or the place for this. You're all upsetting Earl. Grow the fuck up."

Heads swivel toward the double doors as they open and two doctors walk toward us. It's quiet enough to hear a pin drop.

Jackson and Shannon rush to Earl's side and hold his elbows. "Are you Sylvia's family?" asks the doctor whose embroidered lab coat says Dr. R. S. Monti, Cardiothoracic Surgeon.

I'm trying to read her body language. The green scrubs and matching scrub cap accentuate her porcelain skin and large blue eyes.

"Yes, I'm her husband," Earl manages to mutter and shakes in the grip of his grandchildren's hold.

Dr. Krizz, the orthopedic surgeon, speaks up, his expression stoic. "We have good and bad news, sir. The good news is Sylvia's stable. The bad news is she needs more than a new hip. We ran some additional tests and discovered a blockage in one of the arteries around her heart. Dr. Monti will give you more information. It's a good thing we caught it. This could be the reason Sylvia experienced the fall in the first place."

"Before we can go through with the hip replacement, we need to place a stent into the artery to clear the blockage," Dr. Monti explains. "We'll go through her leg to insert the stent. We need to run a few more tests before we're sure she's strong enough to withstand the surgery."

Dr. Krizz takes over. "We've inserted an IV and given her medicine to manage the pain. She's comfortable, but not fully alert. Would you like to see her before we take her in?"

Earl loosens from Jackson's and Shannon's hold and walks toward the door without speaking. Shannon follows behind. "Grandpa, do you want me to go with you?"

He turns around to face us. "You wait here. I need to see my wife alone." Earl turns, stuffs his hands into his front pockets, and walks through the door, a surgeon on each side.

Shannon's shoulders slump, hair falling forward, and tears stream down her cheeks and onto the floor. Solia puts her arm around Jackson and together they head back for the chairs.

Apprehension and sadness hang heavy in the air. My skin crawls with discomfort, and I can't seem to muster up the right words. I follow and place my hand on Shannon's shoulder and feel the heat from Richard's body approaching, followed by the wind from his left hook to my jaw. Shannon and Jackson swivel upon hearing the commotion.

The room spins. It's one thing to get punched, but completely different when you don't see it coming. I manage to lift my head after the blow and find Richard inches away from my face.

"Man, who the fuck do you think you are?" Richard spews spittle onto my face. His eyes are fueled with fire, and he's winding up for round two.

I'm strong enough to hold back, but not today. I push Richard's shoulders and throw his ass into the chair. Its front legs tip into the air, sending the one next to it crashing to the floor and startling everyone into silence. We have the attention of a growing number of onlookers in the waiting room .

"Listen up, you lowlife piece of shit. I'm not the one with the fucking problem. Man up and get the hell out. She divorced you."

He's up, careening toward me. I land a hard uppercut to his jaw. Blood pools on his lower lip. Next thing I know, Richard grips my shoulders and pushes me against the wall. Jackson grapples and pulls his arms behind his back. Someone screams.

A bulky hospital security guard appears and pulls me off the wall and into the corner. Solia's arms are wrapped around

Shannon, a shield of protection from this onslaught of testosterone. Everyone from the front desk, the hallways, and the waiting room back up and watch us with mouths agape.

"Get him out of here," the nurse from the front desk orders the two security guards as she points at Richard.

The first officer pulls Richard's arm behind his back and walks toward the front door.

"Him too." She's pointing the second officer my way.

"Me? You see this guy? I didn't start anything. Man, let go." There's blood splattered on my white sleeves. My shirt is untucked and ripped at the seams. The security guard finally loosens his grip on my wrists. I wriggle free of his hold and rush to Shannon's side.

"He didn't start this. The other guy did." The rawness and defeat are present in her voice. The officer looks at the head nurse, and she nods him off.

Shannon's eyes are sunken, her skin rubbed raw from the hospital tissues sitting on the small end table. "I can't do this right now."

I reach for her hands, but she pulls away and crosses her arms, looking toward the double doors. "I understand," I say. "But whatever you need, I can help you. If she needs extra care, I can help."

Shannon spins on her heels. Anger has pushed the sadness from her eyes. "What do I look like, a tax write-off? I don't need money. What I need is my family! What I need is for my grandmother to come out of here alive. Can you do that for me?" Her hands are suspended in the air, awaiting my response.

"That's not what I meant. Of course that's what you want. I merely meant …"

"I honestly don't care what you meant. You should go."

*How the fuck am I the bad guy?*

"I came to check on you. I had no idea Richard would be here and act like an asshole." I rub my chin, partly in pain and partly to remind her that I got slugged by her psycho soon-to-be ex-husband.

"Yeah, well, I didn't know either of you would show up." A small flash of calm washes over her. "I'm sorry he hit you. Here, let me see. Do you need a doctor?" Her hand cradles my chin.

"Every time I see the guy, he's unhinged. What's gotten into him is the fact that he's a drunken asshole. I'm fine. Nothing a little ice won't fix. The guys at work will wonder what the hell goes on in New Hampshire. And I'm sorry I reacted, but—"

"You defended yourself. Anyone would do the same. Thanks for checking on me, but I'm good. You don't need to be here."

"Will you let me know how she is?"

"Yes. Let me walk you to the door." Shannon's lips are pursed as she gently exhales. Her hair is pulled tight into a low ponytail and her skin's usual rosiness has been whitewashed with exhaustion.

I take the hint and follow her lead to the front and through the double doors. Before she turns to walk away, she holds my hand, looks up, and says, "I got your message about Boston. I do want to go. I'm not sure how things are going to turn out here, but my answer is yes if things with my grandparents have settled somewhat."

"It's two weeks away. Hopefully, your grandmother will be on the mend and back home by then. I can wait." I kiss the top of her head just as I spot bikes approaching in my peripheral vision.

Richard and two other bikers rev their Harleys. Two are dressed in full-on biker gear—leather jackets and patches, no helmets but bandanas—and jeans. And then one in fucking black scrubs. What a loser. Richard slows enough to blow Shannon a kiss and then looks me square in the eyes.

"You're fucking dead, man. Watch your back."

# 9

These past two weeks have been nothing short of a blur. More hours were spent at the hospital than at home. After the shit show in the waiting room, I made it clear to both men that despite their best intentions, I want space. The last thing anyone needs is a royal rumble. My grandfather is strong, but he's not fooling anybody. Worry and despair have settled deep into the creases on his face.

The surgeries went smoothly without any complications. Grandma has been transferred to a postsurgical rehabilitation center where she's resting and recovering. Doctors were able to place the stent into the artery to clear the blockage and then replaced her hip. Because of her age and the extent of the surgery, the rehab facility in Lincoln is the most suitable place for her. The doctors check in, and the physical therapist has her up and on her feet, something none of us could've done at home. Sylvia Christianson is amazing—ninety-one years old, and she's not going to let this knock her down.

My parents arrived from New York a couple days ago. My father stayed until the surgery was complete and headed back home, leaving my mom to hold down the fort. I offered to stay with my grandfather, but Mom insisted she would. Having his daughter-in-law in town relieves some stress for us all. My grandfather at the farmhouse without my grandmother is the equivalent of him walking on foreign soil. He looks like a lost puppy. I've never seen him so sad.

The entire town has rallied around him. We have no shortage of people willing to drive Grandpa to the rehab center or fill his fridge. Gerry organized a town meal train and everyone has been eager to help. The advantages of living in a small town are second to none when it comes to stuff like this.

Earl's days are filled with sleeping, visiting, and people trying to feed him. The love my grandparents have for each other is the kind fairy tales are made of. My father plans on returning when Grandma is discharged, assuming the cider production and distribution are under control.

Richard is a whole other story. I don't have time to deal with him right now. He won't return to rehab, convinced he doesn't need it. His family has made it clear he's not welcome back home. His landlord kicked him out, and his sister has left me nasty message after nasty message about it being my responsibility to allow him back into our house.

My mother-in-law had the nerve to leave me a voicemail calling me a sell-out and a sad excuse for a daughter-in-law. After everything Richard has put me through, she can't seem to recognize her son's culpability in the collapse of our marriage any more than he can. I'm already struggling with guilt over the whole situation; I don't need a delusional ex-mother-in-law crawling up my butt about what I should and shouldn't be doing.

But enough is enough. I put my foot down, surprising even myself. I called them both and told them I tried, that I did the best job I could, but the rest is up to Richard. Neither woman had anything nice to say and ended the conversation abruptly.

Richard has called me several times, but I've sent him directly to voicemail.

Nate texted me the following day to let me know Richard is staying with a friend in Meriden. I told Nate my ex needs to stay away from my porch.

FaceTime rings and Madison appears on the screen. She's sitting on her condo patio, wrapped in a puffer vest with coffee in hand. "Hey, what's going on?"

"Hey. I think I'm staying in tonight but heading to the farm tomorrow to check on Earl and hoping not to run into my ex-husband, who busted out of rehab. You know, just a regular weekend. Oh, and trying to figure out what the hell I'm doing going on a date with Nick. You?"

"Jeez. I didn't get a chance to tell you at work. I'm taking a ride to Winnipesaukee to look at a condo that went on the market."

"What? Wait—you're leaving Meriden?"

"My HOA fees went up again. How much can snow removal and landscaping cost? My teaching salary won't cover it, so I'm going to look. It's cute, close to the water, and the fees are substantially lower."

"You'll be so far away." My heart sinks. Now is not the time for my best friend to leave town. "Do you want me to come with you to check it out?"

"No, I'm good. My mother is coming with me. And listen, stay clear of Richard. It's only a matter of time before he fucks up again. Go out with Nick. I'll call and check on your grandfather. Go to Boston."

"Sylvia is making progress. She doesn't have her wits about her yet, but physically, she's right where they want her to be. We hope she'll come home within a week or two, god willing. Earl is lost without her. And I'm having second thoughts about this date."

"Wait, why?" Her eyebrows scrunch up in disappointment.

"There's so much going on. I don't know. What if someone needs me? Jackson is still pissed off about me talking to Nick. Everyone in town cringes when they see him. What am I even thinking?"

"I'll tell you what you should be thinking. You can't do anything more for your grandfather than you already are. Plus, your mother is there to help him. Jackson and I can take turns checking in. I'm sure Gerry is even on it. Richard is not in the picture, nor is he your problem. And as far as what other people think of Nick, who gives a shit? Do you really? I know Jackson's opinion is important, but he'll come around.

"And speaking of coming, you drool every time you see Nick. He's sexy as fuck, and you know it. So, things got off to a rocky start with the wind turbines, so what? Things happen for a reason. The deal fell through, he's interested in you, and did I mention sexy as hell? He's not the cold-hearted asshole he presented as this summer. You've learned a lot about him, and I think he might be learning a little something about himself in our tiny little hamlet."

"Yes, you mentioned sexy." I roll my eyes, but the thought of Nick's body next to mine sends a shiver down my spine.

"Then it's settled. What time are you guys leaving tomorrow?"

"Around four. It takes about an hour and a half to get to Boston. The cocktail hour starts at six, followed by dinner, and then we'll head home. I don't know what I'm wearing. The whole thing has my stomach in knots. I don't do cocktail parties and fancy dinners. I do campfires and red Solo Cups."

Madison's laugh rings through the speaker. "You'll be fine. Think of the movie *Pretty Woman*. Channel your inner Julia Roberts."

"Except I'm not a prostitute, Madison." I clutch my stomach to hold back the laughter.

Finally catching her breath, Madison says, "You know what

I mean. She goes from simple to sexy and fits right in. That's what I meant. Although if he has a tub like that, go for it." She winks into the camera.

"She actually goes from trashy to classy, but nice try. Real slick."

Madison does a forward bow into the camera, laughing hysterically. "Okay, text me when you leave. Send a pic and wear something sexy. I'll text Jackson and your mom, and we'll take care of Earl. Enjoy yourself. Everything will be fine here in Meriden."

"Thank you, Maddie. Let me know about the condo. I hope it sucks. I'd rather you stay in town."

"Ha! Thanks, Shannon." She closes her eyes, shakes her head, and ends the call.

Upon pulling my phone off my charging pad the next morning, I see a text from Madison. To my delight, she hated the condo, and I selfishly rejoice.

I kick the blankets off and head to the bathroom. I could've used a couple more hours of sleep, but the butterflies in my stomach took flight. I grab my robe off the bathroom-door hook just as the first aromatic waft of percolating coffee hits. Setting a timer on that machine each night has been a game-changer.

I pour a cup and go out to sit in the front porch rocker, my coffee held with both hands to embrace the warmth. My phone buzzes in my robe pocket.

Coffee set on the only straight porch plank, I pull out my phone. An unknown number appears on the screen. I answer.

I immediately recognize his groggy voice. "Hey."

"Richard?"

"I knew you'd come around."

I lift my cup, take a deep breath, and tilt the lukewarm liquid into my mouth. "I'm not coming around. I'm answering the damn phone from an unknown number. Something I'll never do again."

"Well, isn't that sweet. I wanted to let you know, work took me back."

"Great, that's great. Okay, well …"

"Come on, Shan. You miss me. Just admit it. I'm out, I'm clean, and you don't need that rich prick. Don't throw away all the years we had together." His voice inches toward desperation with every word.

"I'm not doing this, Richard. I hope you stay clean, but this —us—is over. It's not about Nick. We both signed. It's time to move on."

There's a pause. I brace myself for what's next. If time has taught me anything, it's that Richard is not a fan of losing, and right now, he sees this as a game. "Your family is my family. I'm not leaving town. If you think for one second you're finished with us, you've got another thing coming. The only reason I signed the papers was so those assholes wouldn't press charges and I wouldn't get my ass thrown in jail. I'm all you've ever known. Who the fuck picked you up off the floor every time you couldn't get pregnant? Huh? Me. Who the fuck fixed shit around that house of ours? Me. Who the fuck let you have summers to do whatever you wanted while I worked my ass off?"

"Excuse me. You don't *let* me do anything. And how dare you throw not being able to get pregnant in my face. You're a bigger asshole than I thought. Fuck off, Richard." I hang up and toss the phone into my robe pocket, tears streaming down my cheeks. I'm crying so hard, I'm hyperventilating. The anger inside me is almost too much to bear. He's a fucking monster. The Richard I knew, the one I loved, isn't in there anymore.

He's gone. He would never have said those things to me. Who the fuck does he think he is?

I replay Madison's words in my head and calm my breathing. I am going on this date. I've made the right decisions. Period. End of story.

$\sim$

My priorities are confirming my outfit for tonight and visiting Earl when he and Jackson return from checking on Grandma. A quick FaceTime with Solia, who always looks good, solidifies my choice. I've had a short (but not too short) navy-blue baby doll dress hanging in my closet for over a year, and I've been dying for somewhere cool to wear it. I can't recall why I bought it in the first place, but tonight presents the perfect opportunity.

All the anger and disappointment have fueled my need to prove I'm worthy of more than that piece-of-shit loser. Even if Nick doesn't stick around, I deserve a night out with a man who wants and respects my time.

I lay my dress out on the bed with a pair of tan heels I found at Marshall's, and then head to the apple orchard. This farm has been in the Christianson family for three generations. Our family never discusses what will happen next. We're aware of the circle of life, but sometimes I think we're willfully ignorant of how fast time ticks by. One of the byproducts of my grandmother's fall is the reality of their age settling in. They won't live forever. What will we do then? I hate thinking about it.

Jackson will take over the daily operation of the farm, but other than that, the family has been living in a state of denial. Ever since my parents moved to New York State a couple years ago to work with the hard cider production end of things, they have been disconnected from life here in Meriden. My parents have zero intention of working or living in Meriden. They love New York. The production facility and brewery are a huge success.

Driving up the dirt road to the farm, I sideline these concerns with the dirt spinning off my back tires. We'll figure something out. We always do.

I pull into the pebbled driveway and spot my grandfather rocking on the front porch. What hits me straight in the gut is seeing the empty white rocker by his side. My heart breaks thinking about how lonely he must be without her.

"Hey, Grandpa!" The warm sun heats my back. The leaves around the property are turning brilliant shades of red, yellow, and orange. Living in the Lakes Region of New Hampshire takes your breath away with each passing season. I love summer for obvious reasons, but autumn has a special quality.

Tourists retreat to their home base and our population contracts to the usual year-round residents. The summer shops close their doors and trap the heat inside. The air stays warm during the day but has a crispness at night. Evenings are for bonfires, and marshmallows fly off the grocery store shelves. Schools reopen, the classrooms full of bright, shiny faces. The only thing different this year is I'm living on my own for the first time.

"Hey, my sunshine. You're checking on your old grandpa again?"

I kiss his cheek and slide into the empty rocking chair. "Sure am. How was she today?"

"Same as the day before, with a tad more energy, if you can believe it. You know your grandmother. She's a rocket raring to blast off. She wants to be home and is doing everything she can to get here. She's a tough cookie, barking orders at all the nurses."

I'd like to say I'm surprised, but far from it. My grandmother is an enigma. She's got more energy than I do. If she's not weeding the garden, she's sweeping the barn or filling the compost bin. She's simply amazing. "She'll be home before you know it, Grandpa. Wolves couldn't hold that woman back from you." His eyes light up and he rests his tired head against the wooden plank of his rocker.

"I sure hope you're right, honey. So, tell me what's going on with you. How's Richard doing?"

My grandparents have struggled with my marriage ending. They've lived through difficult times. They came out on the other side together and expect everyone else to do the same. I'm not about to upset him anymore than he already is. "He's fine."

Grandpa stops rocking and looks my way. "What do you mean *fine*?"

"We're getting divorced. I'm not going to pretend we can fix this. I'm sorry."

"Those two boys caused quite a scene at the hospital, and I know he's going through hell. I also know you've made your decision, but Richard is family."

It's not worth disagreeing with him right now. Grandpa has enough weight to carry around, and there is no way I will convince him of anything.

"You know, there's something we've never told you, Shannon."

I stop rocking when he says my name. He never calls me Shannon.

"A long time ago, well before you were born, hell … it was just after your father was born, your grandmother gave me an ultimatum. Back in the day, my six-pack and I were the best of friends. It's what I turned to at the end of every day. Sometimes I would think about those six cans more than I thought about her, I'm ashamed to admit. Anyway, your grandmother and I were starting a family, we'd inherited the farm, and she'd had enough of my bullshit. Pardon my

French. It was either clean up or she was taking off. That's all it took.

"Thank god I saw the light. I quit, got myself to my first AA meeting, and haven't picked up a drink since. Marriage is tough, but it's worth working for."

His words hit me like a sucker punch to the gut. Never before has anyone in our family mentioned anything about a drinking problem or AA. How am I just learning this?

"Wow, I had no idea. Thank goodness you took Grandma seriously. I've never even really thought about why you never drank—you just don't. I'm proud of you, Grandpa. Richard never took steps to help himself, no matter how much I begged, pleaded, and tried. Maybe it's because we didn't have kids."

My grandfather takes my hand in his. "I wasn't trying to upset you. I can't help but see a bit of myself in Richard."

"This is all making a lot more sense to me, why you've been sympathetic to Richard's situation. But it doesn't change things. Our marriage ran its course, and I need to start living my life instead of trying to save someone else's. You need to trust me. I'm doing the right thing."

"Of course," he says and squeezes my hand. "We love you very much, Shannon, and I just want my grandchildren to find the same happiness your grandmother and I have had all these years."

"I love you too, Grandpa."

"I'll be okay here on the homestead. Your mother will be back any minute from the store. Don't you worry. Oh, and how about we keep this conversation between you and me—sound good?"

I reach for my keys on the side table and look into my grandpa's drooping eyes. He looks so tired. "You betcha. My lips are sealed. I'm proud of you." His eyes lift and his lips curve into a smile. "I'll see you tomorrow." I kiss the top of his head.

As I pull out of the driveway, I keep one eye on the road and one on Grandpa. His other half needs to come home.

~

The weather is getting cooler, so in case we're outside, my dress has loose long sleeves that gather at the wrist. A low V-neck reveals a peek of skin, but stops shy enough to elicit wonder, and the hem sits at mid-thigh. Having the summer off has its advantages. I suntan easily and this dress allows me to show off my bronzed legs. I wash and straighten my hair and leave it loose on my back. I slide on heels and even though I walk like a newborn giraffe in them, inspection in the mirror pleasantly surprises me. There's a reason women wear high heels. My legs look way hotter. Simple studs and the regular makeup routine and I'm as ready as I'll ever be.

My nerves are shot by the time I'm ready for Nick to pick me up. My body temperature has to be a hundred degrees. I'm officially second-guessing my decision to store the air-conditioning unit in the basement for the winter. I grab deodorant from the bathroom drawer and reapply for the third time, careful to avoid the fabric of my dress. I swear if I start sweating, I'll break out in hives and the entire night will be in the toilet.

I turn down the music and hear a soft knock on the door. I open it, and the sight of Nick behind the screen almost drops me to my knees. Nick would look hot in a paper bag, but he's leaning against the porch post, sunglasses on, hands in his pants pockets, ankles crossed, sporting a black suit and a crisp white dress shirt with the top button undone.

"Hey, sexy," he says in a low growl. He pulls off his glasses and lifts an eyebrow.

My throat constricts and my heart pounds. I don't think a man has ever turned me on more. I register he's walking toward me, but it's like I'm a teenager again and unsure of how to move. He reaches for the door and is within inches of my body. Heat floods between my thighs while I sink into the depths of his eyes.

Leaning his shoulder against the open screen door, he holds out a hand for mine and leads me onto the front porch. "You look amazing," he says. I step closer to the edge and the wind blows the hem of my dress. I wonder how much I've let him see. I'm thankful for my choice in underwear if, by chance, he gets a peek.

"I hope you like it. I wasn't sure."

His eyes trail my neck, my chest, and down my thighs. I swear he can hear my heartbeat. Our eyes meet, and the devilish look he's displaying makes me want to pull him inside the house. He tilts his head in the direction of the black SUV in the driveway, reminding me Harold is waiting patiently to drive us.

Nick slides his glasses on and bites his bottom lip. "Shall we?"

"We shall." I turn and shut the door behind me. I then think better of it and lock it. I'm not sure when I'll be back, nor does it matter, but I'm not leaving the house unlocked overnight. Not that I'll stay with Nick overnight, although a few parts of my body catch fire with such possibility.

"Let's get out of this town."

Something about the way those words land in my ears doesn't sit right.

# 10

Nick

My phone blows up for the better part of the drive. Turning it to silent is bound to send my team into a panic. I'm never unavailable. But my attention is on Shannon and her alone. A woman like her would find it rude for me to be on the phone.

She sits legs crossed, facing me, and talks about everything from work to family (I'm happy to learn her grandmother is making remarkable progress) to sports while taking in the city scene flashing by. I can't remember the last time I spoke to a woman for so long without inadvertently tuning out of the conversation midway through. With my hands free from my phone, I'm having trouble keeping them to myself.

Taking her tonight is a gamble. Shannon made it clear she prefers a bonfire with red Solo Cups. My usual dates attend high-profile events every week and know exactly how to work the room, and the night always ends the same. Honestly, my usual has gotten monotonous, and being in Meriden and around Shannon has me wanting more. Not that I don't want to get her naked, but it's not the only thing on my mind when spending time with her. And when we're apart, I catch myself thinking about her.

Harold pulls to the curb in front of Davio's, a five-star restaurant in Boston's Seaport District. It's the perfect night for an outdoor cocktail hour—the air is warm with a slight breeze blowing off the harbor.

You'd never know Shannon was out of her element when she steps onto the sidewalk, hair and dress drifting back from the wind. She could command a runway with her looks. The best part about it is she has no idea. Having her here is a whole different ball game. I'm concerned about her seeing Hogan and Lambert because the last time was the town council meeting when Shannon's family orchard was on the line. Those fucks better keep their mouths shut.

Once Harold drives off, I offer Shannon my hand, and the hostess escorts us to the back patio overlooking the harbor. Several patio heaters are scattered among the dark wooden planks. Each high-top table is within range of one, so no guest gets a chill. Hogan and Lambert are leaning on the outside bar, seemingly placing an order. I spot their wives at the nearby high top, carbon copies of each other. Both are hot, city hot—bottle blonds, painted acrylic nails, and dresses hugging their sculpted bodies perfectly, leaving nothing to the imagination. Our clients seem to be missing in action.

Shannon walks a step behind. Her hand tightens around mine, reminding me there's a chance she's nervous. Both women smile, but their eyes are glued to our hands. I don't usually hold a date's hand. I glide straight past and into the ring of fire.

"Hey, Nick, glad you made it." Mark leans his back against the bar and doesn't attempt to hide the fact he is checking out the woman by my side.

I shake Hogan's hand tighter than usual. "Mark, Tim, you remember Shannon?"

"Sure do. The apple orchard granddaughter."

I shoot daggers. He better stop right there.

Shannon slides from my grip and shakes Mark's hand, then Tim's. "You got it. The woman whose family successfully kept their orchard and homestead. Nice to see you again."

Her tenacity and quick wit are an instant turn-on.

"Touché." Mark winks and stiffens his shoulders. Tom remains silent. The conversation turns to the night's business. I order Shannon a glass of wine and a soda water with lime for myself. Drinking during business is off-limits.

"Are we going to seal the deal tonight?" Lambert asks.

Shannon's eyes dart from Tim to me, her mouth open. I could sucker punch him. No doubt he did that on purpose. I respond, "The turbine deal, yes. I think we'll secure the location." I wink at Shannon, knowing she thought he was referring to us.

Our clients arrive, two men from Chelsea, a town across the Mystic River from Boston. Despite spending days in a classroom, Shannon blends right in. She introduces herself and makes her way to the high top and joins the other women. From the corner of my eye, I watch her sip her wine and chat away as if she's known them her whole life. I've underestimated her.

The cocktail hour flies by, and it's time to escort our clients into our private dining room.

Lambert comes up behind me. "You are serious about his redneck chick?" He nods his chin toward Shannon walking inside with the other women.

"Don't be such an ass, man. And don't call her that."

"You and I are cut out for a different slice of woman, and she isn't it. She's got the body. Please tell me you're at least getting a blow job. Maybe she likes it rough, since she's from the fucking sticks."

My stomach muscles tighten, and I'm shocked at the

resistance it takes to not slam a fist into his face. "Seriously, shut the fuck up," I hiss in the lowest tone I can manage.

"Good evening, everyone. I'm Sienna. I'll be your server for tonight. Right this way."

I cringe as my two colleagues watch Sienna's ass as though it's being served on a platter. We file into the secluded room in the corner, the interior lined with thick red curtains. Shannon waits alongside the table, unsure where to sit. I reach for her hand and have her sit next to me, across from the clients.

Lambert winks and sits on Shannon's other side. He'd better keep his mouth shut and concentrate on business.

The menu is predetermined. Wine is delivered, and I order another soda water with lime. "I'll have one also," Shannon requests and rubs her lips together against the shiny gloss. "I need to be on my A game here," she whispers, brushing her hand along my thigh. I'm now hard as a rock.

*What is it with this woman? Maybe bringing her wasn't such a good idea. My mind is on one thing and one thing only—those shiny lips on …*

As if she's read my thoughts, a sexy sliver of a smile creases her lips as she takes a dinner roll and reaches across my chest to lift the butter. She then butters her roll, and mine. I'm not sure anyone has ever buttered a roll for me. Apparently, watching the way a woman spreads her butter is a new turn-on.

During dinner, I manage to focus on the task at hand. Everyone seems pleased, and by the end of the night, despite having one ear to my clients and one ear to Lambert's comments, I'm confident we've sealed the deal. We shake hands and schedule a meeting for next week at headquarters.

"Do you want dessert to go?" Everyone has departed, and Shannon and I are standing in the lobby.

"I'm good. I have a few things in my fridge at home." Shannon puts her hand in mine, and the host opens the door to the streets of Boston, traffic flowing left to right, sidewalks filled with pedestrians. "This is a beautiful area," Shannon says as she looks up at the newly constructed office buildings and restaurants lining the seaport.

"Besides the Fenway District, this is my favorite." Harold pulls my blacked-out Cadillac SUV to the curb. Before stepping forward, I take Shannon's hands in mine and look her in the eyes. "I planned a little surprise for us back at my place if you're up for it."

Shannon bites her lip. "Your place, here in Boston? I really need to be back in town for my grandmother."

"The lake house." I rub my thumbs over the tops of her hands. "Have you checked on everything back home?"

"Yes, she's stable, thank god. And I love surprises. Let's do it." She lets go of my light grip, swings her arms by her side, and steps toward our ride.

I didn't realize I'd been bracing myself for her reaction until I was in the clear. My chest muscles relax. I unfasten my top button, loosen my tie, and remove my suit jacket, breathing easier as I settle in next to her in the back seat.

Harold presses the button to raise the privacy shield between the front and back row when Shannon's head rests on my shoulder. He's a mind reader. I need to give him a raise.

"We're here." I cradle her head off my shoulder. I hadn't expected her to sleep the entire ride home. However, after all the nights at the hospital and worrying she's been doing, I'm not surprised.

"Oh, Nick." Her eyes are puffy and she wipes the corner of her mouth. Upon lifting her head, she spots the little drool puddle on my shoulder. She rubs the fabric. "This is embarrassing. I didn't mean to fall asleep and drool, for god's sake." Her cheeks redden three shades darker than usual.

Women don't fall asleep on me. Quite the opposite. The last time I fell asleep during a date, my date was on her knees in a compromised position, and I'd been served one too many beverages that night to enjoy it. I woke up to an empty bedroom, legs hanging off the mattress, and a scribbled note that said "Fuck off."

I derived pleasure from watching Shannon sleep on the ride home. She has a softness about her, a calming presence. It's a foreign sensation for me, but I enjoyed it.

Since giving Shannon a tour of the house right after I got the keys, I've added a few personal touches. When I say I, I'm referring to Harold following my directions.

"Did you add solar lights? Oh, and twinkly lights on the dock?"

I cringe at the tightness in my cheeks, excited she noticed. After our night at the Binn, I hung on to the fact she adored the lights hanging from the rafters.

Harold puts the car in park and looks at the Acura parked in the driveway. "Is that the one you want me to take?"

"Sure is, boss." I toss him the keys. "Text you in the morning."

"You bet. Good night to the both of you." Harold tips his hat forward and moves toward the car.

"Where's he off to?" Shannon has both hands on her hips, watching the car reverse and head toward downtown.

"I needed to figure out transportation and lodging. In Boston, we have a system, but Newfound has complicated things. I can't have Harold staying here or leaving me at the house without a vehicle. That's ridiculous."

"Sounds like you might be getting attached to this place already, making plans and all."

I shake my head, realizing I've now portrayed myself as soft. I puff out my chest. "Nah, I figured the safer, the better. Harold has a room at the B&B for the next month, and I have a car if we need it. He's around if I need anything or if I have to rush back to Boston.

"Enough of this nonsense. Come on, I have something I want to show you." I swing my jacket over my shoulder and catch her looking toward the opening of my shirt.

Shannon stifles her laugh, pulls off her heels, and follows my lead along the pebbled walkway around the perimeter of the house. As requested, the back lights are on. "Follow me." I look down at her bare feet. "No shoes?"

"No way. I'll sprain an ankle for sure. I'm good."

The sky is clear, the stars are out, and the air hovers around sixty degrees.

Landing on the second-story deck overlooking the lake, I silently thank Harold for the setup. The deck furniture is laid out like a plush Pottery Barn catalog shoot. A bottle of vino sits on the side table with two newly purchased Newfound Lake Winery glasses. He managed to score a few lake-themed blankets from Basic Ingredients, a popular shop in town, which are placed on the ends of the wicker couch. The telescope I requested is positioned in the corner, aimed at the sky, ready for stargazing, and I'd bet money Harold filled the refrigerator with snacks.

"Look at this." Shannon runs her fingers along the edge of the cushion. "I'm glad I didn't decline your offer."

"Me too. I would've felt pathetic back here alone."

"Are you not accustomed to being alone?" She angles her eyes to meet mine.

I avoid answering. "You feel like swimming?"

"I didn't bring a bathing suit, and the lake's chilly."

"Look inside the bag by the firepit." I point to a small pale blue bag with a ribbon tied in a bow around the paper handles.

Shannon walks right over, unties the ribbon, and pulls out an emerald-green, triangle-top bikini and bottoms. "Well, you thought of everything. How'd you manage all this?"

Something inside me tightens, and for the first time, a tinge of embarrassment creeps in. "I gave Harold a list."

She dangles the bathing suit top by one of the strings. "Harold did all this." It's a statement, not a question. Shannon looks at me with what appears to be disappointment. "What are you doing here, Nick?"

Her question sends a bolt of lightning through my body, grounding me to the deck. She takes a seat on the couch and drops the suit back into the bag.

I sit and prop my ankle on my knee. "Shannon, I bought this house to spend time here. I asked Harold to do this because I couldn't. We were in Boston."

Leaning forward, her glare cuts through the night. "Couldn't or wouldn't? It looks like Harold does an awful lot for you. Why are you so interested in being here when your life is in Boston?"

Her questions leave me gasping for air. "Shannon, I have been living my life at one hundred miles an hour since I took over the company. Meriden is the first place to grab hold of me. Meeting you made it even more appealing. Seeing this town come together like you all did was really something. It took a lot of heart to fight and no one ever backed down.

"That's what's missing in my life. Everything is cutthroat and cold. My mother getting sick and this summer really changed things for me." I look up and see my words have softened the hardness in her jaw.

"Doesn't it bother you not even having time to go to the store or drive yourself anywhere? It's so …"

"Not everyone's life looks the same."

Shannon turns her shoulders toward the lake, grabs the blanket from the couch's arm, and unfolds it across her legs. I lean back and watch her as she stares at the star-filled sky in silence. Staying quiet is not my forte, but I'm at a loss for words. I have no idea how this night took such a sharp left turn.

I remove my tie and toss it over the nearest cushion, undo my cuff links, and stuff them into my pants pocket. I then lean my elbows on my knees.

In the distance, a chorus of frogs croak from somewhere in the tree line. At least someone is attracting a mate. I'm batting zero. The darkness around the lake surrounds us as the motion-detector lights turn off.

Instead of digging for words, I search for the release panel to the firepit between us. *Righty-tighty, lefty-loosey.* Harold's words ring in my ear.

Pushing down on the igniter, I pray to be saved the embarrassment and breathe a sigh of relief when the flames blaze, casting a golden glow over Shannon's face. She is every bit as beautiful, if not more, than the first time I saw her.

"You know what? You are absolutely right. My life is different from yours."

"How about I join you?" I watch for any sign of acceptance and move closer. Rolling my sleeves has the effect I hoped for; she eyes my forearms like a hungry predator. Lifting the edge of the blanket, I sit next to her, reaching my fingers for her legs and lifting them over mine. I can't help but run my palms along her smooth calves, desperately wanting to venture under the hem of her dress.

I figure I'm in the clear when she scoots her ass closer to me and rests her head on the pillow. The blanket drapes over her waist, and the glow of the fire dancing on her skin makes it hard to concentrate.

She reaches for my hand under the blanket and turns her head toward me. "Thank you for this, for making tonight special. It's been a long time since someone did something for me."

"Things have been heavy since we met. I wanted to surprise you."

"I'm tired of worrying. This is the way things should be. Carefree, you know? Being an adult sucks sometimes."

"That's one thing we see eye to eye on. Right here, right now, it's you and me, the trees, and the water. Let's forget about the heavy stuff for a couple hours. What do you say?"

Without hesitating another second, I lift her legs off my lap, kneel onto the cushion, and hover over her, keeping my right foot on the deck. Gripping the couch, I lower myself within inches of her body, a stream of fire glowing between us. I move my lips to her ear.

"Let go, Shannon."

I trail her neck with my tongue, allowing my chin stubble to brush against her skin. As I follow her collarbone, her chest rises with a deep breath. I trace the curves of her breasts displayed above the cut of her dress, and she runs her fingers through my hair, her nails grazing my scalp. I press my forehead into her, our lips barely a centimeter apart, grab the bag from the deck beneath us, and whisper, "Go put this on."

Without waiting for an answer, I push myself off the couch, walk to the sliding glass door, and flick on the interior light. Shannon tosses the blanket aside and accepts the bag. Without uttering a word, she heads inside.

Harold told me he left me a suit. I spot another bag by the telescope and hustle to the upstairs bathroom for a quick change.

When I return, Shannon's tucked under the Newfound Lake blanket with only the tips of her shoulders exposed. "Damn!"

I look down at my bare chest. "What?"

"Looking good, city boy. I knew whatever was underneath those suits had to be good, but this is …"

I work hard for this body. I tilt my head and anxiously

await my view. "Well, small-town girl, let's see what you've been hiding." I reach and grab the corner of the blanket and tug it away from her. She welcomes the challenge and stands in front of the flames.

"It seems our buddy Harold either likes things tiny or doesn't look at sizes." Shannon tosses her head back, hands on her waist, and sways her hips from side to side.

I won't lie—I knew her body was hot—but damn, she was hiding the goods under those clothes. *Thank you, Harold.* This suit would be better described as Band-Aids than a bikini. Lucky for me, the fire is bright enough to enjoy the view of her round tits covered in goose bumps and her rock-hard nipples pushing through the thin, barely there fabric. The emerald-green top covers about two inches around. I could lick the circumference of each tit and not even touch the bathing suit.

I must have been staring for a few seconds too long because she clears her throat. Without lifting my head, I continue to trail her stomach, between her legs, and down to the floor. "You. You look good enough to eat."

Shannon stifles her laugh with her hand and crosses her torso with her other arm.

"Don't you dare cover that body." I walk toward her and take her hands in mine and spin her around to reveal Harold has chosen an equally skimpy bottom, if it can even be classified as that. I'd call it a thong, but maybe it's a little thicker. Each side is tied in a bow high up on her hip, leaving more of her ass exposed than covered.

A movie montage flashes in my mind. I want to take those bows and pull them loose, bend her over the couch, grab hold of her shoulders, one foot up on the cushion, spread those wet lips apart, and take her from behind. However, that movie isn't currently scheduled to play, so I turn her back around and pull her chest to mine.

"How about I take this sexy, small-town hottie to the water?

What do you say?" I sense a slight hesitation, but Shannon starts walking toward the stairs, leading the way. "Let me grab towels."

With several in hand, I walk a step behind and enjoy the view of her ass bouncing while she navigates the lawn. She's at the end of the dock next to the Adirondack chair with her arms hugging her waist. I wrap a towel around her shoulders, leaving her ass exposed and reluctantly covering up my view of the rest of her body.

I light the lantern in the corner of the dock. It provides just enough illumination to stop either of us from plunging in unexpectedly.

"This place is really something." Her head is tilted toward the sky, but I'm having a hell of a time zeroing in on anything but her rear end. I've always been an ass guy. She's got the best I've seen—round, full, toned, one I can grab hold of and ... damn!

"Yeah, it really is something." I pull her close to my chest in an effort to concentrate, but that backfires when my excitement presses against her. I know she feels it when she gently moves in just enough for her bathing suit to shimmy between her ass crack, allowing my cock to fold inside. *Fuck.*

Opening my palms and laying them flat on her stomach, I gently tug her closer against my body. She emits a low growl and leans her head back on my chest. I slide my hands down her thighs and allow my thumbs to graze her lips as they slide by.

"Nick."

I'm stopped in my tracks, hands frozen. I'm swollen against her. I wait.

"It's been a long time. Like, a really long time since I ... since I've been with someone. Don't get me wrong—you are turning me inside out right now, but I'm a little out of practice."

"Baby, you don't need any practice. How about you let me take control?"

Her chin tilts down and she turns around to face me. She widens both palms on my chest, and her nipples are hard against my body. "Not before you get your ass in that lake. This was your crazy idea. You only live once, so let's go." The towel falls to the dock, and she tugs my arm until we are side by side at the edge. "You didn't think I was going to put on this ridiculous suit without making you actually get in the water, did you?"

"Ridiculous suit? I'm thinking about increasing Harold's salary after seeing his choice of swimwear."

She laughs into the night sky, and a strange sensation pools in my stomach. "Ready … three, two, one!"

Without time to process, I follow her lead and immerse myself in the water. The temperature is warmer than the air. We surface with only the light of the moon and a few house lampposts in the distance. It's a cloudless night, and stars decorate the darkness above and illuminate the mountain ridges across the lake. I reach for her hand and swim closer to shore where my feet touch the sand, pull her body into mine, and hoist her up to my waist.

She willingly wraps her legs around me, making it ever more difficult to keep hold of my desire. Her hair is drenched, slicked back, and brushing against my fingertips. She leans her soft lips to mine, warming the night air between us, and traces the outline of my mouth with her tongue, instantly tripping my engine into overdrive. Her nails drag along my back, into my hair, my tongue exploring every inch of her mouth … I don't think I've ever been so turned on.

Most women are willing to spread their legs for a piece of me, so taking my time is something I haven't experienced. I am suddenly aware that earning her desire is my goal.

She takes my jaw into her hands. "For a city boy, you sure know how to kiss."

"Oh, really? What have you heard about city boys?"

"You all look good in your fancy suits, all cleaned up, but I'm sure you're not used to being out here in the wilderness in the middle of the night, making out with a woman you just met."

I lean closer to her ear and whisper, "Do you trust me?" Her body shivers. I don't move an inch, hovering over her neck as I wait for a response.

In the still of the night, I hear her answer. "Yes."

With her secured around my waist, her ass cheeks in my hands, I walk until I'm waist deep in the water and carry her closer to the dock. Her hands grip my triceps as I lift her onto the wooden planks. I reach for a towel and smooth it out next to her and then lift her back into the water. With both our feet planted upon the smooth, sandy lake bottom, I pull her in to meet my lips as I untie the back string of her bathing suit. The fabric separates from her chest, freeing her breasts into the night air, and I toss the suit on the dock.

With her chest cupped in each hand, I take a minute to swirl my tongue and nibble her nipples, causing her to squirm in my arms. "You like that?" I look up to see her nodding toward the moon. I reach for the side strings on her bottom and tug outward, easily releasing them. I toss them, unsure where they land.

"Nick, I'm not sure I'm ready for this. I mean, we just … What if someone sees us?"

I take her chin and angle it toward my eyes. "I asked if you trusted me." I reach down and tug my suit to my ankles and toss the wet garment onto the dock. "Now, you're not the only one without clothes on, baby. The bears don't mind a show." I wink. A smile spreads across her face as I lift and separate her legs around my waist. I feel her skin against my abs and wonder if I have the ability to hold myself back.

I shuffle through the sand as a few house lights go off in the distance, leaving us in darkness, except for the lantern and glow of the deck fire in the distance. I lift Shannon onto the towel. She places her hands behind her and arches her back into the air, nipples solidly pointing to the sky.

I spread her legs and reach to lift her hands and lay her onto the dock. Running my hands from her shoulders to the tops of her breasts, to her nipples, I tug and give each one a little twist, sending her squirming again as she lifts her heels out of the water and onto the dock. I take this as a sign that I'm in the clear. I place a hand under each ass cheek and scooch her closer to the edge, serving her up on a platter for me to enjoy. "You ready?"

"Don't make me wait." Her words take me by surprise. I feel my way between her lips and am happy to find she's wet and ready. I slide and curve two fingers inside and lower my tongue, familiarizing myself with my new playground.

*God, she tastes good.*

She's moaning in rhythm with my fingers pushing deep inside her. I find what I'm looking for and glide my tongue to the sweet spot. You know when you hit it right. A woman momentarily paralyzes under the sensation and then yearns for more. I wait for it, and then …

"Nick, oh fuck."

There it is. With two fingers inside and one pressing against her backside, I lick and suck her dry. She shudders and yells out in the silence of the night. I taste her release, and her body softens against the wood planks. She thinks I'm done, but I'm taking pleasure in surprising her.

"That was amazing." She leans up onto her elbows. Without releasing my fingers, I use my other hand and place it on her chest, applying gentle pressure.

"I'm not done." I see the white in her eyes brighten, accompanied by a smirk.

"Oh really? There's an encore?"

"Baby, the only thing you are getting here is the opening act. Lie back and let me finish." She listens as I explore every single inch of her, back to front. I want to make her beg for me, and I'm not going to give in. I insert another finger and wait for her to adjust and make sure it isn't too much. All signs point to go when she arches her back and moans. Some women think it's one and done, but I like to prove them wrong.

I may not be from a small town, but I will go to town on Shannon.

I leave no inch undiscovered, paying more attention to her every squirm, moan, and whimper than I ever have with any other woman. Just as I planned, she's begging me.

"Please, Nick, I can't take it anymore. I take back what I said. I'm ready, I'm ready, please."

This only makes me work harder. I'm enjoying this more than I ever have, and seeing her get off, sprawled out on full display on the dock, is sexy as hell.

Once I'm satisfied with my performance and confident she's exhausted, I lift her into the water. She collapses against my chest, drunk on her release. "You are perfect."

I leave the towels and her suit behind and walk onto the sand. As much as I want to pound into her, I'm determined to wait. I throw her naked ass over my shoulder like a rag doll. She giggles and squirms, ass up to the North Star. As we make our way to the house, a cool breeze floats across the rear lawn, sending a shiver up my spine, her hands gripping onto my skin.

Without warning, her body stiffens. I stop dead in my tracks and flip her off my back. I look down at her, both of us butt-naked in the grass. "What?"

"Did you hear that?"

"Hear what?"

"I swear I heard a stick break."

"I'm going to go out on a limb to say there are plenty of animals in these woods perfectly capable of snapping a stick." We double-step it to the rear stairs, Shannon's eyes never leaving the tree line, my eyes never leaving her body, watching each part bounce in rhythm with her fast-paced steps.

With her feet on the deck, the firelight illuminates her naked body. I didn't think it was possible to have a hard-on for this long. She reaches for the blanket on the couch and wraps it around her shoulders. "You …"

Then, without a doubt, we hear the sound even I have come to recognize.

The motherfucking Harley.

# 11

"I think I'm still riding the high from that night." I swing my ten-pound teacher bag over my shoulder as Madison and I leave the staff meeting and walk through the deserted hallway.

"Take it, Shannon! Whatever helps us survive the first couple months back at school until we get in the swing of things. I can't believe you haven't seen him since."

"Things got so busy at school and with him in Boston. He thought he'd be at the lake more, but the man works like a machine. I mean, I'm not keeping track or anything, nor is it my business, but I've only gotten a text now and then. He should be here this weekend. I have to keep reminding myself it's not a relationship. Women can do this sort of thing and not get clingy. Right?"

"It sounds like something I'd keep track of if I were you. What's the latest on Richard?"

"After everything went down at the hospital, I'm trying to steer clear. He resorted to using an unknown number and called. He's not getting the hint, but he hasn't shown up drunk, so there's that. I am so over his bullshit." I'm not about to get into the bike I heard roll by Nick's. I can't confirm it was Richard. The thought of him following me makes me want to vomit.

"His shit isn't your problem. And besides, you've done more than most ex-wives would."

"Soon-to-be ex-wife, you mean."

"Whatever."

"I'm heading over to Judy's for some last-minute race stuff for tomorrow." I throw my bag into the back seat where I'm certain it will sit until Monday morning.

Madison says, "You better be cheering for me as I drag my ass across the finish line."

"You're doing the one-mile fun run, Madison. Seriously!"

Madison shrugs, laughs, and heads in the direction of her car.

"I'll have a glass of water ready, so dehydration doesn't set in."

"See you there," she yells across the lot. I slide behind the wheel, take a deep breath, and drive off into a three-day weekend.

Before heading to Basic Ingredients, I'll stop at home so I can change into comfy clothes. As I pull in, Jackson's pickup is in my driveway. My first thought is of my grandmother. His driver's side door is open, Jackson's work boot resting on the running board. As I approach the truck, I spot the Red Sox hat. He glances at me in the rearview mirror and lifts his head.

"Hey, is everything okay?" I lean into the door and grab hold of the top, trying not to throw the door off its hinge with the weight of the week's exhaustion.

"Yeah, totally. Finally Friday, huh?" Jackson lifts his hat, flipping it backward, and slides out of the front seat.

"Thank god, I thought something happened with Grandma."

"Jeez, Debbie Downer. Everything is good."

I release the tension bundled in my shoulders. "I'm happy it's a three-day weekend. I'm running in quick to change and then heading to Judy's. What's up?"

Jackson stuffs his hands in his front pockets, resting his thumbs on the outside, and looks down at the ground with a smirk. I know my brother well enough to know something is off. "Dude, what is going on with you?"

"I haven't seen douchebag around in a bit."

"I assume you mean Richard?"

"Not exactly."

"Seriously, J., you need to let this go. Nick's going to be around town."

"You can't be dating this guy."

"I'm a grown-ass woman, Jackson. We aren't dating … technically … well … even if we are, there's so much more about him that you don't know. Let me have a little fun. You can't be here checking on my love life. So what's up?"

"Yeah, well, I do have something to tell you." He looks up from the dirt driveway and tension replaces his usual relaxed features. "Solia's running the half tomorrow." He pauses and seems to be waiting for acknowledgment.

"Jackson, I helped organize the bib numbers and have gone with Solia on several of her training runs. I know she's running."

"You know things have been great between her and me, and I was thinking …"

Jackson kicks at the pebbles in the driveway and looks everywhere but at me. The realization hits me like a brick, and I drop my bag to the dirt.

"Shut the fuck up! No way! Yes, yes, yes!" I rush my brother and embrace him, squeezing so hard his laugh turns into a wheeze.

"Jesus, Shannon. I didn't even tell you the rest."

"Sorry, sorry, yeah, go ahead." I release him, allowing

Jackson to breathe again, and I wait for him to confirm what I'm already thinking.

"I planned on asking Solia to marry me at the finish line tomorrow."

I again jump into my brother's arms. "Holy shit, this is amazing! Do you have a ring?"

I let go of him again and sit on the stoop. The cheesiest smile is plastered on Jackson's face, but it's no surprise to me he's popping the question. Solia is the best thing that's ever happened to him.

Jackson intertwines his fingers behind his head and looks up at the sky.

"Wait, you're not nervous, are you? There's no way she'll say no. I mean, it is really soon. Wait—did you tell Mom and Dad?"

Jackson's eyes drift back to me. "Not nervous. Actually … yeah, I'm nervous. It is soon, but she's it. We don't have to get married tomorrow, but I would. I don't want to spend one day without her. I have the ring and I asked for her father's permission the last time they were here, so it's me waiting at the finish line and going for it."

"And you didn't tell Mom and Dad?"

"I told Mom before I came here to tell you. If I told them any sooner, Mom would've never been able to keep a secret. We called Dad together. I was scared shitless that they would freak out. Honestly, it's the first time since telling them I was staying in Meriden they seemed to finally grasp why. By the end of the conversation, Dad seemed ready to cut me some slack. Mom knows I've never been happier, and after being around Solia this past week, she loves her."

"She's going to be so surprised, don't you think? This is perfect."

"You can't tell anyone. Top secret—you got it? I didn't even tell Grandpa. I figured I'd tell them when Grandma gets home, which should be soon. I'm sure Mom updated you." Jackson's jaw tightens and he squints at me, waiting for my agreement.

"Totally, hundred percent, my lips are sealed. I love that you'll tell them together. I heard she's doing well with the new hip, but not so much in the memory department. The doctors say it should pass."

"Let's hope so."

"Anyway, I freaking love that the whole town will be there. Do you need me to do anything?"

"Maybe get a few pictures if you can?"

"Absolutely. I'll be done breaking down and cleaning everything from registration long before she crosses the finish line. I'm volunteering at a water station, so I'll be sure I snag the spot where the race ends. I got this."

Jackson stuffs his hands in his back pockets and paces on the lawn, the damp grass soaking the toes of his work boots. I walk over and give his shoulders a good shake. "This is going to be so great. What are your plans tonight?"

"Solia and Mia are hanging out and getting to bed early— well, at least Solia is. Who knows what Mia is up to."

"She is freaking hysterical."

"Sure is. I'll see you at the finish line." Jackson's features have softened, his hat returned front facing, and he heads to his truck.

It's crazy to think a little over four months ago, Jackson was hightailing it out of town for New York. Solia coming to Meriden stopped his plans in their tracks. She carried him out of the hole filled with guilt and grief and helped him heal. He's smiling again, hanging out with his crew, and now he's freaking proposing! I never would have guessed I'd be going through a divorce and my brother would be getting married all within the same time frame. Life is so unpredictable.

I'm not where I thought I'd be, but I'm charting a new course and my mind has never been clearer. Before the night on the dock, I assumed my wild days were long gone. I was mistaken, and I'm not turning back. More, please.

After a quick change, I inhale a pack of hummus and pretzels. As I lock the door, I can't help but hope that Judy will surprise me with some actual food. That woman always has a hot meal ready in case an army arrives.

Before I back out of the driveway, my phone beeps.

NICK

My meeting is running late ... plan to head to the lake in the morning. I'll be at the race. You free after?

How the hell does a simple text message flood me with desire? My mind travels back to his chest against mine, my heels digging into the dock, and his name filling the silence around the lake. Nick has twisted open a valve I thought had rusted over, and I'm not interested in turning it to the right.

The race is scheduled for an eight a.m. start, which has me cursing my alarm when it goes off at five. Once I'm showered and alert, the excitement of Jackson's proposal—and finally seeing Nick—flusters me, and I find myself anxiously searching my underwear drawer.

This is pathetic. I'm thirty-two and have the underwear of an eighty-year-old. I own one pair worth the hype buried in the corner—navy-blue panties with lace trim on the top. I don't think I've ever worn them.

On second thought, I'll wear shitty underwear now and save these for later. I can't believe I spent ten minutes debating something that will most likely go unseen.

The finish line is located in the middle school parking lot this year to allow for more room. Participation has increased since we had another NFL coach buy a piece of property on the lake. The uptick in business is great, but we do like to keep our lakeside paradise a secret.

In the early-morning hours, a thin layer of fog lifts over the mountains and rolls up the curtain to display Mother Nature's show of bright red to pale yellow, a scene worthy of a feature film. People travel here for the summer and a ski weekend here or there and miss the real autumn show Mother Nature saves for the locals. Sure, there are leaf peepers, but you need to stick around to soak it in.

Tables and tents are already set up, dozens of parked pickups, and people running around in hoodies gripping cups of Joe provided by Brown Bean. There's enough chill in the air to see steam rise above their heads. I hope the volunteers stationed at Sculptured Falls, the starting line for the half-marathon, grabbed a hat and coffee before heading out. A race this large takes a village to pull off, and Meriden always delivers.

Not only is it marathon weekend, it's homecoming. This town loves to cram everything into three days. No doubt the high school is gearing up and decorating for the football game. Everyone who's able comes home for the weekend. Each person is either running, going to watch the football game, helping out at the town bonfire tonight, or chaperoning the high school dance.

I grab my bag and swing the strap of my father's camera over my shoulder. He left it with me before he and Mom moved to New York, and while the buttons on this thing are beyond my comprehension, I can certainly snap a photo.

"Hey there, good-lookin'!"

Wearing a blue winter hat and matching flannel, Gerry walks over. His winter stubble is growing in with streaks of white, and his smile lights up any dismal morning. I'm not sure he meets the minimal sleep requirements—he's anywhere and everywhere in this town on the daily.

"Hey, Gerry!" I tug off my hood and embrace him.

"Is Mr. Windbag planning on showing up for our grand event?"

I can't help myself. The wisecracks this town has come up with since Nick's company attempted to install wind turbines on our land are quick-witted, I'll give them that. "Yes, Gerry, he'll be blowing into town any minute. Come on, let's grab a coffee before I keel over." I loop my arm through his and take a step toward the school gymnasium.

"You go ahead, honey. I've got a few more boxes to unload from my truck."

"I can help."

"No, I got it. There are a few old geezers waiting back there for me."

"All right. See you in a bit."

The gym door is propped open. Inside, two women from town are assembling a photo backdrop for the race. Little steel rods start rolling away and laughter erupts. "We got it! It may not look it, but rest assured, Shannon."

"I never doubted you, Mary." I smile and squeeze by another woman in a volunteer T-shirt. Shit, I need to put mine on.

Rectangular banquet tables have been set up to form stations for sign-in, T-shirts, and swag bags. I spot the Brown Bean trademark in the corner. A local high school student I vaguely recognize from walking the elementary school halls years ago is manning the station, looking like she's already wired on too much caffeine. It's so hard to recognize them when they're all grown up. "Morning!"

"Hey, Miss Shannon. I'll get your regular. Where's the hottie?"

There are zero secrets around here. I might as well post my

love life on the Newfound Lake announcement board and update it regularly. They'd love to hear about us getting down and dirty dockside.

"Now, that would be none of your business, don't ya think? Thanks for the coffee." I give her a smirk and shake my head.

"You bet," she responds, sitting back down to resume her crossword puzzle.

After greeting folks at each table, I'm out the door, ready to set up my water station and see where I'm needed.

"Judy! Good morning!"

"Hey, Shannon, everything is looking good. I asked Gerry to take a ride to Sculptured Falls to make sure everything is a go there. Nate is off duty today and offered to fire the starting pistol, and the library ladies are setting up the tables there. He's also going to phone the bus company and confirm … never mind, the buses are here."

The drivers of our fleet of five yellow school buses honk their way into the parking lot, announcing their arrival and startling everyone who hasn't finished their first cup of coffee. The half-marathon runners will be bused to the starting line to end up back here, whereas the full marathon runners start and end here. The complete loop around the lake is 26.2 miles. Every step is as beautiful as the next, not that I could run it— maybe bike, but certainly not run.

"Check! The buses have arrived."

"I see someone else has arrived."

I spin to see Nick walking toward me, his brown hair loose on top, more unkempt than I'm used to. The rest of the scene fades away, and I am locked in. Despite the obvious tiredness surrounding his eyes, a smirk appears on his lips when he sees me. Gone is the three-piece suit, and instead he's got on tapered gray sweatpants and a fitted T-shirt with a black unzipped hoodie slung over his shoulder.

Holy hell. Laid-back Nick is even more appealing. I didn't think that was possible.

Nick in a suit is dangerous. Nick in formfitting joggers gets the juices flowing. The way his white T-shirt hugs his biceps and displays the tattoos running down his arms has me wishing I had chosen the other panties because I am ready for what he's got displayed under those sweatpants. He held out on me the other night. Now I'm dying to get hold of the package I snuck a peek at. Let's just say I'd gladly pay expedited shipping for the delivery of his goods.

I don't realize I'm frozen until Nick is dipping down and wrapping his arms around my back.

"Hey, sexy." The words whispered into my ear are enough to send a heat wave through my body. Before I can catch my breath and regain my composure, he lowers his hand below the waistband of my pants and pulls me into his hip. "This is Evan."

A man as tall as Nick stands in front of me. He offers a sweet smile and a handshake. "Hey, you must be Shannon. My boy Nick has mentioned you once or twice."

I can't help but smile at Nick, who tosses his fist into Evan's shoulder. "Keep it cool, man."

"Oh, right, right." Evan tilts his head and looks down at me. "Sorry to crash the party, but Nick keeps talking about the lake, this town, and his new crib. I told him enough was enough, I'm going up this time."

I know I'm going to like Evan. He exudes a welcoming energy and has kind eyes. He reminds me of that friendly, cute, dorky kid from high school but with muscles. Deep brown curls cut short sit on top of his head with the sides trimmed close. His brown eyes are set back, and he has the whitest teeth I've ever seen. Of course, he's also sporting the uniform for gray sweatpants season. I'm not complaining in the least.

"Hi, Evan. Everyone is welcome, but I'm warning you, you may be put to work."

"Not a problem." Evan crosses his arms over his chest. It's clear this man hits the gym.

"What's with the camera?" Nick asks, fingering the strap on my shoulder.

"Does she know how ..." Evan attempts to finish his thought, but Nick steps right in over his words.

"No."

I look from Nick to Evan and back, unsure of what just transpired.

"This is my dad's camera. I'm planning on snapping some photos of the finish line today."

"Nice." Nick's arm leaves my back as he does a three-hundred-and-sixty-degree survey of the area. "You're not running today, correct?"

"I am not running, but I'm in charge of a water station and clicking photos. Are you boys sticking around or heading to the house?"

"I wanted to stop by and see you before going to the house. We'll go drop off our stuff and then either I'll be back or we both will. You can tell me where you need me."

Where I need him? If I tell him where I need him, we'll be in the back seat of my car, participating in some other kind of marathon, one that I know I'll be coming in first.

Nick clears his throat, and I snap back to reality. "Yeah, sure. That sounds great." I'm not sure if my cheeks look as red as the flames that have ignited inside me.

A small pinch to my ass cheek takes me by surprise. "Oh!" I giggle like a freaking teenager. Nick and Evan walk away, and I'm admiring the view when Cindy, everyone's favorite bartender, and Solia, my soon-to-be sister-in-law, crawl into the parking lot behind a gaggle of kids on low-rider bikes sporting lawn equipment strapped across their chests, no doubt former students of mine. Nick looks over his shoulder and winks, instantly making me want to follow him wherever he's going. *I need to get a fucking grip.*

Cindy, Solia, and Mia shout over to me, and I force my eyes off Nick. "Hey, ladies! You ready to run, Solia? Cindy, are you running too?"

"My feet are staying put on the finish line today. I do enough running around the bar, I don't need to pound the pavement around the lake. Is Harold here with Nick?"

"Are you hoping to hang on to Harold? And what, Shannon? You don't ask me if I'm running?" Mia's shoulders bobble with her laughter.

"I haven't seen Harold, but I assume he's here staying at the B&B like usual. Are you hoping to see him or avoid him?"

Cindy weaves the loose pieces of hair back into her ponytail and shifts her balance to her left hip. "I'm not sure. He's stayed in touch, super sweet, a little older than I'm used to, but definitely worth the time." She winks, and we are in a fit of giggles.

Taking the heat off Cindy, I turn to Mia. "Mia, you're wearing sandals." I point at her red-painted toenails sticking out of her summer footwear.

"True, true, you got me there. Who's the hottie with wind boy?"

"Honestly, his name is Nick. The guy made a shitty first impression, but it seems like he's redeeming himself," Solia says.

"Oh, for sure." The words slip out before I can stop them.

"Spill it! I haven't seen you since before you went on that Boston date," Mia adds.

My chest constricts and tingles spread to my fingertips as I replay the dock adventure in my mind.

"Leave her alone, Mia. I'm sure we'll get the scoop at some point. Right, Shan? Who was the other guy?"

"The other guy was …"

"A sweet piece of ass, that's what he was," Mia interrupts, hands on hips as she nods her agreement with her own statement. "He looks like a man who needs to get a little roughed up. Sexy as hell, but innocent. A good combination."

"For the love of god, Mia. What about Tyler?"

"Listen, Tyler is my lake lover who I'm still deciding on. It's never a bad idea to tuck another bang in your back pocket for safekeeping."

"Jesus, just stop." Solia shakes her head.

"Well?" Mia looks back and forth between Solia and me.

"I honestly don't know much, other than he's a friend and coworker of Nick's and is up for the weekend. He may be back. At least I know Nick will be."

"Okay, cool, cool," Mia says, hands out with fingers spread wide. "So, what can I do to be helpful around here while these people run their brains out?"

Solia turns to Mia. "I'm going to grab my number and get on a bus. I'll meet you back here when I'm done."

"Sounds good. What time?"

"What time? Why? Are you leaving?"

"No, I want to be ready to watch you run through the parking lot. Seriously, how long?"

Mia and Solia's friendship is hysterical, reminiscent of the Golden Girls or a scene from *Sex and the City*, and Mia is Samantha all day long.

Solia laughs and looks at me. "I'll be back around ten-ish."

"Have fun running forever to get back here. Why would someone put themselves through such torture?"

I don't bother answering because I know Mia isn't looking for an actual answer.

By this point, runners flood the parking lot. I need to get set up. "Why don't you go inside? I'm sure they need help passing stuff out or maybe you can assist runners taking photos by the sign. Help out wherever you can."

"Got it, I'm on it. Let me know if you see my boy toy and have him see me before he heads out."

Tyler, Jay, and Ryan are running in the half. "You bet."

The next hour is spent setting up a few more tents, chairs, tables, and trash bins, filling water containers, and prepping cups to fill. The fog has lifted, allowing the sun to shine over the mountain ridges and cast warm rays upon the marathoners. They're busy pinning on their numbered bibs and are gathering at the starting line.

The buses are just completing their trips back and forth between Sculptured Falls. The church ladies, finished with helping the runners onto the buses, are heading over to take charge of the snack table.

If Tyler, Jay, and Ryan showed up, I missed them. But I spot Evan next to Mia, assisting with photo ops by the sign. Men are drawn to her like moths to a flame. Even with the distance between us, their body language oozes flirtation. And if Evan is here, Nick must be too.

As if on cue, Nick materializes next to me. "Looks like everything is under control." He takes the camera off the table and investigates the buttons. "Canon EOS. This is one of their first DSLRs." He sets it down and looks around. "So, this is quite the production. Everyone is running around like headless chickens."

He gestures as if displaying a scene of chaos. Family members line both sides of the street, holding signs and balancing coffee cups. The runners have assembled in their assigned heats for the full marathon. Steven, our resident winner over the past several years, is up front with his signature bare feet, desperate to keep his title. I'll never understand how someone would be willing to run over twenty-six miles barefoot.

The energy in the air shifts, and a silence falls over the crowd. The starter pistol fires, and the runners take off in a fury, met by the cheers and applause of the crowd. Thirteen miles away, the same scene plays out for the start of the half-marathon.

And Solia has no idea she's running directly into a proposal.

"This chaos is the official marathon of New Hampshire, here in the little town of Meriden. It's a big deal in these parts."

Nick runs his fingers through his hair, hiking his T-shirt just enough to reveal the trail to the treasure. Out of the corner of my eye, I spot Mia and Evan approaching the table. Evan walks with his arms by his side, full attention on Mia as she skips alongside him while appearing to maintain a full-blown conversation.

Quiet enough for only me to hear, Nick nuzzles into my neck and whispers, "I have a feeling Evan doesn't know what he's in for."

"Hey, you two." Mia slams both her hands on the table. She's looking way too cute for a marathon event at eight a.m., sporting a tight gray V-neck tunic and black leggings. She manages to look like a fitness model without any intention of breaking a sweat.

"We're going to have to put you younglings to work over here." Gerry appears from behind the crowd, nursing his cup of java. "Everything went as planned at the other start line. The PTO needs a little help with pinning the bibs on the kids for the Fun Run. Any takers?"

Mia rolls her eyes and steps behind Evan in an attempt to hide.

"Mia, you've been around these parts long enough, there's no hiding at this point. You're an honorary resident. Let's go, missy, and your tall friend too. Oh, and Shannon, I stopped by to see Earl this morning and brought him a cup of coffee. He seemed in good spirits. He's got the food you left him. I'll drop by after the race, so you and Jackson don't have to worry about anything today." Gerry signals in the air for Mia and Evan to follow him without waiting for a response.

*Does Gerry know about the proposal? It wouldn't surprise me if he did.*

Without saying a word, Evan allows Mia to drag him by the arm and follow Gerry toward the crowd of bouncing children. Evan doesn't utter a word in response.

"What's his story?" I ask.

"Evan? He's a good guy. Known him since elementary school. He practically grew up at my house, was there when we lost my dad, and has been working for the family business as long as I have. He's brilliant. Runs our tech department. Thank god he knows what he's doing because I don't have a freaking clue how things work in that respect. He's quiet, the reserved type."

"Well, he's met his match. If he's not careful, Mia will extract any shyness from his pores."

"I'd like to see her try." Nick laughs and turns his chair toward the crowd of parents fussing with their children's laces and giving last-minute high fives.

I always thought I'd have a little runner of my own by now. My hopes were high during the early years. After things started to decline, I was thankful. The last thing our marriage needed was a child.

The Fun Run goes off without a hitch, and the next hour is spent handing out water, placing medals around the neck of each runner, and unfastening safety pins from the little ones' shirts. I notice Nick snagged my camera and is crouched taking photos of the kids crossing the finish line.

I'm a little in awe of his willingness to help out at such an event. This city boy is making quite an effort. I'm hesitant to let myself fall for this man, but he isn't making it easy.

I decide not to point out that Dennis from *The Laker* is here volunteering his time to take event photos. Nick seems to be enjoying himself, but I need to make sure I get the camera back in time for Solia. The first runners will be crossing the finish line soon.

The Fun Run committee swoops in and shuffles the kids and parents off to the playground area for candy apples my grandfather insisted on having ready. This is the first time my grandparents haven't participated in race day. They're usually a staple behind their Christianson's Orchard table where they hand out treats to the local kids. Today, though, Lucas and Brynn stand in for them. I try to ignore the pang of sadness caused by their absence.

A whistle blows and the Run Your Buns committee assembles to set up the finish line. I take out the box of medals that somehow became my responsibility and realize I can't hand these out and take pictures for Jackson. "Hey, Nick."

He turns after finishing his conversation with Greg from the farm, who nods a hello in my direction. "What's up?" How he manages to say the most basic things in such a sexy way is beyond me.

"Would you mind handing out the medals as runners cross the line? I'll take care of the water, and I need to snap a few pictures."

"How are you going to take pictures and hand out water?"

"I only need to take a few."

Nick pulls the camera off his shoulder and slips it over mine. "I believe every favor needs one delivered in return." He slides both hands onto my hips, melting me from the inside out. PDA is not something I'm used to. There might as well be a spotlight shining on me with the heat I'm exuding.

"Hmmm" is all I can manage. Nick laughs, slicks his hair

back, and flashes a prize-winning smile. He manages to grab the box of medals from the table without taking his eyes off me.

I pull my phone out of my back pocket and check the time. Any minute, the first runner is due down Main Street. Jackson is walking toward me from the direction of the hardware store. You'd think he could ditch the work boots for the day, but nope —and he's got on his backward hat, his flannel button-down open, and well-worn jeans, and I'm fairly certain Solia wouldn't have it any other way. He's grinning from ear to ear. I can't believe my little brother is proposing today.

Several half-marathon runners cross the finish line in record time. Then the crowd begins to erupt, and to no surprise to anyone, Steven's poor bare feet slam the pavement as he runs around the corner and into view. He's done it again. How? The crowd goes wild and chants, "Steven! Steven!"

I look back to Jackson, who has positioned himself on the left side a few yards in front of the finish line, directly opposite the water station I should be sitting at. I flash him a thumbs-up and he shakes his head. I know nervousness when I see it. I look across and see Nick standing in front of the water table, medals ready, Mia and Evan now alongside him. Mia is chatting away, and Evan seems to be absorbing her every word.

Steven breaks through the finish line, and I snap a few test shots to avoid failing my mission. I'm not sure who's more nervous, me or Jackson. Several other runners have rounded the corner and approach. The streets are packed on both sides. I recognize and can name almost every face in the crowd. The few I don't know are here visiting family, I'm sure. No matter who crosses, the crowd goes crazy, kids jump up and down, adults wave their homemade signs, and each runner crosses with a smile plastered to their face.

I spot Tyler, Jay, and Ryan rounding the bend. They must have made a pact to stick together. They've been running since the school cross-country team. I look over at Mia, and she has her back to the finish line and her eyes on Evan. This should be interesting.

I yank out my phone and voice-text Tyler's name to her, hoping to intervene on what could be a shitty moment. Jackson high-fives them, and I watch as they approach the water station, each fist-bumping Nick. That's a step in the right direction. I notice Tyler eyeing Evan up and down and then he scoops Mia into the air. Evan looks like a lost puppy searching for his water bowl. Mia wraps her legs around Tyler's waist and recklessly jams her tongue down his throat.

I hear my name and turn to see Jackson's face tense, his focus straight ahead. Oh shit, here she comes!

Camera ready, I step forward to get the shot, careful not to be rude and block other runners from their moment to shine. Solia is running alone and takes each stride as easily as the next. From the looks of her, you'd think she started the race ten minutes ago. All her training has paid off.

She's beaming and looks at both sides of the street as several residents shout her name, clap, and shout. It's quite an accomplishment. She's wearing a bright yellow tank and black running shorts, ponytail bouncing. She's beautiful inside and out, and it's easy to love her. Her hands go into the air as she sails across the finish line.

I step forward as Jackson approaches from the side. He says something and gives her a hug. They release and she's wiping the sweat from her brow and eyes as Jackson gets down on one knee. My eyes blur behind the lens as I try to steady the camera and snap away.

The crowd has caught on, and all eyes pivot to Jackson and Solia. I step closer. Jackson takes Solia's shaking hands and reaches into his pocket. The crowd reacts and signals everyone to hush.

Words are exchanged and Solia's chin crashes to her chest.

Jackson looks up into her eyes. Solia drops to the ground and embraces him in a hug that can be felt for miles. I'm so screwed—I snap as many pictures as I can, but I can't see a thing through my happy tears.

"What the fuck just happened?" Mia is in my ear and startles the shit out of me.

"Your best friend is getting married." I return the camera strap to my shoulder and wipe my eyes.

"Holy shit! Did you know this was going to happen?" Mia doesn't wait for my answer. She's halfway to Solia.

Everyone hugs the newly engaged couple as runners continue to cross the finish line and the crowd resumes their hooting and hollering.

Jackson and Solia are meant for each other—no one can deny that.

My brother waves me over to them. Tears and sweat stream down Solia's face, bright with elation. A sister-in-law. I love the sound of that.

"Welcome to the family, Solia! And congrats on an amazing race."

Solia welcomes my embrace and rests her head on my shoulder. "I've always wanted a sister. Your brother is the best thing that has ever happened to me, and to have you as family is more than I could've ever dreamed of," she says, each word barely audible between her tears.

"Right back at you. Love you."

Jackson sneaks between us, hugging us both.

"I'm proud of you, little brother. You're marrying up, for sure."

"That I know, Shan."

"Oh my god, people! We need to celebrate. I hear there is a free after-race beer at Caitlyn's. What do you say we grab that and have a party back at the cabin tonight? Who's game?" Mia looks from Solia to Jackson. "If that's okay with you guys, I mean—I'll take care of everything."

Solia shrugs and says, "Why the heck not?"

I look around and spot Nick passing out medals to runners, oblivious to the commotion ensuing on this side of the finish line. This is going to be interesting—Nick, Evan, Tyler, Mia, the newly engaged, and half the town at Solia's place.

Sure, why not?

# 12



Today was more than I bargained for. I don't recall a time I've spent that many hours outside among so many people sweating and cheering. I met everyone in town, from the resident plumber to the woman with the terrifying chin hair who runs the bridge club at the church. Everyone in Meriden knows one another; therefore, they all knew me by name and formed an opinion before I ever had a chance to make a positive impression.

If I were a betting man, I'd say my chances of turning their opinion around is slim. I'll try like hell, though, for Shannon. There's something about her I can't walk away from.

I think I fist-bumped over a thousand runners and handed out medals that inspired reactions comparable to Olympic wins. I was happy to do my part. It was a welcome change of pace, and I think Shannon was impressed. Somehow Evan got sucked into Mia, and that is a train wreck waiting to happen. I love the guy, but he can't find his way out of a paper bag. Smart as fuck with no common sense. She's clearly into Tyler.

And to top it off, I witnessed Jackson's proposal, which, if I'm being honest, was pretty damn sweet. Not the most romantic of places, but Solia dug it. I didn't get a chance to talk to Shannon much after. It was a family moment, and I maintained my position outside the circle. From what I gather, Mia is throwing a party at Solia's cabin tonight and made sure to let Evan and me know we should stop by.

I'm not exactly sure what a house party in the woods looks like in our thirties. My weekends are five-star restaurants and bottles of Moët. I'm sure this evening will be quite different.

"Dude, this place is insane." Evan is on the second-floor deck, his arms extended toward the lake in front of us. More than half of the autumn foliage has fallen, giving an expansive view of the water. He's right—the surrounding nature is insane. Insanely quiet. I'm still not accustomed to the lack of sirens and honking. But it's growing on me.

"Right? It's quite the score, enough room for everyone to stay, and it'll kick ass in the summer."

"What does Shannon think of it?"

"I think I convinced her it's pretty awesome a few weeks ago." I wink and head inside for something to drink.

"Spreading your charm comes naturally to you, my friend." Evan follows me in and grabs a hard cider from the fridge. We then move back out to the deck, and Evan drops into the end chair facing the water.

"There's something different about her. She's worth it, but I'm hoping she feels the same. However, I do love it here, and if I can keep her warm at night, I'm happy to offer up my services."

"Ever the gentleman. If you ask me, it sounds like you've got it bad for her. Speaking of bad"—Evan walks over and uncovers the shiny new grill in the corner of the deck—"my hunger pangs are killing me. You want me to grill those burgers we grabbed at the market before we head out? What time were you thinking?"

"Yeah, man. I'll shower, you grill, and we'll leave here

about seven? She lives right down the street. We could walk, but the wildlife is enough to scare me shitless. Did you hear the lady at the register talking to the bagger about bear-proof dumpster locks?"

"They've got bears, we've got rats. Which do you prefer?"

I've never thought of that before. "I'll take my chances with the bears. At least they hibernate."

Showers, dinner on the deck, and a couple beers later, we head over to Solia's. Between my lake house and her cabin, we don't pass one car, one streetlight, or one business. The only signs of life are house lanterns glowing along the mountainside, spotted through the trees now that the leaves have fallen. You could play connect the dots from one to the other and form an intricate constellation. The only other lights casting a glow are the stars themselves.

I hear the music before the cabin is visible. Trucks line the dirt driveway—clearly no one is worried about getting blocked in. The bonfire on the hill blazes and people are scattered along the front porch, side porch, screened-in porch, and by the fire. It's a sea of backward baseball hats and red Solo Cups. I can't tell who's who.

"Well, here goes nothing." I park as far away from the house as I can in case this ends up being a fucking disaster.

"At least people know you. I'm a stranger."

"Trust me, dude. You have the advantage. Blend in, and don't ask for a glass."

"Right."

Before we're halfway up the stairs, I spot Shannon on the top step. Her outfit stops me dead in my tracks. She's wearing booties, too-short-for-autumn denim shorts, and a flannel button-down tied around her waist. Her hair is pulled into a ponytail and she's sporting a Live Free or Die New Hampshire baseball cap. She puts a high-heeled, matte-makeup city girl to shame. The restraint I'm going to need to get through this night might be more than I'm capable of.

"Are you going to keep moving or stand here like an asshole?" Evan nudges my back and steps in front of me, shaking Shannon's hand like we are meeting for some kind of business dinner. Idiot.

"'Bout time the city boys showed. Come on in and meet everyone."

I'm not sure what it is about this small town and twinkly lights. Maybe they keep the critters away. Either that or everyone is too lazy to put up Christmas lights each year. Solia's got strands woven around the banister of the wraparound porch. We navigate through the row of green wooden rocking chairs and into the screened-in patio located at the back of the house. Thank god for screens—otherwise I'd get feasted upon by woodsy-ass mosquitoes. They grow them huge up here.

"This is the gang."

Several people turn and look our way without much intention of stopping what they're doing. I spot Jackson and a few of the guys I met at the Binn the other night. Solia's friend, Mia, has her arm around Tyler. "Looks like your chick is taken."

Apparently, my voice travels a little too far because Shannon turns around giggling. "Trust me, no one takes Mia. Mia takes whoever she wants." She then turns and weaves us through the group, who nod and acknowledge our presence. Shannon pushes the door open, and we are on the end of the deck where Gerry has hot dogs sizzling on the grill, surrounded by coolers overflowing with beer, cider, and seltzers.

"What's it going to be?"

"I'll take a beer." I enjoy watching Shannon bend to get the cans out of the ice because her shorts ride high enough to give me a peek at what I'm hoping for later.

I catch Evan snagging a look and knock him in the chest. He grabs his ribs in exaggeration and coughs. "Make that two, please."

Shannon reaches back into the cooler and Evan winks as if doing me a favor.

"Who do we have here? New boys in town?"

A young woman appears beside us like an unwrapped firecracker. Shannon hands us our drinks and grabs her for a hug. "Who are these boys, Shan?"

"Brooke, this is Nick and his friend Evan from Boston."

The woman exudes nervous energy, proven when she jumps into me for a hug. "This is Nick? Hi, Nick. Oh my goodness, I've heard all about you. I mean, we don't talk about you regularly, but Shannon has, like, mentioned you. Like, once, maybe. This is so exciting you're here! I'm happy you came to party with us. I mean, how crazy is this weekend? A marathon, homecoming, bonfires, a dance, and now this and an engagement to boot!"

Her five-foot frame peels off my chest, but I'm pretty sure residual energy sizzles on my skin. *Holy shit.*

"Come on, Evan, I'll introduce you to the crew. They love new people." Brooke loops her arm in his, swings her high ponytail to the back, and skips away, dragging Evan down the deck stairs.

"That poor boy's ears are going to ache after Brooke's done with him." Shannon slides her hair behind her shoulder and cracks open a seltzer. "Hungry? Mia decided to go all redneck on us for this one. Wait until you see what she has. She dragged Tyler and the rest of his buddies around the market, getting everything from Cheez Whiz to Twinkies."

I hold open the screen door to the log cabin and follow Shannon inside. The first two people I recognize are Jackson and Solia, huddled in the corner of the kitchen. Jackson's back is to us, but no doubt it's them. They're oblivious to everyone around. Jackson is talking in her ear while she giggles uncontrollably.

I don't think I've ever stepped foot in a log cabin before. It's interesting that the logs are visible from the inside as well as outside. It's dimly lit, but it fits the mood. Maybe a few too many pieces of moose and deer décor for my taste, but it's otherwise cozy.

Shannon squeezes into the crowd around the kitchen table filled with pub cheese and crackers, chips, and what look like baby hot dogs rolled and baked in dough. I'm not sure what the hell it is, but I'm thankful I ate before coming. I down the rest of my beer as Shannon makes small talk with others. Meeting new people comes easily to me when we're dining on filet, our laps draped with linen napkins. This is a different story.

"Nick, you remember Cindy?" I look left and recognize the woman from behind the bar that night and Harold's bed the next morning. She must be having the same thought because her ears turn bright red.

"Yeah, of course. How are you?"

She runs a palm over her slicked-back hair and down her ponytail and smiles. "I'm good, yeah. Is Harold here with you?"

Shannon giggles and grabs my arm. "I'm so sorry, I wasn't thinking. Absolutely, you should've invited him. Give him a call. He's probably bored to tears sitting at the bed-and-breakfast alone."

"Are you kidding me? Harold loves his peace and quiet. I won't be surprised if he ditches me for a condo by the lake. I'll give him a call."

"Oh, Shan. It's okay. I mean, unless he doesn't want to miss all this fun. Whatever you think, Nick."

It doesn't take a rocket scientist to realize Cindy is hoping to see him again. And I'm not going to cock-block the guy. Reaching for my phone in my rear pocket, I look at the service bars and see zero.

"Come on, I'll show you where you need to stand to get reception. We'll be right back."

I follow her through to the front porch, weaving in and out of a sea of flannel.

"Right here." Shannon points to the spot between two rocking chairs. "Everywhere else, you are shit out of luck, but for some reason, this spot works every time."

I'm not even going to question this.

The music from the side porch has been turned up so loud, I figure a text will do. I don't have the widest range of musical taste, but Sam Hunt and Zach Brown are not on my playlists. Instantly, Harold texts back and asks for the address. Damn, at least someone is getting lucky tonight.

I turn to face the inside of the cabin and see Cindy watching us through the window. I throw her a thumbs-up, and she smiles and waves.

Shannon is talking to Madison beside me, so I excuse myself to grab two more beers. I'm going to have to pound a few of these to get through the night.

A slap on the back catches me off guard while fishing at the bottom of the cooler. "What's up, Boston?"

I'd know Jackson's voice anywhere. "What's going on, man? Congratulations are in order." I grasp both cans in my left hand and dry my right on my leg to shake his hand.

"Thanks, man. Is he another company guy?" Jackson points to Evan, who seems to be getting schooled on how to roast a marshmallow over the bonfire.

"Sure is, but much less of an asshole compared to me. He codes the computers. Techy shit like that. He doesn't deal with clients or piss anyone off."

"They save that for you? Got it."

"Listen, man, let's move on. If Shannon didn't ask me, I wouldn't be here."

"Our land is one thing, but my sister is another. Come for my land, I'll lay you out. Hurt my sister, you won't recover. Got it?"

"Cheers." I nod, and fortunately, Jackson clinks his beer against mine. It's a start.

Out of the corner of my eye, I see Shannon smiling at the scene playing out between her brother and me.

"Who do we have here?" A man well over six feet tall approaches us wearing the evening's standard outfit.

"Joe, this is Nick. You remember him from the town meeting this summer. He was the asshole in the suit. Joe is the owner of Gray Lodge Marina. One of the many businesses that would've sunk had you pulled off your deal."

"Damn, I knew you looked familiar. Lucky for us, your mission sank instead of my fleet. So, what the fuck are you doing here?"

Shit, this is starting to get old. Maybe I should hold a public forum, let everyone lash out at me, and then move the fuck on. Or better yet, maybe I should say I ate Jackson's sister on my dock for dessert, and I'm currently obsessed with what she's serving.

Certain both thoughts are better left unsaid, I shake my head and extend my hand. "I'm here with Shannon. She invited me. Rest assured, my company has no interest in any land around Newfound Lake, so from here on, I'm just a part-time resident."

"Well, look at you, slippery little sucker. But hey, every asshole deserves a second chance, right?"

I decide to leave his comment unanswered and throw back half the can and reach in for another. Thankfully, Shannon, Madison, and a pint-size blond show up.

Shannon wraps her arm around my lower back, a pleasant reminder that all the razzing these guys are dishing out is worth it. Liquid courage may have something to do with it when I scoop my hands under her ass and lift her around my waist and pull her in for a deep kiss. Madison and Pint-Size holler in response. Shannon's ass cheeks fit perfectly in my palms, almost too good. I put her back on the deck before my fingers crawl inside her shorts. Even through the darkness, I see desire in her eyes.

Jackson has already walked away, Joe's eyes bulge out of his head, Madison giggles, and her sidekick watches like she's studying for a test.

Shannon buries her face in my sleeve and squeezes my arm with both of her hands. I'll take that as a sign of approval.

"Damn. I want some hottie to lift me up like that. Fuck." Pint-Size reaches into the cooler and heads off with two cans dripping down the front of her legs.

I watch her walk off.

"That's Brynn," Shannon explains. "She works for our family at the orchard. She's a sophomore at Plymouth State."

"Got it. I thought she looked young."

"She is. I think she's twenty. Come on, let's play *Stump*."

"Play what?" I follow Shannon past the outdoor shower and down to the bonfire where a crowd has gathered. I can't make out what's going on. It's a sea of hoisted red cups and cheering.

"Okay, here's the deal. It's called *Hammerschlagen*, otherwise known as *Stump* in these parts. They'll probably start a new round in a sec. Each person gets a nail and a hammer. You have to be the first to drive your nail into the stump or you drink. There are probably exact rules, but this is how we play."

"*Stump?*"

"Yeah, look." She pulls me through a small opening in the crowd, and lo and behold, a fucking tree stump, about two feet high, sits in the center. Several nails have already been pounded into it. Four clearly drunk guys stand with hammers, each taking a turn swinging in hopes of banging the nail in. I'm thinking mixing alcohol and heavy steel tools is a disaster waiting to happen, but I'm not about to say anything. The guy up next, I recognize from the bar. He swings and slams the nail perfectly into the wood.

"Fuck, yeah." He howls like a wild animal. I'm pretty sure any bears that were thinking about stopping by have run for cover. "Drink, motherfuckers."

The other three guys throw back their beers. Shannon looks up at me and smiles. "You think you're up for the challenge, city boy?"

Why is it every time she calls me that I am determined to be as manly as a goddamn lumberjack? She wants me to bang a nail into a stump, I'll swing away.

I pull off my flannel and toss it into her arms.

"Looks like we have a new contender, boys." One of the guys on the outskirts holding a water bottle turns to the side to clear a path to the stump. Shannon's hand drops to my lower back and she inches me forward.

"Ryan," she says an octave above the high fives and commotion and pulls him in for a hug.

"All right, who's in?" some meathead lumberjack yells out, looking in my direction. It's a mindfuck having to prove my masculinity. Where I come from, I blaze the trail. Here, I'm crawling out of the breakdown lane.

"I'm in," I say, edging my voice deeper and rubbing my palms on my thighs.

"You heard him, fellas. City boy wants in. What's up, man?"

I extend my hand with a hope the welcome is sincere. "Hey." No dead-fish handshake, Tyler's grip is assertive.

He tilts a mason jar filled with god knows what into tiny red

Solo Cups. "This is Hunter, Cindy's son. I assume you met her at the bar. And Lucas is the baker at the Christianson's Country Store."

Freaking five degrees of separation is halved in these parts. "Nick." I nod at each of the guys. "What are we drinking?"

Hunter, who doesn't look more than twenty-five on an unshaven day, glances at the jar, to me, and back again. "Moonshine. Shit will fuck you up. Don't lose, bro."

Tyler and Hunter grin at each other. Lucas, on the other hand, elbows me. "It's not that complicated. Hit the nail into the stump. Don't be last unless you can handle your booze."

"Got it." I square my shoulders, stride over to the group, and grab a hammer and nail, despite the fact that the last time I picked up a hammer was in elementary school when a Boy Scout leader hosted an assembly and passed out build-your-own wooden boat kits for each kid. I was so excited, and I recall my mother forcing my father to take ten minutes to build it with me. Pretty damn pathetic.

Tyler goes first. He taps the nail and then slams it in, first try. Mia screams out from behind him. The shit that gets these chicks to tick.

Hunter lifts a hammer out of his back pocket. *Seriously, dude.* He lifts his arm shoulder height and hits the nail on the head, knocking it sideways, stopping it from going all the way in. *Thank god.*

"You're up next, city boy." Shannon slaps my ass. I wonder if she'll deliver a reward if I win. Hammer up, hammer down, on the stump, miss the nail.

"Ooh, damn! Drink up!"

Three, two, one, down goes the moonshine. I've had plenty of booze in my life, but what the hell is this? Trapping the cough inside is not happening.

"You'll get used to it." Tyler knocks his fist into my shoulder hard enough to set me back a step.

At some point between the first nail and the fifth, Shannon must've walked off. I have a full cup of moonshine in my hand that's going down like water at this point. And just like they promised, this shit will fuck a guy up.

"Let's do one more." I rest my hand on Tyler's shoulder and lean to grab another nail out of the bucket and squint to find a spot to place it.

"No way, Boston. You're done. I'm not carrying your ass out of here. Go get something to eat."

As much as it pisses me off, I know he's right. I pass the hammer to Hunter. "Thanks, man." I hear them laugh as I walk away and spot Shannon sitting fireside just in time to see Water Boy tuck a blanket around her lap. Next to Shannon, Brynn again eyes me up and down like I'm an Edible Arrangement. Seeing Ryan dote on Shannon makes me want to knock out his sober teeth.

*Fuck. Sober.*

Water Boy is playing his cards well and might seal the deal instead of my drunk ass.

I straighten my shoulders and pop a leftover mint from the Capital Grill to mask the alcohol.

I survey the circle of chairs. Harold is across next to Cindy, then a few others I don't recognize, and Evan's got Brooke on his lap. That makes me second-guess my eyesight. Evan does have a woman sitting on his lap. Maybe he's drinking the moonshine too. My choices are the empty seat next to Harold or squeezing next to Brynn on the bench, closest to Shannon.

"You mind sliding over so I can talk to Shannon?"

Brynn looks up with her nose crinkled and her head tilted back. "Are you talking to me?"

I look around as if to say, *Who else would I be talking to?*

"The name is Brynn, and you are Nick. That is how people introduce themselves around here."

"Yeah, sure, sorry about that. Hi, Brynn, can you slide over so I can talk to Shannon?"

"Hey, Shannon. You want to sit next to this guy?"

I turn around, and Shannon and Ryan are both laughing. Shannon clinks her cup to his water bottle and nods at Brynn.

"I'll talk to you later, Shan." Ryan places his hand on the top of her head and playfully musses her hair. She giggles, looks back at him walking away, and straightens the strands he tousled. A ping of jealousy stabs me.

"How did *Stump* work out for you?" Shannon grabs the steel armrest and slides her chair closer so she's within touching distance. She then hands me the water bottle laying on her chair.

I look up at the black sky and sigh. "I'm glad you walked away."

"Practice makes perfect. Looks like you could use a little bit of that." She points to the water bottle and stands, revealing the full length of her legs, mere inches from my hand. What I wouldn't give to spread them open again. "I'll be back."

"Shit." My shoulders slump forward, and I take a long swig of the much-needed water.

"Her loss." The heat of Brynn's leg crossed over my kneecap takes me by surprise. "You are looking three sheets to the wind. It doesn't bother me one bit."

Brynn's eyes are watery, her words slurred. She's in worse shape than I am. My drunk ass is sober enough to see that as clear as the fucking sky. She's staring into my eyes like a crazed sex kitten ready to pounce. I look across the fire and make eye contact with Harold, who seems to be getting cozy with Cindy. My eyes travel to the predictable water bottle in his hand and I know I can always count on him for a safe ride home.

I toss the rest of the water back and before I can even swallow, Brynn's knees are wedged on the side of my thighs and her ass is lowering to my lap. My head snaps forward and

I'm inches from her lips, getting more intoxicated by the millisecond from the smell of tequila rolling off her mouth.

"Whoa, honey. Slow down." I put my hands on her hips and lift her forward, and I push myself back. She wiggles in my hands and throws her head up to the sky and laughs, revealing Shannon's silhouette outlined by the blaze.

"You don't wait two minutes." It doesn't take much to lift her from my lap and place her down beside me. Brynn's roar of drunken laughter only gets louder. She folds forward, regains her balance somehow without setting her hair on fire, and stumbles to the cooler.

I grab the knot tying Shannon's flannel together and pull her to me. "The only woman I want on my lap is you. She's trashed and will need a ride home."

"I'm not sure if that's you talking or the moonshine, Nick." Without a trace of makeup, she glows from the fire, her bare lips lifted into a seductive smile, and her eyes tell me she isn't through with me yet.

If I knew she'd roll with it, I'd show her every trick I had up my sleeve and rock her world. But she's different. She's not like the rest. How? I haven't completely figured it out, but sign me the fuck up.

Every muscle tightens as fireworks explode and reverberate through the mountain range surrounding the cabin. It takes a moment for the sound to register, and each muscle begins to loosen in my chest.

Two hands grip my shoulders from behind. "Boston has a lot to get used to. We like to light up the night around these parts. Homecoming, proposals, you name it, we celebrate. And we need to make sure this one"—he nods at Brynn—"doesn't drive home."

He releases his hold and pats me on the back of the neck. I don't need to turn around to know it's Gerry. He walks to our side. A seventy-something-year-old in farmer jeans with a flannel underneath is not something I'm accustomed to seeing, and I can't help but smirk.

"Jackson and Solia have—"

All motion and conversation ceases. It's not fireworks. Everyone focuses on the dirt driveway as five motorcycles kick up the rocks and rev their engines.

Every male in the group lurches forward, straining their eyes through the darkness. I look over at Shannon glued to my side, sizzling with fear. Her fingers dig into my forearm, no doubt leaving an imprint. I sober up enough to realize it's the rumble of bikes she fears.

If Richard is here, this whole night is going to get fucked real fast.

# 13

Shannon

My breath sticks in my throat, and every nerve in my body is on high alert. Richard wouldn't dare show his face here; this can't be him. And if it is, all of us being here together, in addition to Nick, is enough to send him over the edge.

I'm suctioned to Nick's side, practically digging my fingernails into his skin. His opposite arm is wrapped on top of my hand as he peers down the hill through the space between Lucas, Gerry, Jackson, and twenty other men who are raring to charge at full speed.

The bikers kill the engines and a voice at the far end of the attack line yells out, "You motherfuckers showed up!"

All heads turn and face Cindy's son, Hunter, who is halfway down the hill. He turns around to face us, seemingly stunned by our silence.

"They thought it was Richard coming back to start shit, Hunter. For heaven's sake, it's Logan and the crew!" Cindy pushes herself to the front of the blockade and yells down to the bikes, "Get your asses up here, boys, and stop scaring the shit out of everyone! This is a party."

"Sorry, folks, nothing but the boys back in town." Hunter throws his arms in the air and hops down the rest of the hill to welcome his friends.

Brynn adjusts her top, feasting her eyes on the bikes. Thankfully, her eyes are off Nick for a moment.

Relief filters through the crowd. No one utters a word, but it doesn't go without notice the shared fear and protection this town has for me. The party resumes, crisis averted.

Nick peels my fingertips out of his arm and grabs hold of my wrists to face me. We are the only two left on the hill, and everyone else is the backdrop to our scene. "He's not here, Shannon. You are okay." Despite his alcohol intake, he's laser focused on me.

Richard is the only man I've been with, and I know how to handle him. Right now, Nick towers over me, all muscle, protection, downright authoritative. His eyes are locked with mine. I want to run my fingers through his hair and I long for his ripped arms around me.

I've always been the provider, the worrier, the caretaker, and I'm not sure I've ever felt protected. Nick may be a complete one-eighty from Richard, and maybe this will be a welcome change, exactly what I need.

"Yeah, it wouldn't make sense for him to be here. He's an asshole, but I'd like to think he knows enough to stay away. I'm not sure I'll ever disassociate that sound and not expect him to roll up."

"Shannon! Nick!" Solia yells through the voices from the front porch. "Get over here."

Jackson is cuddled behind her and points to something toward the mountain range in front of the cabin. "We are being summoned." Nick squeezes my wrists tighter, pulls me into his chest, and then wraps his arm around my back. His corporate bullshit deodorant smells amazing.

He leads me to the porch, and I think I'd follow him anywhere.

We weave through the group huddled behind the circle of chairs, up the deck steps to the front porch. The view is breathtaking. I can see why Solia was determined to stop her parents from selling this place. A log cabin in the middle of the woods, surrounded by nothing but nature, quiet enough to hear a pin drop? A slice of heaven. The noise you can make out here … I wonder how loud you would have to be for a neighbor to hear you.

The mountain range comes into view and fireworks reverberate through the valley, colors igniting the air. A slight breeze rolls off the mountainside and sends a trail of goose bumps along my thighs. A chill travels up my torso, my shoulders shuddering in response. Nick reads my body and grabs a blanket off the rocking chair to the left.

Holding the corner, he wraps the warm fleece around his shoulders, spins me so my back is pressed against his chest, and gently walks us forward to the open spot against the porch railing. Nick then wraps the blanket across my front and whispers in my ear, "Pull it around and tuck us in." My heart races from his hot breath against my ear. His words are my command.

I pull the blanket and encase the two of us into one tightly wrapped burrito.

His warm, rock-hard body against mine causes my pulse to thump louder than the pyrotechnic explosions. Somewhere nestled in the mountains, locals celebrate the weekend, lighting up the night sky, sending the celebration to the air for all to enjoy. A spectacular show of every color sizzles and penetrates the darkness.

Everyone here is huddled on the porch. Nick closes any gap between us by pressing his excitement into my lower back, and I want to bend over the porch railing for his easy entry. His palms slide down my arms, across my stomach, and settle on the waistband of my shorts. He's not going to … but I want him to. This intense desire is something I've never felt in my life. I never had this anticipation with Richard.

"My hands are a little chilly." Nick sends my body into the fever zone as he whispers in my ear. He toys with the flannel knot in my shirt and slides his fingers into my shorts, resting his hands on the band. He doesn't go any further but tickles my panty line, gently turning my body into a flood zone. I'm aware that no one can see underneath the blanket, but I blush from the naughty thoughts raging through my mind. What I want from Nick right now, I can't have.

Screw these fireworks. Forget my fear. I want more of whatever this man is serving.

To my left are Cindy and Harold, and to my right is Brynn, who looks ready to crawl underneath this blanket and eat Nick alive. She's always been so quiet and reserved. I realize I've never been around her when she's been drinking.

A couple feet down, I spot Solia snuggling into Jackson, his arms wrapped around her. Her eyes are closed, her chest rising and falling in contentment. I couldn't be happier for the two of them. They are perfect for each other, and knowing Jackson is staying put in Meriden makes the future bright. We are a close family, but since our parents moved to New York, my relationship with my brother has deepened, and thinking of Jackson and Solia growing old together warms my heart.

Our grandparents may have acted as if they had everything under control, but Jackson staying and taking command of the family farm has been a relief for everyone. Between my grandmother's recovery process, her and Grandpa's advanced age, and the steady success and increased production of the orchard, it would've been difficult to maintain the farm without Jackson at the helm.

My little brother looks over, as if reading my mind, and

nods with a slight smile. I've never seen him so relaxed. At least one of us has a shot at happily ever after.

I push my head against Nick's chest and turn to look up at him. "Let's get out of here. I'll drive."

Nick doesn't say a word. He grins, removes his hands, and slides them behind me for a squeeze. I'll take that as a yes.

We weave through the crowd, saying our goodbyes, and congratulate the newly engaged couple. Gerry is at the bottom of the staircase, eyeing us up and down as we approach, scratching his beard. "Where are you two kids headed?"

"Hi, Gerry. I'm taking Nick home." In front of Gerry, I morph into a teenager caught by an authority figure trying to sneak off with a boy.

"Hmmm, he's going to leave his car here?"

"Evan is staying for a bit. He'll drive back."

"I'm fine, Gerry. She wants to be in charge tonight." Nick winks and I gently punch him, my hand meeting his granite six-pack.

Gerry crosses his arms against his chest and takes a step forward. He lays his hand on my shoulder and holds my gaze. "You have my number if you need me, Shannon. Make good choices."

I let go of Nick and squeeze Gerry in a hug. His embrace is familiar and reassuring. "I know, Gerry. I'm good." He's as much a part of my family as anyone. He embraces me back, and loud enough for both of us to hear, says, "She's a gift, this woman. Tread lightly, young man."

Gerry extends his hand to Nick, and they shake on it. This is about as close to an approval as Nick is going to get anytime soon. I'm not going to lie—I'm enjoying watching him squirm his way into the hearts of my community.

The chatter and laughter fade into the background as Nick and I settle into my truck. "I'm not typically in the passenger seat. Where to?" He slides his hand on my thigh, spreading his fingers wide and taking hold of my flesh.

"I'm thinking your place." I was hoping to avoid my house, specifically my bedroom. I haven't been with another man besides Richard. If this night goes the way I think it will, I don't want to be in my bed. That would be weird. I cringe at the thought.

"My place it is." Nick rests his head back and leaves his hand on my thigh. If he only knew what was going on underneath the fabric of my shorts.

I strain my eyes through the blackness with the help of my headlights, avoiding every divot in the dirt road while staying alert for a crossing bear or deer.

No matter the time of year, Newfound is stunning. Tonight, the glow of a full moon filters down and shines upon the stillness of the water as it ripples gently in the breeze. Swim lines and most docks have been removed at this point in the season to prepare for the cold weather ahead. The majority of homes are invisible through the darkness, lights out for the night, people tucked away in slumber, and those who have a porch light on are either fireside or waiting up for kids to return home from a homecoming after-party.

I take the corner a little tight and a tire bumps into a small pothole I should've anticipated. Nick has molded into the seat and the bump sends his head careening into the window.

"Hold on, city boy."

Nick lets out a groan, lifts his hand to his forehead, and releases a deep breath. "Hold on? Baby, you tell me what to hold on to, and your wish is my command."

I'm not sure I will ever get used to the phrases that come out of his mouth.

"Here we are, home sweet home."

I look over at Nick, who is already halfway out the

passenger door. *Home sweet home.* I internally repeat the words, and they send an uncomfortable itch through my body. This wasn't supposed to be my life. I had what I thought was my forever home, a lasting marriage, and happiness.

Plans change, people change, and I'm moving on.

I'm shaken out of the looming spiral when the driver's side door opens and Nick is within a foot of me. The motion-sensing light over the garage illuminates the driveway and his body, and every thought about why or how I ended up here flies away. Tonight, I'm going to let my worry go. I want to see what I've been missing.

His hand reaches for mine and with one tug, I'm behind him, climbing the back deck stairs, still in disbelief that he snagged this house.

"Inside or outside?"

"How about inside?"

"You are running the show, Shannon."

With Nick's first step through the sliding door, the recessed lighting kicks on, providing the living space with enough illumination to set a romantic stage. Something inside me pushes away every worry I have about what I should or shouldn't be doing.

"Let's take a shot."

Nick stops mid-stride and turns to face me, fire in his eyes, anticipation on his lips. "You want a shot?"

I run my hand along the side of the soft armchair and allow my gaze to wander from his eyes to his lips to his chest. "I want to let loose. I'm always in charge, the person making every decision, worrying about everyone else."

Between my first word and my last, Nick towers over me, close enough that I admire every inch of his face. "You know what? Shannon, let me. I'll take charge, turn you inside out, and savor every square inch. Just say the word. I'll take good care of you."

The way his long lashes dip over his captivating eyes makes me want his hands all over my body. His deep, sexy growl purrs across my skin, making me want to rip off my clothes.

"Drink first?"

Nick kisses me passionately, his gentle scruff tickling my upper lip. His tongue moves gently around and then he nibbles on my bottom lip with a soft *mmm*. "Let me get something."

I throw myself into the armchair and attempt to regain control of my heart rate and stop myself from acting like a horny teenager. Being in Nick's presence is throwing me back twenty years without a clue about what to do next.

"Honey whiskey or something harder?"

"You pour it, I'll drink it." *What does that even mean? Who says that?*

Nick pulls off his flannel, lifting the T-shirt underneath enough for me to get a view I want to crawl all over.

"Take it off."

"Take what off?" He steps closer, smirking.

*Shit, did I say that out loud?*

I cover my eyes with both hands and tuck my knees into my chest.

"Get up, Shannon."

His directness takes me by surprise. I snap out of my shell, stand, and take the shot glass from his hand.

"Cheers to a great night." Nick taps his glass against mine, and we toss the golden liquid down. The slight burn is perfect, just what I need. He takes the emptied shots and places them on the table in the center of the room.

"Now, what do you want me to take off?"

I look down at the floor, embarrassed to have spoken those words. "I didn't actually mean to say that for you to hear."

His hand under my chin lifts my face to meet his. "Do I get an answer to the question?" He squints and crosses his arms against his chest.

I nod and stand in silence, filled with tension.

"My shirt? You want my shirt off?"

I grasp the bottom of it and pull as high as I can until I can't reach. He takes over. His muscles, tattoos, and chiseled shoulders shift shy Shannon into bold Shannon in an instant.

I grab the shot glasses, walk my ass to the bottle on the island, and pour another two. Nick joins me, his chest in my peripheral view and his hands on my shoulders. "I don't want you regretting anything, Shannon. I had enough tonight."

I toss the liquid courage back and put the glass down. Nick's hands are on my waist, lifting me onto the island. He spreads my legs and wraps his arms around my back. "Tell me what you are thinking."

"This is not something I do. I want to be here, right now, and I don't want to think about anything else. I'm tired of living on the straight and narrow. I think you can show me what I've been missing. Can you do that?"

"There is nothing more I want. Do you have to be anywhere in the morning?" He pulls my ass closer to the edge of the counter.

I tilt my head to my shoulder and jut my chin. "No."

"Good." The steam from his voice powers into my neck as his tongue traces my skin to the back of my ear. "Are you sure you're ready for this?" he whispers in his signature deep growl.

I grab his jaw and pull him to my lips, kissing him with a forcefulness I didn't know I possessed. The need for him to show me is more than I can bear.

He wraps his arms around my back, his palms under my ass, and lifts me off the counter and around his waist. I've never had a man literally carry me to bed.

My head has just the right amount of buzz to keep me from overthinking. Nick's bedroom door is open. He holds me until we reach the edge of the bed and then releases me like a rag doll onto the mattress. He says nothing and walks to the sliding glass doors. He presses a button on his phone and the blinds slide open. Then the gas fireplace in front of the bed ignites with a faint glow. Nick unlocks and slides both sets of doors open and a rush of fresh night air rolls off the lake and through the room, sending a chill over my body.

The combination of the unspoiled lake view and the sight of Nick's chest and soft trail of hair leading to his low-hung waistline is almost too much. I want him to have his way with me.

I can't waste another second. I sit up and yank off his belt, dropping it to the floor. His tongue rolls over his bottom lip. I undo the button and slowly unzip his jeans, and his pants puddle around his ankles. He hasn't moved or said a word. This beautiful man is standing in front of me in only a pair of black boxer briefs, and I know there's more underneath them than I've ever experienced.

I throw caution to the wind and tug on his briefs, lifting them forward in an attempt not to disrupt the package. I lower myself to my knees and pull the briefs all the way to the floor. I'm not sure I've ever admired a man's legs before, but everything about Nick is perfection. He's muscle and class, manly and strong. I want to do this; I want to be wild and devour this man. For a split second, I panic and wonder if I will suck at this—literally.

*Fuck it.*

I'm staring at more than I can handle but go for it. I open my mouth to take him as my hair is gathered and tugged gently upward, bringing me to stand in front of him, his excitement gliding over my body and pushing against my stomach.

"I don't want you on your knees, baby. Not yet."

*Do women really like being called* baby? *Because damn, it's hot coming out of his mouth.*

"Turn around."

I certainly am not going to argue. I turn and Nick rips the knot in my flannel apart and pulls my tank over my head. He unbuttons my shorts next and slides them and my underwear off in one shot, then unhooks my bra and gives my ass a slap. "Get on the bed."

I crawl atop the duvet and freeze on all fours as I feel his tongue between my legs. "I needed to make sure you were ready for me." He pulls back, flips me over, and hovers over my body. "You taste ready." He leans down and kisses me firmly, filling my mouth and exploring every inch. He lowers himself over me and uses his knees to spread my legs.

I'm not sure I can stand the anticipation. If you'd asked me two months ago if I needed sex, I would've told you burnt toast sounded better. Now, I can't leave here without it. This version of Nick uses his authoritative qualities in the best way possible.

He glides over my wetness. A loud moan escapes my mouth, and I giggle in excitement, surprising myself.

"You like that?"

"Like that? I don't know if I can last another second."

"You can let go whenever you want. I've got more than one round with you tonight."

More than one round? Is that even possible?

Before I can comprehend multiple rounds, Nick leans over to his nightstand, rips open a package, and unfurls a condom over himself. He kisses my body all the way to my lips and glides inside in one swoop. The fullness causes me to arch my back in response and tilt my head into the mattress.

Nick slides his hands under me and grips my shoulders, bracing me for the waves I'm about to ride. His eyes never leave mine as he sends my every nerve to the edge. The man knows exactly what he's doing. I'm about to lose all control when he slows his rhythm, stares deeply into my eyes, and runs his tongue on my lips. "Not yet. You okay?"

*Am I okay? Yes, I'm okay. Don't stop.* The words I want to say.

All I manage to gasp is "Yes."

He backs out and kneels in front of me with the fire blazing behind him. He looks edible as hell. "You are beautiful, Shannon. Will you get on your knees?"

*I'll stand on my goddamn head if you ask me to.*

I'm on all fours faster than I've ever flipped a pancake.

"Face the lake."

*Yes, sir.*

I crawl sideways on the bed and feel his knees inching my legs as far apart as he needs to pave his way. He grabs my hips and pulls me into him, again taking me by surprise. There's an urgency and heat that spreads through my body. I gasp for air and tilt my head to the ceiling.

Nick grips my hair and pulls, holding my mane with one hand, the other on my waist. I look out into the night and allow words to come out of my mouth that I've never spoken in the bedroom. He reacts and reads my body like a blueprint.

"I can't wait any longer."

"Just let go."

*Yes, sir.*

He takes his cue and there isn't an inch of me unfilled. His pace quickens, and I shudder and ride the waves while I look out into the calmness of the water and empty myself onto him.

Nick wasn't kidding when he said multiple rounds. A man of his word, he wore me out. I was contorted in ways I'm not sure I would've thought possible, even with years of yoga training. His body is demanding, and I am more than happy to comply. Each time I don't think I have an ounce of energy left to give, and every time I surprise myself, begging for more.

We kiss, he holds me, and leaves me exhausted. At some point, he reaches his limit, and I crawl into the space next to him, our bodies molded together, sticky with sweat, depleted.

Sometime during the night, I wake, dying of thirst. I slide out from under his arm and tiptoe across the hardwood floor. It's before sunrise and darkness fills the room. Normally, I'd have clothes on, but I have no idea where those are at the moment. And I'm swollen between my legs, the fullness apparent when I walk. It's a nice reminder of last night. I'd do it all over again.

I glide down the hallway, knowing the chance of the pristine floors squeaking is minimal compared to my ancient hardwoods. I ease each cabinet open, locate a glass, and fill it with water under the refrigerator light. There's a pile of Green Breeze brochures and a notebook on the counter. Knowing I should mind my own business, and actually following my code of ethics, are two different things.

I take the notebook and hold it under the light. It's a list of towns. Towns in New Hampshire. Some are close, some are up north. Each one listed is one I've spent time in, whether it was hiking, skiing, or visiting. My jaw tenses and my shoulders climb toward my ears.

Every emotion I pushed to the recesses of my mind from the summer's turbine saga comes flooding back. Nick is going to do the same damn thing to another community. We may have saved Meriden, but nothing changes the fact that this guy and his company are ruthless.

"Oh shit." A deep voice penetrates the darkness.

I spin around, spilling water over my chest, knowing the voice doesn't belong to Nick. Standing there like a deer in headlights, Evan's eyes survey my soaking chest and pebbled nipples.

I do the only thing I can. I drop the glass on the counter,

papers falling to the floor, and I spin around to pull open the freezer door. I plaster my naked body inside the opening. "Holy shit, Evan. I forgot you were staying here."

"Umm, yeah. Sorry, I had no idea you'd be in the kitchen. I didn't hear a thing. I'm so sorry."

My wet nipples are surely getting frostbite from being smashed against the ice maker on the back of the door, and my ass is resting on bags of frozen veggies.

"Listen, can you just go away for a minute? I need to get my clothes." I peek at him through the crack in the door. The sun has started to rise and the light filtering through the glass illuminates the shock that hasn't subsided from Evan's face.

"Oh shit, yeah, of course." He hightails it out of the room.

I slam the freezer shut and feverishly rub my nipples to prevent them from falling off.

Back in Nick's room, it's bright enough for me to locate last night's outfit. I need to get out of here. Who am I kidding? Last night was unbelievable, and I don't regret letting him rock my world, but he isn't for me. I don't think I can let this happen again. What if he really is just a rich prick at the core of it all, out to destroy little communities like ours?

"Hey, baby. Where are you off to this early? I was ready to eat breakfast."

Frostbite reversed. Damn it, I hate how my body betrays my common sense.

"I need to go home. Thanks for a great night." I slide my flannel over my arms, and he wraps his arm around my legs, pulling me closer.

"Why do I suddenly get the impression this was a booty call for you?" His grin is enough for me to rethink leaving.

"Me? Booty call? Yeah, no. But I do need to go."

Nick's grin turns to a frown, and his eyebrows scrunch together. "Yeah, sure." He lies back, the sheets resting along his waistline, the cotton molding his package. Seeing the outline of his length and size has me wet within seconds.

I have to get out of here before I let him take me for another ride because that's all this guy might ever be. Don't get me wrong—I don't regret him fucking my brains out—but I'm not going to let him break my heart.

# 14

Nick

Thinking back to my night with Shannon, I played all the right cards. She certainly seemed to enjoy herself. Evan filled me in on the fridge debacle. I wish I could've seen that play out.

Usually, after a performance like that, I have to drive a woman away. I mean, honestly, I know what I've got in the bedroom is talent, but my night with Shannon was more than a hookup. I can't get enough of her, and I wanted her to stay.

But I can't figure Shannon out. She's returning my messages with one-liners, dodging every date I've thrown out. Work is busy, and she spends so much time doing teacher things outside of school. I'm not giving up, but she's making this difficult. I don't know what the fuck to do with myself.

She is taking up brain space, and I can't lie in these sheets without thinking about her. If I'm honest, I don't think I've ever given a woman much of a second thought, and I've been with some real knockouts—tits guys would pay money to play with. But Shannon is different. Underneath her flannel and jeans, she has a body made for me. I crave her ass slamming against my thighs.

This is the first weekend I've been able to get away and spend at the lake since the marathon weekend. Early November in Newfound has a whole different aura once the rainbow of leaves decorates the roads. The town grows quiet, the bears have begun to den, and the locals are holed up in coffee shops and bars or cozied up by fires readying for the first snowfall.

The air has a different level of silence. I'm finally able to sleep through the night without waking and wondering why the world is still. What I haven't gotten accustomed to is the lack of people around. In Boston, you're never alone. No matter the day or time, people swarm the streets and the T, restaurants have a waitlist, and elevators are jam-packed.

You don't see anyone in Meriden unless you're at the town dump, stocking up on books from the library, or you seek them out.

My family should be here any minute. A weekend together has been in the works, and I'm curious to see what they think of the place. Harold is staying in Boston this weekend. He's my right-hand man, but I had to cut the cord, for fuck's sake. I don't need him in New Hampshire babysitting me. He protested because the B&B room is still rented for him, but I think it had more to do with Cindy than me. I even did my own grocery shopping.

I messaged Shannon a few days ago to invite her to have dinner with us. Maybe it's too much, too soon. She fired a text back within seconds, saying she had plans this weekend.

After putting the groceries away, I ignite the fireplace and arrange flowers in a vase. *I'm domestic. I own a house. Flowers on the counter are perfectly normal.*

The doorbell rings, then a knock, and then my sister Ashlyn plows through the front door before I get to the bottom step. "Holy shit, Nick. You are in the sticks!"

Her swinging ponytail swipes across my face when all five

foot two of my little sister pulls me in for a hug. Resting my chin on her head, I smile at my mom and brother walking in.

Ashlyn releases her grip, pulls off her matching cashmere gloves, hat, and scarf, and charges up the stairs, dropping her tote at the top.

My mother, Claire, is next in line for a hug. "Mom, you're dressed for a snowstorm." I pull her winter hat by the pompom and stuff it into the pocket of her winter coat.

"You never know when Mother Nature will dump a storm, Nicholas. I'd rather be prepared."

My brother, Brett, and I clasp hands and pull each other in. "This is quite the place, man."

"Come on up and I'll show you around." They follow me to the main floor and immediately walk to the sliding glass doors.

My mom, whose hair has gone completely white, looks older than I remember. She puts on her glasses and moves closer to the glass. "Oh, honey, what a view."

I reach across her, unlocking the slider, and usher her outside.

"Dude, it's fucking freezing." Ashlyn shuts the door, leaving my mother and me outside on the deck.

"What do you think, Mom?" I wrap my arm around her bony shoulders.

"Honey, you've done well. This is beautiful. Quite a change from city life, but it certainly is my cup of tea. It's quiet. I could get used to this." She squeezes closer. We both stare out onto the lake and listen to the only audible sounds—falling leaves, a car way off in the distance.

"There's something about it. Every time I'm here, I don't want to leave. Does that sound crazy?" I pull her in tighter and wonder what my dad would think of this place.

"Not crazy at all. I've always wondered what life would be like at a slower pace. I would've preferred a little more R & R throughout the years, but you know your father. You seem happy. You look great."

"Work has been insane as usual, but when I'm here, I recharge. The silence is tough to get used to. Nobody needs me. It's a nice escape."

"Speaking of being on your own." My mother crosses her arms over her chest and scoots out from under my embrace. "We stopped at the rest stop on the way up on 93N. I picked up a copy of *The Laker* to read while your brother drove."

I take a deep breath, knowing what's coming next.

"I didn't know you were still taking pictures."

I stuff my hands in my jeans pocket and face the water. "Yeah, neither did I. Who knew almost destroying this place would inspire me to preserve it through photos? I brought my old cameras here, and one night I was sitting out on the Adirondack chair on the dock and knew I had to take a few shots. There's this time of day right after the golden hour—they call it the blue hour. The sun is behind the mountains, the moon is out, the stars too … it's breathtaking. That's the photo you saw."

"I'm proud of you, Nick. I know when Daddy died, you hid your dreams of photography, figured they were impossible. You convinced yourself you had a company to run and a name to live up to, but it's never too late to chase a dream. Life is short. And look, you won *The Laker* contest."

"I didn't expect to win. I think I wanted to know if I was good enough, that I hadn't lost my touch."

"That you haven't, Nick."

"Thanks, Mom." I wrap her in a hug and ask, "Did you mention this to Brett and Ashlyn?"

"Not a word."

"Okay, good." I meet her eyes. "How have you been feeling?"

"As good as new. All is right in the world. Don't you worry

your handsome head over anything. The doctors are keeping a close watch, but for now, I'm in the clear." I'm so relieved to hear her say these words. "Nicholas, this place has what it takes to rejuvenate a mind, body, and soul. You might have company more often than you'd prefer."

Her words fill a void I didn't know existed. This is what I hoped she'd want—more peace and quiet up here by the lake.

It's not a secret photography was the love of my life in my teens and early twenties, but it's a passion I've kept close to my chest. My siblings were too young to remember, and I don't feel like explaining it. I never thought my family would see the contest results. I didn't expect to win.

Until Newfound Lake, I never realized I missed being behind the lens. There's a magic to it. I love the way a camera captures a moment that will never be seen again. A picture freezes time, allows it to last forever. Maybe there's something to dusting off old dreams and wishing for them again. Mothers know best—it's never too late.

After dinner, my mother's exhausted and goes up to lie down. I get her comfortable in the bedroom next to mine and let her know that I'm going to take the two knuckleheads out to the Binn. They are already bored to tears, and if we're going to stay awake, we need to go out.

My sister walks into the kitchen decked out in a black skirt, little black boot things, and a pink cropped sweater. "What do you think? Cozy mountain vibes or too basic?"

She eyes me up and down where I sit on a barstool at the island. "What are you wearing? A T-shirt and jeans? You look like a freaking hick."

I nearly spit out my mouthful of cider and Brett bangs his fist on the marble counter. "You took the words right out of my mouth. I said the same damn thing."

"Listen, guys. You are not in Boston, or any city, for that

matter. People here don't dress up to go out. Relaxed and comfortable is the vibe. It's a local dive bar."

"What the fuck does that mean? I'm relaxed. I'm comfortable. And what does diving have anything to do with a bar?"

I slap my palm against my forehead. "Ashlyn, you'll look ridiculous. Don't you have jeans and a T-shirt?"

Brett pipes up behind me, "Dude, you know that's what she's wearing. Leave it."

I manage to get my brother to switch into jeans and a long-sleeve button-down. Cityside Barbie is going to stick out like a sore thumb, so be it.

Ever since my sister became one of the most sought-after wedding photographers in Boston, her head has inflated to twice its size. I love her, but she's a lot.

"Let's go." I grab my keys from the hand-carved bowl sitting on the counter. "Mom knows we're heading out."

"Silver or black purse?" Ashlyn asks from the top of the stairs. Brett and I are halfway out the door.

"Silver," I reply without even looking because who the fuck cares.

The Binn is a little over a mile from my house, but somehow my sister manages to ask ten freaking times why there are no streetlights or cars anywhere.

"If you ever want to know where serial killers are hiding, bingo! This is it. Seriously, does this lake contain some sort of magical shit? Because why these people live out here is beyond me. Did someone hold a gun to your head and make you buy the place?"

Brett turns around from the front seat. "Can you shut up for a minute? Maybe, just maybe, not everyone likes to live among wall-to-wall people."

I couldn't have said it better myself. Brett left Rosendale right after high school. He could've gotten into any college he wanted, but firefighting has always been his dream. Despite my mother's pleas, he's training to be a hotshot in California. Having her youngest move across the country was tough, but we knew nothing would stop him. He's made for that life. Brett is one of the toughest guys I know.

Ashlyn's head slams against the back seat window when my left front tire dips into a pothole upon turning into the dirt parking lot. I have to bite my tongue to hold back my laughter. The lot is packed. My only choice is to parallel park on the street.

"This place is jammed. Any hotties hiding in these woods?" Brett slaps my shoulder as he walks behind Ashlyn, who is trying to spare her boots from the muck.

"You never know, little brother."

We round the back to the tavern door, where a handwritten sign displays the name of tonight's musical act. I'd forgotten Saturday nights at the Binn offered live entertainment.

Ashlyn turns around once we step inside, eyes wide and forehead crinkled. "There's no cover?"

I wrap my arm around her shoulders. "This isn't the Avalon, Ash. Let's get a drink."

As I expected, every head turns when we walk in. Every stool is fitted with a flannel-and-T-shirt-wearing local. A few raise their drinks in my direction, a couple nod and turn away. A handful of residents have moved to the friend zone from enemy camp, but there are still many more to win over.

Ashlyn snaps her fingers in the air and wedges herself between two men on their stools. Both lean back and give her the elevator. She looks like a walking highlighter, and her skirt might as well be underwear. I move closer, and they take the hint. Cindy walks over, snapping her fingers in response. "Let me guess, another city slicker. Honey, we don't snap around here. We wait our turn in line and chat while we wait."

Cindy smirks at me. "What can I get you folks?"

Ash stands with her hands on her hips, her elbows jabbing the guts of the barstool men. "I'll have a glass of your finest white, and what do you guys want?" She waits for our response.

"We'll take two IPAs. Thank you, Cindy."

"You know her?" Ash's mouth drops open in disbelief.

"Coming right up, sweetcakes. Our finest wine for you." Cindy gives me a wink, takes a clean mason jar out of the dishwasher, and presses a button on the wine gun, filling the jar with a pale-yellow liquid.

Ashlyn's eyes bulge, and she looks from Cindy to me and back. "She can't be serious. No fine wine comes out of one of those."

The man on Ash's left speaks up. "Honey, Cindy's wine is about as fine as you'll find. Take your wine and twirl around."

If she didn't deserve the jab, I would speak up, but she absolutely does. *Has she always been this much of a snob?*

I wink and grab the IPAs from Cindy. Ashlyn hightails it, leaving me with the bill and the two men chuckling. "Sorry about that. Those are my siblings." I hand over my card for the tab.

"No shit, Sherlock. You could be triplets. Has anyone ever mentioned your brother resembles a young Tom Brady?"

Cue the eye roll. "Once or twice." I turn and look for Brett and Ash through the crowd. I spot my sister pulling out a stool at one of the round tops.

"Hey, man. What are you doing here tonight?"

I shove one of the IPAs to my chest to shake Lucas's hand. "Hey, good to see you. I had to get out of the house for a bit. Family in town."

"Nice. I'll let you get to it. Stop by the bar before you leave. Shannon is over there." He tilts his head to the corner of the room. "Is Harold here too?"

*Weird.*

"No, he's not." I follow Lucas's gaze, and sure enough, I see Shannon's back toward me where she stands at the end of the table against the wall. I'd spot her silky black hair and gorgeous ass anywhere. She's wearing tight blue jeans, brown boots, and a long-sleeve white T-shirt that reveals the small of her back as she leans against the table. I know all the women around the table—Solia, Brynn, Mia, Madison, and Brooke.

I'm staring and I know it. Thankfully, the musician onstage switches it up, causing the women to squeal like a pack of teenagers. The energy in the room shifts, and the ladies flood the small wooden dance floor. God, what I would give to ride up behind her.

I place the beers on the high top, never allowing my eyes to leave Shannon. "I Love Rock 'n' Roll" cranks through the speakers. This guy is killing it—he's really good. There have to be thirty women packed onto a dance floor made for ten.

"These women can't be serious. Nick, snap out of it. This song is like a hundred years old," Ashlyn whines.

"Who is she?" Brett jabs me in the chest.

"Who's who?" I peel my eyes away from Shannon moving to the beat, waving her arms in the air. She looks happy.

"You know damn well who I mean. Your eyes haven't left her ass since you got these drinks. You got it bad." Brett takes his beer, tosses it back, and leans an elbow onto the table.

"Her name is Shannon. I'm not sure what's going on. I mean, I'm into her, but she said she was busy this weekend. I didn't know she'd be here."

Ashlyn spins around and jumps off her stool. "You're dating one of them?"

"No, I'm not dating one. I'm …"

"Yeah, man! Nice. Are they wild out here? They probably aren't stuck up and high maintenance." Brett winks with a nod at our sister.

"Definitely not stuck up." I finish my beer and head to Cindy for more liquid courage.

A bar customer spins out of his seat and looks at me. "Hey, sit here and order while I go to the bathroom. Hold my spot for me, yeah? I'll be right back."

I do as I'm told, and Cindy brings me another beer. "Any luck, Boston? Looks like you got it bad."

"Is it obvious?"

There is something about Cindy. She's got that best-friend quality about her. You can spill your guts without even thinking twice. "Yeah, it is. Is she giving you the cold shoulder?"

"Not entirely. She just doesn't seem interested. It's odd."

Cindy takes a wineglass from the washer and shines it with the bar towel tucked in her pocket. "Odd that she isn't interested in you? Or odd that you don't know what to do?"

The barstool man is back, tapping my shoulder. I push myself up. "Both, I guess."

I'm about to walk away when I hear Cindy say my name. "Try being honest with her. Tell her how you feel."

I stare at her. *How I feel? How would I do that?* I shake my head.

"And what's with you leaving Harold back in Boston?" Cindy leans her chest on the bar, scans the row of customers for empties, and waits for my response.

"What's the matter? You miss him?" I wink and don't wait for her answer.

Mia and Brynn are at our high top when I return. "Hey, Boston. I didn't know you were hiding a sexy younger brother."

"Give him room to breathe, Brynn. Hey, Nick. We spotted you guys and wanted to say hi," Mia says, tilting her head to indicate Brynn was the curious one.

Before answering, I look over to the girls' table, and

Shannon's gaze meets mine. I don't utter a word but follow the invisible path leading to her.

My vision lands on the plunging neckline of her white shirt. Her full breasts push through the top, and memories of them slapping against my chest flash in my mind. I force myself to meet her eyes, and a small smile lingers on her lips.

Without hesitating, I place a hand on both sides of the table with her in between and lean in to kiss her glossy, cherry-flavored lips. I want to pry them open and tell her I want her, have missed her, need her.

Her hands press against my chest, pushing me back and away from her mouth. "Hold up, city boy."

I bend and rest my forehead against hers. "I didn't know you'd be here."

She leans closer to my ear and says, "I never expected you to be here either."

She can tell me to fuck off and I'd still have a boner. She faces the table, placing her back against me. The willpower it takes to concentrate on the people around her is considerable.

"You remember the girls—Madison, Brooke, and Solia. It looks like Mia and Brynn are introducing themselves."

"Come on, I'll introduce you to my siblings."

"So fun!" Madison jumps up from the table and heads over with the other two women in tow.

"I didn't mean to crash your night out," I say, leaning closer to Shannon.

I can tell she's had more to drink than the last time we were together. "You didn't crash my night. You're just making it more difficult for me to avoid you."

I gently rest a hand under her jaw and pull her closer. "Why are you avoiding me? Did I hurt you?" Fear runs through me, and I replay our night on fast-forward in my head.

"Hurt me? No." Shannon tosses her head back and giggles. She's definitely drunk. "Listen, the morning after our night together, I snooped in your kitchen and spotted your hit list of towns to destroy next. I'm into you, trust me, Nick. But I have to listen to my gut. A guy like you, with money and a company like Green Breeze, destroys things. I've got enough shit going on, I don't need to be left in the ruins."

Her words are a gut punch. Before I can respond, she's walking toward the rest of the group, ready to meet my family. *This should go well.*

Brynn is already cozying up to Brett by the time we get back. This is no surprise.

"You didn't tell me about all these ladies, Nicholas." Ashlyn throws back a shot in sync with Mia.

"Yeah, sorry. I guess you've already met everyone. This is Shannon."

Shannon walks over and shakes my siblings' hands, winning them over with her smile and obvious charisma. Another popular song begins, and Mia ushers them all back to the dance floor.

"Dude, now I see why you bought a house up here. So, Shannon is the lucky lady, huh?"

"Not exactly. I'm an idiot, but I don't buy houses to chase a woman." I rest my elbows on the table closer to Brett without my eyes leaving Shannon. "I can't figure it out. She's into me, but not enough."

"Maybe she's playing hard to get. You'll win her over. Come on, I'm liking that little one."

I follow behind him, yelling, "Her name is Brynn." It's a lost cause. He's not hearing a thing.

I'm not a dancer. Halfway to the floor, I turn back to spare myself the embarrassment. I pull up a stool at the table to sit and watch. Shannon really is beautiful. Her hips sway in rhythm to the music. She spots me watching her and smiles. Once again, I get that queasy feeling—I want her, but she's afraid I will hurt her?

A cool breeze wafts through the bar as Jackson walks in and over to me. "You alone, man?"

"Nah, they are all on the dance floor." I point toward the stage.

He nods and scans the room. "I figured they'd be here late. Tonight Solia was planning on asking all the girls to be in the wedding party."

The last puzzle piece slips into place. They don't need a reason to be this giddy and carefree, but now I understand their celebratory mood.

"I'm not staying. Just dropped off a case of cider to the back room because Cindy was running low. I don't want to disturb girls' night."

"Yeah, sure thing. I had no idea they'd be here." I notice Jackson leaning uncomfortably and scanning the bar area. I follow his stare and try to figure out what or who he's looking for.

Just as I'm about to give up, I see Cindy swing through the door behind the bar, tucking her shirt into her bar apron. At the same moment, Lucas walks into the bar through the side door, shirt untucked and hair disheveled, looking left to right and landing on Jackson. Jackson turns his hat to the front and sits on the empty stool next to me.

I look at Cindy behind the bar, and she's pacing from one end to the other with beer and wine bottles in her hands.

If this is what I think it is, nothing is going to surprise me in this town. "Listen, man. I don't know what the hell is going on, but—"

Jackson sighs and shakes his head. "Let's just say there are some things that aren't meant to be seen. But once they are, you can't unsee them."

I look back at the bar, and Lucas is sitting there watching Cindy's ass spin from one end to the other.

The girls return to the table in hysterics. Shannon's skin

glistens—clearly the temperature is climbing on the dance floor. "Not a dancer, Nick?"

Jackson stands from the stool and adjusts his belt. "Hey, ladies, we were catching up. I see we have visitors. I'm not staying, but hi, I'm Jackson."

"Yeah! He's the hot farmer fiancé. Let's hear it!" Mia is louder than the damn speakers. People around our table start cheering and Jackson leans in for a kiss from Solia. Even I have to admit, they are perfect for each other.

"I'll catch you later, babe." Jackson smiles, kisses Solia's forehead, and turns toward the door.

"Hey, city boy. I heard you were quite a ride the other night!" Mia hip-checks me to the side.

"Mia. Stop. Seriously." Shannon has her hand over Mia's mouth. "Hello, family is here."

I drop my chin to my chest and laugh. I'm flattered she's told the ladies. I guess there's hope for me.

"So, Shannon, since you've taken my brother for a ride, how about you come out to dinner with us tomorrow night? Claire would love to meet you. Nick has told us a lot about you." Brett is a smooth talker. I haven't said shit about Shannon because *I* can't even convince her to come over again.

"Yeah, girl. Meet the family!" Mia chimes in.

Shannon is put on the spot, but based on her smile, I breathe a little easier. "I'd love to."

"Perfect. I'm not sure how a woman like you isn't already taken. My brother is a lucky guy."

Brett, always one step ahead of himself. Shannon's eyes go from clear to overcast. I'm not sure what changed.

Before I can ask, Tyler, Jay, and Ryan come through the door. "Well, look at this party. Who the fuck knew we were missing out? I thought it was ladies' night."

I shake the guys' hands and introduce them all to Ashlyn

and Brett. Jay looks at my sister a little longer than I'd like, but I'll chalk it up to her pink top.

"Nah, man. We didn't know they were here. My family's in town and my mother went to bed early. We came out for a couple of drinks and ran into everyone."

"It's all good. I'm here to escort these ladies home because, obviously, no one is driving tonight. Right, baby?" Tyler slides his arm around Mia's waist.

"Oh yeah, baby. I'll ride you home tonight." Mia throws her head back, losing her balance and almost crashing into the table behind her. Clearly, they've partied too hard. Perhaps louder than she intended, Mia asks, "Did you get another shower curtain and baby oil? Let's do that again."

I've heard some crazy shit in my life, but what the hell? All heads spin toward the two of them. Tyler throws both hands in the air and shrugs. "What? You only live once, men. Might as well slide into some fun. If you know what I'm saying."

Everyone laughs and shakes their heads. The little I know about these two, their sex life already doesn't shock me.

With tabs settled, the party members grab their coats off the hooks by the door. No coatroom in Meriden, just hooks. I'm not sure I'll ever find that normal.

I throw my keys at Brett and tell the two of them I'll meet them at the car. "Hey, Shannon. Wait up." She lets the others get ahead of her and waits in the dirt lot.

She shivers in the cold.

"You want me to drive you home?"

"No, it's okay. I'm going back to Solia's for a bit. She's excited, and we may be up for a while. Are you sure you want me to come to dinner? I mean, that was a little awkward."

"Shannon, I already asked. You know I've been trying to see you."

She looks down at the ground. "I was trying not to think about you. I'm not sure I can be with a guy like you."

"A guy like me?"

"Yeah, someone who has it all figured out. You're in a different lane. Seeing those brochures stirred up some bad memories. Plus, my life is kind of a mess. What did your mom think about my situation? I'm not even officially divorced."

If she knew I haven't mentioned her name to my mother, she'd never come. "She's the best, Shannon. Dinner will be great. You two will get along. Let me show you I've got more dimension than my company logo."

"I'm not entirely convinced. But I'll have dinner with you." She pouts her lower lip and looks so edible.

How am I not supposed to pick her up and take her home?

"I guess I'll see you tomorrow night. I'll text you a time, okay?"

"Of course. Good night, Nick."

Score. I've never worked so hard to get a woman to agree to dinner. Shit. I watch her walk away and wonder how I'm going to explain this entire backstory before dinner tomorrow. I've never taken a woman home for dinner. Let's just hope this is one of those situations where actions speak louder than words.

# 15

Holy mother of god, my head pounds like I took a cinder block to the skull. I can say one thing for sure—I can't party like I used to. In all honesty, we didn't even "party." We had a girls' night, had some drinks, and I stayed up way past my bedtime. We ended up sleeping over at Solia's cabin, no one sober enough to drive home. Adult slumber parties need to be a routine thing. My stomach muscles are still sore from laughing.

I think we heard as much about Solia and Jackson's wedding as we did about Mia's sex life. After Solia asked us to be her bridesmaids, Mia went into full bachelorette party-planning mode. I'm not sure we are ready to handle what Mia will be serving up. Yikes.

Parts of the night are a little hazy. Nick had no idea we'd be at the Binn, but butterflies took flight as soon as I laid eyes on his chiseled jaw and neatly trimmed stubble. And it's not the divorce that's holding me back from being with him. I have so many emotions running through me at the same time.

In less than eight weeks, I'll legally be a single woman. This isn't supposed to be my life. Being out late on the weekends, sleeping with a cutthroat businessman I met a couple months ago, and going to dinner with his family is not what I envisioned for myself. I'm having a hard time pivoting my life plan.

Maybe that's the problem—I don't have a plan for the first time in my life.

Richard's mother called the other day, nagging once again that he's hitting her up for money and I should be the one he's calling. The whole family has lost their ever-loving minds. Our finances are squared away, and I am not letting one dollar of my hard-earned money go to Richard. Enough is enough.

The house is mine, free and clear. He had no interest in fighting for it. I've done the majority of the work inside and out. I'm here if there's an emergency, but I can't be a landing pad for him. He needs to figure out his life, and unfortunately, I can no longer be a part of it.

With Grandma Sylvia back home, my mother has returned to New York. I'm not sure how we're going to handle everything with my grandparents, but Mom staying in Meriden long term wasn't the plan. She arranged for a visiting nurse to check on them daily, despite the resistance from my grandfather. He is adamant he's capable of taking care of whatever they need and insists that paying someone else to sit around is a waste.

My mother was clever, however, focusing on pill organization and food, both responsibilities my grandfather will hand over without any reluctance. Despite all that, Jackson and I understand the burden will fall on us to make sure everything is okay on a daily basis.

Today is my day to check in on the farm and my grandparents. This time of year can be a zoo between the apples and pumpkin harvest. Along the winding, narrow roads of Meriden, the community displays signs of impending winter. Residents wave while pushing their snowplow poles into the sides of driveways and front yards, hoping to spare the grass. Piles of firewood wait to be stacked on more driveways than not, farmers prep greenhouses, and businesses adjust their signs to reflect winter hours.

Jackson mentioned Grandpa needing a new shovel, so before visiting, I pull into Raubuchon's, knowing full well Jackson and Lucas are the only ones who will be using this shovel. The last thing anyone needs is my grandfather going down in a snowbank. Between taking care of my grandmother and the fear of her being alone for a minute, Grandpa will have enough to keep him busy inside the house.

"I've been looking forward to a visit from a pretty lady like yourself this morning."

Gerry finishes bagging our town librarian's purchases and meets me halfway. "Have a great day, Carol."

"You bet, Gerry. Thank you. Will I see you at the potluck fundraiser?" She eyes me up and down. "Hello, Shannon. Lovely to see you. I saw Richard around these parts the other day. I heard he cleaned himself up. You might be regretting your quick decision." She winks and waits for a response from either of us. I shouldn't be surprised by anyone's nosiness at this point.

"I'll be there, Carol." Gerry attempts to guide her over to the exit. "Who else would call out the bingo numbers?"

Carol giggles and covers her mouth. Flirting doesn't end with age, apparently. No one can blame her. Next to my grandfather, Gerry is the sweetest man I've ever known. He's good-looking, even at almost eighty. I'm sure he was quite the hottie back in the day. He's also a damn hard worker. I've never seen him without dirty hands or sporting a pair of worn hiking boots, always working a job or helping a neighbor. One thing that rarely changes with age is eye color. Gerry's eyes are a shade of baby blue and exude the kindness reflective of the generosity in his heart.

Gerry succeeds at getting Carol out the door and then gives me a hug. His flannel jacket smells of pine and bonfire.

"Don't let that nosy bird upset you. You doing okay?"

"I wish nothing but the best for Richard. And my decision was anything but quick. Not everyone in this town is going to approve."

"You don't have to justify anything to me, dear. We don't get a do-over here. You deserve better."

"Thanks, Gerry." I pull him in for another hug, his unshaven face scratching my cheek.

"You bet. Now, let's get you a shovel." He starts past the registers and I follow, shaking my head. I shouldn't be surprised he knows what I need.

"Pick your fancy." Gerry steps back to display my two choices: red or blue. "We're almost out. *Farmers' Almanac* is calling for Mother Nature to dump lots of white powder this season."

"Blue it is."

Gerry grabs the handle. "Does Earl need anything else?"

"I'm sure I'll be back."

"It's on the house, hon." Gerry waves me off to the exit and stuffs his hands into the pockets of his farmer jeans. "I'm not sure Jackson let you in on the fact I drove over last year's shovel with my plow." He lets out a deep laugh and heads back to the end of cashier line number three to bag more purchases.

"Thanks, Gerry. I'll see you soon."

"Sure thing, kid."

My truck bumps along, the small potholes soon to be much larger after they're beaten by plows all winter.

Long gone are the summer days when my grandparents would rock on the front porch. The air is much too cool for them. Anything under sixty requires a sweater and fire. Their chairs sit empty. One of us should move them into the barn.

The chimes jingle in the breeze, and the leaves blanket the ground and crinkle under my boots.

I knock but don't wait, calling their names into the empty kitchen. Their matching blue coffee mugs and dirtied teaspoons sit on plaid placemats on the wooden snack bar. Creatures of habit.

"Hello! Yoo-hoo, anyone home?"

I barely hear Grandpa's voice from the bathroom. I walk down the tight, dark hallway and stand outside the slightly propped-open door, scared to look inside. I peek into their bedroom behind me and see it's empty.

"Are you both in there?"

"Who's yelling, Earl?" Now I'm certain they're both in the bathroom.

"No one's yelling, Syl. It's Shannon, she came to visit. Be right out, honey."

"Who?"

I stuff my hands into my pockets, unsure what to do next for the first time ever within these familiar walls. It's eerily quiet and uncomfortable. These walls and floors have seen more traffic than a freeway over the years. Before my parents moved to NY, Sunday gatherings were the norm. Dynamites in the Crock-Pot, someone playing the piano, and wine flowing.

Things have slowed, we have all aged, and the family dynamics have shifted, especially as of late with my grandmother's fall.

"Hold open the door please, Shannon."

I open the door and see my grandfather hunched over with his sleeves rolled up to his elbows and hands under Grandma's armpits. She looks so small in her maroon terry cloth bathrobe, brown moccasins, and wet hair dripping onto her shoulders.

"Come on, love. Let's get you to bed."

My grandmother lifts her head, eyes meeting mine. There's

uncertainty and fear filling the spaces where warmth once was. "Earl, who's in the doorway?"

"I told you, sweetie, that's Shannon."

"She needs to get out of here. This is my house." Her mouth wrinkles into a scowl, her eyes never leaving mine while Grandpa ushers her through the doorway and into the bedroom.

I'm speechless, tears beading at the corners of my eyes.

I wait a few minutes before looking into the room. Grandma is under the covers and Grandpa is tucking the blankets around her. Her back is toward me and Grandpa points to the hallway, motioning me to move away.

A few minutes later, he emerges from the bedroom and hoists himself onto the stool beside me at the wooden bar.

"It's eleven o'clock in the morning. What is she doing in bed?" I search his face for some understanding. Puffy bags rest under his eyes and stubble has grown in where he's usually freshly shaven.

"She hasn't been the same since she's been home, you know that. We knew it'd be an adjustment, that she'd be less mobile."

"The doctors said the memory loss would wear off. Post-op amnesia or something?"

"The doctors indicated memory loss might be temporary. The big word being *might*. I'm hoping the sleepless nights don't stick around. Last night was a tough one. The new hip was giving her a boat load of trouble. She was tossing and turning. I walked the hall for a bit and finally settled down after she fell back asleep."

"Oh, Grandpa. You do look tired." I rest my hand on his forearm. He places the opposite hand over mine, closing his eyelids. Seeing my grandfather struggle hurts.

"It's part of the job, my dear. There are good times and there are tough times. Your grandma and I have been blessed

—this farm, our kids, the grandkids. We have what people wish their whole lives for. When you say 'for better or worse,' this is what they mean. I'm happy to take care of her. She'd do the same."

The tears stream down my cheeks. His words hit a chord deep in my soul. I pull my arm away and use my sleeve to wipe my cheeks and rest my forehead in my hands.

"Well, that was awfully insensitive of me, sweetie. I was referring to your grandmother and me, not your situation. You're doing what you need to. Not every love was meant to last a lifetime." He pinches the bottom of my chin like he used to when I was little. It brings a smile to my lips.

"I know you didn't mean it that way, but it's hard. I didn't want a divorce. I don't think anybody does. I tried so hard, Grandpa. I really did. I wasn't a big enough reason for him to get sober. I don't know what else I could've done."

"It's a disease, not a matter of you not being enough. Any granddaughter of mine deserves happiness. You go on and enjoy your day." He rubs my back as if I'm the one who needs cheering up. He's ninety-two years old and caring for his wife, who is getting more forgetful by the day.

"How are you managing all this? It's too much."

"Don't you start on me." He leans across, grabs the metal tin of peanuts, and pops a few into his mouth. "The only way we are leaving this house is in body bags. Your grandmother and I decided that a long time ago. I met your parents halfway and agreed to have that busybody nurse come in a few hours a day for some feather dusting or whatever she does."

"She is doing more than dusting. I think she's taking care of all the medicine and appointments. I was told she helps Grandma with her stretches."

"Yeah, I suppose so."

I shake my head and laugh at his foolishness. "You have food for today?"

"Are you kidding me? Look in the refrigerator. If one more lady from church drops off a casserole, I'm going to have Lucas start selling them at the store."

He's at the fridge, pulling open the door to display the evidence. Sure enough, the foil containers outnumber the apples in the basket on the counter.

"Okay, fair. What else can I do?"

"Nothing. Go enjoy your day. We'll be fine. I've got half the town to call if I need anything. You aren't the first to visit today, and you won't be the last. I'll need a nap soon. I should probably do that now while your grandmother gets some shut-eye."

I stand and reach in for a hug. "Promise you'll call if you need me?"

"You betcha. Go on." He walks me to the door. I kiss his cheek, step onto the porch, and hear the lock click from the inside. Part of me wants to knock and stay, and the other half respects their privacy.

Once behind the wheel, I can't bring myself to put the truck in reverse. I look at the farmhouse, and sadness fills my heart. Things aren't the same and I hate it. I've never seen two people love each other more than my grandparents. Sure, they've been blessed. But that doesn't mean it's not difficult to watch them age. Tears flood my eyes and I'm not sure if I'm crying in admiration for their love or for the love I realize I've lost.

My love life is a high-wire act. The chance of me getting across in one piece is doubtful. I am hanging on by a thread, petrified to lose my balance and equally terrified to trust my safety gear.

I text Madison before leaving to see if she has time to meet up at the Brown Bean. I need a pep talk before I have dinner with Nick and his freaking family.

I spot her leaning over the window of a cruiser parked out

front of the coffee shop. I peer inside and see Nate. He waves, and Madison stands and walks to meet me. We slip into our usual table by the window.

"You look like hell." Madison wipes the side of her coffee with the napkin and nods at the streaked mascara under my eyes.

"It's been a day." I tell her about my grandparents, Librarian Carol's dig about Richard, and dinner with Nick.

"Okay, that's a lot of heavy shit for anyone, but listen. Number one—you, Jackson, and the rest of the town will look out for Earl and Sylvia. Didn't you mention your parents were coming back for another weekend soon?"

"They are." I squeak out with my straw in my mouth.

"That's good. As far as Richard, not your problem. You need to make peace with it. I know I'm as single as they come, but no regrets. Don't allow anyone to make you forget all the moments that finally helped you decide to put yourself first. You leaving may be the best thing that ever happens to him. You deserve more. And as far as Nick goes, you're not marrying the guy, so relax. I know this is new, but roll with it."

"I don't roll with anything."

"After what you told me a few weeks ago, it sounds like you did fine all on your own."

She's got me there.

"Enough about me. How's the condo search?"

"It's on hold. I can't find the right place. Oh, by the way, that Evan guy at the party was pretty cute in a dorky way. Mia seemed into him at the race, and Brynn was all over him at the party, and then Brooke. What's the story with that?"

I did notice Mia flirting with Evan, but I didn't think much of it. "Mia flirts with anything on two legs. She's said it herself. The poor guy probably didn't know what to do with himself. And Brynn and Brooke? Who knows. Evan did sleep at Nick's, so there's that."

Madison sips the last of her drink and tosses it into the garbage. "Is he sticking around?"

I grab my wallet and keys and follow her to the door. "I think he already left. Nick said it's his mom, sister, and brother at dinner tonight—no mention of Evan."

"Good. It'll keep your mind off Richard. Maybe you and Nick can have a little after-party."

I elbow her arm before we split to walk to our cars. "Why did you ask about Evan? Wait, are you into him?"

"Just curious. Talk to you later."

I know that smirk.

Meeting up with Madison puts me in the right state of mind to see Nick for dinner at Fire Hearth. Not many restaurants serve during all four seasons, but luckily, one of our best is always open. It's a perfect choice. My only hope is Nick's mom doesn't ask too many questions and that dinner goes quickly.

NICK

I'll swing by at six to pick you up. They're happy you are coming. I should warn you ... I don't usually bring women to dinner with my family.

I'll meet you there. I have an errand to do. Now you're making me nervous.

NICK

If you insist. See you there.

I don't have an errand to run, but having a getaway car in case I need to leave an awkward situation seems smart.

Deciding what to wear is a nightmare. I haven't gone shopping for "going-out" clothes in a long time. Everything in my closet is teacher wear. I settle on black tights, short brown booties, and a loose beige crocheted sweater with a tight white tank underneath. It's sexy but not over the top, perfect for a family dinner. And I stopped at the Tilton outlets for new underwear, so no more granny panties. Hair is staying down, and simple stud earrings and a silver necklace complete the look.

Gary is at the host station per usual. "Looks like there's a new crew waiting for you in the tavern area."

"Thanks, Gary."

I'm unwilling to dish any details despite his pleading eyes. The whole town will know my plans tonight in about five minutes, so I'll enjoy the short-lived privacy.

Nick's eyes meet mine across the room. His family is sitting toward the back next to the roaring hearth that warms the place, despite the cool breeze outside. I have to pick my jaw off the ground when Nick stands as I approach the table. I'm not upset that he stands out among the flannels and jeans in the room.

His dark brown khakis, brown belt, and his perfectly tailored white button-down tucked in fits just right. The outlined bulge between his legs is not lost on me. He extends his arm and reaches for my hand, and the shine off his watch catches my attention. I have to pull my eyes away from his chest and bury the thought of tracing his tattoos to smile at his mother.

"Hi, you must be Claire. I'm Shannon." I reach across to shake her hand, careful not to burn my sweater sleeve on the candle centerpiece.

Claire stands and leans in for a hug instead. She's a beautiful woman—petite, with short white hair and blue eyes. Right away, I can tell where Nick gets his style. She's dressed in a white cashmere sweater and dark slacks, and a hefty diamond dangles from a silver chain around her neck.

"Okay, Mom. Let her breathe. Nice to see you again, Shannon."

"Hi, Ashlyn. Brett.

This family looks like a cutout of a J.Crew catalog. They are beautiful and dressed to the nines. If Ashlyn were taller, she could no doubt command a catwalk. Her chestnut-brown hair and flawless skin are breathtaking. And Brett, while he doesn't meet Nick's swagger, is certainly easy on the eyes.

Both siblings embrace me and settle back around the table. The waitress arrives, taking our drink and appetizer order. Claire orders a few for the table without consulting anyone, but I'll eat anything.

"So, Shannon. It's a rare event that Nicholas brings a woman to dinner. You must be special. How is a catch like you still single?" Claire sips her water without moving her eyes from mine.

Nick's palm is on my thigh, moving in small circular motions. I gulp my nerves down and remind myself I have nothing to be embarrassed about. "Well, that's a great question. I'm not sure I have a clear answer for you. What I do know is Nick picked a perfect lake to buy a vacation home. What do you think of Newfound?"

I breathe a sigh a relief and will my pulse to slow as my change of subject is successful and the conversation immediately shifts to small-town antics and Ashlyn's distaste for the wilderness.

"I don't know how you do it, Shannon. Where the hell does a girl shop? The local country store can't be enough." Ashlyn pops a stuffed mushroom into her mouth, signaling the waitress for another glass of wine.

Brett has been relatively quiet, but laughs at Ashlyn's statement. "Do you realize how ridiculous you sound? We are from Massachusetts, not Mars. You're a teacher, right? What grade?"

I appreciate Brett's effort to shield me from explaining my shopping habits, or lack thereof. The conversation flows between school, business, and the orchard. My love life never comes into question again. Dinner moves along without my stomach tangling into nervous knots. Nick's hand never leaves my leg unless he needs to cut his food.

"Do you need another drink?" he asks.

"No, I'm all set." I push my chair back and excuse myself to the restroom.

I freshen up and swing open the main bathroom door to find Nick waiting in the hallway. "Is this as awful for you as it is for me?" He pushes off the wall and leans onto his side, one hand in his pocket, one hand rubbing the stubble along his jawline, and eyes me from head to toe.

"Awful?" I copy his stance against the wall beside him and put my hand on his chest. "I think things are going well."

He moves close and cups each side of my head. In a low growl just inches from my lips, he says, "I'm happy you're here, but I'd rather have you all to myself. I can't stop thinking about the other night."

His mouth is close enough to kiss. I breathe in the scent of him. I would be lying if I said I hadn't replayed that night in my mind over and over again.

"Say you'll come home with me tonight. Please, Shannon," he purrs in my ear.

His intense stare and focus break me. Words leave my mouth before I process what is coming out. "Yes." Three letters stating everything I want while also rationalizing how crazy this is.

"Good." He presses his lips to mine, and suddenly I'm in a flood zone. How the hell am I supposed to go back to the table now?

Nick holds my hand and walks me back to the table. I notice a few people smile and nod in our direction. Ninety percent of the people in this restaurant know me and my entire family tree. I simply smile back. What else can I do?

We return to the table seemingly unnoticed by his family, who are debating the holiday schedule and annual Christmas cards. Nick's hand doesn't leave my thigh, sending warmth everywhere. The rest of the night goes smoothly. Their family dynamic is drastically different from my own. They are honest, blunt, and quite funny.

"What do you think about Nick winning that photo contest?" Claire asks after insisting on paying the bill, despite Nick's attempt to take it from her.

The hand on my thigh freezes, and the motion in the room seems to slow. I look at Nick and search his face for understanding. I recognize the look in Nick's eyes. I instantly know a secret has been released.

"I thought we weren't discussing this, Mother?"

"Relax, Nick. She left the paper on the counter. We saw it."

I watch Nick take a deep breath and hold it. His fingers grip my thigh.

"It's awesome, very cool. I'm proud of him." I reach for Nick's hand and squeeze.

"That's what I thought. There's no sense in wasting talent. He's always Mr. Businessman, but if he insists on spending time up here, might as well do something he enjoys. I'm not sure why you need to advertise your name in a local paper and all, but that's neither here nor there." Claire reaches for her coat on the back of her chair.

"Leave him be, Mom. The guy works like a dog. Let him enjoy a few days on the lake." Brett rolls his eyes when Claire's back is turned.

"I hope you at least got a cash prize." Ashlyn flips her hair behind her shoulder and finishes the wine in her glass. "We need to hit the road, Mom. Brett, you ready?" She is already walking away.

Nick looks at me, hesitates, and smiles slightly. My mind reels. I'm thinking back to the camera at the race, and the one I spotted on the bookcase in his house. I'm intrigued. This man has more up his sleeve than tattoos.

Ashlyn paces in front of the large window near the exit, eyeing the parking lot. Brett and Claire look at the Homestead-sponsored soccer team pictures on the wall. Dinner was great, but I'm ready to get to the bottom of this story.

"When will you be back?" Claire and Brett turn toward me. Ashlyn can't be bothered.

His mom looks at Nick. "Whenever my son lets us know his schedule. He's not a man with a lot of free time, but I certainly hope to see that change. Work gets busy this time of year, right? I'm not sure how often he will be here, never mind all of us, but I sure would like to be."

"Brett, start the car. It's freezing." Ashlyn is out the door, leaving nothing but the chilled breeze in her wake.

"I am thrilled you met us for dinner, Shannon." Claire pulls her coat closed and slides her gloves on.

I think I like her. Despite the money and a daughter who needs to rough it a little in life, Claire is down-to-earth.

Nick hugs his mother and brother goodbye, and we watch through the tavern windows as they get into the black Cadillac. He then wraps his arms around my waist from behind. "I have some explaining to do."

I wiggle his arms loose enough to turn and look him square in the eye. The dim overhead lights cast a glow on his strong jaw, making it difficult to focus. He squeezes me tight and dips his head lower, resting his forehead against mine.

"A photo contest, huh?"

He takes a deep breath and releases it slowly, closing his eyes. "Yeah, I know it's weird."

"I don't think it's weird. I'm surprised, is all."

"I've loved photography since I was little. My first camera was a film camera—I burned through rolls and then would beg my parents to get my pictures developed. It drove them crazy. For the longest time, I thought it was what I wanted to do when I grew up."

"What changed?" As soon as the words leave my mouth, I want to stuff them back in. He's told me about his father.

"Life had other plans for me when my father died. My photography dreams were buried with him. Deep down, part of me bought the lake house knowing how beautiful pictures could be here. I spotted the contest in *The Laker* and figured, what the hell? I never thought I'd win."

Reaching up, I kiss his cheek. This is the most vulnerable I've seen him. "What was your prize?"

"A crocheted blanket from some woman called Mae."

Thankfully, Nick is holding me in his arms. Otherwise, I would fall over from the hysterics.

"What are you laughing at? I'm sure it'll be a very warm blanket." Nick joins my laughter. That's as New Hampshire as you get.

"Come on, let's get out of here." Nick slips his Burberry coat around his broad shoulders, grabs my hand, and we walk into the cloudless night, stars shining above. You'd think it was midnight, but it's only seven. This time of year, you need to enjoy the sun when you can because it sets early.

"I forgot—we came in separate cars." My phone vibrates in my pocket. It's Solia, letting me know the whole crew is together. "How does a drink at the Binn sound? Everyone is there."

Nick opens my driver's side door. "Sure, but only if you'll come home with me after." The devilish look in his eyes makes it impossible to say no.

Hooking up with Nick on a school night! What is my life

coming to? I'm acting like Mia. Wild! "I have school in the morning."

"I have work." Nick grins and knows he's made a solid point. "I'll leave and drive to Boston in the morning, and you can drive home five minutes and then go to school. Deal?"

How can I turn him down? Nick has pushed me into my *yes* era. "Okay, you've got a deal. Meet you at the Binn."

Driving along the twisty, dark mountain roads, I'm a stranger in my own skin. My life is predictable and uneventful. I never want or need anything more. Until Nick. Nick is a drastic change of pace, one I didn't realize I desperately desired. I can't get ahead of myself.

The parking lot is half full. We find parking side by side. I spot Jackson's truck, along with Tyler's, Ryan's, and Jay's. I even see Brooke's and Madison's.

"Heyyyyyy," their voices ring in unison from the high top as we enter. Brooke runs over and jumps into a hug as if I didn't see her forty-eight hours ago. Madison smiles, winks, and nods toward Nick.

Nick is more relaxed this time. He stands by my side, squared shoulders and hands in his pockets. The girls say hello and Cindy is over with two ciders. "On the house," she says with a wink.

"Talk about service. Thanks, Cindy."

"My pleasure, my pleasure. It's not every night I get the whole gang here on a Sunday."

"What are you talking about, lady? We are here more nights than not. You must be sick of our asses!" Tyler jokes and then turns to Nick. "What's up, man?" His bro hug breaks the tension of me bringing the "outsider" into our space again.

"Not much. How's it going?" Nick grabs the cider and takes a hearty drink.

"Just another night in paradise, buddy. Pull up a stool. Where are you guys coming from?"

"Didn't you hear? They went to dinner with Nick's family. So exciting! How'd it go? Was it awkward? How was the food?"

Madison drops her forehead into her hand because once again, Brooke has made things awkward as hell. She can't keep her mouth shut. Nick looks at me wearing a sly smile. Thankfully, all the guys ignored her and continued talking. Apparently, Sunday Night Football is more interesting than our date, thank god.

"Everything was great, Brooke."

"Oh man, I shouldn't have said anything. Shoot, foot in mouth. You know me! Sorry." Her lips crinkle in concern. She turns her attention to Madison and rattles on about something else.

I put my hand on her shoulder, knowing how sensitive she is. Brooke wouldn't hurt a fly, but she'd probably start a conversation with one. "It's all good. It went well. So well that after this, I'm heading back to his place."

She clamps her hand over her mouth and squeals in delight. Madison doubles over watching her reaction. "I won't say a word. Lips are sealed." She pretends to zip her lips shut and lock the key. She signals toward the bathroom and bounces away.

"She is insane. Super funny, but don't ever tell her something you don't want the whole town to know," Madison says out of earshot of Brooke and then lifts her chin toward Nick, who is in a deep football discussion. I'm thankful he found common ground with the guys.

"Nothing is a secret around here." I lift my drink and clink it against hers. The background country music is barely audible above the roar of the game and the bar full of men cheering on their favorite team.

"How's my big sister doing?" Jackson shifts to my side and hip-checks me into the high top.

I toss my hip back but it doesn't move him an inch. "All good, Jackson. How're the newlyweds?"

Jackson smiles ear to ear and repositions his hat. "Nothing but excitement over here. We started talking about our living situation, but we've got plenty of time. Speaking of living, how's his new crib?" He edges his chin at Nick, still engrossed in conversation.

"Nice doesn't do it justice. Gorgeous is more like it. The view is to die for, seriously. I'm obsessed."

"Take it easy. Don't go getting obsessed. Remember how he got here."

Jackson's statement earns an eye roll from me. I don't expect people to forget the wind turbine saga, but I'd love not to hear about it for one night. Jackson would kill me if he knew half of how far my interaction with Nick has progressed.

In an attempt to change the subject, I turn my attention to the crew huddled around.

"Dude, you got it bad. Already!" Tyler slaps Nick on the back. Nick looks at me and smiles.

"What does Mr. Ford have bad?" I snuggle into his chest.

"Your man seems to think New Hampshire is for him. I'm not sure if it's the lake or who he might be swimming in it with, but this part of the woods is a far cry from the city."

"Hey, hey. Just because I'm from the city, you shouldn't underestimate my manliness. I might surprise you boys." Nick puffs out his chest and puts his arm around me.

"Do you hear that, gentlemen? City boy thinks he's got what it takes. Remember, we did witness your hammering skills. Just saying. Do we invite him and see what he's made of?" Jay smirks and elbows Ryan.

I roll my head into Nick's chest, shielding my eyes because there's no stopping this train from arriving in the station.

"I think so." Jackson nods and takes a drink of his cider. Solia smiles at him from across the table.

"What's going on here?" Lucas rounds the corner, closing the door to the back of the bar. Odd.

"We were about to tell our buddy Nick that he should join us next weekend." Tyler rolls his lips inward, wide-eyed. Lucas whips his head and squints toward me.

"Yeah, yeah. Sure, great idea," Jackson shouts across the table to Tyler and folds his arms over his chest.

I fill my cheeks with air and grab an empty stool to get comfortable. This is going to be interesting.

Tyler clears his throat, demanding the attention of the group. He holds his pint as if he's at the podium addressing a crowd. "Well, Nick, in an attempt to celebrate the change of seasons, we Newfound boys have an unofficial 'First Frosty Freeze' event on the shores of the lake. Despite winter officially starting in December, the frost and sometimes snow arrives much earlier. A bunch of us put up tents and camp on the shore. We have a fire and shoot the shit. You in?" Tyler's stare at Nick holds strong.

Solia pipes up. "Ty, give him the whole story. We all do it, but the guys take it to the next level. They have these ridiculous man challenges. I can't remember half of them, but there's log splitting and don't forget the morning swim."

And that's when Nick breaks his confident posture. "Swim? That water has got to be fifty degrees by now."

Tyler laughs. "See, I knew it'd be too much."

"Hell, no. I'm not saying it's too much. Muscles aren't only grown lakeside, boys. I can handle myself anywhere you put me. I'm in." Nick asks me if I want another cider and heads over to the bar, leaving the men speechless.

I watch him lean on the counter, waiting his turn to order. Confidence is sexy as hell. Nick is turning me into a sex-crazed kitten. *Yes, please.*

Cindy walks through the door behind the bar, and she and Nick start chatting. I wonder if she's asking about Harold.

The men are high-fiving and seem to be looking forward to the Frosty Freeze. I'd be lying if I wasn't excited to spend the night huddled in a tent next to Nick. Body heat is always the answer.

A couple hours tick by. The men have stopped measuring their manliness, and the conversation has moved back to football.

"You want to get out of here? It's getting late," I whisper in Nick's ear. He turns and puts his arms around my waist.

"Hell yes." A devilish look overtakes his face as he slides his coat off the chair.

"We should get going too." Jackson nods at Solia whose eyelids are already beginning to droop.

"Yes, we could stay all night, but Monday morning calls. I'll go settle the tab."

"I got it this time, on me. See you later, guys." Lucas pulls out his wallet and walks to the bar.

The night air sends a chill through my body. It will forever surprise me how quickly the seasons change around here. One minute we are swimming and boating, the next we are lighting the fire and stocking up on hand warmers. A half-moon lights up the parking lot, a few clouds skimming across the sky. The only lights are the lantern Cindy will soon turn out and the homes in the mountains.

Nick pulls me into his waist, and I relax into him. I no longer care where this relationship is going—I want to live in the moment. For once in my life, I'm more concerned about getting reckless between the sheets than I am about cleaning up someone else's mess.

Keys jingle in the air and doors slam shut as our group disperses. Nick waits for me to open my door and slide in, his eyes fixed on my every move. I've never had someone look at me with such intent.

I let out a gut-wrenching scream when I realize someone is

sleeping in the passenger's side of my truck. I fling myself through the driver's door, crashing into Nick, sending a wave of panic across the parking lot. Nick whips me behind him and ducks to see what the hell is in my car.

Richard.

My brain registered it's him, but my muscles reacted first.

"Baby, I didn't mean to scare you." Richard unlatches the truck door, kicks it open, and crawls out. He's hanging onto the side for balance, eyes crusted over and bloodshot.

I peek out behind Nick. He puts his arm across my chest, shielding me. Jackson, his crew, and everyone else with us tonight catch on.

"What the fuck are you doing, man?" Jackson steps in front of Nick and faces Richard head-on.

Related through marriage, there are strong ties between the two, but they've been weakened because of Richard's alcohol abuse. He leans into the truck, slides along it to the back, and sits on the bumper. His hair is in knots and desperately in need of a cut. He looks like he hasn't slept in days, and something resembling dried puke coats the front of his flannel.

"Listen. This don't concern anyone but me and my wife. You all can get in your trucks and get the fuck out."

"We aren't going anywhere." Nick's face is stone cold, and he takes a step forward in line with Jackson.

"Oh, no you don't." I reach out my arm, grabbing hold of his shirt. "This will not be a repeat performance."

Richard squints and he edges to the end of the tailgate, the knees of his jeans dirt-stained. His shirt is only half tucked in. He leans forward and stumbles.

"Man, you're drunk. How did you get here?" Tyler surveys the parking lot, pointing at Richard's bike propped against the dumpster. "Unfuckingbelievable. Did rehab not teach you anything?

"Fuck off, dude. Come on, Shannon, baby, listen. Things

are better now. Look, I'm here, you're here, it'll be like old times. You don't need this creep and all his money. You know I have what you need. I came to talk. Your truck was warmer than the bike. I fell asleep. But I'm up now." Richard throws his head back and howls into the night, slamming his head against the back of the truck. The impact sends him ass down on the dirt lot. "Shit, man."

It is as though the light of a million stars shines upon me. My choice is as clear as day.

Things are never going to get better. I've made the right choice. He's sick and I can't fix him.

"Richard, we are over. We are fucking over. Do you hear me? Stop. Get the fuck out. I'm not doing this. You can't do this to me anymore." I'm not sure where the strength comes from, but every word comes screaming out of my mouth. I've never had stronger feelings than I do right now.

"Actually, I can. This prick isn't going to walk into this town and think he's going to get to fuck my wife and steal you out from under me."

My blood boils. I restrain myself from hauling out and punching him in the face. "I am not your wife. You don't own me. We are through."

Richard shoves his hand down his pants and scratches, making me want to heave every piece of food I ate earlier at his feet. "This is the only dick for you, baby. Come on, you know it."

Before he's able to utter another vile comment, cruiser lights speed around the corner into the parking lot. "Looks like your jig is up, man." Lucas extends his arm.

"Seriously! What the hell? I'm not bothering no one. I came to get my wife." His words are slippery and slurred.

"I am not your wife." The words fall out of my mouth like rain, splattering and disappearing into the dirt. "It's over."

"Honey, I signed, but we have time to change our minds. You know you made a mistake."

All I can do is shake my head and let the tears soak into the dirt with my words. "No one will be changing their minds. Let's get out of here, Nick."

I surprise myself and hold Nick's hand, hoping my strength will carry me into his car and away from this life of unrelenting hurt. Nick squeezes my hand and hesitates to look at Jackson.

"You got this, man?"

"Yeah, get her out of here." Jackson motions to Nick's truck and turns back to deal with Richard, who has moved away from the officer and onto his bike.

Within seconds, Richard's bike revs, reverses into the lot, and peels out. Nate talks into the radio mic fastened at his shoulder. "Fifteen to dispatch, white male suspect leaving the Binn lot on cycle, intoxicated, heading east on Lake Road."

"Copy, officer en route. Ten-four."

"He's letting him go?" Solia's voice booms over the rumble of the motorcycle.

Throughout my years of dealing with Richard's drunk ass, I learned unless a drunk driver is actively driving, they can't be charged. I'm sure this is what Nate was waiting for. Richard's lucky he hasn't killed anyone in his path over the years, including himself. People from town have reported him over and over, but somehow nothing ever sticks. Nobody wants to see someone they love arrested and thrown in jail, but deep down, I know this is what has to happen.

Officer Nate slams his cruiser door shut. I assume he's heading to the scene I will actively avoid.

"Are you okay?" Nick folds me into his arms. The heat from his body removes the chill.

"I will be," I whisper.

# 16

Nick

For a guy who's supposedly out of the picture, Richard has managed to ruin just about every night I've had with Shannon so far. He's probably the biggest douchebag I've ever met and deserves to have his teeth knocked out for the way he speaks to Shannon. I don't chase women, nor do I have time to deal with fuckups, but Shannon has a grip on me I've not experienced before.

Jackson stares at me from across the lot, nodding toward our vehicles. I need to get Shannon out of here.

"Let's go, okay? Do you want to leave your truck here? I can bring you by in the morning."

"I'll drive to your house. I'm okay." She dries her eyes on her sleeve and backs out of my arms.

"Are you sure?"

"One hundred percent. Honestly, this is the best thing that could've happened. A small part of me hoped that maybe he'd clean up and change. But even with everything, he's right back where he started. If this isn't a sign I'm doing the right thing, I don't know what else can be. I want to get out of here."

Shannon walks over to Jackson, they exchange a few words,

and then she slowly pulls herself into her truck. I'm not sure I'll ever get her scream out of my head.

~

It's like a switch has flipped. We haven't even made it off the walkway to the backyard and she's got her hand in my ass pocket. Her eyes tell me she's not interested in behaving. I tried talking to her about the way Richard speaks to her, and she wouldn't have it. She seems to have grown a tougher skin as a result of the encounter.

Instead of throwing her over my shoulder and tossing her on my bed, I choose this moment to put a woman's mindset before mine. I'm not convinced she's thinking clearly after everything that transpired.

I pull her hand out of my back pocket and spin her around. Her jacket is unzipped, and her body reacts to the cold breeze rushing across the lake. I loom over her and place a hand on each hip. I lean in and nibble her earlobe. She shivers in the dark. "I want you tonight. But …"

"But?" She looks up with worry.

"Tonight was a little nuts. I don't know how you could be thinking straight."

"What are you saying?" She folds her arms into her body and walks across the back lawn to the dock I have yet to pull from the lake for the winter. The solar lantern glows faintly due to the changing of seasons. She's standing at the edge, crossed arms resting against her chest. I sit in the Adirondack chair and watch her back widen with every deep breath.

"Listen, if you asked me a few months ago if I wanted a relationship, hands down, the answer would've been no. Watching you go through what this guy is putting you through has me wanting to protect you." I clear my throat and find the words working their way to the surface. "I care about you. This is probably a normal circumstance for most people, but I don't get deep with women. Let me rephrase that. I am all about getting deep, but you are taking up some serious headspace."

She looks at me with tears in her eyes. The wind picks up; leaves rustle and blow off the trees. The water laps onto the rocks in the distance. Other than the sounds of autumn, there is silence, and for once, I welcome it.

"I want you. Don't think for a second that I don't. Believe me when I say this is the first time I'm trying to think about emotions other than my own. Come on, you're freezing. Let's get inside."

She doesn't budge. "Is this where you took the photo? The one for the contest?"

I follow her gaze toward the silhouette of the mountain ranges in the distance. "You were right. Everyone was right. This place would've been destroyed by the turbines."

The words are in the air before I process them.

She wipes her eyes without saying a word and turns to walk across the lawn to the deck. I follow close behind and stare at her ass while we climb the stairs, and I'm not even thinking about slapping it or ripping off her pants. I'm not sure what's going on, but I want her in my arms, safe and protected from the outside world.

I slide the glass door shut and ignite the fire, welcoming the wave of heat.

"I'll be right back. I need to use the restroom."

I take this opportunity to grab glasses of water and put them on the table by the couch facing the fire. The room has about five different blankets to choose from. I gather and toss them along the side of the huge sectional. The room is warming, enough to remove my hooded sweatshirt.

I'm not sure how to play this evening. The fact that I'm even thinking ahead is foreign. She's not simply a beautiful woman I want to sleep with. She met my family. She's tough, not fragile. She's sweet, but strong. She makes me second-guess what's going on in my head and my pants.

Flipping through my phone, I choose Bruno Mars to play in the background. I don't even know what kind of music she prefers; I need to ask. I rest my head on the back cushion and cross my feet on the table. This house is fucking nice. The penthouse in Boston is high end, but there's peace here, solitude, knowing it's just us and whatever animals roam the woods.

Shannon's feet grace the hardwood floor. I lift my head toward the hallway. She appears before me wearing nothing but a mischievous smile. *Holy fuck.* Go figure, the first time I'm ready to restrain myself, she walks in bare-ass naked. There's only one part of my body that reacts to the scene in front of me. I am frozen in shock, waiting for her next move.

"Are you going to sit and stare?" She leans against the wall by the fire, loose hair covering her shoulders, and crosses her ankles. My eyes roam her entire body, not sure where I want to start. Her perfect, full breasts, nipples pebbled and ready. The trail between them leading down to her stomach and between her thighs.

My legs spring to life, and I lean over her, pressing my arms against the wall above her.

"I was not expecting this. You are fucking gorgeous."

"I don't do these things, Nick. I don't go to a guy's house, take off my clothes, and ask him to do things to me that will blow my mind. My life is predictable, uneventful, and usually clothed." She giggles at her honesty, somehow making her more adorable.

"If it's any consolation, this is not my life either. My life is unemotional, cutthroat, and I'm usually the one avoiding anything other than a one-night stand."

"What I'm hearing you say is…" She reaches up, slides her

fingertips against my chest, and wraps her arms around my neck. "You want me for more than one night?"

Her chest is firm, poking through my T-shirt. "That's exactly what I'm saying. I don't do feelings, but you have me very confused." I slide my hands under her arms and skim my fingers over her shoulder blades, caress her soft, smooth skin, trail her back, and land on her firm behind. She's putty in my hands. I grip her ass and lift her off the ground and around my waist. The warmth between her legs soaks through my T-shirt, telling me she's ready.

I back her up and sit on the couch with her arms locked behind my neck. I reach for a blanket and wrap the red fleece around her back the best I can. She's Little Red Riding Hood, naked on my lap.

"I think deep down, you are a softie," she whispers in my ear.

This sounds like a challenge. I reach for her hands, pull them apart, and bend them behind her back, creating a space between us and leaving her chest on full display. The fact that I'm able to restrain myself is award worthy.

"I'm definitely not a softie. I am as hard for you as they come." I take a deep breath and play the next words in my head on repeat a few times to make sure I want them heard. She waits patiently, hunger in her eyes. "I want more from you than sex." That sounds fucking ridiculous.

She throws her head back in a fit of laughter and arches, the fire illuminating the front of her body. Her hair slides back and covers her breasts when she returns to me. "City boy, I think this is new for both of us. And for once in my life, I've never been more certain I'm right where I should be. So"—she dips her fingertips below my waistline—"if you'd do me a favor and save the gushy stuff for another time, I want you to show me how much you want me."

*This is not the Shannon I expected tonight, but who am I to deny a woman's needs? Game on.*

Not another second is wasted. I slide my hands behind and underneath and pull her forward. Her body leaves my hands wet. She pushes her mouth on mine, and we go from zero to a hundred. I toss her onto the couch in a fit of giggles as she bounces on the cushions. I waste no time getting my clothes off. She surprises me yet again, moving to the end of the couch, spreading her legs wide and grabbing hold of my readiness. She tempts me forward, closer to the couch, and uses her tongue in ways that force me to lift one foot onto the cushion to maintain balance.

*Holy shit. She wasn't kidding.*

Before I embarrass myself and let her finish me off, I show her how much I want her. I grab the back of her hair and pull myself out of her mouth. Her lips spread wide with surprise and a dare to show her what's next. I toss a sea of blankets onto the floor in front of the fireplace. "I want you down there, hands and knees."

Her smile lifts, telling me everything I need to know. I sit back on the couch and watch her follow my directions. She's got a wild side she didn't realize she had, and I am here for it. Never mind the fact she has no idea how smoking hot she is.

I sit back and admire her from behind. She listened to my request, her knees and palms on the blanket. The fire lights up all the right spots. Her breasts dangle and the firmness of her ass has me reeling. I make her wait for a minute, and she is patient. She arches her back, tipping her ass up, and flicks her head with what I hope is anticipation. "Are you going to sit and stare?"

"I'm admiring the view."

"Is that all you plan on doing?"

*Oh, baby, no, no I don't.* I crawl onto the floor and push the coffee table off to the left, allowing for more space. Who am I to deny her? I reach for my pants, grab the wrapper out of my pocket, slide on the condom, and toss the empty foil aside.

I approach her from behind, crawling on all fours, like a tiger on the prowl. Her ass twitches in surprise when my tongue makes certain she's ready. Her soft moaning and arched back have my dick throbbing. I want her to say my name just once.

I flick her bundle of nerves with the tip of my tongue, listening to her body, letting it guide me. I hit the right angle and speed, and she's sliding against my face and then, bingo! I hear it.

The way my name rolls off her tongue with need is what I wanted. I crawl back and she shudders from the absence of my warm mouth.

"Nick?"

I can't get enough of her vulnerability.

"Nick?"

"I'm here."

Her ass gently bobs, her wetness glistening between her legs. I kneel behind her, my thighs against her, just centimeters from her opening. I grab hold of her hips, sending her head down to the blanket, hair sprawled out in a fan in front of the flames. She moans softly, her thighs tight and ass pitched upward. I gently tap her opening with my tip.

"You're teasing me," she groans into the blanket.

"You want me to stop?" I freeze behind her, holding steady, and leave her exposed.

"No. No. No."

My hands haven't left her hips. She strains against my grip, trying to inch herself closer to my cock. She almost succeeds. I have no doubt she's ready.

I slide into her, teasing her, pushing against her tightness, guiding her closer with my hands on the small of her back.

With every inch, she arches her back, opening up wider. "Let yourself go."

I'm done. I can't. I push myself in, and she moans in response. She's tight and perfect. I listen to her body and ride in rhythm to her moans. I take a fistful of her hair and wrap it around my hand and tug. If she wants more, I give her more. I can go all night if she wants. I want her begging.

With one hand on her hip and her head tilted to the ceiling, I have her at the angle I want. I hit that sweet spot and push as deep as I can go. Her body reacts, her knees sinking into the blanket. She's dripping with desire.

I release her hair, and she slides her elbows down and rests her forehead on the floor to steady herself. Her jet-black strands fan out on the white blanket, her breasts pressed firmly to the soft fabric. I grab hold of her hips and lift one knee off the floor to get as deep as I can.

In a matter of minutes, I have her right where I need her. Her back and my chest glisten with sweat. The mouth on her surprises me. Hearing "Nick, harder" sends me into overdrive. I don't stop until I know she's shuddering in release, but I'm not done with her. I pull out and lower her body to the floor.

"Holy shit. That … That was amazing. I don't think …" She lifts her head up, resting on her elbows, and wipes a little drool off the side of her mouth. "Can I have that glass of water?"

Her wish is my command. I'm still fully erect and ready. I deliver the water, taking mine and gulping it down. She drinks, rests onto her back, and releases a small exhale.

"I'm not done with you. That was round one."

Her smirk is all I need.

The next couple hours, she is game for everything. I never thought this country girl had it in her, but she's surprising me —and maybe herself.

I almost take her temperature when she suggests the back

deck. It's November. Apparently not getting my cock inside her by the dock last time has her wanting more outside action.

I won't say no to this woman. We are drenched in sticky sweat. She opens the door and heads right out onto the deck. Never have I ever had sex outside. That doesn't happen in Boston, at least not to me. The only privacy is in an actual bedroom. Here in Meriden, everything is spread out, secluded. I'm eager to add our mating call to the wilderness surrounding us. Even with the majority of the fall foliage on the ground, I can't see a house through the darkness. I turn on the propane firepit.

I thought she'd had enough, but she's raring to go. I'm pretty certain I banged every negative thought, emotion, and fear right out of her and left her with nothing but satisfaction. I take her into my arms, run my tongue on her upper lip, and whisper in her ear, "I want to eat you alive."

Her body relaxes in my arms and I know what I want to do. I continue to kiss her and lead her to the deck railing. I spin her around and tell her to grab hold. I kneel behind her and make sure she's ready for the next round. When I'm satisfied, I don't provide any warning, just grab her ass, slam into her, and cause her to yell out into the night air. I'm in as deep as I can. She throws her head up toward the night sky and when she starts yelling my name, I don't hold back. I go until she falls completely silent and limp on the deck railing, convincing me I've satisfied her fully.

I leave her there and shut off the fire, allowing the darkness to fall onto us. I reach behind her and feel the goose bumps forming. I scoop her into my arms and kick open the screen door. She's slippery with sweat and satisfaction.

"Are you okay, Shan?"

She rolls her head against my chest. "I'm more than okay." She smiles and tucks her naked body against me. I walk up to my bedroom and place her on my bed. Within minutes, the night fades away, and for the first time, I pull a woman closer to me under the covers.

⁓

I forgot to shut the blinds last night, so the morning glow wakes me. I slip the remote off my nightstand and press the button to close out the light. Shannon is wrapped in the covers. I slide out from under the blankets without disturbing her. The only time I've had a woman spend the whole night was when I was too drunk to call her a ride.

As the coffee brews, I grab my camera and jacket. Other than the percolating pot, the house is silent. I pour a cup and slip outside to the dock, thankful for each wooden plank.

So much of my day-to-day is go, go, *go*. I thought I had my life and career planned out. I'm good at my job, and lord knows I make enough money. The absence of chaos in this town, in my new house, makes me realize how much I'm missing in my life. I want whatever it is I'm feeling right now. I want the silence, the mug of coffee by the lake, and the same woman in my bed. I want to know that someone thinks of me for reasons other than closing a deal or making a buck.

The steam from the coffee drifts over my eyes and visions of last night's steamy sexcapades filter back. The mountain peaks in the distance begin to lighten under the rising sun. The desire for more in my life has never been stronger. I want more than the money. More than the women who throw themselves at me. I want more nights like last night.

I wonder what my dad would think. He'd probably tell me to shut the fuck up and be a man, to run the business and enjoy the money. But what good is money if I have no time to enjoy it? I've made more money than I'd need in a lifetime, but I'm sitting in a high-rise with other people finding my dates for me. It's fucking pathetic.

I pull my phone from my pocket and text my assistant:

I'm going to be late today.

She takes a few moments to respond. I've never sent such a message. After reassuring her no one has abducted me and stolen my phone, she is convinced and lets it be.

I relax into the chair and tip my head back, breathing in the frosty air. The smell of the lake and morning chill hits different up here. It's pure and clean and has me breathing more intentionally.

After a while, the sun rising behind me casts a soft glow onto the water. I'm in awe of nature's display. Sure, artists can try, but nothing is as beautiful as seeing this firsthand. Each minute a new layer of the mountain lights on fire and shows off the brilliant shades of color hanging onto the forest. The air is still and a mild frost clings to the grass and surrounding trees.

I sit at the edge of the seat and snap away. With every click, my heart swells with emotion. I've tucked this passion inside, forgetting the stronghold it once had. The angles, the light, and the beauty take my breath away.

Growing up in and around Boston, I've always had more city-based opportunities. Although each time we went anywhere, my camera was with me so I could seek out nature's beauty hidden among the concrete. People said I had raw talent. I was never quite sure of the truth in their words. I don't think I believed a word of it until I won that silly contest. If I'm being honest with myself, I think about taking pictures more than my upcoming meetings.

I kneel on the last plank to capture an angle. I don't hear her approach. Her leg grazes the side of my arm.

"Hey there." I drape the camera strap around my neck and stand. She's holding two mugs of coffee. I take the one she offers; my first cup sits empty on the dock. Her standing beside me wearing my hoodie and sweatpants, the lake and mountains as the backdrop, is breathtaking.

She follows my eyes and smiles. "I hope you don't mind. I borrowed a few things from your drawer."

Not many things surprise me anymore, but the sight of this gorgeous woman standing here with her bedhead and in my clothes has me more excited than heels and a short skirt ever could. I don't think I've given a piece of my clothing to a woman since the ninth grade. And I'm even more excited by this now than I was then. I guess we change, but parts of us remain as vulnerable as the day we first discovered the laws of attraction.

"Don't let me stop you." She lifts her mug to her lips, the steam flowing over her skin. "But you really need new mugs. These suck." She takes a sip and focuses on the view unfolding around Newfound Lake.

Looking at the Green Breeze mug in her hands is a little unsettling. I'll have to ask Harold to replace them. I put my coffee down on the arm of the chair and capture more moments.

"You are crazy talented. The way you caught the light in the contest photo was unreal. I'd love to see your other work."

"It's funny how you forget about things you love because life gets in the way. You know what I mean?"

"I do. It looks like you are working it back in." She rubs her palm against the mug and stares out over the clear mirror of the water.

"What can I say? There's something about this place. You guys living at 43° north have the best view I've ever seen. I'm inspired."

"You know our latitude? Impressive. Wait until winter sets in. You'll be shocked. Most people think this area only shines in the summer, but on days when the sky is clear, the view is breathtaking. The ice huts slide out on the lake, the smoke rises from each one, and snowmobilers travel across."

I look out and try to envision the scene. New England puts on a different act each season. "I always planned on closing the house during the winter. I find myself wanting to rethink that decision more and more each day."

"You'll miss out on Mother Nature's ice and snow spectacular." She looks away and again sips her coffee.

She's cold and has to get to school. "Come on, let's go in." Her hand reaches for mine, our fingers intertwine, and again the queasiness floats into my stomach. This sensation is starting to become regular.

I offer her breakfast, but she insists she's fine and needs to head out. I want to tell her to stay in my bed all day. I let her go with the promise of seeing her soon. I'll be back this weekend, just in time to prove my manliness to these New Hampshire lumberjacks.

Her kiss lingers, and she tells me how much she enjoyed last night. I swear she's walking a little stiff. I secretly love that I wore her out and hope she replays last night over and over again. I've had a lot of women in a lot of places, but last night was unforgettable, and I will not settle for anything less.

# 17



I'm speechless. An alternate being overtook my body last night. Oh man, I never knew how boring my sex life was until Nick. I like the guy. I like him a lot, probably too much.

For reasons unbeknownst to me, a confidence and fire consumed me last night. Maybe it was my drunk ex disappointing me for the thousandth time, or the desire to have every ounce of hesitation sucked from my soul.

Whatever it was, for the first time in my life, I didn't hesitate, didn't allow myself to second-guess. I wanted what I wanted and went for it.

And boy, did he deliver.

At one point, I wasn't sure I was going to last. But when Nick told me to bend over the railing, I'm glad I listened. How hot is it when a sexy, tattooed, composed businessman tells you exactly what he wants? Fucking hot. Every time I thought my body would collapse, he held on tighter.

I haven't looked at my phone since last night and find twenty-five new messages waiting for me. Everyone has checked in, but while I wait for my truck to warm up, I open the text from my brother first.

JACKSON

It's a good thing last night happened. I talked to Nate. Richard is in the slammer. But it won't last long. I'm sure one of his buddies will bail him out, but it's something. Maybe a night or two behind bars will wake his ass up. And for the record, I still think wind guy is an ass, but he may not be as bad as I thought.

Thanks for everything. I'll call you after work and stop by the farm.

A pit opens in my stomach upon thinking about Richard sitting in a jail cell. For the first time, there isn't an ounce of guilt weighing on me. He brought this onto himself. The only positive to his drunken antics is that Nick is starting to win over a few of my friends.

I look up and spot Nick standing at one of his front windows, watching me. He's dressed in nothing but sweatpants and holding a mug. I wave and shift into reverse before I kill the engine and back up into what he's got under those gray joggers. I have to get to work. He smiles devilishly and lifts his chin.

*Fuck.*

I need a cold shower. And I've got one hour to plaster on my teacher face and be ready to face the day.

I'm not two steps into the school building when Madison pulls me into the staff room. "Dish it, bitch. You look exhausted."

I put my oft-neglected teacher bag on the chair. This bag pretty much goes on a field trip to my house every weekend and then comes back. Maybe one day I'll open it. I pull the zipper of my coat down, but it snags at the bottom. A couple other teachers walk in and say good morning, and there isn't a chance I'm spilling the details in here. "Later. This is a conversation for later."

"I knew it. That good, huh?" Madison rubs her hands together with enough friction to start a fire.

I free the zipper and yank my coat off my body as another two teachers walk in with orange shirts. I look from them to Madison and back. "Damn it. It's freaking spirit week." I look down at my black shirt and black tights. I look like I'm in mourning.

Katie is warming up her coffee at the counter. "Shannon, you need a shirt?"

"Apparently, I can't remember a damn thing." I throw my hands in the air. She reaches into her bag. Unlike me, she apparently opened her bag over the weekend. She tosses me an orange T-shirt.

"You are a lifesaver. Thank you."

"You bet," she says, grabbing her mug out of the filthy microwave. Ever since Sue left, no one has been willing to pick up the extra chore. "I knew someone would forget."

"I'll get it back to you."

Madison ushers me down the hall toward our classrooms. "Okay, you can tell me later, but on a scale of one to ten, one sucks and ten mind-blowing, how was it?"

"An easy eleven." I turn my back, walk through my door, and leave her standing in the middle of the hallway with kids careening by on all sides, filling our rooms with chaos.

Usually, I don't hear from Nick during the workweek. By ten a.m. snack time, I check and hope to see a text. Nope.

Madison and I arrange to eat lunch in her car. It's the only way to give her the full story. She's in the worst dating slump of her life, so she is living vicariously through me.

This is a reverse UNO if there ever was one, because I never have anything salacious to share. We pile into the front of her car and grab the blankets from the back seat.

"I can turn on the heat."

"Nah, I'm good. Don't waste the gas." I pull out my sandwich and relay the events of last night.

"I can't. I cannot believe you went that wild, Shan. Look at you! Get it, girl! What's next?" She finally picks her jaw up off her lap and begins eating her lunch.

"I have no idea. This is fun and all, but …"

"Don't you dare start with the buts." She waves her finger at me as if I'm a student in her class.

My text-message chime interrupts. I pull my phone from the side pocket of my leggings. It's Jackson. Richard made bail. A lead weight drops into my stomach, every neck muscle tightens, and I bite my bottom lip hard to stop the tears from escaping.

"What? What's wrong? Who was that?"

I shake my head. "He made bail. I knew it was too good to be true. I bet Judah paid the money to get his pathetic ass out. What a sucker." I'm heaving deep breaths and trying to center myself, but my calm is slipping further away.

"What was I thinking? Why did I think I could simply walk away without Richard making my life hell? I'm counting the days until I'm officially divorced. I have a raging drunk of an ex-husband who manages to show up unannounced at the worst possible times who is now free from jail. What good did that do? And falling for Nick is careless. He hasn't even decided whether he's staying here through the winter."

"Wait, slow down. What?" Madison drops her sandwich on the paper towel across her lap.

"Nick is winterizing the house. He bought it to be a

seasonal home, like many on Newfound. He committed to the campout weekend, but he wasn't expecting to be up here after the marathon weekend."

"Yet, here he is. Still here and returning next weekend. And as far as Richard's concerned, he is not your problem. Stay clear and don't take one ounce of his shit. Hopefully, Judah will talk some sense into him. He's the only sane friend Richard ever had." Madison rolls her eyes.

"This situation is a total clusterfuck. Nick's got a crazy-busy job, and the commitment he made to his father is ironclad. Come on, our luxurious lunch break is over. Enough of my drama." I roll up my paper towel and baggie and shove everything into my brown paper bag, toss the blanket to the back, and hop out.

"For what it's worth, at least one of us is getting laid." Madison laughs and holds the side door open for me.

"If you weren't so damn picky …"

"Picky? Every guy here I've known since the age of five. The dating pool isn't expanding anytime soon. You and Jackson just happen to land the newbies before the rest of us."

I shrug and wonder what will become of Nick and me.

～

The chaos of the day puts me over the edge. I'm exhausted and want nothing more than to crawl into bed. Jackson has been on grandparent duty for the last couple weeks while he gets the farm ready for winter. During the school year, I rely on him, and the guilt builds. He has a lot on his shoulders. We've convinced my parents to stay Thanksgiving weekend this year. They need to see the reality of the situation. Despite the doctors saying my grandmother's memory would recover, it hasn't.

The trees surrounding the farmhouse have all shed their

leaves and blanket every square inch of grass. The field in the distance looks bare and ready for hibernation. Jackson must have put the rocking chairs in the barn; the porch looks empty without them. One year he forgot, sending my grandparents into a tizzy. That year we had early snow and having them buried was somehow triggering. He won't make that mistake again.

Jackson's truck is parked out front, and I hear the tractor off in the distance. What would we have done if he'd left for New York? We were ready to support his move, but there's no way this place would've been the same.

"Hello?" I push open the front door to a darkened space. I switch on the lamp in the front room next to the cordless phone. *Antiques Roadshow* would have a field day with this place. I hear shuffling in the kitchen. Earl is in his gray lined flannel and dirt-stained jeans carrying a soup can to the counter. "Hey, Grandpa!" I turn my voice up a few notches, hoping I'm loud enough for him to hear me.

He sets the can down and looks up. "Oh, look it there. Next time, say hello when you walk in, dear. I didn't know you were here."

I nod in agreement and smile. I fold him into a hug, noticing a stale smell and an unshaven face. "Whatchya doing? Where's Grandma?"

"She's sitting in the other room. She had a rough night and is calling for tomato soup for dinner." I look at his worn hands folded around the aluminum can and see his tired eyes.

"This can't be dinner, Grandpa."

He proceeds to put the can under the can opener and dump the congealed contents into the cast-iron pan on the stove.

There's no debating the menu with Earl. When he's made up his mind, it's set.

I walk into the front sitting room, piano keys dusty from

neglect, board games in the corner from the years we were small enough to play and enjoy, and knickknacks from yard sales crowding the shelves. Earl and Sylvia are famous for walking miles through the town, hitting up every sale along their path and collecting random treasures. These inexpensive purchases either made it to one of these shelves or were wrapped up for Christmas.

The running joke in our family is always about who's going to unwrap the weirdest gift. Grandma means well. According to her, there's no sense in wasting and spending money on new things. I blame it on generational thinking. They grew up in much different times.

My grandmother sits in the recliner and doesn't move when I approach. I take a minute to survey the scene. She's slumped forward, bones protruding from her shoulders, the small of her back against the padding of the tall maroon recliner. The plaid blanket covers every inch of her besides her shoulders and slippers. Her glasses are resting on the wooden coffee table next to the Sunday crossword puzzle they do together each week. Her eyes stare into nothingness and water at the edges.

Life is one big circle that never stops rotating. We start out helpless and needy and return to that very state. You know people are going to age, but nothing prepares you for the reality of it.

"Hi, Grandma." I inch closer and kneel by the recliner, knees pressed into the worn braided rug. I try again, louder this time. She slowly turns her head and looks into my eyes, water falling down her cheek. I reach up to wipe away the tear and dry it on my pants. "Hi."

She tilts her head. "Earl! Earl! There's someone here." Her scratchy voice trembles. Her hands shake under the blanket and her eyes grow wide.

"It's okay. It's me, Shannon." I smooth the blanket, searching for a hand to hold on to.

She looks in the direction of the kitchen, darting her eyes from left to right. "Earl!"

"I'm right here, dear. The soup is almost ready," he shouts from the kitchen. "You remember Shannon?" She looks in the direction of his voice, then back to me.

Sylvia stares at me blankly and says nothing. A piece of my heart chips away. Lifting myself off the floor, I see my grandmother's shoulders relax, and I walk into the kitchen.

"Grandpa, what is going on?" My words startle him as he's taking the metal top off the electric can opener and slices two of his fingers on the edge, dripping blood onto the counter.

"Oh dear, heaven forbid."

I grab hold of his hand and turn on the faucet. "You need to be careful." He stands still and lets the water clean the cut. "Where are you keeping the Band-Aids these days?"

"Your grandmother takes care of that nonsense, honey. I have no idea. No need to make a big deal out of nothing. I've got my handkerchief in my pocket. Stop all the fussing."

I know there's no use in handling this any other way. "Why don't you go sit with Grandma, and I'll heat the soup."

"So be it."

He finishes wrapping his fingers with the nasty cloth from his pocket. I won't say it to him, but that damn thing makes me want to puke. There's nothing nastier than blowing your nose or wiping your mouth on a cloth, then reusing and keeping it in your pocket. I'm going to have to get that thing from him and wash it somehow.

I pour the soup into two bowls and search the pantry for something to add to this pathetic dinner. I would suggest going to get something but know better. He will find that insulting.

Behind the rice and cans of beans, I find a box of saltines on its side. I check the expiration date to be sure it was purchased this decade. Jackson, or someone, is running errands for them from time to time. I need to check in because there doesn't seem to be much selection.

I stuff the plastic sleeve under my arm and carry the two bowls to the front room. The sight of them makes me pause mid-stride. My grandmother hasn't moved an inch, but Earl pulled a wooden chair from the corner and is sitting beside her. He has a crossword puzzle in one hand and the other holds my grandmother's hand on top of the blanket. There is no truer example of love than this.

They don't see me, but my heart is so full. My grandfather's hand tremors slightly while he reads aloud the clues to the next phrase and asks her what she thinks. She shakes her head and doesn't reply. He continues on guessing.

For everything they've gone through, finding each other was all they needed. This is for better or worse. This is through sickness and health. This is what I wanted. This is what I don't have. Everyone deserves this kind of love.

"Here we go, you two lovebirds. Dinner is served." My grandmother doesn't say a word, but her eyes watch me place the soup and crackers on the wooden table. I point to the TV trays in the corner and Grandpa nods.

"Here we go." I unfold both tables and slide them as close as possible.

"We could share. No need for two." He waves off the second table and I place it back on the rack. Another point I won't be arguing.

I set the soup on the TV tray side by side and pull open the cracker's plastic packaging. After putting aside the first two crumbled crackers, I add a few whole ones to the table.

"Grab me that pillow on the couch, dear." My grandfather pulls his wife's shoulder forward and stuffs the pillow far down to allow her to sit straighter. The blanket falls to her waist, revealing a tattered green sweater. It's clear she's not wearing a bra. Maybe it's too difficult to hook, maybe she forgot, or maybe it just doesn't matter. I'll mention this to Mom.

Together, they slurp up their soup. The sound is enough to make me gag. I start talking loudly in hopes of drowning it out. I tell them about school and the big Frosty Freeze event next weekend. I leave out the latest encounter with Richard. This will only upset them. Both nod and smile.

My grandmother's eyes are distant and empty, as if I'm a news anchor on a screen. She is supposed to be better. The doctors told us sometimes when people of a certain age have surgery, they experience memory loss but that it usually recovers with time. Yet it's been weeks, and I want my grandmother back.

Clearing the mess is a welcomed distraction. I need to talk to my parents. They are due in town in a couple days, but this isn't right. I'm uncomfortable leaving my grandparents alone. I've never questioned their ability to take care of themselves, but maybe it's time we step in.

"What else can I do to help before I leave?"

"Earl, someone is here. Who is that? What is she doing in the house?" My grandmother's eyes are wide, and the tears flood my vision and fall.

"It's me, Grandma. Shannon. I'm your granddaughter. I brought you the soup and crackers."

She has both hands out of the blanket, rubbing them together in a repeated motion. "I don't understand. Earl? Tell her to leave."

"Grandma, it's me." I edge on pleading, but her eyes only grow more fearful.

"I'll be right back, Sylvia. Don't you go anywhere." My grandpa smiles at her, stands, and kisses her on the forehead.

He points to the kitchen and shuffles past me. I'm expected to follow. I don't say goodbye to my grandmother. I don't want to upset her even more.

"Listen, we are fine. Thank you for helping with dinner. You've got enough on your plate without worrying about us."

"This isn't dinner, Grandpa. You can't do all of this. It's too much. You have this huge house, and now you're trying to take care of yourself and Grandma. It's too much at your age."

He turns to face me. We are now equal in height, thanks to his shrinking in old age. "Now, you listen here. I may be the oldest person in this town, but I am a man who can take care of his home and wife."

"I'm sorry. I didn't mean to suggest you can't. It's a lot for anyone at any age. I want you both to be comfortable, eat well, and we need to take her back to the doctor. She doesn't know me."

"Dear, you've done enough. I know what's best, and what's best is your grandmother and me under this roof. We are fine. Don't give it a second thought. I'm going to finish the crossword, help her to bed, and call it a night."

What choice do I have? There isn't one, and I know it. So many things could go wrong here. He pushes in the chairs around the table and heads to the door.

"Okay, I'll go. Mom and Dad will be here in a few days. I'll call you later, okay?"

"You bet. Now give your grandpa a kiss." He offers his cheek, and I wipe my eyes and comply.

"Good night. Love you."

"Love you too, dear." He swings the door shut, leaving me standing on the empty front porch as the breeze picks up. A stream of clouds cast a shadow over the front lawn. I jog to my truck, wondering if there is rain in the forecast. Jackson's truck is gone. He probably knew he was in the clear to leave when he saw me here. I don't blame him. I've lost count of the times he's stayed late to help.

I pull out my phone and scroll to find the family text between my parents, Jackson, and me and type:

We need to talk about Sylvia and Earl. I'm just
leaving their house. They are okay, but this is
getting to be a lot for Grandpa.

I snap my head up at the roar of a motorcycle engine inching closer. Sure enough, the tires spin into the dirt driveway with the last man on earth I want to see behind the handlebars. The panoramic view around me turns into still frames, each second lasting minutes. I press my palms against the cool metal of the truck door, my focus locked on Richard's red, unshaven, and angry face. My fingers grip my keys in angst; they burn from the indentations of the metal ridges.

More clouds block the sun. Darkness is cast, and the energy shifts in the air.

My body stills against the side of my truck as he stops and swings his leg over the seat, swaying a little too far to the right, nearly collapsing onto the dirt. His wiry beard is unkempt and his usual black bandana is rolled against his crinkled forehead. He's otherwise wearing a ratty T-shirt, soiled jeans, and leather vest. He looks terrible, worse than I've ever seen him.

He rights himself and marches toward me, his fists clenched.

*Why am I not moving? Why do I not simply get in the car?*

My mind blares with alarm, but my body is locked in place. My teeth grind and my head pounds.

"You can't hide from me, baby. I figured I'd find you here. 'Bout time you're alone so we can finally talk." Richard runs his hand under his nose and flicks it into the air.

His sloppy speech and slobber wake me up. "We? You and I have nothing to talk about. How dare you show up here? Leave." I cross my arms against my chest and hold my breath.

Richard's jaw tightens, and he runs his tongue along his top teeth, emitting a slurping sound. He's moving closer. I feel my blood pressure rise and hear my heartbeat in my ears.

"You have no right to be here. You've caused enough trouble. Don't involve my grandparents in your mess."

He's within a foot of me, and the reek of booze fills the air. "You've got quite a mouth on you these days. What happened to those vows we took?"

I'm a tea kettle reaching its boiling point. Every ounce of my soul is sick and tired of running on this hamster wheel. My deep-seated anger boils to the surface and explodes. "You know what happened, Richard? Hell happened. Living with you was hell! I am done. Get it through your thick fucking skull. I am never going to change my mind. You need to pack your shit, get help, and never fucking talk to me again."

Without warning, a mask of fury disguises Richard, and the scene pans into slow motion. His hand reaches out closer and closer, but not slow enough for me to react. His meaty fingers clamp around my throat, every dirty sharp nail digging into my skin. His grip tightens and constricts my airway.

Fight or flight takes control, and I knee him between the legs with every ounce of strength I possess. I gasp for air when his hand releases. He doubles over and drops onto his knees. Without warning, a gunshot rings into the air.

Like soldiers, we pivot toward the front porch where Earl stands on the edge of the last step with a shotgun pointed directly at Richard.

If there is anyone in this town who would cut Richard an ounce of slack, it is my grandfather. He loves him like a son, but right now, at this moment, there's stone-cold anger hovering over the trigger.

"You listen here." Earl has left the porch and walks toward us, gun pointed. "If you ever show up on my property again or step within a mile of my granddaughter, I will shoot you dead. After all these years, you haven't learned a damn thing. Today, you crossed the line. Nobody puts a hand on a woman. You hear me?"

Richard hasn't moved an inch. His eyes dart between the gun barrel and Earl's face.

"I asked you a question, motherfucker." He's got the shotgun white-knuckled against his shoulder.

Now I'm staring wide-eyed at my grandfather. I've never seen him point a gun, never mind curse like this.

"Earl, listen." Richard puts his hands up and takes a few steps back. "This is between Shannon and me."

"Like hell it is. You made it the whole damn town's business, treating her like you did. You don't think I know what you've been up to, harassing all the town folk, driving around recklessly, and now this. Hell no."

I hear the sirens before the cruiser comes careening up the road. In less than a minute, Richard is trapped in the driveway. Two police officers run toward us. I dart in the opposite direction, toward the house. Earl lowers the shotgun, his finger off the trigger. Tears gather in the corners of his eyes and his shoulders slump forward. I wrap my arms around his middle and the shotgun falls to the ground.

"You made the right decision, honey."

I intertwine my fingers against his back and hug him tighter, hoping he can feel my endless gratitude and love.

Everything at the station goes as terrifying as one would expect. Nate never leaves my side. The other officer on duty takes my statement, and I sign the paperwork for the assault charges. They photograph my neck, which has little more than a couple red marks on it. Richard didn't squeeze hard enough or long enough to bruise me, thankfully, but the photos are necessary. Nate insists Richard will be held on a domestic violence charge at least until he steps in front of the judge.

Either way, Richard is off the street for now and they are issuing a no-contact order. Nate put my mind at ease with his promise that my ex will be spending more time behind bars.

I never thought it would come to this. These things happen in movies or books. How did we get here?

I called Jackson prior to leaving for the station. He was able to come stay with our grandparents to ensure them everything would be taken care of. I called my parents, and my mother was ready to drive down to New Hampshire, but I convinced her otherwise. Having Jackson here and Richard likely locked up for a few nights eased their fears somewhat.

Reversing onto the road, I hesitate to put the truck in drive. I continue to repeat the words in my mind: "Everything will be okay." Without a doubt, I will be scheduling an appointment with my therapist soon.

I bump along the side road and onto Main Street where the rest of the world continues to operate as if nothing is amiss. A few people are outside the middle school hanging a sign for the upcoming turkey trot. I honk and wave, knowing one of them is a fellow teacher. The employees from Raubuchon's are bringing in the last of the outside items.

Gerry leans against Mike Kelley's pickup, thumbs behind his suspenders. He spots my truck, and both men wave and tilt their hats. If they haven't heard the news yet, I'm sure it will make its way around real soon.

Thank goodness for Mike. Ever since he took his lawyer skills out of retirement, his popularity has gone through the roof. He's our local celebrity. He was even asked to announce the homecoming king and queen during the game, which he graciously accepted.

The natural spring fountain is loaded with cars. People are lined up by the spigot with containers. There isn't a moment on any given day that I've driven by this spot and found it empty. Despite having the best drinking water around, we locals will forever be obsessed with getting our water directly from the source. We don't bottle this stuff and say it's from a spring; we fill our containers, know it's from a spring, and keep it a secret. That's how we roll in Meriden.

I breathe a sigh of relief when I pull into my empty driveway. No bike, no drunk man on my deck, nothing but silence. I kick the truck door open with the little strength I have left and slide off the seat. Exhaustion from the altercation is setting in as the adrenaline fades. Nate promised he'd take care of everything, but I'm certain my phone will soon be ringing nonstop.

Opening my back seat to lift out my school bag, I laugh and leave it there. Who am I kidding? Shower, shave, pj's, and I'll be ready for dinner. I slam the truck door closed, climb the creaking porch steps, and unlock the front door.

Tossing my jacket on the chair, I pour a glass of water from the faucet and look in the fridge, coming to terms with the reality that my selection is as sad as my grandparents'. We only have one restaurant in town that delivers, and I'm sure Pat is the only one working the deliveries on a school night. I'm sure she's hoping to get home early, so I'll join the soup crew. Except mine has a plastic tab. I don't own a can opener.

Tomato basil soup, two pieces of toast, and my chair in just the right spot to get a signal, and I am a happy girl. As exhausted as I am, I need to reassure everyone that I'm okay.

> I'm home, everything is fine. The officers took care of everything. I should have more information tomorrow. I'm sorry you were so worried.

DAD

Hey, honey, don't you apologize. You did the right thing. I talked to Mike and he's looking into the legal end of things, just in case. Jackson keeps us in the loop. Your mom and I will be in town Wednesday.

Good, because we have to talk about Grandpa and Grandma. It's getting bad. She is so confused.

MOM

You need to take care of yourself right now. Jackson is there too. They are getting older, so this is expected.

JACKSON

Did something else happen before Richard showed up? Shan, I saw your truck here and left. I figured you had things under control. I'm still sitting with them. I was going to wait until they were asleep.

Yeah, it's fine, but Grandma still doesn't know me.

MOM

Honey, it's going to take time. You heard the doctors.

JACKSON

She recognized me today.

She did? She knew you?

JACKSON

No, but she didn't yell at me. She usually does that when she is confused. She's better in the morning hours.

Okay.

MOM

Kids, you are great. Don't worry. We are a phone call away if you need us. Jackson, you can head on home. They will be all right.

Night.

DAD

Night. See you soon. We love you both.

A new message buzzes through.

SOLIA

Hey, Shannon. Good news, Mia is coming to town this weekend last minute. She got Friday off. I want to schedule a girls' night before Tyler plans set in. Are you free? I could ask Madison, Brooke, and maybe Brynn if she's around.

Yeah, that sounds great. I only have the campout Saturday night.

SOLIA

Oh! How did I forget to tell Mia that? This is going to be good. Can you imagine, Mia camping out on a frosty beach? Ha! Okay, let's plan on Thursday night. Good?

You want me to start a group text?

SOLIA

Sure!

I don't have the energy to tell her what happened. I'm sure Jackson will give her an earful when he gets home.

I eat several spoonfuls of soup, immediately regretting my

choice of not bothering Pat for a delivery or driving my butt to pick up food. My phone buzzes again. Pressing the notification, I drop my spoon into the bowl—it's Nick. I don't usually hear from him during the week. He does his thing, I do mine.

NICK

> Thinking about you.

This is interesting. Escapism exactly when I need it. Nick doesn't text feelings. Should I write back? Wait a few? Screw it … For just a minute, I want to pretend my life isn't a shit show. I can fill him in on the ordeal next time I see him. I can't do it right now.

> That's nice to hear…

[DELETE]

> How are you?

[DELETE]

> Thinking of you too.

[DELETE] Finally, I decide on:

> Really?

Shit, that's pathetic too. Really? Who writes *really*? Too late to delete that one.

NICK

> After the other night? You bet I'm thinking about you.

> I like the sound of that.

Who the hell am I? I think the only remotely sexy message I've sent to Richard in the past five years was a picture of an eggplant from the grocery store, and the joke was completely lost on him. I thought it was funny.

NICK

I have a crazy week, but I'm hoping I can see you Friday night. Is the campout still on for Saturday?

I'll keep Friday open and yes to Saturday.

NICK

What will you keep open on Friday?

Clever, very clever. I need to up my game. Where is Mia during a conversation like this? That girl always has the words.

My mind and my ...

I'm not ready to type dirty things over text—hell no. I can barely say them.

NICK

Excellent, I'll be ready for you. Clean-shaven or a little stubble?

Is he asking about him or me? What? Shit. He must mean him. His face. He must mean which do I prefer because I commented on the stubble last time. It was just the right softness. Hoping my understanding is accurate, I type back.

I like the soft stubble.

NICK

Sleep well. 

I release a deep breath. That was like, what—a ten-second text exchange—and I'm turned on? What is wrong with me?

I flip on BookTok and scroll while I slurp my shitty soup and pretend my life is not a blazing dumpster fire. I'm going to attempt to focus on the positive the best I can. I have four more days to think about what that stubble will do to me.

# 18

Nick

Instead of staying for drinks after our dinner meeting, I went home. It's ten o'clock, and I've been lying here for hours staring out into the city. The motion of the traffic never ceases, the steady stream of people bustling on the sidewalks doesn't have an end, and sirens are the backdrop to the night.

I texted Shannon earlier and haven't been able to stop thinking about her. Normally, I'd contemplate texting Evelyn down the hall to get my mind off things. She's always down for a quickie, but the thought doesn't even appeal to me. I'd be going through the motions. I can take care of things myself if I need to. All I really want is Shannon.

We haven't been able to talk much because of my work schedule. However, she was able to fill me in on Richard's latest. That piece of shit is lucky I wasn't there. I'm not sure he'd be breathing if I'd gotten my hands on him. If he ever tries that again, I'll be in jail for life.

How a man could ever put his hands on a woman in anger is beyond my comprehension. After hearing the play-by-play, Shannon sounds like she's in a good headspace, centered and looking forward, without an ounce of lingering guilt.

I think about driving north to surprise her, but I figured that's over the top and might seem slightly pathetic.

These feelings are all new to me. One minute, I'm picturing her bent over the deck railing and the next I want to cuddle with her on the chair by the lake and watch the sunset. Shit. When did I start thinking about fucking cuddling? I've never had time for this. Work, fuck, sleep, repeat. That is my schedule. Right? That's what works. I'm successful, filthy rich, and happy.

Am I happy?

Maybe not as happy as I could be.

I throw my phone across the mattress and sit on the edge of the bed. My entire wall of windows overlooks the city. It's a sea of lights, billboards, and chaos. Boston never sleeps. Its pulse is the honking of cars, the beeping of the crosswalk signal, the city-dwellers always in a rush. You can't be anywhere fast enough; everyone is always running out of time. I'm starting to wonder what the hell everyone is racing for.

I stand by the glass and try to picture Shannon here. Would she hate it? For every modern convenience this city and apartment provides, it lacks meaning. I never realized how cold money can feel. I live among people who never have enough. Enough money, enough cars, enough women. And never enough time.

During my short stays at Newfound Lake, I've learned that everyone in Meriden has much less, and yet so much more. I never would've noticed how fast I was moving until I was forced to slow down. Thank god Green Breeze wasn't successful. I'm starting to understand why I am the number one asshole.

It hits like a bolt of lightning. I reach for my phone. I have decisions to make. It's ten thirty. I can't bother my mom this late, so I'll wait until morning.

❧

The rest of the week is filled with meetings, dinners, clients kissing my ass, and some chick who tried to pick me up at the bar after a business dinner. Normally, I would be happy to oblige. Evan's been cracking on me all week, calling me pussy-whipped. I knew I should've kept him away from the lake. I haven't heard the end of it.

He's got it bad for Mia, Brynn, and maybe even Brooke. I think I've finally managed to convince him Mia's not his type, that she's got her claws dug into Tyler. Evan wants a picket fence and brats running around. That's not happening with Mia, from my vantage point, anyway. And Brynn is too young. Brooke, who knows?

I instruct my secretary to leave my Friday afternoon open. I haven't texted Shannon after the other night. I don't want to seem desperate.

My meeting wraps up at two and I want to beat rush-hour traffic. Harold asks to drive me this weekend. In truth, he insists. He is determined. I play dumb, knowing full well this is more about Cindy than me. I confirm his room is available at the bed-and-breakfast but insist on driving separately so I can have my car. I tell him he can run my errands if necessary. He seemed satisfied with that and headed out about an hour ago.

Harold and the small-town bartender. This was not something I saw coming.

I text Shannon when I pull off the exit and tell her I'll be at the house in a few. She doesn't respond, but then again, Meriden's service is shit. I could go by her house, but I'm not Richard. I have so much to tell her. I don't know how she will react.

The minute I pull into the driveway to my house—yes, it is still odd to say—my pulse slows and muscles relax. Harold shopped for a new wardrobe for me this week, also making sure I had a few womanly items in case Shannon sleeps over.

The lake house smells different from my apartment. I throw my bag on the island stool and open the blinds. The sun is about to disappear behind the mountain range, and now with daylight savings time in effect, more hours of darkness are ahead. I grab my camera from the corner table and head out to the water. The wind has picked up, forming the biggest whitecaps I've seen since discovering this place. There isn't a visible soul around the lake. I'm not sure how many homes are occupied in the winter. I know mine wasn't supposed to be.

The golden hour has always been my favorite. The light filtering out, dipping underneath the horizon, slowly blanketing the world in darkness. It's surreal. Hopefully, I snapped a few good ones.

I pull out my phone and see Shannon's response.

SHANNON

I'm free whenever. Let me know if you want to grab dinner. Was thinking maybe Caitlyn's. And great news, Nate called … formal charges were laid. Richard is being held at the county jail and will stay until his arraignment. He's finally off the streets.

He better be. Thank god. I'll be there to get you. How about 7? Casual or dressy? Haven't been there.

SHANNON

It's New Hampshire. We are always casual.

Right, got it.

I forgot to turn on the overhead fan during my shower, so the bathroom fills with steam. Thankfully, I don't need the mirror to shave. Shannon's request for soft stubble will be fulfilled. I think a two-day grow-in is my best texture. I'll have to ask her later tonight … hopefully.

If you tell me to dress up, I'll be in a three-piece tailored suit in five minutes flat. Tell me to dress casually, I'm stumped. I told Harold to load me up, so let's see what he's got in these bags.

I dry off and drop the towel to the floor. I open the walk-in closet and sure enough, it looks like what I would expect from someone living up here—I unpack stacks of T-shirts, sweatpants, and hoodies. I hang a variety of flannels, followed by khakis, jeans, and a couple button-down shirts and pullover sweaters.

On the other side, I add the pajama pants, underwear, socks, and other necessities in the drawers. Do those pajama pants have moose on them? He'll hear about this one.

I look at my reflection in the full-length mirror and almost don't recognize myself. After five outfits, I settle on jeans that are more on the fitted side than baggy, a random beer brand T-shirt, and an open blue flannel, which I roll up on my forearms. Shannon seems to like the tattoos. I'll put them on display for a few bonus points. I try on a few hats, but impostor syndrome sneaks in. This is as casual as I'm getting.

By the time I'm ready, I crack open a beer—thank you for stocking the fridge last time, Harold—and realize I forgot to have Harold buy condoms. Shit. I look at the time. I can make it. There has to be somewhere I can stop.

I remember seeing a place on Main Street with a sign that said We Sell Everything. Let's see if that's true.

I pull into the dirt lot of Jack's Market for All. Interesting name. Five or six bikers have parked in the corner by the dumpster and one pickup sits by the front door. Before getting out of my car, I squint at the bikes and don't spot Richard.

Even though Shannon told me he's in the county jail, I still look.

The store's front steps are crooked and wobbly. Positioned directly next to the entrance is an eight-foot wooden black bear statue, claws out, ready to attack. The fact these creatures are in the woods around my house is frightening. I remember Solia saying something about a bear bell or whistle. I need to look into that.

"Howdy there," a gruff voice booms from behind the register. I hear him but can't see him through the lottery tickets and flyers taped around the wooden beam hanging overhead. I round the rack of beef jerky and spot the man sitting on a stool, smoking a cigar.

He's dressed in a brown flannel, a black leather vest with a collection of colorful patches sewn on, which I'm sure aren't Boy Scout badges, a beard that is long enough to conceal a pistol, and not a single hair on his shiny bald head. He has to weigh at least three hundred and fifty pounds. I stare a beat too long and suck a cloud of cigar smoke into my nostrils.

"Hi, um, I just need to get a few things." I shove my hands in my pockets and do a one-eighty, observing my surroundings. This was a giant mistake. From the foggy refrigerator case labeled Fresh Worms to the rifles hanging on the wall and the puzzles stacked up underneath them, I am not in the right place. There is no way I'm walking out of here empty-handed. This guy looks like he'd shoot my eye out if I tried.

I wander up and down the rows, searching for something I can buy that is remotely useful. Inflatable inner tubes for the lake? Nope. A tea set? Nope. How about a case of Matchbox cars? Nope. A sweater for my mother with a loon on it? Not a chance! A holiday oven mitt? Sold! I don't think Harold bought one. If I decide to be domestic and cook a meal, this will come in handy.

"Looks like you found yourself a winner." The man puts

his meaty hand on the chipped laminated counter and pulls himself off the stool, using the other hand to stop his pants from falling down. He turns around, revealing more of his backside than I'd ever want to see. The sight will be permanently burned in my mind. His stinky-ass cigar sits in a black plastic ashtray, surely breaking every fire code in the state of New Hampshire. "Looks like someone is in for a wild Friday night. Cooking up some venison or something?"

"Sorry, what?" I pull out my debit card and look for the machine.

"Deer meat. You cooking tonight?" He waves the pot holder in the air.

"Oh, that? Yeah, sure. Actually, the one other thing I'm looking for is condoms. You seem to have everything under the sun in here, but I didn't see those."

"Lucky man tonight, huh?" He wheezes as he inhales and releases a deep, throaty cough without bothering to cover his mouth. "No rubbers in here, I'm afraid. You'll need to go to Cumby's."

"I'm sorry. What did you just say?" I stare blankly at this man whose arms are larger than my head. *Did he say what I think he said?*

"Cumby's?" He's holding out the mitt. "You ain't from around here, are you? Cumberland Farms down the road. You said you need rubbers."

I run my fingers through the stubble on my chin and nod. "Yes, yes, I do."

"Head that way. I think they have all sizes. Large and, of course, small." He releases a deep guttural hack, once again spraying enough germs to infect a crowd. He winks like some secret language is being spoken. *Get me the fuck out of here.*

After stopping at "Cumby's" and purchasing my size large accessories, I pull into Shannon's driveway. She looks even hotter than she did last weekend. Across the distance, her shiny hair catches my eye, draped over her shoulders, long, thick, and sexy. She smiles and her button nose crinkles. Her eyes are warm and inviting. I never thought I'd find a flannel shirt sexy, but here I am getting hard over a button-down yellow and orange flannel. The first two buttons are undone, leaving enough eye candy for me to want to eat what she's serving. She's got it knotted above jeans that sit low on her waistline. When she reaches up to wave, she reveals a shot of her belly button.

"Hey, sexy!"

She spins in a full circle, looking for someone else I might be referring to. Getting a behind view is an added bonus.

"Who, me?" She laughs and puts her arms around my waist. "Look at you, city boy. If I didn't know better, I'd think you grew up around these parts."

"Is that your stamp of approval?" I lean in and kiss her lips. Soft, sensual, and a hint of coconut. I grab her chin, pulling her close. "Are you okay?"

She pulls me against the wall of the house and giggles. "I am now." My hands frame her jaw, knowing if I don't stop soon, there will be no turning back.

I ease my hold and brush soft kisses over her forehead. "If we don't get out of here, I'll end up eating you for dinner instead."

Despite the porch light being the only source of illumination, I see her cheeks flush and she scratches the tip of her nose. I've noticed that habit a few times.

"Well then, we better get to dinner."

Caitlyn's is a small traditional Irish pub in Meriden. The owners succeed in transporting patrons to Ireland once inside. Dark wood, low lighting, and traditional dishes greet each customer just as they would in Dublin.

There's no hostess, just one bartender and waitress. Apparently, speed is not something they are known for.

The resident bartender waves us in. A few tables sit open by the bar.

"Mom? What the hell?" I stop dead in my tracks. I have to do a double take because surely, my mother is not sitting in this restaurant.

"Nicholas?"

"Umm, Mom?"

Shannon appears at my side. "Gerry?"

"Hi, Shannon."

"I'm sorry. What the hell is going on?" My throat is dry, and I haven't blinked since seeing my mother sitting here.

"Honey, you know Gerry." She holds on to her pearl necklace with two dainty fingers, pushes her whisper-white bob to the side, and looks back and forth between Gerry and me.

"Yes, I know Gerry. But I don't know why you are here with Gerry, in New Hampshire. You are in New Hampshire with Gerry. You are sitting in a restaurant in Meriden with the man who owns the hardware store."

"What's wrong with owning a hardware store?" Gerry unbuttons the cuffs on his wrists and rolls them up each arm.

"Nothing is wrong with owning a hardware store, Gerry. This town wouldn't get by without it. Hi, Claire. It's nice to see you again." My mother smiles warmly at Shannon and pats the bench, looking up at me.

"Have a seat, dear."

"How about Shannon and I get these two a round from the bar and let them catch up?"

"We did catch up, Mom. Last night."

"Sure, sure. Come on, Shannon." Gerry holds the edge of the mahogany bench, pulls himself to the end, and wraps his arm around Shannon. "Let's go."

Shannon smiles, shrugs, and walks to the bar with Gerry.

I take his vacated seat. "Mom, what the hell?"

"Last time we were up, I stopped at the hardware store in

hopes of finding you a housewarming gift. Clearly, it's not the place for such things, but I met Gerry. What a gentleman. He didn't realize who I was when we first spoke and exchanged numbers, but we really hit it off."

"Hold up. Where are you staying? Mom, tell me you aren't staying at Gerry's."

"Mind your manners, young man. What do you think I am, some kind of floozy? I had Harold give me the number of the bed-and-breakfast he stays in."

"Wait a minute. Harold knows about this?"

"I've known Harold since before you knew Harold."

"That's beside the point. You rented a room at the bed-and-breakfast in a town where your son owns a house. You don't tell me any of this, despite the fact we talked last night? And you're on a date with Gerry." It's as if we've switched roles —I'm the authority figure and she's the child.

"I'm your mother, but I'm also a grown woman. You've got a lot going on, and after our conversation last night, I figured it'd be best to see how this went and then fill you in. No harm done and everybody can enjoy themselves. I certainly didn't expect to run into you tonight."

"Gerry, Mom? Really?"

"How is this any different from you and Shannon?"

I don't have a response for her. She's got me there. Shannon and Gerry return with two waters in hand.

"I wasn't sure how this was going to go, so we stuck with water." Gerry offers me a glass. "Are we good, kids? Your mother is a lovely woman, and I am delighted to take her to dinner tonight."

He puts his hands in his jeans pocket and smiles at my mother, who freaking blushes. Who is this woman?

"Oh, Gerry. Stop. You're too much." Even her voice is higher than normal. I'll give it to Gerry. My mom is a classy woman and obviously has some underrated game.

"Well, kids, we were just about to take a brisk walk. We don't want to spoil your evening." Gerry holds out his hand toward Mom, and she willingly accepts, sliding to the end of the bench.

"The bill?" My mother reaches for her purse.

"Don't be silly, young lady. I took care of it at the bar."

My mom's hand rests on Gerry's chest and her lips curl into a smile. "Well, that was awful kind of you, sir."

I'm frozen on the bench. "A brisk walk? Since when do you walk, Mom? And it's cold out."

"Oh, that's enough out of you. I'll call you later. You kids have a good time tonight."

Gerry grabs a coat off the hook on the end of the booth and places it over my mother's shoulders. It's like watching life in slow motion.

"Mom, you can stay at the house. I don't understand."

"Honey, I'm a big girl. Let's see how tonight goes. Maybe tomorrow night I will."

"Wait, see how …" Before I can finish, they are halfway to the exit. Shannon is bent over, hands on her knees, laughing.

"Holy crap," she coughs out. "I don't think I've ever seen Gerry with a woman. He's smitten. Did you see the way he's looking at her?"

"Smitten? That's my mother!"

"Yeah, Nick. I get that part. They are on a date. Your mother is on a date with Gerry. I'm digging it. Come on, get up."

She reaches for my hand, and I follow her to an empty table. After a full glass of water, a beer, and a couple of appetizers, my brain seems to be functioning at somewhat normal capacity. Shannon's calming presence regulates my breathing.

"Why do you think she didn't tell you?" Shannon wipes the cream sauce off her lips.

"It's so crazy. We talked on the phone yesterday. I called her, and she didn't mention a thing. That is a big thing not to tell me."

"Because it's a date, or because it's Gerry and this town?"

"Because …" I hesitate and ponder the question. "All three. It's all three. My mom doesn't date. I didn't know my mom knew Gerry. And yes, she's in the town I bought a house in and didn't tell me."

"For what it's worth, Gerry is as good as they get. A gentleman and one of the kindest souls you'll ever meet. And maybe your mom had other reasons she didn't tell you."

This brings me back to the topic I want to discuss with Shannon. I shake my head and excuse myself to the restroom. I wash my hands and look in the mirror. The reflection of the stubble and flannel is going to take some getting used to. I turn to the side and grab my chin. I fit in. Here goes nothing.

Shannon is at the bar chatting with a few customers. She sees me exit the restroom and slides back into the booth. "You want to split an order of boxty?"

"Yeah, sure."

She raises a thumbs-up and our waitress yells over, "On it!"

"You good?" She pushes the empty plates out of the way, slides her arms toward me, and leans forward. Her breasts are propped on the table, nearly spilling out of her unbuttoned flannel. "I'm over here."

Busted. I return my focus to her dark chocolate eyes. "Admiring the view is all."

She smirks and blushes.

"Listen, there is something I want to discuss." I squeeze her fingers between mine. "I've been doing some thinking."

Her arms grow rigid, her expression stoic. "Thinking can be dangerous."

I pull my hands back because the sweat is starting. "When I was in Boston, I was thinking about you." I notice her face muscles relax and a slight smile returns. "I love Meriden, but work is in Boston." Her smile fades.

"What I'm trying to say is I want you to come to Boston. I want you to be with me, at least on the weekends. I can visit more in the summer, but I want you in Boston with me." I hold my breath and sit idle, waiting for a reaction. She hasn't moved an inch.

"Nick, I have a job here, a family, a home. We just met. I'm not ready for any of that."

I reach out for her hands, no longer caring if mine are sticky. "I know it's asking a lot. I'm supposed to close the house for the winter. I can have Harold come and get you after work on Fridays and bring you back. You won't have to worry about anything. I'll have food there and whatever else you need."

She pulls her hands out of mine, shakes her head, and closes her eyes. "I am not leaving Meriden. My family is here. I love this town. I like you, Nick, I like you a lot, but I'm not even officially divorced yet."

"I know, I know." I hang my head low, chin to my chest. Is this what it's like to be turned down? I'm not sure what I expected, but I want her to say yes.

"I'm not saying I don't want to give us a shot, but I'm not leaving my job or my life here. For the first time ever, I'm on my own. I call the shots. I don't want to leave every weekend. I'm not saying I won't from time to time, but not with everything that's going on. It's too much."

I have so much I could say, but she's made up her mind. "Maybe this is all too soon."

"If I didn't know better, I'd say you might be falling for me. I think you might really like me. I think you wanna kissssss me." Her singsong voice makes me laugh, my cheeks warming like I'm a teenager.

"Get over here." I pull her chin toward me and nuzzle her lips with mine. "I'm not letting you go, Shannon."

"I'm not asking you to." She returns my kiss and sits back in the booth. "But I am asking you to bring me home after dinner. I'm exhausted and tomorrow is the campout."

"Seriously?" My shoulders slump forward.

"Yes, seriously. My parents are in town. Jackson and I are meeting them at the house in the morning to talk about Earl and Sylvia. I need a clear head for that convo."

I reach into my pocket to pay the check and finger my purchase from Cumby's. Looks like my large package will stay sealed tonight. Damn it.

I guide Shannon to the car, keeping my hand under her shirt on the small of her back. "Damn, it's windy out here."

The ride is too short for the heat to warm up the inside of my SUV. Shannon's arms are wrapped around her waist. "Wait until winter blows in. You'll need a hat and some good mittens."

"I'm not sure about that."

"I'll find just the right pair, city boy. Are you ready for tomorrow?"

I open her door and follow her to the lopsided porch. "I'm thinking the less I know, the better."

"I have the tent and sleeping bags. But you seriously need to dress warm. Do you have thermal underwear?"

I'm trying to think of a witty reply but come up empty. "I'm not even going to pretend to know what that means."

She runs her fingers through her silky strands and pulls it all back into a ponytail, lifting her shirt up enough to drive me wild. "The stuff you wear under snow pants. I'll come by before we go with a few things for you. Raubuchon's will have what you need."

"You mean base layers? Who calls it thermal underwear? Just send me a list and I'll get it myself. But promise you won't tell the guys you told me what to get."

She reaches up and wraps her arms around my neck. "What's it worth to you?"

"Oh, you're going to play it like that, huh? Are you sure I can't come in for some dessert?"

She releases her hands to my chest and spreads her fingers wide, looking as if she's contemplating my offer. "Not tonight, Nick. But I will see you tomorrow."

With a soft kiss, she turns, leaving me horny as hell on her porch.

～

My headlights create a path through the pitch-black night. Rounding the bend, I look to my right at the bed-and-breakfast. I still can't believe my mother went on a date with Gerry.

*Wait—what the fuck?*

I slam on the brakes, my eyes glued to the parking lot beside the inn. Lo and behold, Gerry's truck is tucked into the last spot.

*You've got to be kidding me.*

# 19

_Shannon_

You up?

MADISON

Yeah.

FaceTime?

MADISON

Sure.

"What's going on?" Madison's head is on her pillow and she's rubbing the sleep out of her eyes.

"Nick asked me to spend my weekends in Boston from now until the summer."

She springs off her mattress and bugs her eyes into the camera. "Shut the hell up. Are you serious?"

"Dead serious."

"Tell me you said yes!"

"Absolutely not!"

"What are you thinking? He's like a hot sugar daddy!

You've got to be kidding me." She collapses back onto the bed. "Ugh …"

"Hello, my job, my grandparents. And we just met. That's nuts." I watch her roll her eyes in response.

"Okay, fine, logistics. Whatever. At least you know he's not playing. He's into you, for sure. This guy has never been married, no kids, shits money, and wants your ass. Shit, don't fuck this up. What did you say?"

I've never heard Madison drop the f-bomb. "Jeez, Maddie, I told him I'm staying in Meriden. He seems a little put off, but that's crazy."

"Wait, why the hell are you home and not in his bed?"

"I'm exhausted, plus I'm going to the farm early."

"Pathetic. This conversation isn't over. Just tabled for later. By the way, it's supposed to rain tomorrow. We are not camping in the rain."

"Hell no. I'll text you in the morning."

As promised, the skies are dark gray and my wipers are on full blast. The pounding of the rain matches the banging of my heart. I spent the last two hours in my grandparents' kitchen listening to my parents act like everything is fine and dandy at the farm. Mornings are typically better for my grandmother; however, it's clear as day this is going downhill. It's too much for a man in his nineties to manage. Jackson is there most of the time, but he's running the farm. And I can't be there every day.

They need help. My grandfather is too stubborn to ask, but they're struggling. Plain and simple. I've convinced my parents to look into a live-in nurse or Meals on Wheels, or at least have those options on standby.

Jackson handles all this much better than I do. All he does

is revert the decision back to Grandpa, as if he knows best. Doesn't there come a time when someone else should make the decisions? I don't want something awful to happen because we didn't step in soon enough. We are balancing on a thin line between not wanting to insult them and wanting to protect them. Most of what I said fell upon deaf ears.

My phone vibrates in my pocket just as I pull into the hardware store.

"Hey, Nick."

"Shannon, I'm sorry," he says, his voice trembling ever so slightly. "I have to head into Boston. There's a huge client disaster, and I need to meet them for dinner."

I want to ask him to stay or ask if he can drive back later, but I know these are completely ridiculous requests. "Of course. Sure, I get it." I push the speaker button, position my phone on my thigh, rest my head on the seat, and close my eyes. "You'll never hear the end of it from the guys, but you can handle them next time."

"If it weren't a work emergency, I'd be there. I'm interested in being wherever you are."

Despite being flattered, I'm kicking myself for going home alone last night. I will never accept his Boston offer, but I was counting on tonight.

"When will I see you?"

"That's the worst part. I have a conference in Chicago until next Thursday. I was supposed to close the house after this weekend, but I want to be up there for Thanksgiving. I'm hoping my family will come up. I'm sure you have plans, but maybe you could squeeze me in?"

I am looking forward to a lot more than squeezing him in, but combining families is not what I had in mind. "We'll figure something out." I open my eyes and look out the window. "I guess I don't need to get those extra hand warmers."

"I was planning on using you to keep me warm, anyway."

Again, disappointment looms over me.

Everything about tonight has lost its luster. I didn't realize how much excitement I'd built up until Nick was subtracted from the equation.

Nick can't make it tonight. He's heading back to Boston—work emergency. I'll be there but not camping out.

SOLIA

You made my night. Perfect! Let's ditch the part where we freeze our asses off outside on purpose.

MADISON

Count me in!

BROOKE

Never wanted to anyway ... Yahoo!

SOLIA

Let's have a sleepover at my cabin instead. All in?

Yes!

MADISON

Absolutely.

BROOKE

100%

If I can't have Nick, I'll settle for a girls' night in.

The rain stopped midday, leaving the air cool and dry, a perfect night for a fire, as long as the sand dries.

I'm dressed in multiple layers because I'd rather sweat than freeze. Sweatpants, boots, T-shirt, sweatshirt, jacket, gloves, and hat complete the look. My camping chair is already in the truck bed. I toss my backpack in with everything I need for tonight, plus a cooler with waters and ingredients for s'mores.

I spot the setup and my crew and park in the closest spot. All that's visible is lit by the roaring beach bonfire, the tents erected around the perimeter and camping chairs set in a circle.

I timed this perfectly. It comes as no surprise when Tyler walks over. "City boy got nervous, huh?" He wings his arm around my shoulders and hands me a beer.

"He had a work thing." I land a soft punch to his rock-hard torso and swig a sip of beer and immediately spit it in the sand.

"What the hell, Shan?"

"This tastes awful. What'd you do? Bring skunked beer?"

He grabs the can from me and guzzles half of it down. "First of all, it's fine. Just a little warm. And for the record, I don't think it's a work thing. It's an 'I'm a pussy thing,' but whatever."

I land another insignificant punch to his gut. "You can even ask Cindy. Harold was in town with him but drove back to Boston a couple hours ago."

In the sea of flannels and winter hats, I see Jackson, Ryan, Lucas, Nate, Cindy (who finally got a night off), and Jay. Brynn, Madison, Solia, and Brooke are also here.

"Bring it in, everybody," Ryan yells from the lake's edge. He holds up his water bottle. "Cheers to being the best crew around. Don't be a bunch of assholes this winter and hibernate. Now that Jackson is sticking around and getting married, we need to live it up this winter."

An echo of cheers bounces off the mountain ridges hidden in the darkness as red Solo Cups collide with beer cans.

Ryan sets my chair up next to his. "Pretty boy had to work?"

"Yeah, he did."

Ryan cocks his head to the side, eyes squinted.

"I swear. I think he's got it bad for me." I take a sip and shrug.

"Oh, really? Confidence is key, my friend."

I've known Ryan my whole life. Being one of my little brother's best friends, I always sensed he had a crush on me, but the line was never crossed. He was the wild child of the group. Trinity's accident put him on the sober path. A lucky girl will snatch him up one day.

"I'm serious, Ryan. He asked me to come to Boston on the weekends."

"Holy shit." Ryan responds loud enough to catch the attention of everyone. Conversations halt and all eyes focus on me.

"Might as well sit for this one, crew." Madison throws herself back into her seat, almost tipping it over onto the sand.

"Damn, I forgot a chair." Brynn looks around the circle. The only empty chair is mine.

Tyler pats his thigh, and she skips over eagerly.

Odd. I steal a glance at Solia whose chair is beside Jackson. She shrugs in between sparks floating into the night. "Where's Mia?" I mouth over the flames.

"Tomorrow," she says back to me.

"I guess you'll all figure it out, anyway." I squirm into my canvas bucket chair and wrap the double blanket I intended to share on my legs and stuff the extra under. "Since my love life is interesting to everyone, I'll have you know that Nick asked me to spend the weekends in Boston when he closes the house for the winter."

If Solia's eyes were to bug out of her head any farther, we would be able to scoop them off the sand.

"You said no, correct?" Jackson rips the winter beanie off his head.

"Relax. I will never leave Meriden. The family is here, you guys are here. I've had enough change in my life for a bit."

"Thank god." Jackson places the hat back on his head, and Solia grabs his hand. Could he be any more dramatic?

"Speaking of change," Nate pipes up from across the circle. "Would you like a Richard update?"

"Yes." I don't miss a beat. My heart pounds.

He glances at Jackson, who nods.

Why not? My life is an open book at this point. I sit back in my seat, shoving my hands under the blanket.

"Richard pled not guilty at his arraignment. The judge ordered him to be held at the county jail until his trial based on his history and prior probation violations. He won't be around for a long while."

After Richard's arrest, I asked everyone to leave me out of the next steps unless I absolutely needed to know. So this qualifies as essential news. I didn't expect he'd disappear into thin air, although that may have been easier.

"I don't care where he is, as long as he stays far away from me." The entire group nods in agreement.

Nate walks over and kneels at my side, draping an arm over my shoulders. "Trust me—that message has been delivered to Richard loud and clear."

Knowing I have this small community at my back is priceless. "I trust you." I wrap my arms around him and squeeze.

"How about we change the subject? We can share wedding ideas with you." Solia giggles to the groans of the crowd.

"I'm going to get more wood from my truck before I gag." Nate stands and walks up the small dirt hill and opens his tailgate. It's funny to see him sporting facial hair for the annual no-shave November. Nate is our clean-cut officer in uniform. Seeing him with this neatly trimmed beard is interesting to say the least. There may be a few gray streaks growing in.

If there were a guy I wish Madison would fall for, it's Nate. I remember thinking he seemed so much younger than us during our school years, but now age doesn't matter. And she's always had a thing for a man in uniform. We set them up one time, but it was a no-go. Thankfully, they've remained friends.

Nate lifts a log over each shoulder and returns to the circle. Lucas meets him and takes one. I watch Cindy's eyes follow him as he returns. She catches my stare and looks away. *Interesting.* I wonder if she'd be here if Harold hadn't gone back to Boston.

Each man tosses a log onto the fire, and sparks flutter into the air.

There's talk of ice fishing, whose snowmobile is going to make it out, which paths they'll cover, and a possible group ski trip.

"Why would we go on a ski trip when we are all within driving distance of the mountains?" Madison asks Tyler, our resident party planner, whose head is bent over the open cooler. Brynn stands behind him, and I watch as she slaps his butt. *Note to self: Ask Solia about this later.* I'm wondering if I missed the memo that Mia and Tyler called things off.

"We could rent a huge house right on the mountain, one you ski right out the front door. February break would be great for the teachers in the group." Tyler tosses a few beers around the circle, releasing droplets of water above our heads. "It'd be like old times, with a few new members. Does Nick ski?"

"I'm going to go out on a limb and say no." I pull my hands free and push the blanket to the side. I'm suddenly feeling the heat as the flames increase.

"I'm in. This will be a blast. Great idea, Ty!" Brynn smiles.

Her long blond ponytail swooshes side to side through some cutout in her winter hat.

"Ty?" I repeat loudly enough to get a snort out of Madison.

The conversation roars to life about all the must-haves of the rental: jacuzzi, firepit, lift tickets, *Twister*. I'm not sure if some among us are having an early midlife crisis or if they need a reminder that this isn't college spring break. Come to think of it, though, this will be the first trip I take as a single woman. I wonder if Nick would even want to come.

I stand and walk to the cooler and grab the marshmallow bag. As I pull it apart, Nate walks over. "When's the last time you went on a ski trip, Shan?"

I lean into his body. "You mean the last time I went on a trip, period?" I pause and look up. "A really long time."

"It certainly has been. This is a new beginning for you. Smile." He holds up his phone and takes a picture.

"Send me a copy." I'll have to add it to my collection. We've been together at countless events over the years— weddings, anniversaries, reunions, you name it.

"You bet." He heads to the next group. I should get a few pictures too. I need more good memories to add to my camera roll.

I trade each person a marshmallow for a picture as I make my way around the circle. Jackson and Solia make out under the tree by the road, even though their assignment was to collect sticks for roasting. After I take a picture with Cindy and Lucas, I shake the third-wheel vibes and ask Lucas to whistle.

I never could, especially the way he does. He puts his two fingers in his mouth and lets it rip, startling the shit out of our resident lovebirds.

Everyone turns in the direction of the target and cheers them on. Instead of being embarrassed, Jackson throws Solia over his shoulder and squeezes her butt. She kicks her legs and giggles uncontrollably.

The scene is adorable. I don't think their smiles could be any brighter.

We eventually do roast the marshmallows, and Cindy takes charge of the chocolate and graham crackers. Despite having the night off, she insists on dishing out the treats.

One bite into my s'more and it doesn't sit right. I toss it in the trash and grab a water from the cooler. Maybe I didn't eat enough dinner.

The guys are three sheets to the wind within a couple hours. Ryan finally convinces them not to take on the polar bear swim until morning because these idiots will freeze to death tonight. I don't know how he manages to keep his sanity around this crew. I'm proud of him for staying sober and truly believe it saved his life. He was in a bad place after the boating accident.

I catch Solia's attention, nod my chin toward Cindy and Brynn, and she reads my mind.

"Hey, Cindy, Brynn. We are thinking of skipping the camping part and having a girl party back at the cabin. You in?"

Madison and I start folding and packing our chairs. "I'm ready." Brooke bounces off her chair, as if the night was hanging on her decision.

"Sure, yeah. I'm in." Cindy looks down in the sand, head wobbling. "I don't think I should drive, though."

"I think I'm going to stick around a bit, if it's okay with the boyzzz. I'm ready to party!" Brynn gets up from her chair, steadies herself but then loses her balance, and lands ass down in the sand.

"Sure, cool. Cindy, you can come with me." I look at Jackson and motion for him to call me if needed. Solia and I agree to drive everyone to her cabin.

The reality of the temperature sets in when I'm off the sand. It has to be hovering around freezing. With the fire blazing, I didn't realize how cold it was.

Solia's cabin is breathtaking, no matter the season. It sits snug between two mountain ranges, made of beautiful dark logs, covered with a tin roof, surrounded by wildlife and woods. Life here isn't for the faint of heart, but the beauty makes every ounce of sweat worth it.

Twinkly lights twist around the front porch banister. Her porch flowers have been removed for the season, and pumpkins decorate the top steps. I haven't asked the lovebirds what their living arrangements will be after the wedding, but I'm confident there is no way Solia is moving out of the cabin after everything she did to save it.

We pile through the front door and throw our bags in the loft. Solia leaves the side door open to grab some wood, sending us into a tizzy as we grab blankets and claim spots on the couch.

"What's up with Brynn?" Madison squeezes next to me, her knees bent to her chin and her long brown hair tied in a topknot.

"I think she's really wasted."

"Really, Brooke? I had no idea." I send a pillow careening across the room.

"Oh my god, totally. She was guzzling the beer like we were going to run out. She'll be okay, right? I can always go back and see if she's changed her mind."

Solia returns carrying several chopped logs in a wood carrier slung over her forearm. "Brooke, she's good. Jackson will call if we're needed. I don't think she'll be sleeping solo tonight."

I shift to the end of the couch. "So, you did notice?"

Solia grabs the fire mitt and tosses the logs into the woodstove through the side door. "How could I not?"

"What am I missing?" Cindy returns from upstairs and joins Brooke on the opposite couch.

"Mia and Tyler are kind of a thing, but it's clear Brynn is interested in getting it on with Tyler."

"Are you going to tell Mia?" Brooke's eyes bulge.

"Yeah, I'll mention it, but who knows what will happen. Mia is not the kind of girl who's looking to be tied down. I love her to death, but I'm sure she's not holding out for Tyler when she's home. I'm not sure it would bother her all that much."

Brooke rests her chin in her hand. "Wait, they don't care if the other is sleeping with other people?"

Solia nudges me and I scoot left, draping half the blanket over her lap. "Brooke, some adults would rather be free to do as they please with whomever they please."

Her cheeks ignite. "Oh, interesting."

"I've been satisfying the men in town for years, and I wouldn't have it any other way." Cindy laughs and throws her head back on the couch cushion and closes her eyes. The room goes silent.

It seems like an eternity before anyone has the nerve to speak. The only sound is the fire crackling and Cindy's deep breaths. I don't think I realized how wasted she is.

"Did you say what I think you just said?" Solia cuts the tension, everyone waiting for a response.

Cindy folds her arms across her chest and pulls her head forward. "Ladies, how do you think I've managed to make a living tending bar for all these years? My bar service isn't the only thing earning me those big-ass tips."

Okay, now we are on the edge of the couch, our eyes bugging, heads shaking. "Hold up. Wait. You are charging men for sex?"

Cindy clears her throat and shakes her head. "Now you're making me sound like a prostitute, Shannon."

Brooke's face is drawn and pale. She looks like she might be close to tears. "Cindy, you don't have to do that. We are your friends. If you need money …"

"Holy shit, you guys are a hoot. I was married to a dirtbag for years. Listen, a woman has needs and things just happened."

"Whoa, whoa, whoa. You can't drop a bomb like this and not give us details. Who needs a drink?" Solia looks at me and signals toward the kitchen. We gather a few seltzers and ciders and pass them around. By this point, the temperature in the room has risen comfortably and blankets are tossed aside. Brooke is sitting cross-legged on the rug in front of Cindy, as if she's bought a seat to the best show in town.

"Start from the beginning," Madison says from the edge of the cushion, drink between her hands.

"I don't kiss and tell, but one night, there was a local left at the bar, and he tipped me and made a comment that my service was excellent. He's good-looking, single, and I'd been in a drought. I told him he hasn't seen what else I can serve."

All of our mouths drop wide open. Brooke gasps. "You did not?"

"Oh, I did. You have no idea how wild a bar area can get after-hours."

"Holy shit, this is getting good." Madison joins Brooke on the rug.

Cindy pulls her legs up and crosses them underneath her. "This shit doesn't leave this house, got it?"

"Got it," we answer with bated breath.

I've spoken to Cindy countless times over the years, but only ever surface-level conversation, nothing deep. My mind is blown.

"I locked the doors that night, he joined me in the back of the bar, one thing led to another, and let's just say, the beer fridge is the perfect height to be bent over."

"Cindy!" Brooke covers her mouth.

"Don't worry, I sanitized everything. After that, he left a hundred-dollar bill on the bar, and we went about our lives."

"You kept the money?" I'm not understanding how this doesn't qualify as prostitution.

"I tried to give it back, but he insisted it was for the excellent service. Who am I to reject a tip?"

"Was that the last time?" Madison asks.

"Honey, that was the beginning. I'm a woman with a twenty-year-old man's sex drive. The more, the better. The less attachment, the better. The last thing I need in my life is drama or a whiny-ass man-baby yapping in my ear. *Wham, bam, thank you, ma'am* is fine with me. I prefer it. And if these guys want to tip me extra, let's go."

"Like, how many guys are we talking? All locals?" I start running through a list of possible men. "These guys are all single, right?"

"Jeez, Shannon. I'm not a home-wrecker. No ring, no problem. And yes, most are locals. I'm not giving up names. But I will say some don't mind extra company."

Madison stops her cider halfway to her mouth. "Are you saying you had a threesome at the Binn?"

"No!" Brooke looks like she's just found someone strangled to death.

"Brooke, relax." I toss a much-needed pillow at her face. She takes a breath. "I wish Mia were here. She'd have a field day with this."

"Don't knock it till you try it, ladies. We were given more than one entrance for a reason. That was a profitable night." Cindy tosses her head back again, smiling.

"What is the craziest thing you've done? How often is this happening? How much are you making? How do you know they are interested? Do all the men in town know? Cindy, this is not okay. I'm worried about you." Brooke's hands wave everywhere. She's shaking her head and looking back and forth among us all.

"You need to get laid, Brooke. Seriously. I can arrange it." Cindy laughs.

"I'm good. It's okay." Brooke shrinks back into herself.

"Trust me, I don't do anything I don't want to do. Do guys kiss and tell? I'm sure some do. Has word gotten around? Maybe. At my age, I do what I want. If I want to take a guy into the back room during a quick break, you better believe that's what I'm going to do. I may be approaching fifty, but they like what I am serving because I have my regulars."

"Holy shit, Cindy. You are blowing my mind," I say.

"Speaking of blowing, that isn't on my menu."

"Wait," Madison interrupts. "You mean to tell us these guys keep coming back, laying out the hundreds, and you aren't doing that?"

Cindy stands and swaggers into the kitchen. "Honey, I'm not getting on my knees for anyone. No thank you. Been there, done that. They can either eat what I'm serving or show me what they can offer." She disappears around the corner, leaving us to wonder if we heard that correctly.

"Did any of you know this was happening?" Solia pans across each of us.

"I've been here my whole life. Never once have I heard of this." I throw my hands in the air and laugh.

Cindy returns. "You better not be waiting for me to spill the details. I'm not sharing any more than I have already. But I can tell you one thing. Shannon, if you decided not to hang on to lover boy, I'd like nothing more than to take him for a ride. Not because he's loaded, although that is a bonus, but there is something nasty about him, in a good way. With that said, I did take his driver for a ride or two, but he might be a little too clingy. Maybe worth it. Shit! That wasn't supposed to come out."

My body temperature rises and I'm surprised to sense a little rage in my gut. "Oh, yeah, well, I think I'm going to keep Nick close, Cindy. And let's say, between us, of course, he is serving it up quite well."

The entire room bursts into hysterics. I'm not dishing details, but I'm drawing the line in the sand. I didn't realize how possessive I'd become. And Harold, really? The guy seems really sweet.

It's well past one a.m. by the time we call it a night. I love Cindy and all, but no one is getting their hands on Nick. At least, I hope they don't.

# 20

Nick

Dinner sucked. The food took forever. This time of year, in Boston's north end, it's impossible to get a seat in the higher-end establishments without a reservation. It pays to have connections, but even that didn't help with the slow service and noisy atmosphere. At the end of the night, Evan and I had a few drinks at the bar. Poor guy tried to talk up a chick, but she shot him down. All he's ever wanted was to find the one and start a family, though I doubt he'll find her in this place.

I wasn't on my A game tonight. Business got done, but Shannon is front and center. Never have I had a woman take up space in my head. What a mindfuck! I also spilled my guts to Evan about my mother and Gerry. He's all for it and couldn't understand why I wouldn't be. It's not that I'm unhappy about it. It's just that I never would've pegged Gerry as the kind of man my mother would go for. She's fine china, and he's a paper plate. She's a lavender bubble bath, and he's a hose shower. Although she seemed happy the other night.

We finish the evening and I'm not even tempted to take

home the blond with the D rack at the end of the bar who's been giving *fuck me eyes* half the night. I only want Shannon.

My suite is cold and vacant. I light the room with the fireplace, but it doesn't warm the emptiness. Looking over the bustling city below, I'm alone among so many. I fly out tomorrow to Chicago. All I want is to head north.

I don't bother to change out of my suit. My jacket gets tossed onto the leather recliner; I hold down the button to shut the lights and blinds. As I scroll through social media, my thumb freezes.

Shannon and I started following each other last week. Neither of us posts often, more snoopers than participants. Tonight, however, she posted a carousel of photos of people I now know. The last picture has me holding my breath. Nate, the local cop from Meriden, has his arm around Shannon. She's smiling at the camera, clutching a water bottle and leaning into his chest. He, on the other hand, is looking at her with eyes that can only mean one thing. I let the air out of my chest.

*Is this jealousy? Is she into him? I know they go way back, but maybe something happened tonight.*

Glancing at the time, I take a chance and text her.

> Just thinking of you. Hope you had a good time
> tonight.

A few minutes later, nothing.

> I'm going to try to get up there sooner than
> Thanksgiving. Not sure how, but I miss you.

I hit send before really thinking that one through. I sound like a fucking pussy. *I miss you.* Who the fucks says that in a text message? I went from wanting to bang her brains out to—well, I still want that, but I also want to hold her after. I don't want her to leave.

~

My flight gets delayed. I'm stuck at an airport restaurant next to a family with three kids. I leave with a headache and locate the closest CVS alcove for some Tylenol. I haven't heard back from Shannon. She probably partied too hard. She's rarely on her phone. I'm sure she's good.

I never fall asleep on planes, but the second I recline my first-class seat, I'm out. My dreams take me lakeside, Shannon tucked against my chest, both of us wrapped in a sense of calm. I wake to the sound of the captain's voice announcing our descent. Reality floods back, my pulse increases, and my agenda overrides the memory of my dream.

After a long day, I arrive back at my hotel room and call my mother. Twisting the tie off my neck and unbuttoning my suit shirt, I take in my reflection in the full-length mirror. Around me is nothing but a cold mattress, a polished desk, and a view of the skyline with no one to share it with. My life is a marathon with no finish line. Hustle, schmooze, dinner and drinks, a random woman, sleep, and repeat.

*Fuck this.* Something has to change.

I sit at the desk with a mission in mind, my decision as clear as day.

"Hey, Mom. Listen, you got a minute?"

"Everything okay, Nicholas?"

"Yeah, yeah. I need to run something by you. What do you think Dad would say if I sold the company?" There. I drop it like a bomb.

Silence.

I move the phone away from my ear to make sure we haven't been disconnected. "Mom?"

"I'm here. Surprised is all."

"Yeah, well, I've been thinking, and a lot has happened in the last few months."

My mother cuts me off. "Honey, I'm surprised it's taken you this long. Your father was a tough man. Strong, smart, and business-minded. He wanted to provide for his family, and he succeeded. This was never your dream. Sure, you're used to having money, but you have more than you'll ever need."

I hang my head and a hundred-pound weight rolls off my chest. "That is the last thing I expected you to say."

"I don't want you living anyone's life but your own. From the time you were five years old, you wanted to be a creative. You have an eye for things that a fast-paced life covers up. Your father expected you to fill his shoes, but I never did. When he passed, I tried to talk to you about selling, but you wouldn't hear of it. I was ready to sign the paperwork."

"I don't remember."

"You wouldn't. We were in shock, dealing the best we could. You wouldn't hear a word I said. I learned a long time ago, my boy, that once you have your mind made up, there's no standing in your way. If this is what you want, we have a whole team of lawyers who can work with us. We'll probably make more selling than you would running yourself into the ground."

"So, that's it? You don't care?"

"Your sister and brother don't want anything to do with Green Breeze. They are pursuing their dreams, and I think it's time for you to do the same. Go get your girl and take a good picture when you do. But make sure you are certain. Don't do it for love—do it for you."

I'm left shaking my head. How does she do that? I swear mothers are psychic.

"Thanks, Mom. I'm going to put in a few calls."

"Be sure you make this decision with total understanding, because once it's done, it's done."

"There's nothing left to think about, Mom. Thank you for your help."

"You don't need me. My stake in the company was secured in paperwork years ago."

∼

I went through the motions at the conference. I shook hands, kissed asses, ate fancy dinners, and pretended to give a shit about green energy for one last time. Once I mentally cut ties with my career, the amount of brain space freed up astounded me. Wild ideas of future possibilities fired through every neuron. I cannot recall the last time I had this much excitement infiltrating my cells.

When I called and told Tim Lambert about my decision, I sensed his hard-on through the wireless connection. He and Mark Hogan were meant for this rat race. I can be a cutthroat asshole if there ever was one, but it takes a little effort. I can take off the mask as easily as I put it on, whereas Lambert was born for the business world.

And his last statement, I will never forget. I quote, "I knew it was only a matter of time before you were pussy-whipped into small-town living."

If roles were reversed, I'd be saying the same damn thing.

The last three phone calls were slightly different. Ashlyn thinks I've lost my mind. She seems to think moving to New Hampshire is the equivalent of shitting in an outhouse. Brett is missing the Ford competitive gene and isn't fazed in the slightest. He clicked with Shannon right away, and the outdoor lifestyle is already embedded in his soul.

Last up is Evan. He's the only guy I can see myself staying in touch with. He didn't seem too surprised and is more interested in visiting the lake than fretting over my major life adjustment.

My entire life plan pivots on a dime. One minute I'm CEO,

the next I'm not. I mean, there's legal wrangling and piles of documents still to come, sure, but a company such as ours operates like clockwork. Everyone has a role, and with me stepping down, everyone climbs to the next rung and the clock keeps ticking. Companies like ours have a contingency in place in case of emergencies. While this may not be an emergency, we have a board set up to run the company in my father's name, and everyone knows their place.

I toss my Armani suit on the floor and slide into the shower. There's so much to do, but yet nothing to do. It's as if I've pulled Pandora's box out from under my bed, dusted it off, and am ready to open it. What lies ahead? Shannon may not want me in the end. I may hate lake life after a little while, but running on this treadmill needs to stop. I grab a towel and look in the mirror.

I'll never forget Shannon's surprise when she spotted my tattooed arms. Spilling ink into every inch of my skin seems like a lifetime ago. I was a different man then. There was no clear path for me, but I was free to live the life I wanted. Photography was my drug. I lived for those photos. Taking a scene into view at the right angle with the perfect light is pure magic. I spent every moment I could behind the lens.

When my father passed, the lens cracked and sat forgotten. It's funny how something you feel so strongly about can be washed over in an instant and disappear under the sand. I had a responsibility, a role to fill, and I did it well. I morphed into someone I never planned to be.

I eventually hear from Shannon but want to surprise her. She seems distant and short, but I chalk it up to stress from work and her grandparents' situation. I haven't brought up the pictures from the campout. I'm not going to become a desperate, jealous type.

Several meetings and signatures later, I walk out of my

office, ready for a new chapter. I agreed to stay on the board through a transitional period as needed. This is the best of both worlds. I'll ease out, and the board will phase in. With the flip of a switch, my life is headed 43° north.

Harold is my biggest loss. He's watched me grow up and has driven my ass around forever. Not having him with me every day will take some getting used to. However, I don't think it'll be long before I see him—and Evan—in Meriden. My mother even mentioned keeping Harold on her personal payroll part time.

My college buddy agrees to list the penthouse condo and arranges a moving crew to relocate my stuff to New Hampshire. I want to make a clean break. The week is a blur of legalities, banking, and rearranging. Everything I need for the time being is packed in my car.

I'm ashamed to admit, I sent Harold on one last shopping trip for more clothes. I have staples, but if I'm going to live up north, I need more options. He is happy to oblige and even offers to drive me. Again, I think there is a certain bartender he wants to see. I decline, but I'm sure she'll be serving him soon.

Leaving the office on Wednesday, I'm ready to head up to the lake. I make a pit stop on Newbury Street. I may not have done my own shopping, but picking out a few items I want to see Shannon dressed in is at the top of my to-do list.

Though my brother is stuck out west, my mother, Ashlyn, and Harold will head up to Meriden Thursday for Thanksgiving. Mom insisted on me finding a place in town for us to have dinner, but that's proved to be a headache and a half. I settled on the Newfound Inn. Without connections, I am lucky a family cancelled and their table opened up.

All that's left to do is find the words to surprise Shannon about my move. The pressure and buildup of this conversation has me more on edge than any billion-dollar business deal ever has.

Or maybe I shouldn't make it a big announcement—more of, "Hey, I'm staying, no more Boston. Cool, huh?"

Why am I sensing this is going to be a colossal fuckup?

# 21



I reach across the toilet and grab a fistful of tissue paper. Luckily, I turned the heat on. Otherwise, I'd be freezing my ass off on the bathroom floor for the third day in a row. Throwing up first thing in the morning wasn't a red flag on day one, but after three days, I can't ignore what's going on.

The number of years I woke up praying I'd puke and now here I am playing a game of tug of war, unsure which way to pull and which side I want to win. It's probably a stomach bug, a nasty virus of some sort. This can't be happening. A wave of nausea consumes me, and my head hangs low in the bowl. That's going to be the last one. I know it. I wipe my mouth with more paper. I need to splurge on thicker ply. This shit sucks.

I've got two options: ignore my gut or get a test. Can I test? Is it too early? When's the last time I had my period? I don't even bother keeping track. I kept a calendar for so many years. I wanted a family. *Wanted*, past tense. But I wrote off that dream a long time ago. As the clock ticked into my thirties and the Richard I'd loved drifted further away from me, I considered no babies a blessing. He's not meant to be a father.

Thankfully, the universe knew better than I did. Bringing a baby into the world with Richard was not in the cards. Imagining the mess I'd be in with a child in the mix breaks me. Would I have found the strength to leave? How would Richard's decisions and my choices have impacted a child?

I hear the coffee percolating in the kitchen, but the smell of the French vanilla beans turns my stomach. I turn on the faucet and look out into the side yard. The first snowfall of the year. A sprinkling of powder fell overnight, enough to hide the grass under the sparkle. The tree branches are bare and dripping as the sun evaporates the precipitation on the tips. The bird feeder is empty and unoccupied and will stay that way until spring. I picture a swing set in the backyard, and my chest swells.

My alarm sounds from my bedroom, dropping the curtain on my mental movie. I'll stop at Rite Aid on the way to school, grab a test, wrangle hyper kids for seven hours, and then lock myself in my bathroom.

"You look like hell." Madison gives me a thorough once-over. I scan my black leggings, brown boots, and TGIF (Thank Goodness It's Fall) long-sleeve tee. My makeup was applied without ever checking the mirror, and I didn't touch my hair this morning.

"Well, thanks, Madison. You look like shit too." I smack her with my armload of copies as we walk into the teachers' room, knowing my comment is completely off base. Madison never looks disheveled. Her outfit is complete with a beautiful yellow sweater and full-length waves in her hair.

The bathroom door swings open. "Hey, beautiful teachers! You know what day is almost here? Turkey Thursday." Brooke tucks her hands under her armpits, pretending to fly, and gobbles her way to the staff fridge, stuffing her lunch box among the fifty others already crammed in.

"Did you seriously glue feathers all over that?" Madison leans on the lunch table, looking intently at Brooke's brown shirt covered in faux feathers.

"Girls! I totally would've made you one! The kids would've gone bananas. Instead of the Three Musketeers, we would've been the Three Terrific Turkeys."

I'm not sure if it's the nausea or the sound of her voice. I can't today. I look over at Madison, who shrugs and laughs. "Thanks, Brooke. I'm fairly confident you are the only one who can rock that outfit."

"Aww, thanks, Madison. You are so sweet. Have a great day, turkeys!" She grabs her coffee off the counter and lets the heavy door slam in her wake.

"Is she serious?"

"Oh, she's serious. Go fix your hair. I'll see you on prep."

I follow her orders.

The day goes as expected. Kids are off the wall, despite bribery of extra recess and board games. The pregnancy test sits at the bottom of my bag like a hand grenade. If it weren't for the energy in the room, the day would've dragged by.

By three thirty, I'm run ragged and starving. "You sure you're okay? You seem off." Madison and I walk through the staff parking lot.

I can't hold it in any longer. I drop my teacher bag on the pavement, and she turns and stares at me. "What?"

"I think I'm pregnant."

Now her bag is on the concrete. The wind whips through the parking lot, sending a chill. "Wait, what? Why? How?"

I pull her elbow and loop our bags on my arm, leading her off to the side to avoid getting run down by staff hightailing into the long weekend. "I never throw up. I've been throwing up in the morning. I don't remember the last time I had my period. As far as the how …"

"I don't mean literally how—I got it. Holy shit. We need to find out. Let's go get a test." She lifts her bag. "Let's go. No use in freaking out without knowing anything."

"Oddly enough, I'm not freaking out. I bought a test this morning. It's in my bag."

"Then let's go! I'll follow you home."

There's no arguing with Madison. She's coming home with me regardless of what I have to say about it.

"**A**re you ready for this?" Madison and I stand face-to-face in my kitchen outside the bathroom, the unused test squeezed in my palm. In a matter of minutes, I will take a big breath in and continue my life as predicted or be thrown onto a path I didn't see coming.

"Pee on the stick and put it down somewhere flat." Madison is talking in a hushed voice, as if someone will overhear.

"I've done this before, remember?"

Her eyes flicker in the light and a shade of regret unrolls over her face. "Right, of course."

"Here goes nothing." I shut the door behind me, lean back on the wooden paneling, and stare at the toilet. I slide my butt to the floor and fill my cheeks with air. My cheeks are bursting with pressure. Part of me wants to see the plus sign; the other half knows this isn't the way things were supposed to pan out. Richard and I were a team, us against the world. Living in our small town, raising a herd of children, and watching them run through the apple orchard. Those dreams went down the drain along with every bottle of vodka I emptied. There would be no white picket fence, no tiny feet running through the dirt.

Now I'm standing in this bathroom with my best friend outside the door, potentially pregnant with Nick's baby. A man who almost destroyed our town, lives in the city, and practically prints money. We are not a team either.

"You okay in there?"

"I just walked in, Madison. Give me a second." I get my ass off the floor and sit on the toilet. Sliding my underwear and pants to my knees, I look up at the ceiling, pee, and let the stick absorb what it needs. I then place it on the tank and flush.

"Are you done?"

"Jeez, yes. I'm done. Come in." I wash my hands. Madison hovers over the stick.

"It takes a couple minutes. Let's go sit."

Neither of us says a word, drumming our fingertips on the wood table as each second ticks by in slow motion. "Okay, it's been three minutes. Let's go."

"Yes, ma'am."

Madison follows me into the bathroom and hovers over my shoulder. I pick up the stick and hold my breath.

"Holy shit. Holy shit. Holy shit." Madison holds on to my elbows. We back out of the bathroom. I'm still holding the stick as I melt into a kitchen chair.

"Say something." Madison reaches back and ties her hair into a ponytail and sits at the edge of her seat.

"I …" I look down at the stick. I see the plus sign. I understand what it means. What I don't understand is how to feel. It's as though every single human emotion is running through my veins instantaneously. I'm excited, terrified, sad, thrilled, panicked, hopeful, and the list goes on. "I'm having a baby." I drop the stick on the table and put my hands to my stomach. "I'm having a baby." I look down at my fingertips. "Holy shit, I'm having a baby!"

Now my ears are picking up on the words, and I'm getting

louder. "Madison, I am having a freaking baby! Holy shit. Holy shit. Wait, holy shit."

Madison jumps to her feet and embraces me in a hug that comes close to suffocation. "We are having a baby! That's right. Holy shit. I mean, we aren't, you are. I'm going to be an aunt!"

We hug, tears streaming down our faces, mascara running, hearts full. "What do we do now?"

"I'm pregnant, not deaf." I back away laughing. "I need a minute. Holy shit."

"Yeah, you've said that once or twice. How far along do you think you are?"

"It can't be long. It's early for sure. Wow, this wasn't planned."

"No shit. Were you guys safe?"

"We were, but apparently not safe enough. Oh my god, I have to tell Nick. What do you think he'll say?" Every positive emotion drains from my body and panic fills the emptiness. "I hardly know him. Our sex has been deeper than our conversations. How the hell am I going to drop this bomb?"

"Okay, let's think this through. Here, let me get you water." Madison runs over and fills a glass for me as if I'm more fragile than I was five minutes ago.

"I'm going to tell Nick first. You're going to have to keep this top secret until then. With Thanksgiving tomorrow, I'll go through the motions. He's supposed to be up here at some point tonight or tomorrow."

"Are you sure he'll make it? I heard the janitor talking about some storm blowing in."

"I heard. Yeah, it should be fine. He's only in Boston. However, he doesn't drive a truck. Maybe I'll text him. Will that be weird if I ask? We don't usually text about mundane details."

"I think now is a good time to start."

She's right.

Hey, are you coming up tonight?

NICK

Yeah, for sure. Why, you miss me?

A tingle passes between my legs. Madison is sitting across from me, and my sex drive kicks into overdrive. What the hell?

I do.

I mean, it's true. I do.

NICK

I like the sound of that.

Do you have plans tonight?

NICK

I was hoping you were my plan. I wasn't sure how busy you were.

Not too busy to see you.

NICK

Good girl.

*Fuck.* What has gotten into me?

"What is he saying?"

I press my phone to my chest, hiding it from Madison's view. I love her, but I don't need to out myself as a complete horndog. I may be throwing up in the morning, but all I can think about is getting Nick under the sheets again.

"Hold on, hold on." I point a finger.

I'll come to you. What time?

NICK

To me? Or for me?

*Dead. I'm dead.* I'm not good at sexy talk.

Both.

I hold my breath, eyes bugging. I watch as the bubbles appear on the screen.

NICK

I'll pick you up at 7.

Okay.

I set the phone down.

"Well, spill it. What did he say?"

"He'll be here at seven to get me."

"Holy shit."

"I think we've set a *holy shit* record today."

"Agreed. What are you going to say?"

"I have no idea. What I do know is I need a shower and to eat dinner. I'm okay. This will be okay. Oh my god, I'm having a baby. Holy shit."

Madison grabs me for another hug. Her happiness seeps into my bones. I can do this with or without him. Women do it all the time. No matter what, I'll be okay.

"Okay, I'll go—and I promise—" She pretends to zip her lips and tosses the key.

"Thank you for being here with me. I'll text you tonight or maybe tomorrow." I wink and walk her to the door.

"Do you really think you'll be into that tonight?"

All I can do is nod, laugh, and close the door behind her.

I'm not sure what my plan is. Selfishly, I'd like to take Nick for another ride before I break the news, just in case he decides to run.

# 22

Nick

The speedometer is way over sixty-five. Once Shannon's message came over the Bluetooth, my heartbeat quickened and so did my miles per hour. She's never asked my ETA. Maybe I've finally gotten under her skin.

It hits me when I pull off the exit that I'm the only one up here. Harold won't be my right-hand man anymore. Pulling into Hannaford's, I snag a spot alongside the building. I have an hour to get what I need, hustle to the house, and pick up Shannon. I push my door against the wind and am blasted by what feels like arctic air. *Holy shit.*

"Here's your cart, sir."

A white-haired woman with a name tag displaying Sheila stands inside the automatic doors. "Thanks, Sheila."

"Are you lost, sugar cakes?" She's pointing to my tie and sniffing around me like a K9.

"No, ma'am, I'm in the right place. Just in a suit, that's all."

"And looking mighty fine in it. Have a wonderful night."

"You too." A few feet ahead, I look back because I sense her stare burning holes in my ass. Sure enough, she raises her hand and wiggles her chubby little fingers.

I throw in a bag of grapes, cheese, crackers, a bottle of wine, and a case of cider. This will do until tomorrow. The store is wall-to-wall people slinging everything from gravy to green beans to boxed stuffing in their carts. There's almost a brawl over the last can of cranberry sauce. Cooking Thanksgiving for an entire family sounds like absolute hell. This is why we have restaurants.

The checkout line is twelve people deep. Time is ticking and no one here is in any kind of rush. A man working the customer service line looks to be finishing up with a woman returning dog food. After she takes her change, he flips on his service light. I'm not fast enough; a mother with one kid in the cart and two trailing behind cuts me off. I'm not a complete asshole. My wait time is at least cut down.

Despite trying to make small talk, Chuck quickly realizes I'm not here to make a friend. He rolls his eyes and picks up the pace. "Have a great night," I yell out halfway to the door.

Louis Vuitton shoes are perfect for the office, but not so much for a slippery walkway. I damn near kill myself walking from the car into the house. I turn the lights on, raise the heat, and throw the grocery bag in the fridge. I pull the tags off the panty set I bought and slide it into the top drawer of my bureau.

There's no time to change, so I throw on the work boots Harold left by the door the last time he was here. The look is ridiculous, but being late is worse.

As I'm walking up her driveway, Shannon meets me halfway. Black vest, gray hoodie, brown boots, and a winter hat loose have never looked sexier. In a matter of a few months, I've traded in high-heeled, long legs for sexy cozy. There's something about knowing what's underneath. I want her to be my gift to unwrap and no one else's.

There's something different about her walk, a confidence, a determination. Whatever it is, I like it.

"Hey, sexy." I hold out my arms to embrace her. She stops and looks from my head to my shoes and covers her cheeks.

"I don't think I've ever seen a man in a suit wearing work boots. This could be a thing."

"If you're digging it, I'll make it a thing." I loosen my tie and undo the top two buttons of my white shirt. I'm in it for her giggles. They drive me wild.

"Stop that." She reaches in and buttons me back up. "It's freezing out here. Come on, let's go." She grabs my hand and walks to her side of the car. I'd follow her anywhere.

Shutting the door behind her, I look up at her home, wondering if I could ever convince her to leave.

"Have you eaten dinner?" I reach across the seat to hold her hand. Her soft, cold fingers slip into mine. I crank the heat.

"I have."

She rests her head on the seat back, looking deep into my eyes. There is nothing basic about her. She has a way of looking through me like no one has before.

Her gaze makes me pause and wait to place the car in reverse. "You okay?" I lean into her. Her hand slips to my waistline. I reach in for a kiss and have to restrain myself from ripping her clothes off. She's a prize I need to take my time with. Not here. Not in this car.

I pull back and reverse into the road. Her seductive smile tells me all I need to know. I force myself to keep my focus on the road and get to the lake house.

Despite her seductive grin in my peripheral vision, I get us home without pulling to the side of the windy mountain road to make out with her like a hormonal teenager.

I've never been so excited to get a woman into my living space for a reason other than to show her what I have in my pants. Men have commented more than once they are envious of the women I can pull. I had no fucking idea that I was missing out. During all those years, I had no clue there was something better to be had.

Something deeper, real, authentic. I want her to know me, and I want to learn everything there is to know about her.

The lights are already on inside, so I grab her hand and lead her up the stairs. "I want to show you something. Don't take off your coat. Let me run and change. I'll be right back. The fire's on and there are drinks in the fridge."

"Yeah, okay." She looks left, then right, surveying the room, her forehead creased.

She's curious. I'm clearly up to something, and she willingly plays along.

After a quick change into jeans and a navy blue hoodie (thanks, Harold), I find Shannon looking out at the view of the lake. I wrap my arms around her middle and gently squeeze. "Follow me," I whisper into her ear. Her body shivers in response.

She interlaces her fingers with mine and follows me down the deck stairs and onto the back lawn. There's a crunch of leaves and frost under our feet. The air is still, not a light to be seen other than that from a brightly lit house across the water. Probably a family finishing up dinner or playing cards. I never thought peace and silence would be something I craved. But here I am, and I don't think I've ever been happier.

The cuff of my flannel jacket covers Shannon's fingertips. Her nails graze my wrist, turning me on. Then again, everything about her turns me on.

The dock has been lifted out of the water, but the one Adirondack chair remains on the grass by the rocks. I walk her a few feet from the edge, so the water doesn't seep into our boots. I stand behind her and wrap my arms around her waist. She's the perfect height to rest her head against my chest, and I kiss the top of her head through her fluffy gray hat.

"It's so beautiful, isn't it?"

Looking out onto the lake, I couldn't agree more. There's

an emptiness without the leaves, the summer commotion, and the crowds. What remains is a secret for those who stay. Tonight is clear, not a cloud in the sky. You'd never see this in the city. Each star shines. The moon lights a path along the still water. I tug her closer and whisper in her ear, "I don't want to let you go."

She turns slowly in my arms and places her cheek on my chest, hugging me closer. She doesn't say a word and yet says so much.

"Turn around. I want to show you something." I pull my camera strap off my shoulder and focus the lens, then place it in front of her, holding it steady. "See how the moonlight is dancing on the water?"

She nods.

"I want you to walk a few feet in front of me."

She spins, places her hands on her hips, and gives me a slight side-eye. "And why is that, Mr. Ford?"

She's never called me that, and it takes every ounce of my being not to throw her over my shoulder and carry her inside. "Mr. Ford, huh? Okay, I'm going to pause on that for a moment." Her words ignite a fire in my core, hot enough to set my skin ablaze. "I want to get a shot of your silhouette against the water. I've had this image in my mind, and tonight is the perfect night."

Shannon presses her hands to her heart and follows my directions—a perfect subject.

I take less than sixty seconds to get the shot I want. With the camera slung over my shoulder, I reach behind her and place my hands on her shoulders.

"I didn't think this place could get any more stunning. I've spent countless summer days taking in the beauty of Newfound, but I don't often stand here in autumn. It's so serene. Don't you think?"

"This city boy couldn't agree more. However, there's someone a whole lot more beautiful than the stars."

She takes my cue and turns. I don't waste a second and lift her into my arms and throw her over my shoulder. Working out has its benefits. She's like a rag doll and her giggles tell me she loves it.

"I can walk, Nick. Put me down!" She attempts to wrestle out of my grip. I give her ass a playful slap and restrain her tighter.

I put her feet on the ground in front of the deck stairs. "Get up there before I take a bite out of that ass." I love messing with her. She's so easy to shock.

Without a word, she shakes her head and charges up the stairs. I don't chase women. Never have. Never thought I would. But here we are.

She leaves her boots and vest by the door and settles into the couch. I unload my earlier food purchases and attempt to put together a charcuterie board. The fire is on. Shannon watches my every move from underneath the blanket she's covered herself with, the backdrop behind her nothing but the dark of the night.

Earlier today, I googled how this board should look, but I am failing miserably. I give myself an A for effort and place the board on the table in front of the couch.

"What are you going to do with that photo?" she asks, pulling off a few grapes and popping them into her mouth.

"I'm not sure yet. I'll find the perfect spot for it."

She grabs another handful of grapes and stands with the blanket drawn over her shoulders. With one knee in the cushion, she crawls onto my lap and straddles my waist. She drops a grape into her mouth and then one into mine. The juice trickles down my throat. I have so much I need to say … I want to say. But she's got me rock-hard and ready.

"Listen." The word comes out way more intense than I

intend. Her body freezes, and she settles deeper into my lap. "There's something I need to tell you." The light in her eyes clouds over and the corners of her mouth drop. She takes a deep breath and looks up at the ceiling.

"Hey, don't do that." I wrap my arms around her waist. "I'm a little afraid of freaking you out, but here goes nothing."

She looks braced for battle and immediately pushes off my lap and tucks herself into the corner. I'm not a genius when it comes to women, but it's clear I didn't prep this well, and now she's expecting disaster.

I don't do feelings. I'm not that guy. But somehow, she's turned me into this man. I want to be the man she deserves.

"Okay, I'm not good at this stuff. I need to say this."

"Sure, okay." She hugs her legs to her chest and rests her chin on her knees. Her eyes fill with anticipation and dread. If a tear falls, I'll never forgive myself.

"This isn't bad news, but I don't …"

"Just say what you need to say." She leans her head back into the cushion, ready to absorb my words.

"I'm not a one-woman type of guy. I'm not even a relationship kind of guy. Somehow, you've managed to change that. I don't mean to make myself out to be a total playboy, but I've never had time for anything other than a date here or there. My career has come first since the day my dad died, and I know I've told you that.

"But being here, being with you, has changed my life." I pause to see the clouds in her eyes drift off and the light return, giving me the strength to continue.

"The faster each day passed, the better. The more money a deal made, the richer I became. The richer I became, the more women were thrown my way. The more women I had, the less I felt. That changed when I met you.

"You're unlike anyone I've ever met. You see the world through a different lens. Where I saw black-and-white, you made it color. You allowed me to uncover a passion I'd kept buried alive for decades. You may not realize the way you look at life, but you have opened my world to so much more than my nine-to-five.

"I've been running for so damn long, I never realized how long it's been since I stopped to take a breath. I see you, I see this place, and I need to change."

I grab her hands in mine. The firelight dances around her sharp cheekbones and water fills the corners of her eyes. "I don't want to pressure you." I pause, knowing that the next sentence will either result in happiness or her grabbing her vest and hightailing it out of here.

"Just say it, Nick. Whatever it is, it's going to be fine."

Her words coat my nerves with calmness. "I'm selling the company. I'm selling my condo. I don't want that life anymore. I miss photography. I want meaning in my life. I'm tired of eating on the go, having Harold drive my ass around. I mean, I don't get me wrong, Harold is the best. You make me want to stock my own fridge and buy more than one stupid winter hat. I want to see every flannel on your body this winter and take every single one off. I want to use this money sitting in my bank for things that matter. I don't want horns and sirens to be the noise in my dreams. I want this. I want you. I am probably freaking you out." I stop, inhale, and hold my breath.

She hasn't said a word. All that's changed is the steady stream of tears rolling down her cheeks.

I exhale and drop my head in my hands. "I'm sorry. That's too much. I know. You are going through shit right now, and you're not even divorced yet. I've never been so confident with a decision before. Whether you want me or not, my life will be better from here on out. I want to open a studio. A photography studio. I've been putting a lot of thought into it. Remember that night we were on the dock? 43° North. That's what I'd name it."

I lean over and brush the tears off her cheeks and ease her back onto my lap. "Don't cry. I didn't mean to make you sad."

She leans her forehead into mine. "I'm not sad. Not sad at all." She presses her lips to mine, and I taste the salt from her tears. She holds my jaw on both sides and pulls me into her, her tongue exploring every inch. I run my hands through her hair, each strand like silk. My hands travel down her back and rest on her hips.

She pulls her lips away and snuggles into the crook of my neck. Her tears continue to soak through my T-shirt.

"Why are you crying if you're not sad?" I whisper.

"Trust me, these are happy tears. I'm not sure you'll love this place year round, but I can't wait to find out."

"You're happy? You aren't freaked out?" I pull my head to the side and try to steal a glance for some understanding.

She lifts her head and takes my face into her hands. "I don't think there are any other words I would rather hear come out of your mouth."

I don't waste another second. I reach my arms to the band of her sweatshirt and pull it up and over her head. Her smile and slight nod indicate game on. She takes off her T-shirt and unhooks her bra, freeing her breasts, and I pull her close and kiss every inch. Her nipples harden under my tongue. She tugs at my shirt, and I'm happy to oblige. Her fingers trace my chest and graze over the tattoos.

"You can stop talking now if you've gotten everything off this sexy chest of yours."

"I have absolutely nothing more to say."

"Good. Take me to bed."

I ease her off my lap so she's standing in front of me with nothing but her jeans. They sit low on her waist and show a toned stomach. "I." I reach for the button fly and release each one. "Have." I tug them off her waist and shimmy them to the floor. "Nothing." I slide each leg off her feet and remove her socks. "Left." I run my fingers along the inside of her legs until I'm over her panties. "To." I slide her underwear to the floor. "Say." I pull her into my mouth and explore every inch until I'm certain she's ready to release.

I pull back and take in the view. "Wait. What?" she asks, standing in front of me butt-naked, near breathless, dripping and swollen between her legs. "That's it? You're going to leave me like this?"

"Oh, baby. No. I'm not going to leave you like that." I throw her over my shoulder, reach my arm around her, holding on tight in just the right place, filling her until I get her upstairs. She moans onto my back.

"Leave the blinds open."

"Yes, ma'am." I toss her onto the bed and ignite the fire. If this is how the rest of my days are spent, I'll die a happy man.

# 23

*Shannon*

I open my eyes. It can't be later than seven o'clock. The sun is rising behind the mountains, a gorgeous view since Nick's spot on the lake is to die for. I'm tucked in close to his chest; neither of us moved after the last round. I don't know what has gotten into me. It's as if my libido has been locked in overdrive.

When Nick told me he was selling the company and moving to Meriden, my jaw almost hit the floor. Granted, he has no idea I'm pregnant, but I needed last night. The fact he made those plans, made decisions without ever knowing about the baby, is more than I could ask for. I don't know what lies ahead, but a newfound strength has bolstered me. I know I'll be okay.

Nick shifts behind me, his excitement pressing between my folds. He groans in my ear and presses deeper. My body reacts to him, but unfortunately, so does my stomach. I cover my mouth, bounce off the bed, and bolt to the bathroom.

I barely make it to the toilet. I'm heaving into the bowl and hear his footsteps approaching. "Shannon, are you okay?"

"Yup, all good here. Just give me a minute." Without a

word, he follows my direction. Thank goodness for his fluffy bathmat and radiant-heat floors. My body shivers in response to the violent projection of everything I ate last night. I sit back on my heels and regain my breath and wrap my arms around my naked chest.

Cleaning the swill out of my mouth, I look at my naked body in the mirror. For thirty-two, I'm proud to say I look good. Nick seems pleased, at least. My nipples are raw and red from the workout last night. I'm not complaining. I turn to the side, running my hand down my flat stomach. There is a life in there. No one would ever know. I'm not alone in this body. There's two of us. I'm hoping it'll be the three of us, but as long as there's the two of us, nothing can go wrong.

I hug my stomach and turn to the other side. It won't be long before this little one will make its presence known.

"Can I come in?"

I put the toothbrush he purchased for me in the holder. "Yeah, sure. The coast is clear."

Nick opens the door wearing nothing but boxer briefs. *Fuck, how did I manage to snag this hottie for a baby daddy?* I smirk at my intrusive thoughts.

"Why are you smirking? Are you okay? Something you ate?" Nick holds out a white bathrobe. "For you."

I hug the softness close to my chest. "This is heavenly." I pull my arms through and tie it around my waist. "Thank you. Yeah, I'm good."

"My mother and Ashlyn will be here soon. We should probably get dressed."

"I'm going to take off, anyway. I'm meeting my family for dinner at the Newfound Inn at four. We usually eat at my grandparents' house, but with everything going on, we decided to go out."

"This will be interesting. That's where we're headed for

dinner too. There was a cancellation, and we snuck in for a four thirty spot."

"Then I'll see you there, kinda sorta." We retreat to the bedroom and I slowly slide into yesterday's clothes. I'll grab a shower—or maybe a nice bath to soak my sore bits—when I get home.

Once I'm dressed, Nick walks me downstairs and helps me into my vest. Such a gentleman.

"Maybe we can meet up later?" He opens the front door for me and then leans against the frame, looking too good for me to leave.

"If you're lucky." I kiss him once more for good measure and shuffle to my truck, pulling my collar against my throat to keep out the morning chill.

With the truck door shut and Nick back inside his house, I slam my head into the cushioned headrest and turn the key. *What is wrong with me?* I should've told him. Fuck. Everything is so perfect. Nick poured his heart out to me. He's staying, and I selfishly want this feeling to last a little longer.

What if the pregnancy scares him out of his mind? What if he doesn't want any part of this? Never in my wildest dreams did I think a baby was in my future. How the hell is he going to react?

My phone rings. It's Jackson. I put him on speaker and back out onto the main road. "Hey, what's up?"

"I think Mom and Dad are finally realizing we might be right."

My heartbeat slows, as well as my speed. I look in the rearview mirror to be sure I'm not holding up anybody behind me. "What do you mean?"

"They found Grandma outside sitting on the front porch this morning in only her bathrobe, locked out."

"Wait, what?" I jerk the steering wheel to the right and pull over. "Is she okay?"

"She is now. They got her to the hospital. No one knows how long she was outside."

"Aren't Mom and Dad there?"

"They are, but at some point during the night, Grandma went outside and sat on the porch step until they found her. She's so confused, she didn't remember Mom when she went to bring her back inside."

"It was freezing last night!"

"I know. Luckily, she's physically okay. Grandpa is a mess. They are releasing her, but this isn't safe. You know it, and I know it."

Tears run down my cheeks. How is this all happening so fast? "Where is everyone now?"

"Grandma should be discharged in the next half hour and then Mom and Dad will bring them both back to the house. Grandpa is insisting on having dinner together."

"What can I do?"

"There really isn't anything we can do. Hopefully, they will rest this afternoon. We're going to have to call another family meeting."

This time it isn't the morning sickness that has me wanting to vomit. "Okay, text me if anything changes."

I hang up with Jackson and drive home, wondering if the doctors got this completely wrong. Maybe Grandma's memory won't come back. The thought of her sitting outside freezing in the middle of the night rips my heart in two. My parents must be so distraught.

I hang my vest on the back of the kitchen chair, grab a sleeve of crackers and peanut butter, and pull out my phone.

Is there anything I can do? How's Grandma?

MOM

> Nothing, sweetie. She's got a little frostbite on a couple of fingertips and dehydration was an issue. They filled her with fluids. She's stable and warm. Grandpa is insisting on dinner as a family, stubborn old bird. We'll see. Stand by.

Okay, love you guys.

MOM

Love you too.

How I'm already exhausted by midday is beyond me. Throwing up and napping are knocking me out. I missed two calls from Madison while I was asleep.

I prop my phone on the pillow next to me and FaceTime her.

"What's up, Momma? Oh shit, are you alone?"

I rub my eyes. "Yes, you idiot. Good thing!"

Madison's hair is done. She's dressed in a pale yellow sweater that brings out her natural highlights. "Aren't you going to dinner with your family? Are you in bed?"

"Yes and yes. I'll be ready. I was exhausted."

"Tell me about last night. Did you tell him?"

"Last night was amazing. He's moving here full time, and the sex was out of this world."

"He took the news well!"

I wrinkle my nose and forehead. "The thing is, I didn't tell him. I was going to, I swear. When he told me he was selling the company and staying in Meriden, he did it without knowing about the baby. I was so relieved and happy. The last thing I wanted was for him to feel trapped, cornered into a life he doesn't want. There's a chance he may not be interested in raising a child with me, but he decided to stay without any pressure. I guess I was so excited, I didn't want to ruin the moment. And I think I want to keep this a secret for just a bit longer."

Madison's eyes widen. "So … what's your plan?"

"I haven't figured it out yet. My grandmother was in the hospital this morning. She's okay and getting released soon. We have dinner at the Inn, which Nick's family happens to be going to also, totally unplanned. I have to meet with the family because Sylvia is going off the rails. She's beyond forgetful."

"I'm so sorry, Shan."

I know she means every word. Sylvia has been a part of Madison's life since elementary school.

"As Jackson would say, it's the circle of life."

"Doesn't mean that it doesn't suck," she says.

"Facts. You're having dinner at your parents' house?"

"Yeah. I'll call you later."

"'K. Have a nice time. Tell your mom I said hi."

I double- and triple-checked. Everyone is still insisting we meet at the Newfound Inn for dinner. My mother told me to give them space so they can get ready and they'll meet me there. Jackson and Solia offer to pick me up. I'm sure he figures I'll have a few glasses of wine at dinner. I don't correct him.

The Inn this time of year is as gorgeous as ever. Without the leaves on the trees, the view of the lake is as expansive as it gets. The pumpkins, autumn décor, and traditional fireplaces create a warm and inviting atmosphere.

Jackson, Solia, and I arrive before Mom and everyone. They have our table ready in the center of the room. The owners are family friends and have set us up beautifully.

"This is gorgeous." Solia runs her fingers along the white

linen tablecloth and cranberry garland between the long-stemmed wineglasses.

"Is this the first time you've been here?"

"As an adult? Yes. I'm sure we came when we were little. The meals I remember were beachside."

Jackson pulls out a chair on the end for Solia, kissing the top of her head. He then sits next to her.

I hear them before I see them. My mother, father, grandfather, grandmother, Gerry, Lucas, and Cindy round the corner. "I had no idea Lucas and Cindy were coming," I whisper to Jackson as we stand to help grab everyone's coats and place them on their chair backs.

"Sorry, forgot to mention that in the chaos."

"Hope you don't mind a few more people for dinner. Your parents insisted." Lucas remains standing and waits for a reply.

"I told you both—we're all family here," Jackson says. "When Gerry told us your mother wasn't feeling well, you weren't going to sit home alone. And Cindy, you know you are always welcome." My brother pulls Cindy in for a hug and then shakes Lucas's hand.

Hugs and kisses all around. We are a circus show in the middle of a busy dining room. The people at the surrounding tables are all locals. It takes a good ten minutes for the room to settle and for everyone to choose a seat.

I approach my grandmother and offer a gentle smile. Her focus is locked on my grandfather, and she doesn't acknowledge my presence. She flinches when I gently take her coat off her shoulders and place her winter hat in one of the pockets.

"What's she doing, Earl?" She hasn't let go of my grandfather's hand since they arrived.

He gives me a half smile and a wink. "She's taking your coat, sweetie. Let's get you comfortable."

"I am comfortable. Why does everyone want to cater to me like some goddamn fragile egg?"

My grandmother never talks like that in front of us grandkids. My mother always says she has a mouth like a truck driver, but I've never heard the evidence.

"We love you, Syl. That's all." He takes her elbow in his hand and guides her to the chair two seats down from me.

She looks so bony and frail. Her shoulders hunch forward, her hands clasped in her lap. Her eyes have a distant gaze. My grandfather uses his handkerchief every few moments to wipe her eyes. She's not crying, but they seem to water continuously.

"Everyone, grab a seat."

Gerry, Cindy, and Lucas sit across from Jackson, Solia, and me. My parents choose to sit across from my grandparents, I assume to keep a watchful eye on them. Wine and cider are set out and passed around. Thanksgiving at the Inn is easy. The menu is preset. They have it down to a science. Everything you'd want, they have it whipped up.

"I propose a toast." My father raises his glass.

I notice my grandmother isn't responding. My grandfather pushes his chair against hers and picks up both of their glasses.

"To family. Without each other, nothing is possible. To Earl and Sylvia, thank you for this beautiful life we are blessed to enjoy."

"Cheers!"

The glasses clink and smiles are abundant. I hear Grandma when she says, "What did he say, Earl? Who's he thanking?"

He hands her the wine and unfolds the linen napkin in her lap. "He's thanking you, sweetie. For everything you've done." He pats her leg and insists she drink up. No one caught the exchange but me.

I pinch my leg to stop the tears. My emotions are all out of whack. The corn bread and appetizers are passed around. I reach across the table and look up. Rounding the corner into the dining room are Nick, Claire, and Ashlyn. Claire is the first to spot me.

"Shannon, what a lovely surprise! Well, hello, everyone! Happy Thanksgiving. I'm Claire, Nicholas's mom." She begins to make her way around the table. Nick's face wears a silent apology for the awkward scene. I'm pretty sure I'm the only one catching Ashlyn rolling her eyes and probably fighting the urge to run.

I introduce my mother and father and the rest of the gang to Claire. Nick gets a hug and a firm handshake. Ashlyn waves from a distance. The only person more uncomfortable than Ashlyn is Gerry. I don't think I've ever seen Gerry squirm. He and Claire exchange a gentle embrace. Nick and I fire a quick glance at each other, and I can't help but giggle.

"Well, there's no sense in sitting separate, unless, of course, you'd prefer. I'm sure we can add to this table." My mother doesn't wait for a response. She calls over the hostess and puts things in motion. I shrug, hoping Nick is okay with it all.

Lucas and Cindy switch to the other side of Gerry, each moving down one and making room for the new crew to sit across from my grandparents and me.

Nick is overdressed, but I could eat him for dinner. He's wearing his tailored black dress pants, black belt, and crisp white button-down shirt tucked in and rolled at both wrists, displaying a hint of his tattoos. He kept the neatly trimmed scruff. His lips look as red as my chest did this morning. I'm having a difficult time paying attention.

"So, he's still here, huh?" My grandfather nudges me and points to Nick.

"Grandpa, he can hear you."

"I know he can hear me, sweetheart. That's the point. If he's here, he better be sticking around. Don't be messing with my granddaughter, you hear me?"

"No, sir. There will be no messing around." Nick sneaks a quick wink. "I'm quite smitten with your granddaughter."

"Well, no shit, Sherlock. It doesn't get much better than her. Except, of course, my Sylvia." He turns his attention to his wife and smiles.

I shrug and pass the potatoes.

The rest of dinner goes smoothly. There's no awkward or forced conversation. I try to involve my grandmother in the conversation, but she has a far-off glance that wasn't there before the surgery. She looks tired, her eyes drawn and glassy.

"What do you all do here for the Christmas season?"

"Funny you should ask, Claire," Solia pipes up from the end of the table.

If there's one thing Solia is on top of this year, it's the town's tree lighting. Because she's a new teacher at our school, she's being evaluated this year. No better way to impress than being in charge of the school's contribution to the event.

"The Friday after Thanksgiving, Meriden has a traditional tree-lighting ceremony in the center of town. There's a small parade with Santa on the fire truck. We serve hot chocolate. The food that's been collected from school gets put on the back of a wagon and pulled by a tractor for the town to see. I'm in charge of the food collection from the elementary school this year. It's really quite precious. And since you brought it up, Gerry, I have a favor to ask."

Gerry, who's been uncharacteristically quiet this evening, gives Solia his full attention. "Anything for you, dear."

Lucas laughs and covers his mouth. "Careful, Gerry."

Cindy giggles and places her head on Lucas's shoulder.

Interesting.

"Lucas's father was our Santa. Since he's sick, would you fill in?"

Smiles and laughter break out around the table. I can't think of a more perfect Santa than Gerry.

"Of course. Who's Mrs. Claus?" He digs into his turkey for another bite.

"That's just the thing. It was supposed to be Lucas's mom. We're stuck. If we can't find one, at least we have Santa."

"You can't have Santa without Mrs. Claus," my mother shouts from the opposite end of the table. "It's tradition."

Nick, who has remained quiet for most of the meal, only delivering sexy glances my way, offers, "Mom, you're planning on staying. How about you do it?"

I'm fairly convinced if daggers could shoot out of an eyeball, she would've fired them into her son. "Honey, I'm sure there is someone much more qualified for such an undertaking."

"Mom, it's a suit and candy canes. I assume all you have to do is wave. Come on, why not?"

I lean closer to be sure I'm hearing correctly, although this could be playful revenge for not coming clean about dating Gerry. At the same time, Nick is scoring points with my crew by offering up his mother for a small-town event.

"Sure, of course. It'll be lovely." Claire's smile tightens. She inhales sharply and shoves a bite of cranberry sauce into her mouth.

"You are not serious." Ashlyn tosses her napkin on the table and stands up. "What if it gets out on social media?"

"What if what gets out?" My mom leans forward, eyeing Nick's pretentious sister from a distance.

"This. My mother dressed up as Mrs. Claus on the back of a fire truck. This is ridiculous. What will my friends think?"

She's a toddler pitching a fit in the middle of the restaurant.

"All the more reasons to suit up!" My father puts his hands on his stomach and lets out a "Ho, ho, ho!"

Ashlyn rolls her eyes again and drops her stuck-up ass into her seat.

"Earl, it's Christmas? Are we going to town tomorrow night?"

"I'll take you anywhere you want to go." My grandfather reaches over and smooths the white wisp of hair off her forehead.

"Grandma, today's Thanksgiving, and the tree lighting is tomorrow."

"Yes, yes. All right." My grandmother's eyes dart away from mine in one blink. The same vacant stare remains. The tether that binds the two of us is thinner than it's ever been. My grandfather must sense my unease. He winks and curls his bottom lip under his front teeth.

He silently mouths the words, "She'll come around."

All I can do is smile. The last time she recognized me is a distant memory. I wish I had known. I wish I had videoed her saying my name or giving me a hug.

I lean back in my seat and notice my parents whispering back and forth. Solia butters a roll for Jackson. Nick and his mother banter. Ashlyn sulks and checks her phone. Gerry, Lucas, and Cindy are in a deep discussion about whether it's safe to throw candy canes into the crowd. Last year, the head of the PTO was there and made a comment that it's too early to sugar up the children. Like that's our biggest problem.

Looking around this table, at this food, at these people, knowing there will be an extra seat at the table next year hits me like a freight train. Whether it's the reality of the situation or the hormones, there's no stopping the tears. They don't go unnoticed by Nick.

He leans his elbows on the side of his plate and winks. "You okay?" he asks soft enough for only my ears underneath all the commotion.

"Shannon, join me in the bathroom," my mother announces over the scraping of her chair.

Her comment freezes the stream of tears. I nod, push my

chair in, and walk to the other side of the table. "I'm okay, thank you." I brush my hand against Nick's shoulder blade and follow my mother to the bathroom.

"Listen, Shannon. Your father and I were going to talk to both of you tonight. I don't want to see you sitting there crying. I know it's difficult to see your grandmother this way."

"Mom, it's …"

"Just hear me out."

"Can I pee while you talk? I didn't realize how badly I have to go." This seems to be a thing the last couple of days. I'm good, but then it hits me and I'm running with urgency.

"Yes, of course," she says. I step into a stall and she continues. "You kids were right. This is too much for your grandfather. I was hoping the doctor would be correct and things would turn around, but after last night, I can't be up wondering if Sylvia's going to die outside in the middle of winter because she's confused. Grandpa is adamant about keeping her at home. But I think he's coming around."

"Hang on." I wait for the flushing to finish.

"We secured a room in Plymouth Center."

"Does Grandpa know? Wait, she'll be by herself?" I pull a paper towel off the neatly folded pile and look in the mirror at my mother standing behind me. "Alone? She's going alone?"

"I know it's awful. But they have a great dementia unit. The nurses are friendly and there's an opening. People wait on lists for a while. We got lucky."

Hearing the words *lucky* and *dementia* mentioned together is wrong.

"Grandpa can visit as often as he wants. It's only about twenty minutes away. Your father is going to head back to New York, and I'll stay for at least another week or two."

"Grandpa's going to be by himself? He'll be a wreck in that house alone. They are never apart." Now the tears are flowing out of control. My mother does the only motherly thing there is to do. She pulls me in and lets me sob into the fabric of her white linen shirt.

"Come on. I'll talk with Solia and Jackson after dinner. Oh, and honey, hold on to him. He looks like he's in it for the long run. The looks he's giving you only come from being smitten." She pries me off her chest, hands me another paper towel, and opens the door for me to follow.

Today has been a roller coaster of emotions, to say the least. Nick is helping my grandmother out of her chair when I return, and I rush to his side. "Did something happen?"

"This young man was helping me to my feet. Cutie, isn't he? A young girl like you would be lucky to land such a hunk. Come on, help me over to the bathroom door."

Nick is all smiles. "Is she okay in there alone?" he whispers to Earl.

"So far, so good in the bathroom. Hasn't needed my help yet."

My grandfather steps aside and watches the two walk to the restroom like a pair of snails.

I turn my attention to Earl, noticing his coat. "Are you leaving?"

"I think it's best. She's exhausted and so am I."

I look over at my father. He nods in agreement. My mother takes Nick's spot and explains the care plan to the rest of the table. Everyone sits at the edge of their seat with solemn eyes. I'm certain each of them understands the sadness behind this dreaded decision. My grandfather stands poised, eyes focused on the bathroom door.

"It's going to be okay." I reach around his waist. He pulls out his freaking disgusting rag and wipes his eyes.

"Yes, dear, it will."

My grandmother exits the bathroom and slides her feet across the hardwood floor, careful to remain steady. "What are we all standing for? Is it now?"

Everyone looks to one another either clenching their teeth or scratching their head.

"We're going to head back to the farm, honey. You ready?"

"If you say so, then it is so."

Grandpa lifts her maroon wool coat off the back of her chair and weaves her arms through the sleeves with a gentleness you'd use to handle an infant.

After a round of hugs and goodbyes, the four of them leave arm in arm.

The rest of us sit in silence for a minute until Claire breaks the tension. "They are precious, aren't they? You don't see love like that every day."

Solia leans into Jackson. I'd throw up at the cheesiness if I weren't so in love with their happiness. Nick's foot taps mine and our eyes meet. Maybe they aren't the only cringy couple at the table.

The waitress drops off a bread pudding at each setting and leaves the check in the center. "Do you mind wrapping those four to go?"

Wanda, who I've known my whole life, shakes her head. "I'm not sure what I was thinking. I saw the four of them leave and didn't put two and two together. I know how much Earl and Sylvia love their pudding. Of course. I'll toss an extra side of whipped cream in the doggy bag."

"Thanks, Wanda. They'll love that."

"First of all, what is bread pudding? And second of all, what on earth is a doggy bag? Who the hell has a dog that eats bread pudding?"

There is no stopping the wave of laughter roaring from the table. For once, being an outsider has backfired on Ms. Ashlyn. Her face is the deepest shade of red I've ever seen.

"Welcome to the back country, sweetie." Gerry chuckles, his belly bouncing to the beat.

"I don't get it." She looks at her mother for an explanation, who in turn shrugs and smirks. This is freaking priceless.

The rest of us dig into our dessert and let Ashlyn spoon around for some understanding.

"Looks like we have a busy weekend ahead, folks." Gerry reaches and puts an arm around the back of Claire's chair.

"Tell me about it. Everyone who left town comes back for Thanksgiving. The Binn will be mobbed."

"Are you working all weekend, Cindy?"

I don't miss the underlying meaning of that question or the wink Lucas throws her way. I will forever picture Cindy bent over the bar after hours.

"Sure am. Friday and Saturday until the wee hours."

"What else do you do?" Ashlyn pushes her uneaten pudding forward and waits for an answer.

"Slinging drinks is my only gig."

A lump of dessert almost projectiles out of my mouth. Drinks aren't the only thing on the menu this weekend. Both she and I know it.

"On that note, I hate to bust up the party, but I'm going to head out. What do you think?" I slide my hand over Nick's thigh.

Wanda takes the check and card from Nick. "Nick, you aren't paying for this. Wanda, give me that." I reach across the table, but he waves Wanda off.

"I'll be right back," says Wanda with a smile that is meant for Nick.

"Let me. I want to."

"Thank you." I squeeze the muscle under my hand and smile. He may shape up to be a family man after all.

Jackson clears his throat to get my attention. "Mom just texted me from the car. Grandma is rambling about leaving the house to pick crops again. This isn't good."

"Why is everything going downhill so fast?" I slump in my seat and a heaviness settles in my heart.

"Nighttime dementia, dear. It's real, and it can happen to the best of us. It's the most difficult for the loved ones watching them slip away." Gerry reaches across the table for the coffee Wanda left.

"Jackson, it's going to be Christmas. She loves Christmas. Their old-fashioned tree, the houses that light up, the village she sets up, the traditions." The tears again flow. "It's never going to be the same. Will she be able to come home for Christmas?"

Solia leaves her seat and folds her arms around my back. "We will figure it out. We can make new traditions, Shannon. I'm sure she can come home and be with us."

Claire and Nick nod in agreement.

Nick's eyes are frozen on me. I'd do anything to fold up in a ball and let him help me forget all this sadness.

Ashlyn, whose ability to read the room is about as sharp as a butter knife, abruptly shifts the conversation. "I guess we'll be going to this Christmas thing downtown. Please tell me there's wine. And then we are heading home right after, correct? Mom, I need to be back. I have brunch with the girls on Sunday."

"Yes. Of course. If I want to stay longer, I can always have Harold come get you."

Cindy's body goes rigid when Harold's name is mentioned. Everyone else is none the wiser besides Nick and me.

Fantastic. We've got about fifteen different major events and life-altering situations occurring in the next forty-eight hours. Oh, and I need to tell Nick I'm having a freaking baby. What could go wrong?

# 24

Nick

"Holy shit. Why did we sit with them? It's Thanksgiving. What the hell?"

"Ashlyn, honestly. You need to calm down. Dinner was lovely. You might want to get used to it."

The fact my mother attempts to come to my rescue and save me from the wrath of my sister is admirable. "It's okay. She'll get the pole out of her ass eventually." My mother chuckles when Ash storms off to the bathroom.

"Come on, let's go down to the water. The sun is setting, so it's perfect. Meet us down there," I shout loudly, certain she won't take me up on the offer.

My mother settles into the chair I've left out on the lawn. "This spot is beautiful. Your dad would be really proud."

I stand by her side, her hand sliding into mine. Looking down at my mom, she seems so small, and I think back to dinner and remember how short time really is. "I know I gave you a hard time about Gerry. It's weird—I'm not going to pretend it isn't. But it really isn't any different from Shannon and me."

"Thanks, sweetie. It's just a crush right now."

I have to pull back and stare down. "A crush? I don't think I've heard anyone over the age of thirteen use that term."

"Well, now you have. It is what it is."

"It's freezing down here!" Ashlyn walks down the lawn, wrapped in every blanket from the living room.

"You better get used to it if you plan on seeing your big brother. I hear the winters here can be brutal."

"You're seriously going to live here? They eat bread pudding out of doggy bags." She huffs, sending a billow of steam into the air above her head.

I wrap my arm around Ashlyn's shoulder. "Afraid so, and not only that, but you are going to help me with a special project tomorrow."

Without having to twist Ashlyn's arm too tightly, we head down Route 3 toward Walmart. Convincing them to help me decorate the house for Christmas to surprise Shannon was easy. We don't have a large family. My father was always working or on business trips when we were kids. My mother did the best she could. We always had a tree and presents, a plate of cookies for Santa, and a handful of carrots left out for the reindeer.

Once I heard the news about Shannon's grandparents, her eyes said it all. If decorating the hell out of the lake house gives her back some brightness, I'm in.

I throw a ten in the collection bucket for a local charity and push a cart toward my mom and sister.

"We need three?" Ashlyn eyes the cart as if it's a petri dish.

"Grab a wipe and get over it." I flick my hand toward the dispenser. "Shit, it's Black Friday." I point to the sign up ahead. No wonder there were only a few carts left. The automatic door opens to a goddamn circus. Red and green have exploded, candy canes hang from the ceiling, every cookie laced with red dye number forty is on full display, and a Santa who appears half in the bag is waving people in.

"I've never been here before. This is going to be interesting." I look over to my mother and sister who stand frozen, staring ahead at the wall-to-wall people who appear to be in their pajamas, running circles around one another.

"Let's get to it." My mom white-knuckles the carriage and steamrolls ahead, clearing a path. Weaving through the underwear aisle and dodging the strollers is a challenge. The Christmas section is another story. People are everywhere. Kids run past with garland wrapped around their necks. Moms toss plastic containers of Goldfish into strollers. Women hurdle over each other for boxes of lawn decorations.

The three of us exchange glances and head in three different directions. In an effort to keep this as pain-free as possible, I made a list for each of us. The tree, ornaments, and stockings are on my list. Ashlyn has to find a snow village or something similar. Shannon mentioned loving the one her grandparents put up. My mother is in charge of garland, wreaths, twinkly lights, and candles for the windows.

Two hours and three carts filled to the brim later, we finish in the aisles and head to the front of the store. I'm sweating, exhausted, and need to get the hell out of here. If the two hundred people playing bumper cars in the self-checkout lane is any indication, this is going to take a while. I hear Ashlyn sulking behind me.

We manage to fit all the bags into every available inch of the SUV, except I didn't think ahead, so I have to angle the tree box to hang out the rear passenger window.

"Are we seriously going to drive around with the window down? I'm going to freeze to death!"

I want to take a picture of Ashlyn, but I also want to stay alive. She is crammed in the back seat, covered in plastic bags with her head pushed to the side to make room for the tree box. Where is my camera when I need it?

"Something funny?" She clenches her jaw and delivers a vicious side-eye to both of us.

Mom and I turn back around and giggle. I'm going to enjoy this ride home a little too much.

**M**om and Ashlyn go into the house in hopes they'll figure out what to make to eat while I start to unload the car. My phone buzzes in my pocket.

SHANNON

My parents moved my grandmother in, and Grandpa is back at home. I'm going to stay the afternoon.

How are they?

SHANNON

As good as can be expected. It's sad.

I'm sure. Do you have your car there?

SHANNON

I came with my parents.

I'll come get you.

SHANNON

It's no bother?

I'm happy to pick you up. What time?

SHANNON

It's 12 now. How about 2? The tree thing is at 7.

Perfect.

If there's anything I excel at, it's working under pressure and meeting a deadline. We are going to whip this place into a winter wonderland, eat, and surprise the shit out of Shannon.

In under ten minutes, all the bags are in the house, Claire is warming the leftovers Gerry insisted we bring home, and Ashlyn has her bags in hand.

"Where the heck are you going?"

"Listen, I'm all for family bonding. It's been great. I went to freaking Walmart. I'm going to Uber home. There's a ride on the way. A few of my friends want to hit the bars in Boston tonight. So many people are home for the holidays. As much as staying and watching a rinky-dink tree get lit sounds amazing, I'm going to go."

She has a point.

"Let her go, Nick. You only live once."

"I'm not going to stand in her way, but she can set up the houses on the table in the living room while she waits."

Ashlyn salutes and gets busy.

I shovel a few bites of mashed potatoes into my mouth and lay out all the color-coded branches of the tree. I debated between a fake or real tree. Maybe I'll get both, but I'm starting with a fake. I have no idea what's involved with a real one. Do I have to cut it down? How does it stay upright? It's too much too soon.

In about ninety minutes, this place goes from lake chic to Christmas on the lake. We put the tree in the corner next to the floor-to-ceiling window. You can see it from every angle. I went with white lights, random colored ornaments, and a white circle rug thing underneath. Ashlyn left ten minutes ago but was able to lay the fluffy faux snow on the long rectangular table behind the couch and place the winter village pieces.

Each house and store has a battery-operated light shining through the window.

We keep the candles in the bag because I'm an idiot and don't have windowsills. I have floor-to-ceiling windows. Five decorative stockings hang from the mantel. Why five? I have no idea.

There are a few snow globes in the kitchen, a festive tissue holder in the bathroom, and a red velvet blanket thrown over my bed and the couch.

It's not quite how I envisioned it, but it's impressive nonetheless. I think Shannon will like it too.

"I'm going to head over to get Shannon, and then we can figure out dinner."

"About that." My mother is arranging a strand of cranberry garland and twinkly lights around the mantel. "I'm going over to Gerry's. He called. The costume is at his house, so I'll get ready there. I'll let you and Shannon have your privacy tonight."

I'm searching through the lakeside restaurants to see where I can order takeout and stop mid-scroll. "I'm going to pretend you didn't tell me you're staying at Gerry's. How about we'll see you at the town tree thing, and I'll pretend you went home?"

"Whatever you'd like, darling."

I'm hoping to avoid any further thoughts about my mother and Gerry.

This place smells absolutely horrid. A mixture of antiseptic and bleach fills the air. I pass by the round wooden counter where a handful of nurses in scrubs scurry around with brown trays and towels in their hands.

"Excuse me? I am looking for Sylvia Christianson's room?"

"Well, hello there, you sexy doll. It's not often we see a strapping young man like you roaming our halls. Do we, ladies?"

"Dolores, let the man be." A woman whose name tag reads Mary shushes Dolores, who looks close to becoming a nursing home resident herself. "Follow me."

The rest of the nurses giggle. I turn and throw them a wink for kicks.

"She's right in there."

"Thank you."

I peek my head into the room. Shannon's back is to me. She's sitting in a folding chair near the edge of Sylvia's bed. I'm a few minutes early. I take a seat in the wooden chair outside the room.

The hallways are silent except for the faint beeping of machines and the murmur of patients in their rooms. It's depressing to know that when you move into this place, it's the last stop. You're not going anywhere else after this. It sucks.

"I'm going to come back."

Shannon's words are loud enough for me to hear.

"You're not alone. We'll visit all the time."

"Okay, dear. You're not alone either."

"What do you mean, Grandma?"

"Your secret is safe with me. It's going to be wonderful."

My eavesdropping is interrupted when one of the nurses with a brown tray stands in the doorway to Sylvia's room. "You can go in. Come on."

"Oh, I didn't want to interrupt."

Too late. Shannon's already looking toward the door and smiling. "Hi, Nick. Come on in."

How she manages to look good while sitting in a nursing home is beyond me. She's wearing her snug jeans and beige crocheted sweater. Her hair is slicked back in a ponytail. I smile and take an extra second to make sure she feels my stare.

"Hi, Shannon. Hi, Sylvia." I bend down closer to make sure she can hear me.

"I'm not deaf, just old. Who are you?"

"This is my ride, Grandma. I'll be back."

Shannon leans to kiss her cheek and reaches for my hand. She's biting the inside of her lip and pulls me out the door. I'm not sure what's going on. We don't speak a word until we are in the parking lot.

"Ugh, thank you for coming." She releases my hand, covers her eyes, and throws her head up to the sky. "That was awful. No matter how much I understand why she needs to be there, it's awful. One minute she's sleeping and the next she's arguing. Today was the first time in so long she remembered me. Like, really remembered me. I wanted to hang on and tell her not to let go, to make it somehow stick. What if we are making the wrong choice? What if she'll forget even more because she's not at home? She's going to miss my grandfather so much."

Shannon stops to take a breath and begins to cry. I'm totally out of my element here. I do the only thing I can think of—I pull her into a hug and hold on. Her breathing eventually slows. She's no longer shaking and sobbing.

"Thank you," she whispers into my chest. "We can go now."

She looks out the window for most of the ride home. I'm hoping this doesn't turn out to be a Christmas décor disaster. My timing might be way off.

"That was tough, huh?" I grab her hand and squeeze her fingers tight.

"Yeah. It's going to be an adjustment for everyone. She's safe, and that's what is most important, but my heart is breaking, knowing our family will never be the same. I don't like seeing her there."

When we pull into the driveway, I look over at Shannon to see if she notices the Christmas tree in the front window. Her eyes are distant, however, and I again worry that maybe I should've waited to do this.

I lead her up the stairs and unlock the door, hesitating before opening it. "So, listen. I'm not sure if this was a good idea or not, but I did a thing. Well, we, meaning my family, helped me do something this morning. And I'm not sure if the timing is great, but …"

She squints up at me and smirks. "I love surprises. Yes, the timing couldn't be better."

I let the air out of my lungs and push the door open. All the lights are off in the house except for the decorations. Despite the fact we need to walk up a couple steps to the main floor, the brightness illuminates the foyer. Shannon's looking for the source of the lights. She turns with an adorable giggle, tugs off her boots, and rushes up the stairs. I'm right behind her.

She doesn't move and her hands cover her mouth. For the second time today, her tears roll.

I walk behind her and wrap my arms tight. "Do you like it?"

"Do I like it? No. I love it." She spins around to face me. "You did this for me? Why?"

"I heard you mention the traditional Christmas stuff your grandparents do every year. I know this year will be different and thought this would make you happy."

She lays her head against my chest and hugs me tighter. "This is the sweetest thing anyone has ever done for me. I love it." She reaches up and presses her lips to mine. "Thank you. I can't believe your mom and sister, especially your sister, did this with you. Where are they?"

She pulls away and moves to investigate the snow village piece by piece.

"I didn't want to say this aloud, but Mom is at Gerry's. Ashlyn went home to go out with her friends."

The porcelain tree in her hand is gently placed back in its position. "We're alone?"

"Yes, in fact, we are. How about a cider? I stopped and got your favorite."

I crack open a can and walk over to the couch.

She follows and settles against the corner cushions, knees tucked into her chest like the last time, wrapped in the new red holiday blanket.

"Here." I offer the drink, but she doesn't move.

"I'm okay. Maybe some water." Her expression hardens and jaw tightens.

I step closer, eyeing her like a fragile doll. "Why are you smiling?"

She grabs my hand and pulls me onto the cushion next to her. "Come here, sit down."

I sit sideways next to her. My eyes drift to her chest. The blanket slopes down, revealing the fullness of her breasts peeping out of her V-neck sweater. Her eyes follow my stare. She giggles and pulls the blanket higher.

"Sorry." I grin and look up.

"No complaints here."

She releases her knees, crosses her legs, folds her hands over the blanket on her lap, and straightens her back. Now, I'm getting nervous.

"What I'm about to say is a lot. I should've told you last night. I'm not sure why I didn't. Forget that—I know why I didn't. The other night was amazing, and I didn't want anything to ruin it. You've made so many huge decisions. I selfishly love each one you've made, but …"

Now my back stiffens and I turn to face her. I take her hands in mine.

"Whatever you say to what I'm about to tell you is okay."

I brace for my first breakup.

"Shannon." I squeeze her fingers. "I spilled my guts last

night. I knew there was a chance you'd be scared away. But you're here. Just say whatever you want to say. You won't hurt me." I know full well that can't be further from the truth.

She tilts her head to her chest, avoiding eye contact, and clears her throat. "I'm pregnant."

I look up to meet her eyes. Every single muscle backfires, and I'm frozen. I'm not sure my ears are working.

"Nick, I'm pregnant."

Still nothing. My body won't move. My eyes drop to her stomach.

She presses her hands into my cheeks. "Breathe. Nick?"

I finally blink, reach across, and pull the blanket, allowing it to fall to the floor. I undo one sweater button at a time and ease the fabric off her shoulders and down her back. I'm moving involuntarily, unable to speak. I open my palms and hold the fullness of each of her breasts. My fingertips trail along her torso and onto her belly.

I stop and leave them there. "You're pregnant?"

"Yes, I'm pregnant." She says it again.

I remove my hands, stand, and walk to the sliding glass doors. I cross my hands behind my head. My back expands and the stiffness of each muscle relaxes on the inhale.

A wave of panic cascades over my body. I'm not sure if seconds or an eternity pass. I'm not in control of my body as my hands reach my knees and I bend over. I hear her clear her throat and snap back to reality.

I turn around, walk to the couch, and drop to my knees in front of Shannon. I slide my arms around her back and inch her to face me.

The silence is thick, the anticipation breathtaking. I pull her sweater apart again and spread her knees, inching myself between. I reach up and kiss her neck, wrapping my arms around her waist. I sit back onto my heels, and drop my head onto her legs.

"You're pregnant." It's barely a whisper. A soft utterance against her thigh.

She takes the silent cue and steps in. She guides my head off her leg. I've never experienced a moment so raw.

"Sit down next to me. I know this is a lot to take in. I'm in shock too. You don't need to decide anything right now. I want you to absorb it."

I'm shaking my head feverishly from the second she starts speaking.

"You don't understand. I don't need to absorb anything. I hear you. I hear every word you are speaking. I was afraid I'd scare you away by moving here. I was afraid you'd think I was crazy. But you stayed, you're here, and if I'm hearing you correctly, our baby is inside you. Like, right now. There's a baby inside you that I put there."

Tears form in my eyes. I am no longer a cutthroat businessman in charge. I'm cut down to my knees. A puddle of mush.

"Yes. Yes, Nick. Your baby is inside me."

"Can you stand?"

Her body lengthens before me, and I'm in awe.

"Come here."

She stills while I unbutton her jeans and shimmy them down. She's breathtaking in nothing but her bra and underwear.

I admire the view. There will only ever be one moment in time like this. I pull her closer and drop to my knees. I place my lips on her stomach, gently kissing every inch of her skin. I see the tears flooding her eyes, down her cheeks, and along the length of her body.

I stand and hold her chin in my hands and kiss her with an intensity I've never known. "Did I hurt you the other night? I wish I had known. Is that why you're sick?"

"No, Nick." She pulls me tighter. "I wanted it all. Knowing

you decided to move here without knowing about the baby meant more to me than you'll ever know. You didn't hurt me. I don't think it's possible. And as far as the throwing up, it's been a daily thing."

"This is so weird."

She blinks and looks sharply up at me. "Weird?"

Shaking my head and covering my eyes, I want to backtrack. "This is going to sound really off, but … here, sit down. Get comfortable. You're probably freezing."

I wrap Shannon's sweater over her shoulders and tuck the blanket around her, pulling her into my chest and down onto the couch.

"I've never given pregnant women much thought. I know that sounds awful, but it's true. The second I touched your stomach, something shifted. Knowing I helped put a life inside you—like, my baby is growing inside you—has made me so hot, it's actually slightly disturbing."

A laughing fit ensues. I'm not sure if she's laughing at me or with me. "So, you're okay with this?"

Gently, I spin Shannon to face me, tucking another fleece around her, as if the cold will damage her perfect skin if I wait another second.

"Am I okay with this? Fuck yeah. I don't think you understand. I laid it out gently last night because I didn't want to scare you away. I want you in my bed every single night. I don't want to see another woman in my bed for as long as I live.

"I fucking love you, Shannon. And that's saying something, because I can't remember the last time I said that to someone other than my mother. I knew there was something about you the first time I met you. You make me want to be a better man. Did I expect to start a family? No. But here we are. Did I tell you this makes you twice as sexy to me?"

She places her hands over her exposed chest. "Yeah, you did mention that."

"You are the fucking sexiest woman I've ever seen. I want to be that guy for you. I'm here and not going anywhere, if you'll have me."

"Yes, Nick. I want you. And I'll have you know that for some reason, this pregnancy has made me hornier than I thought humanly possible."

I cock my head to the side, liking what I'm hearing. "Oh, really?" I slide out and kneel over her. "What are the rules regarding this? Because your wish is my command."

"That is music to my ears, city boy. Get naked."

"You got it." I strip in record time but hesitate. "You sure there aren't any rules?" My cluelessness is on full display.

"No, the baby is protected and untouchable. You can have your way with me, and I'm going to love every minute of it. The dirtier, the better." She looks between my legs and licks her lips in anticipation.

"Who am I to deny my baby momma? Flip over on your hands and knees." I don't need to tell her twice. She's spread wide and ready.

This Thanksgiving, I am thankful for more than I ever imagined and I surely let my gratitude show with every thrust. I've never been so invested—I think I shocked her. We end up in the shower, swollen and content.

I hold her in my arms. I've never wanted to protect someone more than I do right now.

"So, what's next? What do we do, Momma?" I lather up her belly and reach for the nozzle to rinse it off.

"We go kick off Christmas. And I think we keep our little secret from everyone for a while, at least until we're in the clear."

I wrap my arms around her, our bodies pressed tighter than we've ever been.

# 25



Life certainly doesn't always go according to plan. The longer I live, the more I learn. Am I scared? Absolutely. Will everything be okay? Who knows? But right now, right here, I'll soak this in. It doesn't matter how cold the chill in the November air is, I have a man standing behind me, his arms wrapped tight around me, ready to walk into the future hand in hand. Is this a fairy tale? No. Will Nick and I make it? Time will tell. But I'm willing to walk forward and let whatever is meant to be simply be.

The dark of night is lit by the lanterns hanging from the lampposts and kids running with Santa hats and glow-in-the-dark bracelets around their wrists. Everyone I know and love is standing along the Meriden sidewalks for the tree lighting. If anyone told me five months ago I'd be standing here with a Green Breeze executive, I would've laughed.

The only people missing are my grandparents. Navigating this new normal will be a process. I'm not sure I'm ready for the road ahead, but there are parts of life that are simply out of my control. Richard is on a healing path of his own, my grandparents are aging, my brother is getting married, and Nick and I are having a baby.

As if reading my mind, Nick slides his hands under my sweater and rubs my belly.

I look to my left and smile upon seeing Jackson and Solia. Madison winks and turns to join the countdown.

"Three, two, one!" The crowd breaks out in applause as the mayor lights the tree in the brick circle in the middle of the street. He lifts the microphone. "Let the festivities begin!"

The fire truck roars around the corner, lights flashing. Nick pulls his arms out, slings his camera off his shoulder, and steps in front of everyone. "Sorry, guys. There is no way I'm missing this shot."

Gerry and Claire are perched on top of the truck. Gerry is rocking the full white beard and Claire the red dress and round, black-framed glasses. The kids in the crowd go wild and mini candy canes are tossed into the crowd. I'm sure the sugar police is going crazy somewhere.

I smile, thinking about how in a few years, our little someone will be catching candy canes too.

Nick snaps away with his camera. As the truck passes us, Claire and Gerry wave and toss a few candy canes in our direction. Gerry lets out a big "Ho, ho, ho."

"Did you get the shot?"

"I sure did. Wait until I post these."

Nick puts his camera behind him and works his way behind me.

"Since we're keeping secrets, do you want to hear another one?" He snuggles close, whispering in my ear.

I nod in response, wondering how much more my heart can handle.

"Once things settle, I think I found a building for 43° North. Everything will be exactly as it was meant to be. You will never regret giving this city boy a chance. The both of you," he says, sliding his palm over my belly, "are my true north."

**The End**

# acknowledgments

What a dream this has been! Every sentence written, every post created, and every friendship made has been a blessing in my life. Not one minute of this has felt like work. The online community has embraced and cheered me on through every word, and I am forever grateful. I knew becoming an author would change me in unexpected ways, but this is almost more than my heart can handle.

I love the community of Newfound Lake, and being able to share these fictional characters in a place I love is a dream come A huge thank-you and all my love to my editor and friend, Jenn Sommersby Young. You are a guiding light and an amazing wingwoman. I could never have done this without you. Thank you from the bottom of my heart. You truly are Superwoman!

My ARC team, you have my heart. Many of you have been with me since day one. You took a chance on a brand-new author and have stuck by my side. Thank you for being the best ARC team out there. Any author would be lucky to have you on their team.

To every single reader and follower in the #BookTok community, what a ride this past year has been! I started out extremely nervous to post, and now I'm a full-blown maniac. Together, we've laughed, cried, and shared some beautiful moments. I am in love with this community because of the readership, the friendships, and the endless positivity and laughs.

To my small town, colleagues, and friends, thank you. You

are the biggest cheerleading squad a small-town girl could ask for. Your support, words of encouragement, and assistance in spreading the word about my work is the true essence of small-town magic.

The biggest thank-you is reserved for my family. You've never once wavered. I am the luckiest girl in the world to be able to spend this lifetime with you. Even when I'm sure you thought my dreams were too big, you've made it a point to ask how things are going each and every day. You've celebrated every new reader, clapped for every new review, and encouraged me to continue. I love you all. Each of you is my true north.

I look forward to sharing more stories with you on this journey. Thank you for being one of my readers.

# about the author

Alanna Grace has spent most of her summers falling in love with the Lakes Region of New Hampshire where her Newfound Lake series is set. When she isn't writing, Alanna is an outdoors enthusiast. Skiing, hiking, and paddleboarding are among her favorite activities. She lives in New England with her husband, children, and two fur babies.

Visit her website for the latest news and to sign up for her newsletter: https://alannagraceauthor.com/